Sonya & Jack

Sonya & Jack

a novel

DAVID HOMEL

David Homel (signature)

HarperPerennial
HarperCollins*Publishers*Ltd

First Edition: 1995

Canadian Cataloguing in Publication Data

Homel, David
    Sonya & Jack

ISBN 0-00-224374-1

I. Title.

PS8565.064S6 1995   C813'.54   C95-930433-9
PR9199.3.H66S6 1995

---

95 96 97 98 99 ❖ RRD 10 9 8 7 6 5 4 3 2 1

Printed and bound in the United States

Rules are made to be broken, lies are made to be told, especially the family variety. History is made to be, if not rewritten, at least improved in novels. Though the characters and events in this book are real, and true to their nature, some have been shifted in time to obey the novelist's demands. This is always the case when miracles and romance are involved.

BOOK I

A GUIDE TO THE PERPLEXED

1

AN ARK AMONG THE FLAGS

The tale of my miraculous origins begins with a joke. All the best ones do. A joke on a man I scarcely remember, I who remember everything. Though I am told I lived with him as a boy, briefly, through a season or two in the welcoming wilderness of Alma-Ata, a city that is now, God preserve us, the capital of one of those overnight republics. I am told that this man even played the role of my father, returned from afar.

My tale begins with this man, whose name is Jack Gesser, walking down Sangamon Street. It is Chicago; it is the cold early spring of 1932; it is the Depression, and now people have just begun to call it that. Gesser has a hole at the bottom of each pants pocket. These holes allow no filthy lucre to accumulate there, but they do let him reach down and touch his own skin and convince himself that, despite all the evidence around him, he still exists, that he is a man, a human being even.

The tale of my miraculous origins begins with a joke, and that joke is the one history played on this man Gesser, and my mother, and on the other brave, foolish and prideful idealists and adventurers you will meet, including my true father, whom I never knew. A vast, extended joke that crossed decades and continents, and used the most outlandish props to make its point.

Now, I know what you are thinking: every child wants to claim extraordinary origins such as these. Saint Sigmund said it all before, and before him, the Book itself, from which he stole everything, worthy thief that he was. Every child wants to be the baby Moses, set in an ark among the flags, drawn from water by Pharaoh's beautiful daughter one day as she went strolling, bored with her privilege under a parasol, then taken back to the palace to become the greatest man ever to walk the earth. But such prodigies sometimes turn out to be ungrateful, for did he not return later with his rod to fill that same palace with frogs and vermin?

Believe me, I did not go questing for these origins. They came to me, and they are as much a part of me as this scar on my jaw, faded to near invisibility for everyone but the wearer. Many times I've wished I'd been spared these origins. Because, except for this latter-day passion for roots, which has become a commerce in this country, you are always better off with regular features, smooth skin and a quiet past.

But I am not here to fill the family palace full of green, stinking frogs—far from it. I have come to celebrate the adventurers who gave birth to me, not assassinate them. Don't count on me to perform the central ceremony of the current age, and hunt down my parents and dispatch them in a bitter, undignified bloodletting. Why would I do that, since they have endowed me with such rich and complex gifts? One of which is a gift for jokes. For stories, if you will. Like the one I am going to tell you.

So there was Jack Gesser, reaching down through his pockets where the money was not and finding the hole, and touching his skin, and warming his fingertips. At least my skin still works, he consoled himself. Today, on this first of the month, moving day again, Gesser was terribly down on his luck. In the New World, his old learning had proved useless. His mastery of several languages—those of daily commerce and those of argument with the Almighty—had no currency here. He found himself as useless as the knots of other jobless men he strolled past. For Gesser, that thousands of others along Sangamon Street shared his fate was of no comfort. If anything, it made him feel worse. What else should we expect from a man schooled to believe in his originality, in the importance of his parcel of thought, his crumb of chosenness?

Jack Gesser, slim and dark and eel-like, patrolled Sangamon Street. Lines of ropy muscle, surprising in a man raised on books, moved of their own accord under the skin of his arms. For a man who was down on his luck, he still managed a predatory step, his eyes so black that the pupil and iris merged to form one single dark pool of questions.

He passed a shop, slowed and lingered by an open-lidded barrel of schmaltz herring awash in dark, inviting brine. He freed his hands from his pockets, wondered just how sticky his fingers were and whether a fish would stick to them. Then he heard a fleshy tap-tap from close by. The storekeeper was tapping the blunt side of a cleaver against the meaty heel of his hand and wearing a "try-it" smile. Gesser declined.

"What are you doing, showing off with that thing?" he challenged the shopkeeper. "Is an honest merchant afraid of thieves?

Everybody on the street knows you put your thumb on the scale. A cholera on your wormy fish, anyway!"

The shopkeeper went on tapping his cleaver against his fleshy hand, the smile fixed on his waxy, swollen, Teutonic face. Gesser moved on, hands back in pockets. That was the trouble with the mixed ghetto of Sangamon Street. When you insulted someone, you could never be sure they would understand your language. A man could waste a lot of good invective that way.

Piles of trunks and suitcases sat on the sidewalk at regular intervals. Some families were moving of their own free will. They moved because the paint smelled fresher down the block, or so they thought. They moved to spite the landlord. They moved because moving had become a habit. Their children played house around the stacked luggage as they waited for a horse-cart to carry their belongings a few blocks or a few doors further on, to a flat that would be uncannily like the one they had just left.

Other families were not on the sidewalk of their own accord. Their stacks of crates and trunks were crowned by silent, unmoving children who clung to rags that took the place of teddy bears. These were the month's latest evictions.

Jack Gesser felt a kinship with the latter group. It wasn't only his natural affinity for the underdog. He was short of a roof, too, which was why he was out strolling on Sangamon Street this early morning with his eyes and ears open. Another month, another move. He was like the other inhabitants of the neighborhood: none of the flats he occupied was quite to his satisfaction. The principal complaint was that the landlord demanded money for them.

Not that Jack Gesser was without instruction or pride, nor was he a coarse man. Those black, piercing eyes made that clear enough, and his small hands, despite the calluses he'd grown, were those of the aristocracy of book-readers. In another country, earlier in the century, he had received excellent training in the interpretation of the sacred texts. When he was younger, barely a man, he was deemed to be a good learner, a star learner even, the best in the village of learners. A great future was predicted for him. Not that anyone ever specified *what* he was good at learning. That was not the point. Learning was a profession in itself. True learning was without object, only the process mattered. By the time he was fifteen, in the village of Soukenai, on the soggy, acidic Lithuanian plain, he could argue away the day with the village elders about why, for example, were you to drop an onion sandwich on black bread on the floor, it would always land butter-side down.

Therein lay, it was felt in Soukenai, the mystery of the universe, the key to its perverse and unfair nature. Onions, bread, the luxury of butter. They all held a kind of symbolic power in the village. Soukenai was a magic place. Every parcel of ground was invested with law.

After hours of such strenuous interpretation, the rabbi's wife would tiptoe in with a tureen of *shchi* and some of the black bread in question, then slip demurely away, lest the proceedings of the great village minds be interrupted. And soon they were, as the amateur exegetes and arguers with God fell upon the broth in its common bowl, the soup rolling off their spoons and down their beards into the bowl again, in a movement of eternal return.

Too bad there was no call for this kind of trade in the New World. Profession: learner. It would not fill your belly on Sangamon Street. Yet there were many such excellent ex-learners in this part of the New World. *Luftmenschn*, they were called, men who lived on and in air, the air of ideas, theories, possibilities, arguments with the Almighty, even if they had given up believing in him. Liars and rewriters of history who frequented the cafés with their tea and poppy-seed cakes and the occasional manna of schnapps, forever debating over their own uselessness. It makes no sense, Gesser decided; seeing as there are so many of us, perhaps we should join together and create a circle, a syndicate, a union. That in itself was a perfectly *luftmensch* thought. The Fraternal Circle of Dreamers. We would hold unscheduled, unproductive meetings at Steinstein's Leisure Palace and Poolroom. We would compare our dreams; the most extravagant and unfeasible one wins. There is no prize beyond the knowledge of one's triumph. We would band together with other fraternal circles of *luftmenschn* across the country, around the globe. So uplifted by our own verbal prowess and ability to remake the world with our words that we'd never be disturbed by having to *do* anything.

Gesser was enjoying this interlude of bitter self-assessment when he first gazed upon Sonya Freedman. Nearly as tall as he was—though that was no accomplishment—a little square-shouldered, her jaw and neck a bit fleshy, but that was a good thing, for a skinny woman is an abomination in the eyes of the Lord. And the most extraordinary red hair, all wound in a bun as skillful as a sailor's knot, and white skin to match, and freckles scattered across her cheekbones.

Freckles, Gesser thought. *What purpose do they serve?*

And that tunic, the top button daringly undone at the neck, an enchantment in such straitened times. A bag, crafted in better times by a Budapest leatherworker, sat at her feet next to an instrument case.

Gesser circled around her again like a hawk over prey, though, in truth, the thing most hawk-like about him was his nose. This was too good to be true. Here was a woman without grimness, even while she bargained over the rent and the privileges that came with it. On an upended trunk that served as a table, on the Sangamon Street sidewalk, a new collective household was being created. Exactly what Gesser had been looking for. Such delicate negotiations could be carried out only by women. By the trunk stood the Poklub matriarch, stout, distrusting, and her three daughters, who may or may not have reached puberty, for their buttoned-up clothes hid their bodies in expert fashion. Other matriarchs, equally stout and grim and distrustful, argued over the fine points of the flat. All were in agreement that the landlord was a thief, lower than a thief, he was scum, the lowest form of life, his flat wasn't fit for a pig, but, all in all, it was not such a bad deal.

Sonya Freedman, with her complicated red hair, once-fine suitcase and instrument box, was not yet part of a household. But no household could be assembled without her and her kind. She would sign on with a family as a roomer, and perhaps she would graduate to boarder status, depending on her resources. She represented the difference between what the Poklubs could afford and what the landlord wanted. She was that which made ends meet. On Sangamon Street, it did not matter that she was a stranger to the Poklubs. The common ground of rent and race would soon bind them.

Jack Gesser hovered at the edge of the gathering, close enough to hear, far enough away not to be noticed.

"What would a case like that hold?" the Poklub matriarch demanded of Sonya Freedman.

"A clarinet."

"And you play?" the Poklub woman asked, disbelieving.

"No. My husband plays."

The Poklub woman looked relieved.

"Well, if you like, you will bring a little music into the home. At least it is not so common as a fiddle. So, if you agree, it is done. Happy to make your acquaintance. You can carry your own bags, no? The heavy ones we will leave; my eldest will look after them until my husband comes back from the cemetery."

Gesser peeled away from the crowd with the address of the empty flat secure in his memory. From his days as a learner, his memory was still powerful, the strongest muscle in his body, he liked to boast. So, the woman had a clarinet-playing husband, he thought as he moved resolutely towards Racine Street and Steinstein's poolroom. What can you expect from a woman without grimness, that she be available on top of it? Don't dream, he admonished himself. Before romance comes a roof.

Jack Gesser's worldly possessions were stored in their usual spot: under the pool table at Steinstein's Leisure Palace. The same suitcase he had come over with as a boy twenty-five years ago, though now it needed considerably more rope to keep it in one piece. He crawled among the legs of the billiards players to retrieve it from the other bags in temporary storage, and heard a curse as someone above him missed a shot and blamed it on him.

"How's my favorite member of the intelligentsia?" Steinstein called out from the counter. "Got something this time?"

"If I move fast," Gesser told him.

Steinstein shook his head in wonderment.

"More nerve than brains. But if that's what it takes . . . Tell you what, if it works this time I'll stand you to a little something. You'll have earned it."

Gesser waved as the heavy glass and oak door closed behind him. He covered the few blocks from Racine Street back to Sangamon at an easy trot, not running too hard to avoid the interest of the friendly Irish beat cop. *Back from the cemetery*, the matriarch had said. It augured ill, did it not, to attach your fate to a grave-digger's flat? But at least the man had a job, one in a calm, quiet place to boot, where a man might contemplate matters of mortality. He would have traded for it, had he had something to trade.

The door to the third-floor flat at 1225 Sangamon was locked, but not prohibitively so. Ear to the door, shoulder to the frame. Amazing what circumstances can teach a good learner. From a reader of sacred texts to a persuader of locks. A stiff elbow, a skillfully aimed knee. Gesser walked inside.

The empty flat was filled with a rare quality in lodgings of this kind: peace. The quiet was so astounding, so unexpected and intimate, it had something positively sexual to it. Gesser turned into the parlor, visited the master bedroom, travelled down the hall to explore the dining room, the kitchen, the back porch. Empty and glorious. The flat held its breath and waited for the next assault of disappointed tenants. The windows were streaked with soot that attenuated the raw glare of day. There was the pathos of temporary peace. It was like being on a stage before the beginning of the play.

He went to work, distributing the contents of his bag in different locations through the flat. He would occupy the front parlor; no need to place anything else there but his own mendacious bones. He put his empty bag in the bedroom and hung his winter coat on the hook on the back of the door. He draped his handkerchief on the kitchen table, as if it were a tablecloth and he were expecting dinner guests. His small collection of books went on the kitchen table. Riding on top of the stack was the populist poetry of Walt Whitman who, in the frontispiece, wore a beard worthy of the prophets and a peasant's battered hat.

When the masquerade was done, Jack Gesser returned to the parlor to sit on the floor. He leaned gingerly against the wall, testing it to see whether it would hold his weight. Whatever happens now, Gesser decreed, is beyond my will.

With that comforting thought, he closed his eyes and fell into a deep, sudden, bottomless sleep that seemed to stretch all the way back to the very origins of fatigue. Gesser could sleep anywhere, in any position. After learning, it was his greatest skill, and certainly a more useful one in this kind of life. When he slept, even if it was for a minute between streetcar stops, his memory never failed to deliver the same nightmare. So familiar was it that he'd stopped being afraid. It was part of him, like his smell or the color of his eyes, and it carried him back to an afternoon in the village of Soukenai.

It was early in the year 1906, the revolution in Moscow had failed, and the time for revenge had come again. The Czar's men burst into the printing shop where Gesser was apprenticed, where without his master's knowledge he had printed tracts in Russian and Yiddish calling for the uprising to spread to their sleepy province. The avengers wrecked the presses, set fire to the building, threw the elegant little lead letters into the snow. Gesser escaped through the back and the men, heavy with alcohol and the high boots they wore, lumbered after him. He ran through the village and stole unseen, so he thought, into the slaughtering shed where the ritual slaughterer was sharpening his knives after dispatching a steer. Gesser heard the doors fly open and the leader of the pogromists shout triumphantly, "Look, the Jew has a knife!" They fell upon the *schochet*, a man in his sixties with flecks of blood and bone in his beard. Gesser fled deeper in the shed. There was no shelter except the steer's freshly gutted carcass. He climbed inside. *My feet!* he realized in terror, then he scaled the rungs of the steer's ribs until he was safely curled inside its still-warm cavity. He heard, and imagined, but did not see the butcher's death by his own knives, which he had so recently asked the Lord to bless, and the satisfied puffing of the pogromists.

He stayed inside the animal long after they had gone, leaving the village to its habitual outrage and mourning. A fifteen-year-old boy curled inside a slaughtered steer, paralyzed with fear and guilt as its tissues went cold under his fingertips. He huddled there that evening and night and through to the next morning, when the villagers came upon him and shook him out of his hiding place, the wounded inside the slaughtered.

Now he was being shaken awake by a sound: the banging of trunks being bumped up the stairs, and the sight of two Poklub girls, their eyes wide and their mouths forming little circles of horror, as if they had stumbled upon a fairy-tale monster.

Twins, Gesser saw. *Twins bring bad luck.*

The girls shot out of the parlor into the hall.

"Mama, mama, it's not true, this isn't our house. There is already someone living here!"

"What? Such a thing!"

A moment later the Poklub matriarch appeared in the doorway, a picture of outrage, hands on her hips. Jack Gesser sat up, looking as dignified as a man sitting on his butt in an empty room can be. He placed his palms on the floor to indicate possession.

"Here am I," Gesser told the woman.

She stared at him incredulously. She knew those words from somewhere. The Almighty himself had used them to tease Moses with the burning bush. The Poklub matriarch, however, was not one to be teased with riddles.

"This is my flat. I rented it," Gesser said, but his voice lacked conviction. "I am here. You must have made a mistake. Do you have the right address?"

"Twelve twenty-five Sangamon, third floor!" she wailed. "How many places with that address can there be? What did I do to the Lord to make such a thing happen?"

The Poklub matriarch cut short her lamentations. A look of conspicuous triumph came over her face.

"You say you rented this flat. You, one man, you need all these rooms?"

"Me, no. But they are for the others, who are coming later."

The Poklub matriarch frowned, then recovered. She displayed the key to the flat.

"I have this key. I suppose you have one, too?"

"No. The flat was left open for me. An honest man has no need of keys."

The woman snorted. "I don't know what world you live in, mister, but it is not the same as mine."

"I'm sure that's true, madam."

"And I'm sure this is our flat, not yours."

"But here am I," Gesser said triumphantly, palms on the floor, willing himself to grow roots into the boards.

"Yes, I can see that."

An oversized cloak flapped against a narrow thigh, and the smell of perspiration blew in. Maxie, the oldest Poklub issue, stuck his nose around the doorjamb. He gazed upon Gesser, then ducked back to safety. The matriarch and the son huddled in whispered conversation in the vestibule.

The next time Maxie Poklub, whose ambitions hovered between the rabbinate and clerking in a haberdashery, appeared in the doorway, Gesser was no longer a simple squatter who had taken up residence in an abandoned flat. He had been elevated to the status of philosophical obstacle, logical impossibility, a challenge to Maxie's young powers of reasoning. Here was a human creature in the apartment that the Poklub family and its boarders had already rented—at least for the next month.

"Logically, you cannot be here," the boy told him, staring in a scholarly manner over his glasses.

"Indeed, how is it that I do exist?" Gesser asked. "But I do, and I exist in your life. And here is the proof."

He tapped the floorboards.

"You did arrive before we did," Maxie acknowledged. "But does that mean the flat is yours? Can the matter of justice be reduced to a footrace?"

"He is a thief!" the Poklub matriarch shrieked. "He is stealing our apartment! I am going to get a cop!"

Before the Poklub woman could make good on her threat, there was more bustling at the door and the sound of two suitcases being set down heavily.

"Thief? Cop? What kind of house is this?"

The voice belonged to Sonya Freedman. She stepped into the parlor where Maxie, the Poklub matriarch and the twins all stood, gazing upon Jack Gesser. For the daughters, Gesser was one of those fearful, restless spirits wandering in search of a soul to inhabit, a being that had stepped out of a fairy tale and into their flat. For the Poklub woman, he was a scandal, an attack on her sense of propriety. For Maxie, he was a logical absurdity, and as such, a test of his reasoning.

Of all the Poklub family members, the twins were closest to the truth.

"I am so terribly sorry," the Poklub matriarch wailed to Sonya Freedman. "I had no idea . . . Don't worry, he will go. And if he won't, I will get a cop. I will! He says it is his flat. But I have the key, I have the paper that says—"

"You can't just throw him out," Maxie protested. "That wouldn't be proper. He *is* one of us, I'm afraid. I can tell by the way he speaks."

"Here am I, the stranger in your gates. The Lord will bless," Gesser said to prove Maxie's point.

"But we have no room. We don't even know him. He hasn't presented himself to us."

Then Sonya Freedman stepped into the parlor at 1225 Sangamon, which had been transformed into a theater of sorts, and in a most surprising way for a woman in those days made a decision that changed everyone's life.

"You say the flat is yours," she told the scripture-quoting stranger who had not yet presented himself, and who was gripping the floor as if it were a life raft. "We say it is ours."

Sonya Freedman paused. The squatting intruder waited. His fate was in the balance.

"But why must it be one or the other? Since you will not leave, and since it would not be right to throw you out, especially in these times, since you are *here*, as you say yourself, you might as well stay. We will *all* stay. You will stay as a roomer. The rest of us will stay as what we already are."

Maxie Poklub whistled appreciatively.

"For a woman, you certainly know the dialectic. Where did you learn it?"

"Not in Chicago," she told the boy.

"But we don't know him," the Poklub matriarch lamented. "And we don't have the room."

Sonya Freedman gave her a quizzical look.

"Room?" she echoed. "How much room is needed?"

Then Jack Gesser spoke the first reasonable words he had said all morning.

"I'll take the back porch," he announced.

"It's true," the Poklub matriarch mused, "I wouldn't spit on the extra money. I hadn't thought of the porch. But there is no heat there."

Gesser shrugged. A shrug, he knew, wins the argument every time.

"It is almost spring," he reasoned. "After, you have summer. The heat will take care of itself."

And that was how Jack Gesser took his place in the Poklub collective flat. The man who should not have been there, and who would not go away. Gesser rose from his undignified position on the floor, shook the stiffness from his knees and went to gather the possessions he had scattered around the flat.

"Masquerader," Sonya whispered as he walked past her.

Later, when no one was looking, he pulled off his cap and said to her, "I am much indebted to Sonya the Red, mistress of the dialectic."

"You see," she answered confidently. "Philosophy *works*."

At day's end, two more men joined the Poklubs' collective flat. A bone, some root vegetables and a handful of barley were being boiled into an alliance when Joe Poklub dragged in from the Waldheim cemetery. He walked into the dining room, found the bottle of homemade schnapps and his favorite shot glass and collapsed into the head chair at the table, in front of the ashtray. All this, in a flat he had never seen before. He didn't need to. Where else would things be, but where they were? What choice did these objects have?

He raised his shot glass to no one in particular.

"May the bastards croak," he toasted, then whistled off the contents.

"Daughter," he said to Dorothy, his eldest, who had come in with the trunks in mid-afternoon. "Time to tend to the dead. Time to call the barber to come and snip their long green hair."

Dutifully, the girl took a sheet of paper from her school note-book and sat down at the table next to her father, pencil at the ready. She knew the work of madness that awaited her. He poured a second schnapps and emptied the glass, then stored the bottle with great care in the cupboard.

"My dear and anonymous friends," he began to dictate in Yid-dish, "the stone that stands over the place of your beloved, which of course you want to maintain until such time as the Messiah comes and makes such monuments unnecessary, this stone is in sad need of a further contribution of two dollars to ensure that the weeds of time will not take root there . . ."

Old Joe Poklub paused and chuckled at his own pyrotechnics.
"What do you think of that, daughter?"

"Very nice, Papa."

Encouraged, the old man went on.

"So that oblivion in the form of crabgrass, dandelion, lamb's-quarters shouldn't swallow it up . . . Yes, to maintain the stone against these predators."

He gazed towards the ceiling in search of another mocking, flowery formula. Then he turned to Dorothy.

"Plants are in the realm of predators, too, you know that, daughter."

"The Venus fly-trap," she volunteered.

Her father frowned. The plant was unfamiliar to him.

"For my profession has acquainted me with death and its child, forgetfulness," he dictated. "It is a strategy of a kind. I familiarize myself with death, and that way I hold it outside the gates. I frequent it. Death gets so used to me being around it doesn't even know I'm there any more. Clever, yes?"

"I should write all this?" Dorothy asked timidly.

"Of course! You think I'm wasting my breath?" her father said emphatically. "And sincerely yours and respectfully so, too."

The eldest Poklub daughter picked up her pencil. She wrote, she translated into English, she changed her father's ravings into something acceptable that a family with a loved one in the ground who owed money to the groundskeeper might receive. It was a rare education for a child.

Old Joe Poklub looked up and caught Gesser watching the proceedings.

"See? Never let it be said that schooling for a girl is a waste!"

A little later, the member of the collective flat whom Gesser least wanted to see came in. The soup was cooling on the table when Sammy Spielerman walked nonchalantly through the unlocked door and turned into the parlor. A few minutes later he came out, followed by Sonya the Red, who was holding his hand.

"This is my husband, Sammy," she announced.

"Good," said the Poklub matriarch. "Now we can eat."

"Eat and get it over with," Old Man Poklub added cheerfully.

"You, too," she said to Gesser. "Even if you're just a roomer. For just this one time. This man was in the flat when we arrived," she explained to Spielerman apologetically, "and since he wouldn't go away, we decided to keep him. He's rooming in the back porch."

"It was my flat," Gesser said automatically.

Sonya the Red turned and looked at him. "You can stop that now."

Never let it be said, when there is little to eat, that the diners draw out their sustenance. The opposite is true. The assembled members of the collective flat fell upon their supper like locusts upon Pharaoh's crops. And the very minute the last drop of soup was sopped up by the bread, and the last flecks of marrow extracted from the bones at knifepoint, the dishes were collected, rinsed and stacked. The Poklub matriarch herded her daughters into the dining room to sleep. Maxie went off to his night class. With laboring fingers, Joe Poklub struggled to build a cigarette. Freedman, Spielerman and Gesser watched in suspense. It would have been an insult to offer help.

When the task was completed, he drew the smoke into his lungs, enjoying the bitter rasp in his throat. Then he turned to Spielerman.

"So, Mr. Benny Goodman, are you going to play some music for us and make our hearts glad at the end of the day?"

"It would wake the children, I'm afraid."

"The children? Forget about them. They can sleep through a pogrom! They are trained that way. How else do you think we can live like this?"

19

"Do play us something, Sammy. That's why they wanted to have us. To have music in the house."

Spielerman could not resist that argument. He fetched his case and took out the clarinet, battered but serviceable. Joe Poklub leaned closer as if hard of hearing, his cigarette hanging from his lower lip, eager for the kind of music that would carry him far from Sangamon Street and his trade as grave-keeper, to his glorious youth when he danced on the tamped earth of the village square before the temple, when his fingers were straight.

But something unexpected came out of Spielerman's clarinet:

> I went down to St. James Infirmary
> I saw my baby there
> She was stretched out on a long white table
> So clean, so cool and so fair.

Poklub held up a hand to stop Spielerman.

"That music doesn't make my heart glad. It casts my heart down even deeper."

"Aha! That's called the blues. That's what it's supposed to do. It uplifts your heart by casting it down further."

"Makes no sense," Poklub grumbled.

"But it does. It works."

"Not for me it doesn't."

"It's like the dialectic," Sonya Freedman pointed out.

"The devil take the cursed dialectic! It sounds like *schwartze* music to me."

"*Schwartze* and Yid music. We're making it together."

"I know it makes no sense, maybe," Sonya Freedman admitted, "to lift up your heart by casting it down. But that's the way this music works. Klezmer songs can be sad, too."

"Yes," said Joe Poklub. "But when they are sad, they are sad. They even say they are sad. They say, 'Danger, sad song coming up, steel your hearts!' They don't pretend they are sad just to make you happy afterwards. They are not afraid to be what they are: sad."

"All the klezmer players in town are going to the blues," Spielerman insisted. "It's the music of the century."

"A century I won't be around to see, and that's just as well," said Old Joe Poklub.

He went back to building his cigarettes. What did it matter to him? He was no musician and he'd never be one, not with his fingers. Just to hold a garden shears was an accomplishment, and soon that pleasure would be taken from him.

"So, the evening is over," said Poklub once Spielerman had finished his paradoxical tunes, and he had finished assembling a supply of cigarettes. "Not for me, for you. I'll stay up and keep watch on things. Make sure the world keeps turning. To do this, I need company." He pointed to the cigarettes.

The boarders and roomers and rightful renters rose, the Poklub matriarch to the bedroom, the couple to the front parlor, Jack Gesser to the cold back porch, all going carefully past the sleeping Poklub girls who, as their father had said, had not even stirred.

Gesser set about making his bed. He lined up the Poklub family trunks which, mercifully, were fairly level. He discovered a length of padded fabric—a furniture pad, or a quilted job-end for making a winter jacket. He threw it over the trunks. His sweater made a proper pillow, and he spread out his blanket on top. And his jacket over that.

Lying in his new bed, he contemplated his fate. Naturally, his outlook was influenced by the stab of trunk ridges through the layers of fabric. If he had not left Soukenai, he wondered. If he could ever return, he speculated. If he had not printed those tracts when he was still a boy, twenty-five years ago . . . No doubt the result would have been the same. History would not be changed by such accidental details. After all, consider the butcher. He had offended no one. He had lived in accordance with the law; each of his actions had followed a sacred plan—and what was his reward?

2

MITCHELL BERG'S SCHOOL FOR DISGRUNTLED IMMIGRANTS

In those days of little money, it would have taken a truly daring man to question Comrade Mitchell Berg about where he had found the cash to open and maintain his school for disgruntled immigrants. Jack Gesser did wonder, but he kept the thought to himself as he trudged west up Division Street a few evenings later, the streetcars clanging mockingly past him, their bells taunting him that he could not afford the fare.

Mitchell Berg's school was not your usual institute of higher learning. Tonight, for example, the subject under consideration would be the building of international socialism and, as always, the class would be presided over by Berg himself, the new Messiah of the Ghetto, just in from the Soviet Union and already attracting crowds with his workmen's circles. The times were desperate, right for a new Messiah, and even a local one would do. It was rumored among the circles and fraternal orders of the unemployed that the princely Berg had swapped lines of Shakespeare with Chiang in Shanghai, while on one of his many journeys in the service of the Revolution. All this added to Berg's renown and assured him of a full house.

Berg's institution was not really called the School for Disgruntled Immigrants. The name was one of Gesser's private jokes. In that grandiose fashion the Soviets loved, ignorant of irony, Berg had baptized his school the People's College of Trades and Vocations. Gesser considered the name as he worked his way up Division Street. A trade. A vocation. Gesser had the latter, but not the former. Eternal studier, he was acquainted with the treacherous nature of the word *vocation*. It was neither synonym nor complement to *trade*. A man who had a vocation and followed it faithfully could scarcely be expected to practice a trade at all, precisely because he had a vocation: a calling, an impulse he followed, a self-appointed mission.

Now, being a learner—that was a true vocation, and Gesser had it. Random learning was his way of shoring up his sagging dignity. As he idled away his time at Steinstein's Leisure Palace and Poolroom, he always had his notebook at the ready for the collection and committal to memory of the wonderful jargon of the place. *I chalk up. I run the table. I break first. I shoot stripes. I shoot solids. I sink the eight ball.* All of it going into the pages of a little pad, much to the hilarity of the pool-shooters, all unemployed members of the intelligentsia like himself.

In the upstairs hall of the People's College of Trades and Vocations, Gesser was greeted by that particular smell that the chronically unemployed give off. It was not human sweat or the effluvia of rough food. In fact, there was hardly a smell at all. Only the odor a passing ghost might leave behind, as if the men and women in the hall had no material existence, as if they were an unrealized idea.

Gesser chose a seat at the back. Berg's hall was lined with the kind of chair that forced you to stay awake during the lecture. The kind of spartan, hard-backed contraption that just dared you to try to catch forty winks on its butt-breaking seat. Gesser took the challenge. He put his head on his chest and stole into himself, the man who could sleep anywhere, and who did it best without a bed. The day had been long and unfavorable, starting early with the Poklub matriarch's stare as he tried to slip unnoticed past her and her mountain of laundry at the sink. She already regretted letting herself be swayed by her son's charity and her star boarder's verbal sleight of hand. She eyed Gesser expectantly, the way a peasant might size up the golden goose. So, I didn't slaughter you the other day like I should have, so now, show me the reason why—fork over the dough!

But there was no dough. Gesser couldn't make the rent, even the porch-roomer's share. He shrugged and dug his hands into his pockets, then headed for the door.

For a few precious seconds, he beat the hard-backed chair at its own game and caught those forty winks. Then a cheerful voice shocked him into the present.

"Rise and shine, comrade, we have a world to win!"

He opened his eyes to the great artful red construction of Sonya Freedman's chignon. Then she laughed, a great peal of unrestrained, frank, free laughter. Gesser had never heard a woman laugh that way. He hadn't even imagined that laughter like that could exist on this earth.

25

"What are you doing here?" he stammered.

"The same as you are. I've come to listen to the great Mitchell Berg."

"He's that great?"

"Okay, I confess, I'm only here for the sandwiches."

She laughed again and took a chair next to Gesser's. Then Berg appeared at the front of the hall without introduction or ceremony. He leaned forward and put his weight on the lectern, as if daring it to hold his importance. Immediately, the hall went silent.

If Mitchell Berg had a single fault as an orator, it was that his presence sometimes took the audience's attention away from his words. He issued from a family that had loved God and brokered wood along the Dvina River on the same green and water-logged plain where Gesser had known his misfortunes. But his body was that of the woodsman, not the log-counter. The loose white embroidered Russian blouse he wore proclaimed the authenticity of his origins, and a drooping black mustache drew a thoughtful frown above his mouth. His eyes were set halfway into his skull, behind the great bony ridges of his cheekbones, as if he were trying to look ahead and behind at the same time.

Every man in the hall saw in him his rival. The women in the room could have told them to save their jealousy for more worthy targets. The man was cold; there was something priestly, finicky in his gestures. All his heat was saved for ideas.

That evening, as he had done on both sides of the Atlantic, with sewn-together strips of Russian and Yiddish and English, his voice made melodious by elocution classes he had taken in the New World, he exhorted the audience to build the workers' movement in their new land. He exposed the falsity of capitalism and the dreariness of their lives, a fact they did not need to be reminded of. He offered them a tantalizing vision of that society on the other side of the ocean where all were equal and everything was shared, misery and riches alike. Berg was the Messiah of the New. The new society, the new man, the new woman. The old country of tears, Russia, had made itself new through revolution, which they all must do, as individuals.

To one man in the hall, Jacob Spolansky, the FBI agent who'd been assigned to cover Berg ever since he arrived in America via the West Indies, it was clear that he was preaching sedition. Then Spolansky surveyed the room, noted the weary eyelids, the drooping heads. He knew these people, knew their fatigue and exhausted hopes, their love of talk—the bigger the better. They were his people, he understood them, which was why he'd received the unlikely distinction of being enlisted as the first Jewish G-man. So well did he know them that he could not imagine the Constitution of the United States of America ever being overthrown by such a dispirited, quarrelsome, tea-drinking, poppy-seed-cake-eating lot.

With that matter accounted for, and his conscience at ease, Spolansky crossed his legs at the ankle and his arms over his barrel chest, and sat back to enjoy the sermon that, by now, he knew by heart.

His attendance at the Messiah of Division Street's college was no secret to the Messiah himself. When Berg first materialized in Chicago, Spolansky dropped in on him unannounced at his West Side apartment and invited him to a café. There, over poppy-seed cake and several schnapps, offered at government expense, he told Berg everything about the Russian's short career in America. He described Berg's own errand to him: to convince immigrants to start thinking of themselves as revolutionaries. Spolansky had it all, right down to the grades Berg had received in the junior college classes he'd taken in elocution, shorthand and civil government. "The only one in Lenin's gang who knows the Pitman system, I'm willing to bet," Spolansky added, a black constellation of poppy seeds between his front teeth, and whistled off a third schnapps.

Berg blanched with terror. He imagined deportation, prison, beatings, all punishments he had known in the past. Then he giggled with unbecoming, nervous disbelief. How could this Spolansky be a United States government agent sworn to stamp out Communism, yet possess every trait and tick of the Russian immigrant, down to the way he poured his tea into his saucer to drink?

Yet both things were true. This was Berg's first introduction to the wonders of liberal bourgeois democracy, wherein opposites are allowed to thrive, a system much trickier to understand than the new society Berg had struggled to build in Russia. As they swapped stories and ordered more cake and schnapps, Spolansky pandering all the while to Berg's taste for Shakespeare, the Jewish G-man let it be known that he would be happy with an amiable compromise, an unspoken agreement. Berg would remain active and please his masters, but not so active as to get Spolansky into trouble with his superiors, who had no appreciation of the ironies involved; after all, Spolansky could just as well have been on Berg's side as against him.

It took Berg a time to get over his amazement. Here was an agent of capitalism offering him a compromise. He thought of trying to win Spolansky over to his side, then realized that would have been a mistake. The G-man was more valuable where he was. As he recovered his wits, Berg realized there was one part missing from Spolansky's recital of his New World career. The trunks he had carried to the tropics, and had had to leave there because he feared the surveillance of someone like Spolansky—that episode had disappeared. Whether that was out of ignorance, or as a trap, Berg could not tell.

In the same unspoken manner as it had been made, Berg agreed to Spolansky's proposal. Falsely so, of course. No sooner had Berg made the agreement than he began making plans to violate it. He could not help it; it was in his nature to want to win. He was an idealist; Spolansky was not.

The applause was hearty at the culmination of Berg's talk, with those who had slept through it applauding most lustily. The chairs scraped and everyone moved towards the buffet with heavy but efficient strides. You wanted the sandwiches, but you did not want to look too hungry.

Gesser and Freedman were part of the movement to the buffet, which was anything but revolutionary.

"Did the speech give you an appetite?" she teased him as he snaked his arm out for a hard-boiled egg halved on a piece of unbuttered bread.

"An appetite?" he mused. "An appetite for debate is more like it."

He popped the egg and bread into his mouth. That turned out to be a mistake. Not only was the combination utterly dry, but Berg showed up at that very moment. He moved fast for a big man.

"Debate?" he echoed Gesser. "Excellent! Is that not why we are here? I welcome the opportunity. Too many people in this city have been beaten into silence by the circumstances. Debate is the last thing on their minds. So, let us begin!"

Berg gave Gesser a comradely slap on the back. He opened his mouth to speak, but found that was impossible. His mouth was as full as a squirrel's in an autumn forest.

Sonya jumped in.

"Mr. Gesser likes to debate. He is a philosopher of sorts. We owe our acquaintance to the practice of the dialectic."

Berg looked skeptical.

"Oh? As far as I know, there is not much practice of the dialectic on the West Side of Chicago."

"I assure you, there is an underground, informal practice of it. In our world, it is called doing something you did not know you were going to do. This occurs all the time."

Berg was completely mystified by Sonya. Quickly, he brought the conversation around to more solid ground.

"What kind of philosophy does Mr. Gesser profess?" he asked.

"Where I come from," Gesser told him, having gulped down his dry egg on dry bread, "philosophy consists of answering one question with another."

"If only philosophy was that easy," Berg said gloomily.

"Some say it is our people's ethnic trait."

"I am sorry," Berg countered, "but in my world, there are no ethnic traits. We are not satisfied with those kinds of explanations any more. If you answer a question with a question, it is because you cannot bear the answer. To answer is to act. This so-called ethnic trait is simply the trait of those afraid of action. Which is what the Revolution sought to change. To bring the timid into action. To demonstrate to them that the world can be theirs."

"In our method," Sonya argued, "the answer is secretly contained in the return question. You just have to know how to read it."

"Know how to read it?" Berg laughed. "Is this a gathering of mystics?"

Berg's Kirghiz secretary came up and pulled on his arm. They exchanged a few brief, whispered words, then crossed the room together as the ravenous crowd worked the buffet.

"I don't think he cared for our explanations," Gesser concluded.

"Maybe not. Funny, I've never been accused of being a mystic before. There's a first time for everything . . . But tell me, do you always pull off that trick?"

"Trick? What trick?"

"Now don't go answering questions with questions with me!

You know what I'm talking about. I see a man circling around me like a crow when I'm haggling with the Poklub woman over the room. Then, a miracle, the same man shows up in the flat I've rented, glued to the floor, insisting for all he's worth that the place is his. A coincidence, don't you think?"

"A very odd coincidence, yes. Life is made of such coincidences." He looked Sonya in the eye. "Why didn't you expose me for the thief that I am?"

"Thief? Property is theft, isn't that what they say? What did you steal, anyway? A few feet in a room that was not being used. Besides, I admired your trick. Shouldn't I have?"

"It doesn't always work."

"I can imagine! Sometimes, I bet, the old lady really does call the cop."

Gesser nodded. "It requires an appreciative audience."

Sonya smiled. "Someone who will play along."

"Of course, I intend to pay my share," Gesser added quickly.

"Of course you do," Sonya agreed mockingly.

Someone had opened the window a crack to let the five-cent cigar smoke escape and from below, on Division Street, Jack and Sonya heard a streetcar bell clang as the car rumbled off. A fine mist rode the wind that blew off the lake. There is something about gazing down upon a deserted thoroughfare that brings two people closer together, even when they are strangers to each other. *You and I against the world*, that particular romance runs, against the pale streetlamps, the long shadows that run to darkness, the color of hunger. A gust of wind on Division Street blew a man's cap off his balding head, and the cap chose to land in a puddle of water. Gesser felt a pang of grim satisfaction at the cap's choice of landing spot, for in that choice he recognized the usual way the world did its business.

Sonya opposed that world and all that it contrived with something entirely new. A kind of playfulness, a disrespect for one's own miseries. Gesser, the serious one, was disarmed by it.

"I don't believe I see Mr. Freedman," Gesser said.

"Mr. Freedman?"

"The clarinet player. Your husband."

"Freedman is my name. Spielerman is his. Spielerman of Sammy Spielerman and his Roving Band. He's not here this evening. With a roving band, it makes sense that he shouldn't be here, right?"

"I suppose so."

"And no, I didn't take his name. We're cousins, we're close enough. We don't need to get any closer."

Gesser gave his philosopher's shrug. A cousin marriage said nothing about the partners. His parents had been cousins, too, first cousins or second, who could tell? It happened often. In a little village, there were not that many choices, and it never hurt to consolidate the family holdings, the broody hen, the hay-rake, the slightly lame ox.

Having exhausted the buffet, the crowd began to thin. No one particularly wanted to go down onto Division Street and have his weary bones buffeted by the lake wind, but there were no compelling reasons to stay on. As Gesser and Freedman drifted towards the door, Berg reappeared and gave them one.

"Our debate was interrupted," he reminded them, placing his bulk between them and the exit.

"You left us on the word 'mystic,'" Sonya pointed out.

"Yes. Well, the mystical cannot be debated. It is not of much use."

"The issue, Comrade Berg," Gesser said, "is this. You have told us to organize the revolution here, yet in the same lecture you tell us we'd be better off giving up on this place and building socialism in the Soviet Union, on the other side of the world. The Old World."

"I did?"

"You did to those who listened to you. The Soviet Union needs skilled workers, the Soviet Union needs to industrialize, the Soviet Union is calling us home. I'm sure that's all true. But the same worker can't build socialism in two places at once. So where shall we dedicate ourselves? Don't you think that's a contradiction?"

"Yes," Berg admitted happily.

"And?"

"I'm surprised a philosopher like you can't live with contradictions."

"Trust me, we can. It is our daily bread. Only this contradiction interests me personally. We want to know what you think. We have a right to know, don't we? At this college, may we not question the teacher?"

"So my argument is not falling on deaf ears," Berg concluded.

Gesser said nothing. He was too busy admiring how Berg, too, could turn a person's question on its head. Truly, they were brothers in their method, no matter what Berg said.

"Which place would you choose?" Berg pushed on.

"Choose?" Gesser repeated the word as if it were meaningless. "Choose? Right now, I'm not choosing anything. I am here, but I am not here. I am in the air. I am speculating. My condition even extends to the work I do: my job is looking for a job."

"Being unemployed is no shame." Berg jumped on the subject of work. Work was concrete, and he felt at home in the world of concrete things. "In this system," he told Gesser, "it is almost a badge of honor. Do you have a trade?"

"I was a learner." Gesser smiled thinly. "But that is more a vocation than a trade, as you surely know. I was a printer, or more correctly, a printer's apprentice. We lost in 1905, and slaughter is the lot of those who lose the uprising."

"I know the story well."

Gesser nodded. "Since I have been in this city, I have had many trades. I have butchered unclean animals without the benefit of blessing, as befits them, of course. I have repaired umbrellas door to door. I have gathered things that nobody else wanted, then sold them to people who didn't know they needed them. I carried ice to people's iceboxes in the summer, and coal to their furnaces in winter. In between, I ground horseradish root in front of fish stores. For a while I tried turning wood poles into broom handles, but the machines to do these things did not like me. My last full-time job was selling watermelons off a cart. Lately, I have been the eyes and ears for a Jewish blind pig. But my mind has not been idle during these wanderings: all the while, I pondered the mystery of how a man with a learner's vocation came to adopt such a variety of trades."

"The superfluous man," Berg summed up, "made superfluous by his system. This constant self-ironizing. I noticed it immediately. Is it also an ethnic trait?"

"Which you don't believe in?" Jack teased the Messiah of Division Street. "It is more than joke-making. It is a way of telling a story. It's the paper around the package that lets it go through the mail undisturbed and reach its destination."

"It is the mark of the defeated. The self-defeated, at that. You have turned your talents against yourself. This is typical for the worker under capitalism when the system falls into crisis, and he with it. It is a squandering of yourself."

"Perhaps," Gesser admitted. "Of course, you're not telling us anything new, though it's always good to hear it from the outside. But I suppose when you are a believer, a . . . missionary, you always have something to do. Some *use*."

"A missionary? You are overstating the case."

"Some people call you the Messiah of Division Street," Sonya told Berg.

"Preposterous! I can't help what people say," Berg sputtered. "This is work, not religion. Besides, the Messiah is of the next world. I am of this world."

"With their hope in the Messiah," Gesser commented sadly, "our people are very vulnerable to false prophets. Then again, who can blame them? Our history is the history of false messiahs."

Berg's assistant began pushing the chairs across the floor and stacking them with a racket that made all conversation impossible. Berg never did find out whether Gesser was actually accusing him of being a false messiah. As the remains of the crowd dispersed down the stairs and out onto unfriendly Division Street, Berg had the distinct impression that he'd just lost a clean intellectual argument. He had been on the losing side before, and more than once in more than one country, but only because behind his opponent's winning argument stood the authority of a gun or a jail cell. Here, in his own College, he found himself outmaneuvered, or at least out-talked, by a laughing red-haired woman and an unemployed, self-ironizing philosopher.

He wanted a rematch.

And he got that rematch. Over and over again. It was the first of many evenings Jack Gesser and Sonya Freedman spent at Berg's College. Berg's *Salon des Refusés*. Gesser and Berg were natural combatants, brothers of a kind. Sometimes, as an evening ended in a draw, as all their debates did, Gesser thought he'd spotted a light of recognition, even admiration, in the eyes of the Messiah of Division Street. Berg, it was obvious, had underestimated his opponent. Their roles would have been different, even reversed, if not for an accident of history, and both knew it. From the countryside, without any resources but his youth, Gesser had no choice but to flee when defenseless Souke-nai came under attack. Berg, the issue of a merchant family, had been caught and imprisoned in the port city of Riga. Through little virtue of his own, he had stayed on to fight through to the Revolution, then helped direct the new nation it had formed. From the positions that history had given them, they argued with an age-old pleasure in the process. Gesser undermined Berg's convictions with his trademark self-defeating irony, even though he shared the same ideals. Berg retorted by portraying Gesser as morally lazy and politically nihilis-tic. Gesser eagerly agreed with Berg's accusations; Berg pointed to his eagerness as just the kind of complacency that must be avoided. And Sonya, the third term, gaily subverted each man's arguments with a light and graceful touch, whenever it pleased her.

Who was most changed by these days and evenings? Gesser. He pictured the new society, and himself within it, solidly anchored, protected, useful, and he began to believe. The best part of belief was that you got to feel that the world was yours to change.

As the three argued and fenced and grew closer together, the cold Chicago spring turned to summer, suddenly, overnight, in that yearly miracle of the midwestern climate. Some nights, as they walked home from one of their sessions, Jack and Sonya could feel the warm air pouring up from the Gulf of Mexico to waken the smells of summer in the Sangamon Street neighbor-hood. Not necessarily pleasant smells either. The smell of people airing out their poverty in the early summer of 1932.

One warm night, as he and Sonya neared the Poklub flat, Gesser brought up the question of Sonya's matrimony, which was unlike any marriage he had encountered.

"Why doesn't Mr. Spielerman ever come to the College?"

"You mean Sammy?" Sonya asked.

She gestured southward, towards the black districts, the great avenues bordered by tall blocks of flats and mansions that had been divided into ever smaller apartments.

"Sammy's out searching for that music of his."

"The kind that lifts up your heart—"

"Yes, by casting it down," she interrupted him. "If you ask me, all music does that, in one way or another. For Sammy, it's turned into his reason for living. It's his America."

Gesser had been a quick learner when it came to the study and interpretation of sacred texts, wherein the Almighty plays hide-and-seek with the minds of his creations. When it came to the labyrinth of the human heart, he was a good deal slower. In Soukenai, he had been taken in by a peasant woman whose husband was off serving in the Czar's army. Gesser was young, indefatigable, curious, even pliant. He knew nothing about love, had made no prior judgments about it and was willing to be steered by her. After their copulations, and there were many, the woman would jump from bed, squat on the floor and put her finger in her vagina. She turned her finger as quickly and roughly as if she'd been beating eggs, pinning his sperm against the walls of her vagina, then whipping it out of her body onto the plank floor. The young Gesser beheld his product there, feeling slightly diminished, as the woman cackled over the folk ingenuity that gave her mastery over her body.

When the husband returned, young Gesser was put aside, despite his youthful energy. The physical equation was simple: on the Baltic plain, no two men could fill the same spot simultaneously, any more than a herring could be both smoked and pickled.

That rustic affair was poor preparation for a woman like Sonya Freedman.

But Gesser was beginning to see one thing. In a time so poor in everything else, an ideal was the last bit of wealth in the neighborhood. A good ideal could get you adventure and escape from the grind of Sangamon Street. The philosopher's shrug, the perpetual, static ironizing of the *luftmensch*, though it might win arguments in the cafés and poolrooms of the intelligentsia, was the enemy of love.

With summer, the watermelons returned. Jack Gesser, unemployed philosopher, was back on a borrowed cart again, behind a borrowed horse that looked as though it had been lent by the glue factory, riding through the near West Side and Maxwell Street, waking up the dead with his call.

"Vah-ter-mee-loans!"

He could have pronounced the word better than that, but figured the accent was part of the job. As he rode the alleys, selling a product that was a luxury in a time of no spare cash, he began to see the poverty of his neighborhood with new eyes. It suddenly seemed senseless, criminal, against history, for tens of thousands of people to have crossed the ocean, only to live no better, or even worse, than they had in their villages and towns in Russia. True, the floors were not dirt—how could they be in an upstairs flat?— and there was real glass in the windows. But along Sangamon Street, they suffered through a chaotic existence that had no center, no order, no purpose, no *use*.

One evening, Gesser admitted his impressions to Berg.

Berg nodded. "This is what I have been telling you. When at last a person opens his eyes, what has always been normal suddenly becomes intolerable."

A few days later, Gesser reported the same feelings to Steinstein at the poolroom. The good bootlegger threw up his hands in disbelief.

"There's always lots of opportunities, everywhere. There's always a way to make a buck and get ahead in this line of work, even when there's hard times. People pay to forget, don't you understand?"

"Yeah. I do. I understand you and that damned clarinet-tooter named Spielerman."

Steinstein looked perplexed. "Sorry, don't know the gent."

"It doesn't matter," Gesser assured him. "I'm not talking about making a buck."

"But you're talking about being useful," Steinstein countered. "Making a buck or two is being useful. To yourself, to your family, to your neighborhood, to the way things are meant to be."

Gesser shook his head. "I don't know. I don't think I'm cut out for this place after all."

Steinstein shrugged. Something approaching melancholy came into his eyes for the first time.

"They say not everybody is," he admitted.

As he made the rounds of the pool tables, he discovered that for many of the shooters and idlers, immigration was an experiment that had failed. That should have been no surprise to Gesser, considering the circumstances under which most of them had left their countries. But unlike him, their dissatisfaction had deadened them to the possibility of ever doing anything about it. Slowly, Gesser detached himself from life at Steinstein's. It was a nihilists' club—there was Berg's word again. A totally pleasant place with its chirp of billiard balls and camaraderie inspired by the good bootlegger's schnapps. But a dead end all the same.

Which didn't stop Sonya Freedman from wanting to explore the Leisure Palace. In her furious iconoclasm, ostentatiously free, she insisted on learning how to shoot pool. It was a momentous day when she passed through the heavy oak doors of the Racine Street establishment. Not only did the Leisure Palace see its first woman, but the table itself felt upon its green surface the caress of its first woman shooter.

"Who will teach me how to play this silly game?" she demanded of the surprised men, who hurriedly pushed down their cowlicks and straightened their caps and collars.

But they were all too dumbstruck with admiration, lust and amazement to take up her offer.

"There's no use asking Jack," Steinstein kidded her. "When the blind lead the blind, neither shall fall into the pocket."

The bootlegger's joke broke the ice. At last, one brave man stepped forward. A short, powerfully built man whose long wavy black hair was combed back to touch his collar. Had he been taller, he might have looked like some manufacture from Hollywood. And that, at Steinstein's, would have been a handicap.

Sonya took the cue from the man's hand, then examined him freely.

"I know you from somewhere."

"Impossible," he laughed.

"No, I do know you. I've seen you. You go to Berg's."

The man narrowed his eyes.

"Berg's? What's Berg's?"

"The College of Trades and whatchamacallits."

The man shrugged. "It's possible. Who doesn't go there?"

"A lot of people don't. Most people don't. And you know it."

The man kept his eyes down as he racked up. Her words sounded like an accusation, and he was particularly sensitive to that tone. The man, of course, was Jacob Spolansky, the Jewish G-man, idling away a Sunday afternoon at Steinstein's, or conducting surveillance of possible seditious activities—it depended on how you looked at it.

"So?" Sonya asked him. "Are you a fellow student at the College?"

"Simply a fellow player." He gestured vaguely around the room. "It's a small world. A little study at the College, a little playtime here . . . it's a circuit of a kind."

They got down to the business of pool. All of Steinstein's watched the event. Jack Gesser led the cheering section for Sonya. The crowd hooted when Spolansky—who was just "Jake" around the table—sunk a shot, and applauded wildly when Sonya did the same, the result of her partner having left her in an outrageously good position after one of his misses.

Spolansky put it off as long as he could, but at last the inevitable happened. He won. Sonya demanded a revenge match and he accepted. Little by little the Leisure Palace returned to its normal rhythm of desultory talk, and soon it seemed almost ordinary for a woman to be there, playing pool. Sonya enjoyed the easy evasiveness of her partner, his joking tone that kept all important subjects at bay, outside of the position of the balls on the table. Spolansky admired her, but knew it was hopeless, at least for now. The double game he played with Berg and his followers, and with his own employer, the United States government, was bad enough. He was not about to extend it to his love life. Besides, he was keenly aware of Gesser watching him, and he did not like being watched.

A couple of games later, the novelty having worn off, Sonya and Jack were out strolling in the street again.

"There, I did it," Sonya announced.

"You're not going to become a regular?"

She laughed. "Oh no! I can see the appeal of the place, but when all is said and done, it's like being locked up in a cage."

"Most of men's refuges are that way."

She took a long strand of hair that had come loose from her chignon and sniffed at it.

"Besides, the place stinks of stogies!"

Sonya glanced at Jack and saw how much he wanted to do what she had just done. To have that familiarity with her body, her hair, her crowning glory. For a moment, they slowed to a standstill on the sidewalk, then stood, but moved on a second later. Neither had the vocabulary for this kind of encounter. There weren't any words for love in their experience, not from a culture that offered them arranged marriages.

As he rode through the alleys with a congregation of flies circling around a split in a melon, Gesser thought of that moment on the Racine Street sidewalk. Then he pictured the dispirited shooters of Steinstein's Leisure Palace, and understood that Sonya was connected to them in this way: she was their opposite. For some reason he recalled an old Jew from Soukenai, a devout Jew, the kind that could not be found any more. Even after the incursion of the Czar's men into the village—the event was really too local and disorganized to deserve the name of pogrom—this man refused to leave and go into immigration. That the Czar's irregulars would return did not change his mind. He had heard, or understood somehow, that a man could not truly be a Jew in America. And so he died in the next random raid on the village, a man who could be who he was in only one place, and one place alone.

Gesser wondered about his kinship with the man. Perhaps he, too, could be who he wanted to be in only one place. If that were so, he thought as he covered the West Side alleys, the place would surely not be here.

Vah-ter-mee-loans!

Sonya Freedman had taken a job, too. She found it the same way she had found herself in the Poklub apartment, or in America, for that matter. Through happenstance. The Poklub matriarch took in washing and repaired torn garments. There was a pile of dirty clothes on the kitchen table, ready to be thrust into the two kitchen sinks that were as deep as wells. Sonya had a pair of free hands. What could be more natural?

Such were the career choices on Sangamon Street.

*　　　*　　　*

Quite late one evening in that early, tentative summer, a most unusual and pleasing sound was heard in the Poklub collective flat. It came from the white soles of Sonya Freedman's feet slapping on the grimy wood hall that ran the length of the apartment. She was going from the parlor, where the star boarders dwelled, to the back porch room. This was Sonya's path: she loosed herself from the couch in the parlor, picked up her gown and crept out of the room, past an upright cedar wardrobe that held the family's few effects. Past the straight chair where Maxie slept in rigid posture. Through the dining room where the three Poklub virgins lay wrapped in unknowing, as tidy as sprats in a tin.

At the entrance to the kitchen, Sonya stopped. She had come upon something monstrous. Old Man Poklub was sitting at the kitchen table, rocking slowly back and forth like a devout Jew in prayer.

But he was not praying. He was composing his lunatic letters to the delinquent proprietors of the stones under which moldered their dearly departed. "The long green hair of the graves," he was muttering in a state of exaltation. "It is I who am charged with the responsibility, and you have to pay the piper, yes, sir. I am death's right hand. Actually, I stay slightly behind his right hand, and there he cannot see me, though why I am so determined to stay out of sight I do not know."

Poklub's cigarette flared in the darkness, giving off the smell of tobacco and pocket-lint.

"Where's my scribe? How can I write these things when I can't write? Blessed be He who has masked the shame of my ignorance with crooked fingers!"

Sonya clasped her nightgown to her body as Old Man Poklub cackled with satisfaction at his own joke, the butt of which was himself. She beheld the dereliction of the immigrant dream and of the dreamer himself, at ease nowhere, with nothing to do but tend graves and unloose the lifetime of madness inside him. And where did that madness flow? To his scribe, his translator, the one who must make sense of him: his eldest daughter, now locked in rigid sleep in the next room.

Poklub sat and rocked and composed in smoke. But Sonya would not retreat. It had taken her effort enough to come this far. One folly calls for another, she decided, and when the flare of Poklub's cigarette faded, she sprinted recklessly across the kitchen to the back porch room.

She need not have bothered. Old Man Poklub, even if he had seen her, would not have believed his eyes. A naked woman, a spot of light in the dimness, an angel of desire with her dark red bush in the center of her glowing skin, trailing her nightgown behind her like a second Sonya she was about to slough off. Her storm of loosened hair that connected her to the darkness—what was all that if not one more irritating vision the New World afflicted him with?

Poklub's cigarette threw off another flare. A piece of wool rolled in the tobacco, no doubt. Sonya Freedman passed safely into Gesser's room.

In that room, she came upon another extraordinary image. Truly, the Poklub flat was a house of surprises. There sat Jack Gesser, eating watermelons.

A knife was in one of them. A half-dozen more were lined up on the floor. He stood up formally, awkwardly, from his hard pallet.

Sonya put the sleeve of her gown in her mouth to keep from laughing.

"Do you want a slice?"

"Are you opening up a store back here?"

"No one will buy them. I end up having to eat them myself."

Sonya accepted a slice, then bent the edges back till it snapped in two. She let her nightgown fall. It dropped neatly over the fruit on the floor.

"Spielerman?" Gesser asked anxiously.

She moved to his pallet and when she got close enough, she stuck a half slice of melon in his mouth.

"You are hopeless."

Gesser nodded in agreement. He had sense enough, at last, to bite into the fruit. He was at a loss, but he understood this much: when a vision of beauty appears at your bedside with a slice of watermelon, don't waste time asking for her credentials.

3

INVITATION TO A VOYAGE

When he decided that he knew enough about Jack Gesser and Sonya Freedman, the Messiah of Division Street proposed that they take a trip on his behalf. Not only would they have his blessing—they would have his money, too.

"You are a man coming into awareness," Mitchell Berg told Gesser one day in his office, separated from the College's meeting hall by leather-lined double doors. "It's time for you to move one step further."

"With that superior tone of yours," Sonya answered, "and the way you never speak to me because I'm a mere woman, I think it's time for us to get the hell out of here."

"That's the only problem with your talk about equality," Gesser put in, ashamed at lagging behind Sonya. "There's no equality to it."

Berg smiled thinly. "You see why I trust you," he lied. "You are candid and open in your thoughts. I appreciate that."

The truth was elsewhere. Berg was forced to trust someone. In his calculations, for he was nothing if not a calculating man, he wagered that, since he had to put his trust in someone, he was better off choosing this pair of good-hearted neophytes who believed in roughly the same revolution he did, and who would blurt out exactly what they thought and how they'd acted, instead of counting on more qualified professionals like himself who might have the intelligence to turn against him.

Besides, the only qualified professionals he knew lived under the same surveillance he did.

Berg's office was a permanently cluttered, shabby affair, an intersection of technical manuals on plumbing and electricity, dictionaries, manuals of elocution, textbooks on the systems of government of the capitalist nations and their treacherous laws, stacks of drafting paper on which some essay or other had been scribbled. Berg, of course, knew exactly where everything was, down to the last bent paper clip and chewed pencil.

As did that Jewish G-man, Jacob Spolansky. He had experienced a little shiver of historical delight the night he discovered that the Messiah of Division Street was Lenin's translator. Spolansky never bothered reporting this fact to his superiors. Why should he? It was only a literary fact, and his superiors were not literary people. By the wavering light of his break-in lamp in the empty College, in the dark intimacy of the wee hours, he puzzled over Berg's English version of Vladimir Ilyich's awkward, obscure, tortuous prose. Berg himself had done the same puzzling in the course of his duties. He had wondered whether his rendering of "an infantile disease" was an adequate translation for Lenin's critique of the Left. It wasn't, Spolansky decided, dismissing Berg with a failing grade. Then again, Spolansky could not come up with anything better. There was simply no way you could put Lenin into English. The goateed little dictator's pen was just too Russian to make any sense over here, in the world of the pursuit of happiness. His ideas would never catch on, not with language like that.

Spolansky breathed an ideological sigh of relief. Such obscurantism coming from the king of revolutionaries made his own job a lot easier. How could a man be so obtuse and still represent a clear and present danger to the Constitution of the United States?

Jack Gesser was a preoccupied man the afternoon Berg ushered him and Sonya Freedman into his sanctuary. He had awoken early in his curtainless room and looked out over the rooftops to see that summer had retreated during the night. The day was blustery with cold sunlight, and Gesser understood why the blacks called the wind that blew off the lake "The Hawk." He swatted the wrinkles from his trousers and stepped into the kitchen, only to be confronted by the Poklub matriarch, bent over her eternal washing. The philosopher enters the world of dirty nightclothes. To his good morning, she loudly declared her regrets at not having called a copper when she'd turned the key in the door of her rightfully rented flat and discovered him sprawled on the floor, the very image of a reprobate and a cheat, a *goniff* and a *goslin*, which he had unfortunately turned out to be. Gesser made his habitual promise to come up with his share of the rent, and something extra for her trouble, then skittered out the door in humiliation.

At least Sonya had not been there to witness the scene. A fine gallant figure he would have made, scolded by the lady of the house as he slipped out the door, the very picture of the vaudevillian fool.

In his office, Berg swept the papers off a pair of straight-backed chairs so Jack and Sonya could sit down. Once they were warming their hands around cups of weak tea, he made his proposal.

"I would like you to do something for me," he began, then interrupted himself. "For me? It is not really for me. It is for the building of socialism."

Gesser and Freedman waited.

"I would like you to go to Haiti, to the town of Cape Haitian, and pick up two trunks for me. I would get these trunks myself, but there is the College . . . and, honestly, I am too well known by the capitalist police. You are not. You enjoy the privilege of anonymity. Haiti is no more than an American protectorate, as you may know, and it is not safe for me to be crossing borders with these trunks. I'm asking you to go to Florida, find your way by boat to Cape Haitian on the northern coast, locate the trunks and return with them. It is simple. The documents, the tickets—I will see to that."

Gesser nodded in silence. He did not even know where Haiti was. Though coming from Berg, the unexpected, even the absurd, seemed normal, a necessity, even noble. That was the skill of the professional revolutionary: to make the impossible appear plausible and within reach.

"Do we know what is in those trunks?" Sonya asked.

The question took Berg aback. A question about contents was the last thing he expected.

"Plans . . . blueprints," he muttered. "Property of the proletariat."

"And how will it be normal for us to be travelling to such a place?" She clasped the dark cloth of her jacket between two fingers to display her poverty. "We are travelling people, but not the sort who would go to these kinds of places. We'll stick out."

"I will make it look normal. Haiti is a tropical island, a beauty spot. Believe me, I've been there. You will be newlyweds, on your honeymoon." Berg raised his eyebrows in the slightest suggestion of a leer. "Believe me, it will make sense."

"Honeymooners going to Haiti in the middle of the Depression," Gesser countered. "This makes a lot of sense."

"It may be the Depression for you, but not for the rich. There are plenty of people still travelling to such places, I assure you."

Through the window, Sonya Freedman and Jack Gesser considered the thin sunshine devoured by smoke and clouds, and the Division Street trolley that ground over its rails the way life was grinding over them. A voyage to a tropical island, even one they'd never heard of, was preferable to all these things. Add to that the honor of retrieving the lost property of the proletariat, whatever that might turn out to be.

"When is all this going to happen?" Sonya asked.

"I don't know. It depends on when you're needed. A cable to Cape Haitian, the time it takes for an answer, everything that might make up the situation there . . . I wouldn't cancel your other plans."

"Our other plans? Our dance card is full, as you can imagine."

Berg rose from behind his desk and smoothed his walrus mustache. The interview was over, but for a final warning.

"It is a great privilege to handle the property of the proletariat. And a great responsibility, too, enforced by proletarian justice. The first time, through no fault of my own, I was forced to entrust these trunks to someone. Someone who betrayed my trust. As a result, the trunks are still down there. I can't have that happen again."

They nodded, properly chastened. Berg watched them exit his office as he chewed on the ends of his mustache. How absurd it was that his fate should be riding on these two innocent, insignificant immigrants. Freedman and Gesser—that they could save him was a measure of his desperation. Couples honeymooned in Niagara Falls. He knew that much about America. Whether they did the same in Haiti was a matter for conjecture. He, and they, would find out.

*　　　*　　　*

"It's better than selling watermelons off a cart," said Gesser. "Anything is."

"The property of the proletariat. That must mean it's our property, too."

"I doubt it. I don't think we're the proletariat. I think we're somewhere underneath."

As they walked down Division Street, Jack and Sonya were both perplexed and exhilarated. They were nobodies, yet they'd been chosen for what seemed to be a vital revolutionary errand. But in the making of the revolution, was it not said that even nobodies would have important roles to play?

The street presented its usual grim prospect of apple-sellers, straggly knots of the unemployed, papered-over storefronts, greasy fires in oil drums where men stood with permanent cold in their bones. But Jack and Sonya had a mission now, and it raised them above the common misfortune.

A streetcar bell rang behind them. They flagged the car and splurged on two tickets. They settled into their seats, grasping transfers in their hands as if they were ten-dollar bills.

"We don't have to look for work any more," Jack said as he watched the city parade by the streetcar window, a perspective vastly different from walking.

"How's that?"

"We've got a steady job."

"We do?"

"Yes. Waiting for Berg."

On Sangamon Street, they entered the flat with Sonya's key. Jack's position as delinquent roomer disqualified him from having his own.

"You go first and distract the old lady." He nudged Sonya forward. "I don't like seeing people I owe money to."

"There's no one here."

"How do you know?"

She stopped, listened, smiled. "The air. Feel it. It's too quiet."

She was right. The flat was a miracle of silence. Old Man Pok-lub was at his cemetery, combing the long green hair of the graves, gazing in puzzlement at his fingers that refused to grip the grass-cutting shears. The Poklub matriarch was on her laundry rounds, picking up soiled, dropping off clean. The daughters were at school, honing their English that would serve the family enter-prise, which was to protect the world from their father. Maxie was pounding the pavement, sweating under his great flapping cloak, not yet having understood that everything about him made him unemployable, beginning with his comical name. And Spielerman . . . Sammy Spielerman was out roving with his Roving Band.

The privacy was astonishing. The silence was breathtaking. Miraculous. Sonya and Jack had no other choice: they went at each other. Their clothes made a sad heap of patched woollens and overwashed underthings on the wooden floor in Gesser's boudoir, where The Hawk blew vengefully off the lake and rattled the windowpanes in their anchors of cracked putty.

Sonya lay gingerly on the hard pallet. Jack loosened her hair and her face swam in a great stream of red beauty.

He nodded to the poverty of the surroundings.

"I'm sorry the room is not more fitting," he said.

"You don't understand a thing, poor man."

The water groaning through the pipes from a neighboring flat startled Gesser awake. He lay still, his eyes closed, fearing detec-tion, by whom he was not sure yet, but knew he would soon dis-cover. Then he felt Sonya's arms around him, and remembered he was not in a slaughterhouse in Soukenai. A watery, mid-afternoon sun lit up his room. This was the New World, where such miracles as Sonya Freedman occur.

Sonya was awake. She eased herself away from him and stood up. "Come."

She pulled him to his feet. Emboldened by nakedness, they toured the Poklub collective flat, the soles of their feet turning black as they went. They stole past the raised Murphy bed where the Poklub virgins slept, and down the hallway to the master bedroom, that shrine to immigrant exhaustion. Sonya pushed open the door; it creaked its dismay. The Poklub couple's room was a small, off-white cube with a drawn shade that looked as though it had not been raised since they hung it there. A particular smell inhabited the room—of camphor, enclosure, the smell older bodies take on that is so repugnant to the young and vital. The bed stood in the center, its spread falling limply around the corners. A housecoat hung on a painted nail, and on the windowsill sat blurry family photographs in which subjects in dark clothes gazed at the camera as if it were a firing squad.

In that dim room, Sonya's naked body gleamed like a jewel. Jack reached down and cupped the wild red bush of hair at the top of her thighs.

"Like the color of sunset on a wheatfield," he rhapsodized.

"Ha! When was the last time you saw a wheatfield?"

"Twenty-five years ago, in Soukenai. It was on fire at the time."

They toured Maxie Poklub's alcove next. The armchair where he slept sitting up, in a state of exhaustion. At the end of every night, after reading himself to sleep, the book would tumble from his hand onto the floor, and he would lose his place. The next evening, unperturbed, he would begin all over again.

Sonya reached down and took the top book off the stack on the floor. It was the Cabbala.

"Here's a surprise," she said. "A mystic among us."

The stack of books tipped over, revealing what lay behind them. A wad of rumpled handkerchiefs, stiff with his seed.

"And here's something that's not a surprise. An onanist, to accompany the mystic."

"Poor boy."

"They go together," Jack said. "First you try to lose yourself in the mysteries of the Ineffable. When that doesn't work, you call on Rosie Palm and her five sisters."

From Maxie's alcove, Jack urged Sonya forward towards the parlor room she shared with Spielerman. He was in the mood for the kind of self-torture that comes from forbidden knowledge: the rumpled bedclothes, the lingering smell of repeated sexual intimacy, the familiarity of clothes hanging off the same hook, the sheer evidence of the man.

Sonya pushed open the door. It flew back on its hinges, dented the plaster behind it and came swinging back.

There were two beds, side by side.

"Happy?" she challenged.

Gesser shrugged. The scene proved absolutely nothing.

"I was born jealous. Not that I've ever possessed anything to be jealous about."

"Don't you know jealousy is a bourgeois capitalist notion?"

"I do."

"That we must eliminate?"

"Most certainly, and with alacrity."

"Through the practice of free love?"

"Free love? *Free love?* I've never seen anything worthwhile that was free, especially love."

"I thought you were an idealist."

"Yes. But I'm not a utopian. I'm a materialist. And this material,"

he said, sketching out the vertebrae of her spine, each one a perfect polished stone, "is so fine that I'm willing to commit counterrevolutionary thoughts for it."

"Whatever shall we do about your contradictions?"

"Anything, my love, but debate them."

Sonya laughed and spun away from him. When she was
younger, in her Budapest period, her body had been a burden to
her, the way a diamond watch is to a rich man who must walk
through a poor neighborhood. Free love arrived at a convenient
time. Here was a way to loose herself from the attraction her body
seemed to exercise. Take this irritating, precious jewel that caused
so much commotion and give it away, make it belong to everybody, nobody. Let those who cared about it so much worry themselves about it. As for her, she wanted no more of the mystery.

She took a few running steps down the hall, leaving the parlor
where her unresolved marriage dwelt, and made for Jack's cold
back porch. In the kitchen, with Jack in pursuit, she turned and
executed a move he guessed to be a ballet exercise. Sonya naked,
on one leg, the other one raised and bent so her foot touched her
knee, her arms high, her breasts better than the ones praised in
Solomon. The set of this strange ballet was a pair of deep porcelain sinks where the matriarch did her washing, and the heap of
carbonized tobacco that her husband the grave-tender left.

"I was a dancer in Budapest." Her voice suddenly went high
and wispy and insubstantial, like a lunatic old woman playing at
childhood. "A student ballerina. I would twirl around and around
and they would tell me, *No, no, not like that!* A little orphan ballerina, and then I grew a body, a woman's body, I was told, and
they let me go, for I could never be a real ballerina."

She fell from her flamingo pose and collapsed to the floor. Jack
rushed to catch her and steered her to their destination, the back

porch and the blanket-covered trunks. He pulled the covers over his bare back to shut out the raw autumn air and she arched up to meet him.

"We are going on a long journey," she whispered into his ear. "To fetch the property of the proletariat." She laughed raucously at Berg's noble phrase. "What property? The proletariat doesn't own a stick of anything! But who cares as long as we don't come back for a long, long time."

By the time they were through, the windows were running with condensation. Jack gazed upon beautiful Sonya the Red. The scattering of freckles across her cheekbones, her pale temples where blue veins pulsed, the hollows of her collarbone, the damp red nests under her arms, smelling of fresh, sweet sweat, the smell of love's labor. Sated with closeness, after a time Jack rolled off her and onto his stomach. Sonya would have none of it. She pursued him and climbed onto his back. He felt his seed running out of her, onto his buttocks. Then he remembered what seed was for, and he got worried.

"What if you get pregnant?"

"Ah, now he asks!"

He tried to phrase the question more honorably, heard how foolish he sounded, then quit.

She patted his head. "Don't worry, poor man. There won't be any little Sonyas or Jacks. Nature has arranged it for us."

"How can nature do something that's against nature?"

Sonya laughed at his outrageous naivety.

"Remember poor Onan, punished for spilling his seed in a place where it could not grow?" she asked.

"Such knowledge from a woman is rare," he complimented her.

"Remember, I'm from Hungary. We do everything differently there. So, do you know Onan?"

"What man doesn't?"

"You are an onanist, too. Because you are with a barren woman." She tapped her belly where their sweat was drying. "Inside, I am like stone."

"Is that a figure of speech or something?"

"Maybe it is. But like some figures of speech, it also happens to be the literal truth."

"But how can that be? How do you know?" Jack protested.

"Budapest is a city of doctors," Sonya said. "I had the opportunity to be examined. To discover."

"Is that why Spielerman . . . isn't here any more?"

"Oh no, Sammy was my protector, my deliverer. I told you, he's in search of the blues, he wants America, and none of that has anything to do with me. Absolutely nothing. When I was born, I came upside down, and sideways, and feet first, in every possible perverted way a child can choose to be born. Sammy was a prescient, curious little boy trying to scoot between adult legs to see what they did not want him to see, and find out if he could help, which he knew he could. When I finally made it into the world, all but killing my mother in the process, everyone was so busy working on her, a woman much respected, that they forgot all about me, that squalling, destructive, female creature in the middle of nowhere, on a plain the Hungarians call The Empty Spaces. Sammy had the presence of mind to pick me up and put me in the village oven, which was in our bakehouse. My mother died, I lived on; both events were my fault. By the time I reached womanhood, and it came quickly and decisively for me, Spielerman had declared he would be a musician, and would pick up no other tool than an instrument. He was a stubborn mule about it. We were betrothed to one another by village decree. It was a perfect match. Both of us were perverse and useless beings, a disgrace to a village like ours.

"And as for my state, whatever it is that made me want to be born the way I was had the wisdom to make sure it would not happen to anyone else, at least not my offspring."

Jack kissed her. "That's not onanism, you amateur exegete! Onanism is on purpose. You know, the stiff handkerchief."

"That's what you say now. But the word *barren* chills most men's bones before too long."

"Does it look like I want to settle down and raise a family? Besides, things can change, no offense to the good doctors of Budapest."

"See! I told you it would get to you, too! Nobody accepts it! Everybody wants to change it! But they can't!"

The matter of the unpaid roomer's share hung over the Poklub collective flat like a pall of linty tobacco smoke. For the sake of honor, that tattered tunic Gesser was trying to fit to his form ever since Sonya the Red had come into his life, he resolved to settle his debt. Gesser saw the payment as a test of his wits, a rehearsal for whatever was to happen once he and Sonya set out in search of the property of the proletariat, where it lay on some obscure tropical island.

He left the flat that evening before the Poklub matriarch could return with her sack of dirty laundry. Sonya was watching over the Poklub daughters' lessons, correcting them with her English, a spicy, eccentric mixture of jazz and jargon. The glow of her skin and the scent that came off her made a wonderful contrast to the grim, buttoned-up girls. Gesser kissed her behind the girls' back, put a hand on each of her buttocks and announced he had an errand to run.

When poverty comes in the door, love goes out the window, or so says Russian folk wisdom. Gesser was determined not to let this one get out the window, even if he had not exactly earned it—but who has ever truly earned love? He walked south along Sangamon Street in the early evening gloom. His errand involved high finance—seven dollars to be exact, though he had promised the Poklub matriarch a little extra for her waiting. Let's say ten. Ten dollars. The chances of finding ten dollars were about the same as those of the Messiah—the real one, that is—walking into Steinstein's, chalking up and running the table for all eternity.

Gesser turned onto Racine Street, towards Steinstein's. No money there, only commiseration, balm for the morale. The chirp of billiard balls, the *zhlub* King Levinsky's oafish, vaguely threatening grin and the heavy blue stink of cigar smoke were propitious to, if not thought, at least scheming. Men lay on the well-worn sofas, sleeping in shifts. Steinstein was at his counter, as round as a beer barrel, prosperous and in a permanent state of contentment. Happy with the Depression, for it helped fill his leisure hall with players and their nickels. Happy with Prohibition, because it had made him a successful businessman with his backroom commerce. Happy should Prohibition end, for he had made plans for that eventuality, too.

Gesser came to the counter.

"A *shikker ist a goy*," he said to Steinstein.

In return for the Yiddish password, which meant that all Gentiles are drunks, Gesser was given a glass of tea that was half schnapps. That, he'd earned; the password was his invention.

"You look down at the mouth," Steinstein said, watching him drink with satisfaction. "Like an old racehorse about to be turned into glue."

"Thanks. I have money troubles."

He paid for his tea. Steinstein made a move to push away the coins, but he wouldn't have it.

"Small change won't make any difference. Remember the apartment I . . . occupied? Turns out it was easier to occupy it than pay for it, once they made me an official roomer."

"There is always the usual midnight solution," Steinstein pointed out. "Or does your honor forbid you?"

"Honor? No. But I'm afraid there's a woman involved."

"*Oy, gevalt!*" Steinstein slapped himself on the forehead. "Not very original. Let me guess, who did you fall in love with? The *mamen*? The daughter? The niece? The neighbor lady? The washerwoman?"

"The star boarder. The *wife* of the star boarder, I should add."

Steinstein shook his head sadly. "Love . . . it's no blessing. You're not a simple man, Gesser."

"When was a Jew ever a simple man?"

The bootlegger and the *luftmensch* considered that one for a few seconds.

"She started it," Gesser said in his own defense. "She . . . visited me in my chamber, at night. In a state of splendid undress."

"Tell that to the judge. Or her husband. Whatever it is, it's always your fault. If a horse runs over you and breaks a leg, it's your fault. Don't you know that by now, or are you not a Jew?"

The very existence of Jack Gesser was proof of God's unfairness, Steinstein concluded. Take this skinny, dark, ropy, unemployed— but who wasn't?—hawk-nosed little kike. He was getting all he wanted, for free, without lifting a finger, under his very own roof, which he did not even pay for. Some people have all the luck!

Steinstein studied Gesser as the whisky glare came over the man's eyes, the sign of an inexperienced drinker. The bootlegger considered Gesser's predicament and thought briefly of helping him. There was money to be made in the whisky trade, but most of it in enforcement. Bashing heads. Or threatening to do so.

Gesser was trustworthy, he wouldn't stiff anyone, but his head was too much in the clouds, Steinstein decided, to use his fists and his feet. It was a dilemma. If the Almighty had combined the *zhlub* King Levinsky's bulk with Gesser's brains, He would have created the perfect rum-runner.

In lieu of help, Steinstein poured Gesser another tea.

"On the house. Look at it as consolation. Maybe it will—what do you poets call it?—inspire you into finding the rent money. There's not much loose cash around here. It's all got strings on it. Chains, more like it. Like the room in your flat. I don't think the table's going to help you either. With all respect, you're a lousy pool player."

By the time he left the poolroom, Gesser was in a cloud of befuddlement, courtesy of Steinstein's spiked teas. On the way out he smiled graciously at the beefy, moronic *zhlub* Levinsky, in itself a sure sign of intoxication. Gesser, in true American style, was drinking his way towards a solution. He felt a dangerous sense of exhilaration as if, from his vantage point on the choppy sidewalk of Racine Street, could he but extend his arms a little further than the end of his fingertips, he might finally grasp the truth. The truth of what to do with himself. The truth of a ten-dollar bill. A sawbuck. Two fins. Ten singles. Lettuce. *Dough-ray-mee*. Spot cash money.

He walked to the edge of the curb and stood upon it, swaying over the abyss a few inches below, praying that no one would recognize him, for truly, he was beyond speech. Then he was struck by inspiration, as Steinstein warned he might be.

If there was money to be found, it would certainly not be on this street. If there had been any, he would have found it. He never understood beggars who panhandled in the poorest districts, unless they wanted a handout of misery. He walked south along Sangamon, out of his neighborhood. By now the darkness was complete, the air raw, the streetlamps wispy and conspiratorial. Under one such light he stopped and read a hand-painted sign in the window of a corner storefront. The Blarney Social Club, Strictly Private Members Only. The social club was a kind of *schul* for Irishmen, in which worldly subjects were examined, and whisky and beer sold. A philosopher's paradise of a kind. The amateur philosopher in Gesser hit upon the paradox of the place: if it was private, why put up a sign at all?

The door to this social club opened and disgorged one of its members, transported on a blare of voices and a cloud of smoke. The man was a smaller version of Steinstein, short and round and thick and red-faced, with red hair, carrying a checked wool cap in his hand. He looked so much like the picture of the drunken *goy* that the Jews of Sangamon Street were encouraged to keep in their imaginations that Gesser wondered if the man was real.

Like a moth, the man gravitated towards a lamppost as Gesser backed away into the darkness. It wasn't light the man was looking for but the post that held it aloft, against which he leaned, getting his bearings. Unsuccessfully, it turned out. He slapped his cap on his head, then slid, back to the lamppost, until he had achieved the seated position, his knee joints cracking on the way down.

The words *rolling a drunk* appeared from Jack Gesser's compendium of colorful expressions. It did not mean what it seemed. You did not force an intoxicated man into an oil drum and send him down a slope. In a state not that different from the Irishman's, Gesser bent over and pried a loose brick out of the sidewalk. Bridgeport Brick, the brick read, and it supplied its telephone number. Bricks that say *brick* on them and give you their phone number, Gesser thought, freeing the brick. What a wonderful place this America is. Even the stones speak.

He stepped out of the darkness with his Bridgeport Brick and stood before the Irishman. Towered over the slumping man, or so he hoped.

"You must give me your money," he told the drunk.

"I must, must I?" he queried. "And why must I do a thing like that, do you figure?"

"None of your business!"

"It certainly is my business." The drunk man looked up at Gesser with weary, watery blue eyes. "I would say it's very much my business, wouldn't you? I mean, here you are, demanding all my money. Don't you think I've got a democratic right to know what you intend to do with it?"

"I'm not going to drink it away," Gesser scolded him. "It's for the rent, not that it makes any difference. Now hand it over."

"Well, how about that? As if you were the only one who needed money to pay his rent. If you take mine, do you figure the landlady will take pity on me? Not at all! She'll say it's all my fault again."

They had been trapped in reasonable discussion for hours, it seemed to Gesser. Crime, he understood, was to be committed quickly. It did not involve exploring the victim's point of view. Like Samson himself, he brought down the Bridgeport Brick onto the head of the little Irish fireplug.

Nothing happened. The man reached under his cap, patted his scalp tentatively, then looked up.

"Now, I seen that brick in your hand, but I never thought you'd do a thing like that."

Gesser did it again. Again, to no avail. The drunk adjusted his cap, and with his back against the lamppost, assumed the standing position, like a snake gliding up a rope.

"Thanks, I needed that," the drunk told him, smoothing his clothes. "Now, if you don't mind, I'll be on my way."

And he did just that, ambling away from the Blarney Social

Club with steady tread, down a residential street of squat little houses. Houses where people who weren't Gesser's kind lived, who could take two blows to the head with a Bridgeport Brick and thank the brick.

Gesser got out of Bridgeport in a hurry. He walked north and east into Chinatown, where there would be fewer chances of a victim engaging him in blarneyed, beery conversation in the English language. Where the skulls would be more fragile, too, he hoped. By the time he reached 22nd Street and Wentworth, he found he was holding a second Bridgeport Brick in his hand, and rage over his failure in his heart.

The Chinese, it seemed, never ate at home. Perhaps they did not have kitchens in their flats. They certainly did not surround everything they ate with all manner of laws and restrictions. Every second storefront was a restaurant, and all were filled with steam and smoke and hurried diners working their chopsticks in furious, private rhythms. On Sangamon Street, it was considered a shame to have to eat in public. You never knew what was in the food. Even modern-minded immigrants like Gesser who had given up on keeping kosher nourished the ancestral distrust of other hands touching their food before it passed through their mouths and into their precious stomachs.

Gesser walked through Chinatown twice before the opportunity was given to him. A man in white trousers and undershirt, with a grey padded pyjama coat thrown over his shoulders against the cold, was locking up his restaurant. He worked the two locks and shook the door; the plate glass trembled. He turned up the street, feeling secure in his possessions. Gesser fell in behind him.

No talk. No negotiations, Gesser reminded himself as he followed the man down an alley that ran off 22nd Street. The Jew of the East will meet the Jew of Europe in a quick, brutal commercial transaction.

Gesser crept up on his heels to keep his loose sole from flapping on the pavement. He was on top of the restaurateur before he could turn around. He showed Gesser an angry mask, work-hardened, hateful, pock-marked, the color and consistency of grease. The face of the proprietor class, Gesser thought briefly, then clapped both bricks over the man's ears. He collapsed with a weak, bird-like cry. Gesser hated him, hated himself. Hated America.

There was a goldmine in the man's loose white trousers. Singles, twos, fives. What riches Chinatown held; how poorly its merchant princes lived. Gesser did not linger over his good fortune. He made a quick moral decision. He took most of the man's money, more than he strictly needed, but left a little, which a common thief would not have done.

I'm an uncommon thief, at least I have that distinction, Gesser told himself as he ran down the alley, his sole flapping angrily against the bricks. Behind him, the outraged Chinaman called for help. But no help came, not even from his own ghetto.

4

THE LOCAL GODS

The Poklub matriarch did not know whether to bless the unname-
able name of the Lord or spit on the ground three times when
Gesser laid the ten-dollar bill on the kitchen table the next evening,
with all members of the Poklub collective flat in attendance.

Old Man Poklub, constructing a cigarette fleck by fleck,
regarded the green bill with mild interest. It was, after all, only
paper, and you could not even write on it.

"Where did you find that?" the matriarch demanded of Gesser.

Gesser was stuck. He could hit a Chink and a Mick with a Bridgeport Brick, but he had prepared no ready lie for the Poklub woman.

"He got it the way anybody gets money in this country,"
Sonya the Red rescued him. "By exploiting his fellow man. In one
way or another."

"Yes. In one way or another," Gesser approved.

Spielerman was making a rare appearance at the flat that evening, busying himself with the maintenance of his clarinet. He was dressed as snazzily as a bootlegger, a successful one at that. Since his last appearance on Sangamon Street he had metamorphized again: he'd changed his name to Smoky Sam and his Red-Hot Band, but as far as Sonya and Jack's needs were concerned, he was still Roving Spielerman.

"Music isn't exploitation," he declared. "One of the few things that's not."

"We can't all be artists," Gesser muttered. "You need a few peddlers to make the kopecks to pay the piper."

"Of course, peddlers are well-known patrons of the arts," Spielerman countered.

"Boys, boys, don't fight," Sonya said. She touched her cousin and her lover on the shoulder. "I see a lot of things in this room, but I don't see any peddlers. Anyway, I'd hate to think that we're no more than the job we are forced to do." She held up her hands reddened by wash-water. "What would that make me?"

No one was foolish enough to answer that challenge.

That evening, a messenger came unbidden to the door, the way messengers always do. The astrakhan hat crushed on his scalp, the almond eyes and black filaments of mustache hair—Berg's Kirghiz assistant caused a sensation whenever he went onto the streets of Chicago.

He bowed slightly at the door, exposing the top of his hat, which looked as though it had seen the underside of the Halstead Street trolleycar.

"Comrade Berg would like to see you."

"When?" Jack asked.

"Now."

And with that, the messenger went stiffly, self-importantly down the stairs, leaving an open door behind him.

"I'm not in the mood," Gesser complained halfheartedly. "I saw enough of this town last night."

"A true comrade doesn't argue over matters of discipline," Sonya laughed. "I'll go with you."

She picked up her coat and put it on, just in time to greet the next visitor. There was a shuffling of feet and a purposeful throat-clearing at the door of the Poklub collective flat. The outside world didn't often come knocking on the Poklubs' door, but when it did, it knocked loud and variously. Sonya turned and found herself staring into the glossy black face of a strong-shouldered young woman, whose hair was swept and styled and teased into the shape of a crown. On top of her crown of hair sat a tangle of rhinestones.

"Mr. Spielerman, please."

She spoke barely above a whisper, as if she had a sore throat. Her soft tone gave her voice a particular dignity.

When she was shown into the kitchen, Spielerman rose to take her hands with exaggerated formality. He kissed them, and she stood still as he circled around her to admire her long red velvet gown.

"Miss Pearl," he introduced her to the astonished Poklubs. "She is the new singer in Smoky Sam's Red-Hot Band."

"But she's black," the Poklub matriarch pointed out in Yiddish.

"Blessed is the Lord, who giveth variety to his creation," Old Man Poklub countered in the same language.

Spielerman offered her a chair and she lowered her dignified bulk upon it.

"It is always a thrill for me to meet the people of the Book," she said to the Poklubs in a perfect, soft, modulated, caressing voice. "For throughout our history, we have both thirsted for freedom."

"She sure can talk," Old Man Poklub complimented her. He motioned towards the open door. "You really found her out there?"

Spielerman raised a finger. "Ah, yes, but you should hear her sing. She *is* the blues, you can't imagine. The very heart and flesh of the blues."

Sonya regretted her comradely discipline, for now it was too late to take off her coat in order to gape at Miss Pearl. As for Gesser, he set out for the People's College of Trades and Vocations with a lighter heart. Now he knew where Spielerman was doing his searching for the blues. Miss Pearl, the very meat of the blues, the new queen of the Jews. That damned horn-tooter, Gesser thought to himself, he certainly has made the most of America. Some people have a knack for fitting in.

Jack and Sonya were positively intoxicated by their newfound sense of mission; it was Berg's little gift to the lovers for the services they would be providing him. The night of Miss Pearl's visit, the Messiah of Division Street had looked somewhat less assured as he handed over the bundle of tickets and instructions, as if the absurdity of the errand had suddenly become apparent, even to him. Postulate an obscure black island, and on that island a beach, no doubt with palm trees, under which was a hut, a thatched hut, why not, and in that hut two large suitcases that held some indescribable treasure, which these two equally obscure individuals—an intellectual watermelon vendor and a sexually free washerwoman—were to recover and return to the proper scheming Bolshevik hands. Gesser and Freedman might as well have invested in the snake-oil futures that were being hawked around the neighborhood as believe in Berg's concoction.

There was one difference. They weren't paying to go to Cape Haitian. It was the other way around. The tickets, the name of the

freighter, the hotel, the overgenerous allotment of spending money—
that's what gave the *true* to their strange but true assignment.

Given the choice, rather than crisscross the alleys of the near
West Side in the icy rain, selling root vegetables now that melons
were finished, why not sit back and enjoy the scenery?

As they rode the train south to Florida, then found the promised
steamer that would take them to the Cape, Gesser and Freedman
discovered the experience called privacy. It dawned upon them
slowly as they sailed on the sluggish, rickety freighter southward
across the glassy Caribbean, the only passengers on the ship. As
the low Florida coast melted away, and they leaned against the
deck rail, gazing in silence at the unbroken blue water around
them, it occurred to them that they were completely alone. No
one was watching. No one was *there*. On the first morning in their
sultry bunk, unrelieved by any porthole or breath of air, Gesser
awoke with a start to hear no footsteps, no voices, no petty human
stirring in the bathroom—just the tired lugging of the freighter's
engines. The experience was intoxicating. Like all forms of intoxication, it contained its share of vertigo, for the irritating proximity and friction of the next closest human being did, after all,
provide a deep and ancient form of comfort.

Privacy is not for everyone. Some people, even lovers, will experience it as an intolerable form of loneliness. Not Jack and Sonya.
It took them only the first night to realize what privacy is for.

Gesser opened his eyes and looked across the damp sheets.
Sonya Freedman was looking back at him. What was in her eyes?
The terror of the traveller, the taste for adventure, sheer disbelief
at their good fortune. She smiled, shifted in the narrow bed. The
good, rich smell of two bodies in harmony enveloped them.

"Newlyweds," she reminded him.

70

"This isn't what I imagined the revolution was about," Gesser admitted.

"Maybe this *is* the revolution. Think about that."

Sonya threw off the sheet and climbed atop him.

"Sacrilege!" he protested in vain. "The political and the personal . . ."

By then she was astride him. She ran her hands over his body and sketched out every part of him as the good doctors of Budapest had done with her young body, back in her victim period. Victim no more. She had always wanted to know how a man's body was put together. Prone on a couch, classified as a barren hysteric by the psychiatric cabal, she had felt nothing but the weight of pipesmoke, the pseudoscientific vocabulary of exclusion and the heavy meal the particular doctor had taken for lunch. In this overheated bunk in a freighter she was free. With her fingernail she traced out the crease where the Lord had sewn Jack and all other men together. She remarked on how the most neglected parts had their sensitivities that weren't to be neglected, that even the hole out of which a man shat could grow smooth with lubrication, the way a woman did under the right conditions. She beheld the way the testicles hung in their fragile sac, one lower than the other, and she was moved by their fragility, as by the glass animals of her childhood menagerie. She took one of his balls in her mouth and tasted its must. She gave him sensations he had not known existed, though she paid him little mind as he pleaded and twisted under her care. All that mattered was to explore and pry and *lead*, as on the dance floor. Jack's body was hard and lean and totally unaccustomed to tenderness, not overfed and smug, which is why she loved him. She came up proudly from her explorations and parted the lips of her sex and showed Jack her bright pink glistening bud of pleasure, something he'd only heard about in stories around the table at Steinstein's poolroom. So it was true after all, he marvelled, that women also had something outside their bodies, something accessible to him. Something he could understand.

This is what privacy provides to those who have never known it. Gesser and Freedman surfaced in the early evening, watched dolphins jump and the sea come alive with phosphorescence, then returned to the burning hell of their cabin.

According to maritime tradition, those travelling into the tropics for the first time must undergo a baptism of sorts. Sometime between the first day and the second of their voyage out, Jack and Sonya crossed that invisible line in the sea. But the crew of the freighter was unused to passengers, and too busy nursing along the ship's engines to perform the ceremony. Jack and Sonya had to attend to their own baptism, in the way they saw fit. They were self-created, self-saved, reborn.

Do not think that Sonya Freedman's liberation was without bitterness. Her exuberant freedom was underwritten by pain, motivated by loss. Sonya became that dark, musky, blooming, burning bush only through an extravagant confession of her barrenness, the very thing that made her useless in the economy of marriage. Her name was Freedman. Never was a name more appropriate, Jack complimented her. A made-up name, she corrected him, an ironic name. Prisoners, she reminded him, are always calling themselves Freedom.

But confession itself won't procure you liberation. You have to glory in your state. No doubt she insisted on it a little too often as she and Gesser sailed the smooth Caribbean. No doubt she fashioned a character for herself. No doubt it was a way of testing Gesser's attraction. Love this, mister: a squalling, mother-killing little package that should have been scraped away by an angel-maker, but instead got popped into a bread-oven by a big-eyed, far-seeing boy, kept alive in the same warmth that baked the Sabbath chala, and rewarded by the barren beauty that had made her the toast of analysts in both Buda and Pest.

More extraordinary origins! It was a regular epidemic!

First, you tell a story to free yourself. It works. Then you tell it again, to be freer still, over and over. Pretty soon it becomes a habit, and you're trapped once more.

Sonya the Red. Sonya the Free. She ran her tongue and lips over the parts of Gesser's body that he was willing to touch in only the most cursory fashion, and pitied men for being such strangers to their bodies. As for her, she had no more society, no exchange value in the man and woman economy, no one watching, no Lord in the heavens, no fear of the body's revenge in the form of pregnancy. She became a wild-haired, sweating creature, on all fours in a hothouse cabin. Even Gesser, the complicated man, always in search of the oblique angle, had to surrender.

Newlyweds, indeed. What a prophet that Berg was!

One evening as the sun began to pool into the Caribbean to starboard, Jack Gesser stood by the rail, alone briefly, and cast his eyes upon the paradise of Cape Haitian. He considered the town, smaller than he had imagined it, and the swift rise of the green hills beyond it, up towards mad King Christophe's mountain citadel. He realized he was debarking at a place that was no more and no less than the geographical representation of Sonya Freedman's body.

The town's reflection shimmered in the black harbor water. The port was a riot of bougainvillea that ran along the balconies of the waterfront stores, of palm fronds stirring like flower petals in a small park where a bandstand stood, covered in thatch, of great stacks of jute bags ready to be loaded onto the freighter for the return trip, of dockworkers chewing stalks of sugarcane, machetes riding along their thighs like a second phallus. Sonya came to stand next to him, her foot resting on the small suitcase they were to exchange for Berg's trunks. Her hair was up to catch the cooling trade winds, and on the nape of her neck she wore a tiny necklace of bruises he had applied with his teeth.

The two buoys that marked the safe limits of the harbor entrance said everything they needed to know about the Cape. Each tilted in the opposite direction, as if contrary currents ran simultaneously through the waters. The blue-green sea behind the freighter thrashed and foamed as the boat began to maneuver into the small harbor. Ships flying French and Dutch flags rocked at anchor.

But Cape Haitian was more than a sleepy tropical port engaged in the banana and coffee trade. If it had been that, its harbor would not have been busy with American troops.

"You have to wonder how Berg's trunks ended up here. It's a long way to Division Street," Sonya said. "There's not even an industrial proletariat here, by the looks of it."

"You have to wonder about a lot of things. Like why we were chosen. I suppose the idea is not to anticipate or look like we know too much."

"That's easy enough," Sonya assured him. "We don't know too much." She paused. "In fact, we don't know anything at all."

As Berg had promised back in Chicago, there was indeed a room for them at the Hôtel Américain, a rum-drinking parlor with wide unscreened windows that looked out on the port. They checked in, contracted to have a fish grilled for their supper on the cooking fire around the back and went upstairs. A bed, a chair, a pitcher of water covered with a circle of lace, a fragment of mirror, a crucified Jesus woven from sisal bound to a cross of rusty metal. They went onto the balcony with its wrought iron railing to look at the place to which they had journeyed.

In the street below their balcony, men played dominoes, their score sheet rippling in the breath of the trade winds. Women smoked and chewed their soft wooden pipes in the doorways, a boy was having his head shaved against pests, schoolgirls were reciting the next day's lessons in flawless unison. Jack and Sonya felt invisible, as if in this country, to be white was to be transparent as a pane of glass, of no consequence to the lives of the people.

That, of course, was not true. The white soldiers in the harbor, anything but transparent with the clouds of shoeshine boys around them, made that clear.

Early that evening, the newlyweds were sitting at a table by the open window, on the other side of which the occasional drunk American Marine wheeled by. A bottle of cloudy rum and two glasses stood close at hand. In this spectacularly rotting paradise, the struggles of Sangamon Street and the building of international socialism seemed to belong to another galaxy, a hollow, tinny, distant, comical system of planets, where people fought to the death for what was given out free here. Light, fresh air, fresh fruit, the easy availability of intoxication.

When the waiter brought the fish, handsomely grilled with gleaming slices of lime and a foot-long banana split up the middle, he sat down at their table with it.

"The grouper is very good," he assured them in stiff Oxford English, as if he were intent on sharing their meal.

He made no move for the fish, but he did pour himself a dose of dusky *clairet* in Jack's glass as Sonya went about stripping the flesh off the central bone.

"I am not a waiter," the waiter said after a liberal sip.

"Of course not," Jack agreed, thinking of tropical illnesses born by human contact.

"My name is White. I am the chief of police." He rolled up his sleeve and set his arm next to Jack's. "Look, I am whiter than you are."

Jack understood he was to compare arms. He set his sinewy, coffee-colored forearm next to White's.

"Definitely, you are whiter."

It was wiser to agree with the man. Besides, he was right.

"That's why everyone in the Cape calls me White."

"We certainly will, too," Sonya promised, chewing the dense flesh of her grouper, which was excellent.

"I piss on White," the man said.

He rolled down his sleeve and the clownish, obsequious tone disappeared from his voice.

"In the Cape we are blessed with great writers and great painters. We are Haiti's city of artists—that is why we are a city of the second order. I am sure you know of the poet Léo Aubin, you who are no doubt a man of culture, for if you were not, your master would not have sent you here. Aubin is the one who will take you to the Austrian's hut."

"What does an Austrian have to do with all this?" Sonya wondered.

White found and picked off a line of flesh that she had neglected to loosen from between the grouper's husky ribs.

"That is part of the story which, even if I knew, I would not tell you. I would not spoil Aubin's pleasure . . . After this fish, which is very good, you will go to the Melomaniacs' Club. Aubin will be there."

"How will we know who he is?" Jack asked anxiously.

The man laughed uproariously, then drained off the rest of the rum, sediment and all.

"Don't be ridiculous. He will recognize you. Can you guess how?"

*   *   *

Sonya wondered what Spielerman would think of the music at the Melomaniacs' Club that evening. Spielerman who worked so hard to transform himself, who would go to any length to become one with the music he wanted to play. Spielerman, whom Sonya half expected to show up one morning dyed black. The music at the Melomaniacs' Club was anything but contrived. It seemed to rise of its own accord from the earth, and use the voices of the instruments to make itself heard. The musicians simply held their instruments up to their mouths and the music issued forth from them, naturally.

Unlike the blind pigs and sporting houses where Spielerman's preferred music was played, there were no obstacles to getting into the Melomaniacs' Club. The place had no walls. The roof was made of coconut fronds lashed together, and sturdy poles held the construction in place. Gesser and Freedman stood at the edge of the smooth wooden floor as the couples eased by them, barely lifting their feet, the men dancing studiously, the women holding themselves stiffly, but wonderfully responsive. A breath of wind stirred the thatch, the fronds rattled like a child's toy and a minute later a heavy rain began to fall, straight down, pouring evenly off the roof. Not a drop reached the dance floor, which a diligent dwarf dusted with talc after every piece.

The band members conducted themselves like priests, which they might have been, in their day jobs. They were elegantly aware of their importance, dispensing the magic of their music with a kind of sensual dignity and discipline. In times of oppression, and it is always such a time in Haiti, rhythm can speak most freely. Jack and Sonya stood in the narrow zone between the rain and the whirling couples, enchanted, understanding nothing of the words and little of the music. Suddenly, Léo Aubin was at their side. The poet laureate of the Cape looked like a figure from an El Greco canvas. Tall and cavernous, with caved-in cheeks and yellow-red eyes, fingers as long as church candles, and clothes hanging off him as off a scarecrow.

"You are enjoying your honeymoon?"

"A charming spot. Far from our troubles," Sonya obliged him.

"But in the very heart of ours," Aubin spoke the obvious.

Then he seized both her hands and took her into his arms.

"In the Cape, we consider it good luck to dance with the new bride. And I have never touched a woman with red hair before who was not for sale."

Gesser watched as Aubin led Sonya, laughing at his racy gallantry, onto the mirror-like floor embellished by dust-trails of white talc. Sonya did not know the mambo. She had never seen the particular drums used here, which were fashioned from wooden crates heavily seasoned with machine oil, with holes drilled in them. She had never heard the instruments she did recognize, accordions and guitars, manipulated and twisted the way they were in the Melomaniacs' Club. But she followed the ease of the rhythms and the vegetal scent of the poet Aubin who swept her across the floor in accordance with the rules of the mambo. She pressed her body against Aubin's, put her head back and laughed at her own boldness. *May we never go back*, she fervently wished, *may we never find Berg's crazy mixed-up trunks*.

But her partner was all business. Beneath the stylized passion of the mambo, Sonya heard his grave voice in her ear, giving her instructions in a gentle, sorrowful tone that was strangely at odds with his message.

"Your husband will march you out of here, with proper jealousy. I will come after to make sure he does not harm you excessively, and we will undertake to dispute the possession of you, but without exchanging blows, of course, for such realism would be unseemly between black and white. As we do so we will walk out of the light onto the dark paths, which does not take long in the Cape. I will lead you to the Austrian's hut. With your shoes, that would be a mile away."

Aubin turned her in Gesser's direction, and as she went wheeling by she caught sight of him, as stiff as one of the poles that held up the roof. He was exhibiting proper jealousy, as Aubin predicted. The rest of the dance followed Aubin's prescriptions to the letter. He released Sonya with a kiss, advising her to seek pleasure on her honeymoon, since everyone knows that a marriage is built on the foundation of those first days. Gesser, realizing that he was in a dance palace and not knowing how to dance, and not owning shoes that would agree to dance, especially not the mambo, escorted her out of the club and across the noisy square where a pig was contentedly roasting over a mountain of coals. Aubin arrived and began to badger the couple in a way so stagy that even Gesser was tempted to laugh. They quickly came to the limit of the electric lights, strung up by the Marines to keep the forest spirits at bay, and Aubin disappeared into the darkness in front of them, as dense and sudden as the tropical rain. Jack balked, but Sonya urged him forward and they stepped into the blackness.

Sonya and Jack moved like sleepwalkers at the edge of a precipice, afraid to wake up and fall. Candles and lanterns burned in shacks set back from the muddy road, but the humidity devoured their light. Something skittered underfoot. Sonya jumped and stifled a cry, then discovered she had stumbled over a family sleeping on grass mats by the side of the path. Even on this tropical night, the sheer resignation of these people chilled her.

Mercifully, Aubin interceded from the darkness, holding a lantern.

"We here in the Cape have attracted some attention, as you can see by the soldiers in the harbor who have come to stay with us. I am still not sure what it is they see in us. Do they care so much for bananas and pineapples that they must send soldiers with guns to help in the harvest? By now we have gotten used to the white man, but we will never understand him. We did not understand the Austrian either. No man had ever done anything like that, except a madman perhaps, but I did not think that the category of white could also contain the category of lunatic, though I am not so sure now. One morning the Austrian stepped down from a ship, dragged his trunks along the beach and took over a hut. We wondered how many clothes one man, even a white man, could possibily need, but he soon told us that the trunks weren't his, and neither did they contain clothes. He was keeping them, he said, for someone else. We stopped asking questions, and waited. At one time the hut had belonged to the woman who gathered oysters, but when she saw a white man in a golden uniform with golden hair coming down the beach towards her, she thought it was Death himself, or some spirit worse yet, and who could blame her? She ran into the bush."

Aubin stopped and turned up the wick on his lantern.

"Now," he said with priestly ceremony, "we will try to find his dwelling."

They began the passage to the Austrian's hut. Two boys fell in behind them on the trail, a discreet distance behind. Jack and Sonya could only hope they were with Aubin. They followed the bobbing yellow glow of the poet's lamp, and the cloud of mosquitoes that wheeled around it. Jack thought of malaria, or diseases worse, leeches that would attach themselves to his sex; Sonya, of the woody resistance of Aubin's body under his overwashed, shapeless shirt, picturing his body slashed out of palm trunk and whittled down to its essential matter. Bats materialized around the lamp to skim off the mosquitoes. The velvet wings of these unnatural mammals swept by their faces, and the air was full of their primitive radar that humans cannot see but can feel in the hollow center of their bones. In a minute, the bats had cleared the air around the lantern, and disappeared. The forest was full of the cries of higher beasts, predators and hunted, and those opportunists in between. From behind the animal cries came a sound that issued from the earth itself: that of dozens of pairs of human hands striking the taut brown skins of drums in every quarter: in forest clearings, in the smoky courtyards of the Cape, in the makeshift temples along muddy paths. This music was not made to please or transport couples across the polished floor of the Melomaniacs' Club in strictured passion, the women with hibiscus in their hair. Once the drumming entered your ear, you could hear nothing else. It was insistent, maddening, it left no peace, it was as much part of the earth as the strangling vegetation or the humidity that rose through the reglued soles of their boots.

The strangest fact of this passage was that no one was pursuing them. The evil that had this night humming with anticipation was not devised by men. It was in nature, in God's creation itself. It taught folly; it taught that to love is to possess and devour. As a boy, Gesser had walked from Soukenai to the port of Gdansk, in Poland, sleeping in the barns of people who would have killed him had they known he was there, but he had never passed through a night like this one.

Finally, they emerged from the forest onto the beach. Aubin extinguished the lantern. A few moments later the slapping of the boys' machetes against their thighs also stopped.

Aubin took off his shirt and shook it out.

"Do as I do. That's how you get the ticks out."

Jack obeyed, then he and Aubin averted their eyes so Sonya could do the same. She turned around, took off her blouse and shook it, and found herself face to face with the boys who were her escort. Naked from the waist up, she smiled indulgently, then slowly put her shirt back on.

The beach stretched between two promontories. A few huts were scattered at the far end, under a rocky headland, darker shapes with pointed thatched roofs against the pale sand. Inside them, no lights burned. Gesser and Freedman fell in behind Aubin as he moved easily over the sand towards the huts. The sky swam with stars, phosphorescence cut drunkenly through the sea and land crabs scuttled underfoot, heavy, blind creatures that never touched the sea.

Then without warning, halfway to their destination, Aubin stopped. The slap of metal on flesh, a sound to which Sonya was attentive, also fell silent. Aubin began to declaim with the madness of a poet long deprived of an audience, whose speech is often rehearsed but rarely pronounced.

"You know me as Aubin; probably you don't know who I am at all. In truth, I am *le duc de l'Avancé*. The Duke, you would say it. Which is why the Austrian confided in me, why his master, who is also yours, confided in me, and why I am in a position to help you. The natural call of noble blood. The Austrian and I understood that. I knew that only a member of the nobility would go to the extremes he did." He paused and considered the word *nobility*. "A nobility that no longer means much here."

Aubin waved his doused lantern at the empty beach and the wall of noisy forest behind it.

"Imagine it, a white man, *here*. But I am more than the Duke. I am the poet of the Cape, which is why I hate the white soldiers, and why I am helping you. The soldier has turned me into folklore.

Under his orders my songs must be accompaniment to his tavern rowdiness. I aspire to the higher forms from Europe, from France, which I use to speak of the grandeur of my soul. How can we poets speak of the grandeur of our souls with the cries of fishmongeresses and cane-cutters?"

A few anxious seconds elapsed before Gesser realized that Aubin wanted an answer to his question.

"We used to have the same argument in Europe," Gesser said cautiously. "Some people maintained the language of the common people was not suitable for high drama and noble sentiments, and that we should use the sacred language. Others said that the sacred language should be kept for dealings with the Almighty, and not for our passing human miseries. Then there were others still who held that the sacred language should not be used at all until a sacred time dawned, when it would become the only appropriate speech. Their detractors wondered why, then, had we bothered to learn a sacred tongue if we could not use it, since such a time as they were waiting for was not likely to come, and if it did, perhaps all speech would be ruled out entirely. The populists maintained that if high sentiments could not be spoken in the language the people could understand, then such sentiments were useless."

"Fascinating! And what was decided?" Aubin asked breathlessly.

"Nothing. Nothing is ever decided in such matters. People go about living the way they wish to, or can, believing what they need to, and practicing their beliefs if they're brave enough. And then, so many people went to America, where the whole question soon became too petty to interest any but the most philosophically minded."

The prospect shocked Aubin.

"But such things *must* be decided! How could such a question go undecided? How can the poet speak with the raucous screeches of the mango-ladies, especially when there are noble forms available for his use?"

Gesser shrugged. "That *is* the question," he agreed.

"The question is one of profanation!" Aubin declared.

"Profanation is an unfamiliar idea for us," Sonya put in. "At least as far as art is concerned."

"That's true. Either you believe that all art is profanation, because it is idol-making, or you rule out profanation altogther. If you admit art, you admit profanation."

"They want me to sing tavern songs," Aubin wailed, ignoring Jack and Sonya. "By order of their bayonets."

Behind them, still at a discreet distance, their machete-bearing escorts had sunk to a squatting position on the sand. They were used to such lamentations about the world's ungratefulness, which seemed to be part of the glory and misery of the poet's lot.

"Here, at least, in this nocturnal refuge, I can let my true voice be heard."

And Aubin began to recite. His voice was beautiful, a high fragile tenor, an astounding voice in an ascetic's body. *Cœur, rossignol, vigile, repos,* Aubin sang on this narrow beach to an audience of two baffled Chicago Jews and the same number of eternally patient bodyguards.

When the recital was over, Jack and Sonya did not dare applaud. They were too afraid of committing profanation.

"My heart is a nightingale that sings all night to protect your sleep," Aubin explained.

A poem, like a joke, always loses something in the explanation.

Then a terrible howl rose up in the forest behind them. High-pitched, outraged screams travelled through the trees like lightning. It could have been monkeys disturbed by a predator; it could have been a woman in the throes of religious possession. Behind the chaos, as always, the drums continued their impassive thrumming.

"As you can hear, there are no nightingales in my woods," Aubin admitted as the commotion subsided.

Then, dejectedly, he led the party the rest of the way along the beach, to the Austrian's hut.

Jack and Sonya waited at the open doorway of the hut while Aubin lit his lantern again. Inside, a singular scene awaited them. On the sandy floor carpeted with bat droppings, two trunks sat, of the size and color Berg had predicted. But there was more: all around the hut was the sloughed-off skin of decadent European nobility. The wreckage of empire, costume discarded after the ball. For Gesser and Freedman, the appearance of uniforms was always a prelude to devastation; not this time. The gold braid was cast off, the leather of the high boots devoured by mildew, the ceremonial pistol rusted into harmlessness. Nobility reaching its logical end: decrepitude, Gesser thought, but he decided it was safer to keep his reflections to himself.

"The Austrian left everything he no longer needed to live a simple life," Aubin explained. "He set out along the coast, to the west. A white wanderer in a black land. He came here as a messenger, as you two have, but he never completed his mission. He found his own first."

"His failure," Gesser summed up, "is why we are here. I suppose we owe him thanks."

"Failure?" Aubin jumped on the word. "How can finding one's mission be a failure?"

"He abandoned the trunks in the middle of their journey," Sonya pointed out.

"A messenger is a slave to his message," Aubin said darkly. "He did not want to be that slave."

"We, as messengers, will keep that in mind as we work," Gesser said.

Aubin displayed a hurt silence. He did not appreciate his fellow nobleman, this enigmatic Austrian who may or may not have existed, being treated as a failure. Especially since he, too, as a poet in Cape Haitian, under an occupation, could never be anything but a failure. A magnificent, volubile one, yes, but a failure all the same, drowned out by the screeches of the mango-ladies, as he called the voices of his fellow citizens.

"It's amazing how everything has stayed untouched in this open hut," Sonya said.

Aubin smiled. "The Austrian had time to build up enough superstitions around his white person to keep everyone clear. And we kept an eye on the hut, knowing that these were the kinds of effects that sooner or later would attract white visitors. The way our coffee and pineapples seem to."

Gesser bent down and gave an experimental tug on a trunk handle. The trunk was remarkably light. Lighter than empty, really, almost immaterial.

"It is not recommended that you open the trunks," Aubin cautioned.

The little party returned along the beach, through the forest passage, then back to the town, the two bodyguards carrying one trunk, Aubin and Gesser the other, with Sonya sandwiched between them. The party passed undisturbed under the string of dark carnival lights the Marines had installed around the center of the Cape, for the lights went off at their curfew. Undisturbed but not unseen, though anyone who was up at this hour to see the procession was wise enough to adjudge it none of his business. No doubt there were some who saw the party as a procession of spirits; perhaps there were souls locked up in those trunks. They moved through the square where the domino-players drowsed in their chairs, past the smoldering charcoal with its smell of seared pig meat. Aubin preferred the rear entrance of the Hôtel Américain to the harbor promenade, where the Military Police strolled with their nightsticks, on the lookout for anything abnormal, with no belief in the spirit world.

The machete boys stacked the trunks in a corner of the upstairs room, by the washstand. Gesser gave one of them an exploratory kick.

"Somehow we expected more of a struggle," he said.

"More of an adventure," Sonya added.

"That is not the trunks' fault. It is because we have kept a good watch. Your job is over, but it would be dangerous to leave too soon. Remember that you are occupying the role of newlyweds. How short can white people's honeymoons be? Unless, of course, you wish to stage a public breakup. In which case perhaps I can be of service."

"What you don't understand," Gesser explained to Aubin, "is that we really are newlyweds. That's why we play the role so well."

"So I have seen," Aubin acknowledged.

Then he and the bodyguards, absentmindedly chewing on sugarcane, went out the door. Jack Gesser latched it shut behind them.

Sonya and Jack sat on the straight-backed wicker chairs in the silence that the poet and his cane-chewing friends had left. The Cape Haitian night drew tighter around them, the distant drumming approached, worship of all kinds surrounded them. Moths flew around their kerosene lantern. The night seemed to have lasted for several days.

"Now what?" Jack asked.

"Why, we open them, of course."

"Despite comradely discipline?"

"Don't be silly," Sonya teased. "We're going to put our bags inside these trunks for the trip home. You don't think we can do that without opening them first?"

The trunks, it turned out, were unlocked, which went a long way towards reducing Gesser's quandary. He threw open the first one and took a step back, as if afraid that something venomous might pop out. Inside the first, and the second, they discovered graven images of the local gods wrapped in bolts of dyed cloth. Mask after miniature, scowling mask, all swathed in the bright fabric the Cape women used to construct the platform on their heads for carrying their burdens. Some of the gods, Jack and Sonya saw, had already been attacked by wood-eating larvae.

"Property of the proletariat?" Sonya questioned.

"Somehow I'm not surprised."

"Unless Aubin made a mistake."

"What can you expect from a poet?" Gesser asked.

"Poet? Clown is more like it," Sonya said.

"A man made ridiculous by his circumstances, as our Berg would say. That's what makes him a clown. If he wasn't after you all the time I'd feel sorry for him."

"Our first brush with nobility. Completely ineffectual," Sonya laughed. "But his voice was immensely pleasing to me. And could he dance!"

"One more mambo and I'd have circumcised him with my nail clippers."

"And me? Aren't I equally guilty?"

"Of course you are," Gesser admitted. "But tradition demands that I proceed that way."

Talk of jealousy is an aphrodisiac, for it speaks of possession. Gesser raised the glass chimney and blew out the lantern, much to the frustration of the cane-chewing machete boys, who were idling in the street below, having lined up a good view of the hotel room through the open balcony door.

"We have an obligation to be newlyweds," Gesser reminded her. "Your Aubin said so."

"It is for the revolution," she agreed.

Sonya raised her arms for him to draw her blouse over her head, showing him the two pale red nests under her arms, which he kissed, which tasted so pleasantly of talcum powder and spicy sweat from the night's adventure. Gesser thought he smelled the poet on her, around her, like a cloud of mosquitoes, but there was no percentage in arguing over possession, not at a moment like this. Outside, the Marines' generators rumbled in the harbor, churning out the electricity to illuminate and protect their installations. Inside, the room was velvet-black. Jack and Sonya went naked to the open louvered balcony door, their bodies pale stains glowing in the night. The astonished bodyguards had never seen anything of that particular shade before.

How strange and sweet it is to be the only one of your kind in a country, how much more authentic it makes your experience! Naked and daring, Jack and Sonya took a step onto the balcony, all the way to the wrought iron balustrade. Against all logic, as most things in the Cape seemed to be, a single streetlamp burned at the corner by the little square, taking its wary, yellow electric current from who-knows-where, from the electricity in the air itself. In its glow, sheaths of bats passed, cutting swaths through the cloud of fluorescent moths that whirled in its light. Under that light, the light of communal study, a second formation turned: a half-dozen lycée students, each with his battered paper Larousse copy of *Phèdre*, reciting in unison the drama of destructive passion. *J'adorais ce dieu que je n'osais nommer*, they chanted, I worshipped this God whom I dared not name, and it seemed as though Racine had

written those terrifying lines for this very place and time: the soldiers with their beachhead, the mass of incomprehensible jungle
behind them, mad King Christophe's citadel capping that sav-
agery, the students' young dreams of refinement and self-respect
that Aubin had twisted with his clownish insistence on nobility.
Gesser and Freedman did not understand those words any more
than they had Aubin's poetry, but here and now, naked on the balcony with the dark rump of the treed mountain rising at the end
of the street, they felt as though they understood the message of
that play, and that message chilled them. *C'est Vénus tout entière à sa
proie attachée*, they heard, Venus has latched herself onto her prey.
They drew away from the chanting, into their room, and shut the
louvered doors to the street.

In their eager abandon, the lovers had forgotten to hang the mosquito netting from the bed frame. Their precious postcoital surrender was broken by biting insects. Gesser rose, swatting at the
mosquitoes, which made easy targets, since all were bloated with
their blood. He carefully draped the sheath of tulle around the bed
and prepared to climb under the net. Then he stopped. Something
was watching him in the darkness.

He wheeled around to where he guessed the washstand to be.
Utter blackness. He did not feel the usual fear, for the watcher was
not human. He lit the lantern. The trunks were gaping open, the
wooden gods deployed upon the fabric, their hollow eyes cast in
his direction. Inside their hearts, worms were silently tunnelling;
such is the fate of idols. Gesser went to the corner and averted
their staring eyes. He stood over the trunks, empty now of the
exotic bric-a-brac that the Austrian nobleman had amassed.
Unless the collection had been Berg's—though the prospect of the
austere, driven Berg gathering scarves and lengths of dyed fabric

and masks of jungle divinities on the way from Moscow to Chicago made Gesser smile.

He knelt down and ran his hands around the rim of the suitcase. Beneath his fingers he felt bumps inside the fabric lining, as if gravel had been sewn into the material of the suitcase. But it could not be gravel. These bumps were unnaturally smooth and rounded.

Let me not be the slave of my message—Gesser recalled Aubin's words and smiled. The poet was right, he had to admit. Still, he was not about to go and copy the Austrian, for he did not put that much stock in self-exploration; he had other, greater causes than himself. So he settled for a compromise. He would investigate. He would acquire knowledge. He went to his bag and found the nail-clippers he had threatened to use on Aubin's foreskin. Then, neatly, he sliced open the lining of the first trunk, then the second, a slit just wide enough for his little finger.

He eased out the first object. It was smooth and polished and deep-red, and despite the weakness of the candle flame, it shone magically as if lit from within.

It was a ruby. And it was only one of many.

There on the floor of the Hôtel Américain, in the inhabited zone between jungle and sea, on the north coast of Haiti, history, with its usual keen sense of the absurd, had arranged this meeting between Jack Gesser and the Czar Nikolai's crown jewels. Nikolai, the last Russian czar before the Revolution. Gesser finally understood why he had been placed here in the Cape, in the middle of the clinging, mosquito-ridden night, with two seemingly empty trunks. He had an advantage over his charges: the jewels that had been pried off the late Nikolai's crown certainly didn't know what they were doing there. They weren't used to the climate. As the new inheritance of the proletariat, they had been transiting from the Kremlin to

Chicago, on their way to being changed into precious American dollars, no doubt with the complicity of some revolutionary West Side pawnbroker, when they'd gotten terribly off track. It hadn't been their fault. They were just dumb stones that had gotten mixed up with the wrong crowd. Now, perhaps, in anonymous hands, they might be able to continue their journey north.

History, that old mischief-maker and ironist!

Gesser pried out a few more stones from the slit lining. Some were green, most sparkling white. He knew such riches existed; he knew that from stories where they brought ruin and misfortune to all who came in contact with them. Their wealth was unimaginable, useless to him. What would he, Jack Gesser, do with the Czar's crown jewels anyway? He began to slide them back into the lining.

Then there was one left. The ruby he had come upon first. It winked softly in the candlelight. He went over to the heap of their clothes and slipped the stone into his pants pocket. Why not? It wasn't for the money. It was a souvenir, a good luck piece. A gift for Sonya, some day. Commemoration by a little man of the big part he'd played, for one moment, in the secret history of the century.

He sewed up the lining again at the point where it was bunched together to meet the frame of the trunk. An excellent job. He admired his work. One of those skills he'd learned in Soukenai. If this doesn't work out, he mused, I could always be a tailor. Then he went and squeezed the lucky stone safely stowed in his pants pocket.

To be complete, the rescue of the property of the proletariat needed several more days of newlywed activities. Jack and Sonya lapsed into a kind of enchanted idleness that had nothing to do with the dispirited routines of their old life on Sangamon Street. Like the mysterious Austrian, they were being swayed by the indolent country. In the heat of the day they rarely ventured further than the shaded balcony of their room, from which they watched the commerce of the street, and gave their bedsheets a rest. In the evening they stood at the edge of the circular dance floor at the Melomaniacs' Club, where Aubin studiously ignored them, now that the exchange had been made. Gesser suspected that they were being allowed to play out their role. Yet their masquerade seemed so clumsily transparent that even the most myopic observer could have seen through it. Besides the soldiers and the mysterious Austrian, they were the only whites on the northern coast, and certainly the only whites who lived among the blacks. Why would they be in Cape Haitian if they weren't on some errand? Newlyweds? Ridiculous! In their rough clothes and battered shoes, they looked more like Quakers come to alleviate the local misery than newlyweds. But there was no Quaker mission in the town.

Finally, one evening, the fish-waiter in the downstairs restaurant served them their grilled grouper—the only fish available, but fish enough for them—with the information that it would be appropriate now for them to leave the country, and that a handy freighter was available for just that purpose.

"There is no sense in your staying on," the waiter who wasn't a waiter told them. "You have done your part. And my boys have been bored with watching you ever since you started closing the balcony door," he added with typical Cape Haitian gallantry.

The return began. In Miami, Gesser sent a cable to Berg as instructed, cryptically reporting their easy triumph. Now the two trunks were riding in a sterilized cloud in the train's baggage car; the only government surveillance they had had to undergo was a cloud of insecticide applied to them in the Miami quarantine zone. "Souvenirs," Gesser and Freedman told the customs man as he sprayed the trunks. He nodded approvingly. Why else would anyone travel, if not to bring back souvenirs?

As for Gesser's personal souvenir, it rode unmolested in his handkerchief.

The erotics of return are wholly different from those of the voyage out. The erotics of return are those of satiation, the desire to be alone that closes the amorous encounter. These are, in truth, no erotics at all. When is our next departure? Jack wondered spitefully as he watched Sonya retire to the narrow bunk beneath him by the discouraging glow of the nightlight in the Pullman sleeping car. As he and Sonya rode the rails north through the green horse and whisky country of Tennessee and Kentucky, Gesser stared dully out at the leafless trees and lowering sky. Sonya read his copy of Whitman, or engaged in the rare pleasure of thoughtlessness born of movement. They faced the dilemma of all travellers: no sooner had they returned to their country than the extravagant landscapes of the voyage began to fade.

The train schedule conspired against them. In Chicago, as the cab from Union Station wheezed to a stop in front of the College of Trades, he and Sonya considered the shuttered doors and windows and realized it was Sunday. There would be no presenting Berg with the trunks. No triumphant return.

Berg's Kirghiz assistant observed no Sabbath. As the cab idled in front of the building, the meter ticking away and Gesser and Freedman wondering what to do with themselves and their precious cargo, the assistant appeared on the sidewalk in front of the College as if he had been waiting there the whole time, train schedule in hand.

"The trunks," he stated in Russian. "Comrade Berg will be interested in the trunks."

The man opened the cab door and swung a trunk easily onto his shoulder.

"Can we see Comrade Berg?" Sonya asked.

"It is Sunday. The comrade is with his family. Or he is working. In either case he is not available. I will bring these upstairs. I suggest you come back tomorrow when the College is open. Comrade Berg will surely want to hear about your travels."

The man returned for the second trunk and swung it effortlessly onto his shoulder, as if he knew how light it would be. Then he disappeared up the stairs, towards Berg's office.

"That's a fine welcome," said Sonya.

Gesser stared silently at the shuttered facade.

The next day, too, was a day of rest, at least as far as the People's College of Trades and Vocations was concerned. At nine o'clock they were at the door, inquiring after Comrade Berg.

"The College is closed," said his assistant. "It closed yesterday."

"But the trunks . . ."

"Of course, the trunks. There is a letter for you in Comrade Berg's office."

Jack and Sonya were left free to wander into the director's old office and inspect the premises. First, the trunks. They were sitting on Berg's worktable, their linings slit, the contents removed. Gesser noted how hastily the fabric had been ripped open, the wide slash Berg had made in it. The bolts of cloth and masks were of no interest to Berg, who cared little for souvenirs, especially from a country that had witnessed his failure.

The letter addressed to them lay in a sealed envelope on an empty trunk. Gesser read it out loud: *The People's College of Trades and Vocations has fulfilled its purpose and is now closed. You carried out your mission with exemplary comradely discipline. In the Kremlin, they will hear the names of Jack Gesser and Sonya Freedman.*

"Well, at least we'll be famous in the Kremlin," said Sonya.

"Famous, yet abandoned. An unusual combination."

Sonya gathered up a length of brightly colored cloth from Berg's old worktable, where once he had translated the great Lenin himself.

"I think I'll keep this. Something to remember the local gods by."

Gesser nodded. Now both he and Sonya had a souvenir.

5

THE LEAVING PARTY

The dullness of the Poklub collective flat was duller still after the grilled grouper and the glistening slices of lime, the stylized passion of the Melomaniacs' Club, the jabber of the street that would envelop their siestas as surely, sweetly and gently as mosquito netting stirred by the trade winds. Gesser and Freedman found they had been rendered unfit for the daily indignities of their old routine by their exposure to the extravagances of Cape Haitian. It was a kind of trick Berg had played on them, a historical displacement, and they both resented the man for it. As if he had engineered the entire adventure to make them share in his conviction that life on Sangamon Street had no meaning beyond whatever petty triumphs the individual might win for himself: shooting a respectable game of pool, selling the whole cartload of watermelons, stealing a half-hour of lovemaking in the furtive nocturnal atmosphere of the Poklub flat.

What was the meaning of these petty triumphs but meaninglessness itself? No man or woman of their ideals could live with that self-appraisal.

Now that you know this, Berg questioned them from afar, from whatever ship's deck he stood on, overlooking whatever grey seas, now that you know this, what are you going to *do*?

Since their travels, the Poklub matriarch regarded this unsolemnized couple with even greater distrust than before. Not even paying the rent in advance silenced her discontent. Apparently, travel from east to west, Old Country to New, was all that was permitted Jews. North to south was pure scandal. Against the flow of history.

In a way, the sour old matriarch was right.

Gesser turned to routine for comfort. The old ways of passing his life. He strolled along Sangamon Street but found the autumn air cold and unfriendly. He stopped in at Steinstein's, refused to admit he'd been away at all, then quickly got drunk on the bootlegger's spiked tea. Steinstein watched suspiciously as Gesser pulled off money from a roll of bills. Then, in that inebriated state, he wandered up Roosevelt Road and looked desultorily for Help Wanted signs, safe in the knowledge that there weren't any, and that he wouldn't have gotten a job anyway in the state he was in. He walked aimlessly through the streets, considering the life he was tolerating, and whipping himself into a rage of self-contempt in the process. He'd abdicated his parcel of chosenness; he'd squandered the light of his intelligence. Now he blamed himself for those twenty-five lost years on Sangamon Street.

Sonya's re-entry was not much different. In those gloomy, autumn afternoon hours, she sat in the flat, helping the Poklub matriarch sort through strangers' washing. She marvelled at this thing called immigration. Just who is it for? she wondered. Or, as Berg would ask, *Who profits from it?* with that smugness of his that let you know he already had the answer. She hated the smugness, but she had to admit that his was the key question.

Sonya longed for a talk with Spielerman, her life-saver, her confidant, the man who knew the progress of her life from the Puszta to Debrecen, from Budapest to Sangamon Street. But Spielerman, who still contributed to the rent at the Poklub collective flat as a kind of insurance policy, hadn't been seen there for weeks. Smoky Sam's band, which used real black people instead of minstrelized Jews in blackface, had become the toast of two ghettoes.

Berg was gone now, called home to the Kremlin, but he did leave a legacy with his newlyweds, his messengers. Surplus material wealth. Spot cash money. Something unheard-of in those days. Despite the poverty around them, the Gesser–Freedman treasury bulged with ill-gotten gains. The money left over from robbing the Chinaman, and Berg's cash. Born hoarders, Gesser and Freedman had spent almost nothing of the generous travel allowance the Russian had provided for them before their departure, a sum so unnecessarily generous it could only have been an advance reward for the discreet exercise of their comradely discipline.

Discipline they had failed to keep, Gesser chided himself as the single red jewel gnawed away at him in his pocket.

The stone was uselessly valuable. Gesser kept it in his pocket, an omen, a reminder of a moment of folly. Superstitiously, he hoped it would make something of itself, spontaneously, that it would metamorphize and change him, its bearer, in the process, like a magic stone in a fairy tale from his childhood.

Jack and Sonya decided to travel again, though in the autumn, around Chicago, there is not much of anywhere to go. But Venus must have her journeys if she is to retain her sting. Love desires adventure, love wants to travel, love demands a project greater than the lovers themselves, a project that will carry it away from itself if it is to endure. If love has nothing to contemplate but its own splendor, it soon sickens on its own sweetness, mad with claustrophobia in its boudoir.

Jack and Sonya sensed this. They peeled off a bill from their treasury and bought two tickets on the Illinois Central electric line.

Gesser carried his knapsack with the copy of Whitman inside and a towel, though it was much too cold to think of bathing. They each bought an apple from a vendor at the station entrance, a bit uncomfortable with the idea of bestowing charity. Gesser carried the little jewel in his pocket. All right, so it's not Cape Haitian, he admitted to Sonya as they settled into their seats, but at least it's somewhere, it's some kind of travel. They rode across the state line into Indiana, as far as Chesterton, on the Lake Michigan shore, where the lake had deposited its sandy bottom in long, delicate beige strands.

The train rocked, the trees moved in slow parade past the window. Sonya bit into her apple. Hard on the outside, mealy on the inside. She reported this to Jack. He shrugged; after all, it was a Depression apple. The trip took on the solemnity of a retreat, though neither of them was very well equipped to think about the future. The idea that a person might actually plan for the future had no currency in their world. Didn't the future just *happen*, the way a ditch happens to a road?

It was just that passive philosophy, they realized, that had turned them into melon-vendors and sorters of strangers' dirty linen.

At the Chesterton station, they stepped down from the coach and began to walk in silence under the scoured blue, autumn sky. Both were uneasy in the open countryside. In their blood they recognized that all a deserted field needs to become a rough graveyard is an encounter with the wrong sort of person. Both Jack and Sonya had known the landscapes of that residual, ancestral terror. For Sonya, it had been the empty, waterlogged, acidic Hungarian plain. For Jack, the wheat fields around the slaughterhouse where the village cow had been fattened.

Not a good beginning for a retreat. But there was no other way to get to the lake.

"'Aloof and light-hearted, I take to the open road.'" Gesser quoted his favorite poet as they trudged along, the poet of the people. "'The open road before me wherever I go.'" Sonya stopped and considered the sandy track that led over the low dunes, with scrubby pine and tough grasses, and at the end of it, that particular emptiness the sky takes on over a large body of water. *Some open road.* She turned and looked at the distance they'd covered, and the line of telegraph poles that ran along the Illinois Central right-of-way. We've been on that road once already, she said to herself. It's closed. We might as well try the one in front of us. At least that one's still open.

They neared the lake, walking into its wind that smelled strongly of alewives. Jack watched that wind as it pulled slyly and playfully at Sonya's dress that stuck out from under her short, bulky leather jacket. A fishy lake wind that pressed the fabric against the graceful fork where her thighs met, and lifted and tossed the hem to her knees. At that moment, willing plaything of the winds, she was so gloriously, so carelessly beautiful that it seemed natural that he would lose her. He didn't even need to think about whom she would be lost to. To Spielerman, or another, it mattered little. Anyway, it wasn't to *whom*. It was to *what*. To history. The force that ground them down. Because no woman or man could be expected to love themselves, and love another, in the world as it was.

In the off season, the Johnson's Beach Hotel looked like a monstrous freighter driven aground by a Great Lakes storm. On the vast porch, the swings swung empty on their squeaky chains. On the other side of the hotel was the heaving, slate-grey water, heavy with wind, and the circling gulls crying for food. Jack and Sonya had their choice of rooms; the only guests were those on whom the climate made little impression. Some of those unseen guests— First World War veterans, perhaps—were careless, or disoriented, or believed that fresh air was a curative. They left their windows open and the hall doors slammed open and closed, as if the corridors were peopled by ghosts. Jack and Sonya's room was spartan, two cots and two coarse blankets, something from a dormitory in a lumber camp, but it offered privacy and novelty. Gesser hung his knapsack from a nail driven into a wood beam. Sonya reached under the blankets; the clammy sheets made her shiver. On the other side of the window the lake heaved, sand-devils chased each other up and down the beach. The glass rattled in the dry sashes.

Later, they went for a walk in that vast foreign place called nature. They attempted conversation, but the wind blew their words away. In spots, the beach was heaped with alewives, those silvery fish that swim out of the water by the thousands and cast themselves upon the sand in a kind of terminal immigration. They came upon a collection of tumbledown cottages, no more than shacks, really. They had sprung up on the unclaimed, unincorporated sand flats beyond the hotel, rickety creations on stubby stilts, settling at all manner of cockeyed angles, no glass in the window, only screens against the mosquitoes and wood shutters against the wind. There, on the flats, the now-departed cabin-dwellers had squatted through the summer in their Depression vacation homes. Little models of Sangamon Street. Sangamon on the Strand. Wind and cold weather had driven them back to the city.

In the dining room that evening, Gesser and Freedman sat at a long table, overseen by all manner of maritime decoration: nets, lanterns, painted driftwood in the shape of animal heads, mobiles made of fish bones and crab shells, objects whose use they could only speculate on. The owner made the rounds of the empty tables. It turned out that the Johnson of Johnson's Beach was really Jonas, a Hungarian Jew happy for the conversation this time of year.

Sonya glanced around the dining room.

"Where's everybody else?"

"You're it," he congratulated them. "You have my undivided attention." He mimed a waiter preparing to take an order. "May I suggest the fish? It's all we have."

Gesser peered out the window that opened onto the black expanse of the lake.

"At least it's fresh," he remarked.

"I caught it with my own hands."

When he returned with their dinner, Jonas asked, "I suppose you like to fish?"

"If you want to teach us."

"My help went back to Chicago. Too cold for him here. Too windy, he says. Imagine somebody from Chicago saying it's too windy. Why don't you come out with me tomorrow morning? You'll eat what we catch, no charge."

The next morning before dawn, he was rapping on the flimsy wood partition that passed for a door. They rose from their cot and pulled their jackets on over their clothes. A few minutes later they were helping Jonas dump his nets over the side of his heavy, stable wooden boat, in search of lake whitefish. Afraid of the water, they kept to a low, defensive crouch as Jonas rowed the boat free of the trailing nets that spread as they submerged. During the night the wind had dropped, the fog rolled in, and now they were drifting into the mist, the hotel disappearing into greyness, the gulls wheeling above them, invisible, crying the same single scavenger's note.

Jonas rowed into the fog, straining against the oarlocks to move the bulky boat forward. With the water beneath them motionless, it was impossible to tell where the shore was.

Every immigrant builds his own world, and most of that world is memory. But Jonas did more than remember; he reconstructed. He had found a lake to remind him of his Lake Balaton in Hungary. He fished in his new lake as he had in the old. He made a semblance of wine from the Concord grapes that grew out of the sand and up the trellis of his hotel. He was, in a word, *happy*. He had adjusted. He related this to Jack and Sonya as they dragged in the nets heavy with whitefish, flipping and struggling and astonished, their delicious bodies silver-grey in the dawn.

Jack and Sonya considered his strategy. It was comforting, but it would not work for them. Unlike Jonas, they had nothing to reconstruct. And what they had to remember, they were better off forgetting. They congratulated Jonas on his ingenuity but said nothing more, happy enough to work, to be out on the water, pulling in the nets full of dull silver whitefish.

Back in their room after a breakfast of fried fish, Sonya went to the window. The mist had burned off and the lake sparkled. She lifted the sash and the wind blew in with the smell of alewives. A smell of lake rot that, curiously, piqued her appetite.

Jack came up behind her and loosened the intricate knot of her chignon that had taken a beating from the lake wind. When at last her hair had fallen free, she turned in his arms and faced him.

"I'm mad at Spielerman," she announced.

"Spielerman? Here, in this room, on our second honeymoon, you have to be mad at Spielerman?"

"I'm mad at Spielerman," she pursued, ignoring him. "Mr. Jonas made me think of him. I'm mad at Spielerman because he figured out how to fit in. He has something to do. That's more than we have."

Jack released her. "He can play music. That's a gift."

"That's not the point and you know it. He came over here and started playing a different kind of music. He figured it out. Like Jonas did. He understands the New World."

"So does Steinstein the bootlegger. Should we praise him?"

For a moment, they watched the lake rising and falling, its dark surface sparkling like diamonds on a slate, its surface scored by the wind.

"That's the choice, maybe. A musician or a bootlegger. Art or business. Or muscle—though I don't think King Levinsky asks himself too many questions. That's my problem: I don't have a trade like those men do. A man of the Book, a man of books, too. A man of many books cannot be a man of the Book. These are bad days for that trade. There's just no demand for it. Steinstein is selling something everybody needs; he understands. Your Spielerman, too. He's lifting up people's hearts, or casting them down, or both at the same time, but whatever it is, it seems to be something people need. With both of them, it's forgetfulness they're selling. Self-forgetfulness. My problem is that I'm rotten with memory. I don't have anything people need. Not here, not in this world, anyway. Some people, I know, that wouldn't bother. Unfortunately, I'm not one of them."

Sonya threw her arms around him and pressed her body against his. Her body, the best argument there was.

"Please, don't talk like that," she told him. "You're not being fair to yourself."

"Fair? *Fair?* What does that change? Can you honestly tell me that America, or Chicago, or even Sangamon Street needs the *luft-mensch* Jack Gesser?"

"Can I say it? No, I can't. But who *does* America need? Does it really need your Steinstein, or Sammy?"

"Self-made men, the both of them," Gesser mused. "Rugged individualists. Good Americans, in their own way. Funny, isn't it? There's plenty of good Americans among us. I never would have thought so. Maybe immigration isn't such a bad idea after all."

"So, it can't be so hard finding something to do. Maybe not like Steinstein or Sammy, but *something* . . . something else. Something new . . . A lot of people are going to California, I hear."

"California?" Gesser recoiled in mock horror. "Never! That's where watermelons come from, and I hate watermelons! Besides, what's the point of California, if it's the same system? What's the point of another Sangamon Street, but with palm trees this time?"

"That's the problem with you," Sonya grumbled. "Whenever a new idea comes along, you're against it. But what do you have to put in its place?"

In this historical impasse, Jack and Sonya turned to the exercise of the flesh. Marx was not thinking of the plight of the lovers Gesser and Freedman when he composed his famous aphorism *first time tragedy, second time farce*. But he could well have been. That which is glorious at first turns to empty repetition when removed from its proper moment. Every romance has its foundation, no matter how unearthly it might seem. Gesser and Freedman's was built on the new ideology by which the world and the self would join in the great crucible of the century's romance. Its change. That was a tall order for any two people. But that was what they demanded of themselves. To be heroes. To join the march of the century, and not waste away in self-contempt.

Watermelons, Gesser thought as Sonya's brilliant red hair swam around him. It was a prosaic hour for love, and the lovers still had the taste of fried fish on their tongues. He watched condensation forming on the window glass and realized he should not have spoken of watermelons. He could feel his mistake in Sonya's body, the way she was absent even as she gave herself to him. The desperate mechanics of her lovemaking. No woman wants to tie her fate to a man who sells watermelons, and hates it, but dismisses the whole thing with a shrug.

Towards the end of the afternoon, the dinner bell called them for another fish meal. Baked, this time. They gazed upon the room. The sheets were bunched on the floor, as were the covers. One of the two Army surplus cots was lying legs up, in the attitude of a slain beast. Usually, lovers are proud of the chaotic power they unleash. But in that disorder Jack and Sonya pictured their own, and were not happy.

"If we don't go to California," Jack said abruptly, "why don't we go find Berg?"

"Berg?" Sonya repeated dully. At this point, the lure of the Messiah of Division Street was so distant it seemed to belong to another age.

"Yes. Berg," Jack told her. "If we went there, we wouldn't be the only ones. It's in the air, you know."

"As much as California?"

"No," he admitted. "But it's different. *Truly* different."

"Different, it is."

Downstairs, the dinner bell rang a second warning. Gesser paid it no attention.

"Why not? Nothing is working here. The country is falling apart. As far as we know, this might be the end of capitalism. Do we want to be around when it collapses? It won't be a pretty sight. There won't be anything to replace it, not in this country." He reached out and wound his hands in Sonya's hair. "The system isn't working. So neither can we."

At that moment, a strange new logic entered the room. As if the spirit of Mitchell Berg were hovering among the rough wooden rafters, bathing it in the seduction of a totally unexpected solution. The charm of an astonishing third path. It was the dialectic again, up to its old tricks. *Do something crazy*, the dialectic ran. *Do something unexpected, something you did not know you were going to do. And why the hell not, since nothing else works?*

Once you consented to that romance, the rest was easy. A mere matter of documents.

Sonya didn't say yes. She didn't say no either. Outside their door, along the wind-swept hallway, a few mystery diners shuffled their way downstairs, towards the fish. Sonya suggested that they skip the meal.

"If we get hungry later, Jonas will always heat up a piece for us. After all, we caught it."

They spent the rest of the evening in their quarters. Jack took that as a good sign.

But their good fortune was temporary. On the train that carried them back to the promiscuity of Sangamon Street, the skin on Sonya's forearms begun to itch, then break out in angry, pus-filled red welts. She sat in the coach on the electric line, scratching until her arms bled.

She had touched poison ivy in the dunes behind the Johnson's Beach Hotel, but didn't know what it was. *Nerves*, she thought as she rode the train back, rubbing her skin as Jack looked on, powerless. *Hysteria. Nerves—small wonder.*

She told herself that something had to be done.

In the raw early spring of 1933, a winter after their short honeymoon at Johnson's Beach, Sonya Freedman was pushing a heavy iron baggage cart along the platform of another train station. The LaSalle Street Station. On her cart rode her single piece of luggage, and keeping watch over it, the three Poklub virgins, their legs dangling, enjoying the novelty and good fortune of being away from the family cell and the grumbling soup-pot at suppertime.

Steam shot from the valves under the Pullman cars of the New York Central, and Sonya disappeared into the cloying, metallic cloud. Briefly hidden from their procreators' eye, forgetting their spinsterish decorum for a moment, the Poklub girls squealed with delight.

Inside that cloud, Sonya thought about return. It was a fiction as far as she was concerned, an excuse for travel. Jack wanted to return to his old country, and remake it and himself in the process. She simply wanted to go travelling. But what did it matter, as long as their destination was the same, and besides, when do two people ever do anything for exactly the same reason? Jack wanted history to vindicate him, and for that, he was willing to cross the ocean again, going backwards, the wrong way, to the country where he'd suffered his greatest tragedy, the original one by which childhood is spoiled. Sonya would never have agreed to return to the muddy, spongy, acidic, wind-whipped plain of the Puszta, where she'd squalled and bullied her way into life. She didn't even want to set eyes on Budapest again. Why would she purposely expose herself to a city where she'd been probed and examined and declared hysterical, a prime candidate for that fashionable disorder—or so she'd been told—considering the weight of guilt she must be bearing? The doctors' diagnosis had been confirmed by the lack of effect their thick seed had on her, despite how often they'd pumped it into her, in their offices, on their analysis couches, all imitations of the original Couch, joylessly, for scientific reasons, or so they had maintained.

But Moscow, yes. It was new. It was not the Puszta or Budapest.

A pile of soiled laundry. That's what had tipped the balance. On one particularly blue afternoon in the dead of winter, with The Hawk blowing straight through the grimy, uninsulated bricks of the three-storey flats of Sangamon Street, and the radiators clang-ing noisily and ineffectually, calling attention to their uselessness, Gesser had come back to the Poklub collective flat to find Sonya with her face in a pile of strangers' soiled whites. Unaccountably, she was crying. Yes, the city, the flat, the country was a strait-jacket, the winter was endless and it had just begun, but why today and not another day? Crying was a dangerous sign in a time when endurance was prized over all other qualities.

He stood before her. The same offer was in his eyes. She gazed up at him through her tears and nodded, *Yes, we'll go, why not?*

He dug into his pocket.

"There's another reason."

He opened his hand and she saw the ruby, sparkling deep and blood-red in spite of the dimness of the room, definitely out of place in the Poklub flat, with the heap of soiled laundry.

Sonya's eyes widened and her tears dried quickly.

"Is that what I think it is?"

Gesser nodded.

"Do you know how much that's worth?"

"No. Yes. I know it's worth so much it's useless."

"So, why did you . . . ?"

"A souvenir. A whim. A moment of pride. I intend to give it back to Berg."

"Proletarian justice," she reminded him.

He shrugged. "I'm sure he'll be happy to get it back."

She shook her head in admiration. "You're as crazy as a cock-roach!"

That afternoon, they celebrated in the midst of the threadbare sheets of the Sangamon Street laundry business. They'd barely had time to pull their clothes back on before the funereal Poklubs dragged in from their daily rounds.

*   *   *

Which is how Sonya came to be moving down the platform of the LaSalle Street Station, under the majestic cupola, into a cloud of steam with the squealing Poklub girls she knew she'd never see again, towards a berth on the Century Limited with Jack Gesser, both of them greatly renewed by the erotics of the voyage out. She emerged from the cloud, thinking of Spielerman. At this critical time, where was her other lover in America, her cousin Spielerman? He seemed to have dropped off the face of the earth. She'd gone from one hot club to the next, to the bathhouses, blind pigs, speakeasies, honky-tonks, sporting clubs, wherever Smoky Sam and his Red-Hot Band might have been expected to play. But the messages she'd left him had all gone unheeded.

Jack Gesser, swinging his bag, did not share in the Poklub virgins' girlish delight at the clouds of steam. The air in the station was damp and clammy. Part of that was the clouds' fault. Gesser was a superstitious man, and no time is more critical for such a man than the moment of departure. He did not like these clouds of steam. The way Sonya disappeared into one a few steps ahead of him, and by the time he entered it to join her there, she had already gone out the other side. Gesser could congratulate himself at having freed his imagination from the Almighty, and having dismissed His prophets as so many gesticulating peddlers of faith, but he had still not given up his belief in the thousand malevolent influences that attend each of life's moments, the potential for disaster that attached itself to every event like a skeleton strapped to a mule.

Clouds, he thought, as he entered the next gritty escape of steam. Clouds of oblivion. In the heart of that brief cloud Jack Gesser had a premonition. A vision of a man and a woman, separated in frozen clouds of ice, waving in slow motion as they pulled out on separate, endless journeys. A false premonition, he told himself, for once he had endured the last of the clouds, wasn't his Sonya waiting for him, and next to her, the farewell party? The Poklubs, funereal as ever, and the eternally jolly Steinstein, with Jake and Abe and Hy, three of the more philosophically minded pool-shooters from the leisure hall about whom he knew nothing but their *noms de cue.* The one called Jake, he recalled, had been daring enough to beat Sonya at eight-ball the afternoon of her initiation into the mysteries of the game. Only King Levinsky was missing; the *zhlub* was minding the store.

Everyone was there, he noted with relief, but Spielerman.

Jealousy was one bourgeois trait Gesser would not surrender. He defended it with his particular brand of sentimental philosophy. There is no love without jealousy; jealousy is a form of worship; true, noble jealousy—his kind—needs no object. When he would expound this way to Sonya, usually in the warm island of his hard bed in the freezing back porch room, she would lift her arms and arch her back and stretch, as if to display to him exactly what there was at stake, and how glorious it was. Then, sweetly, she would remind him that all he gazed upon with such admiration was her possession, not his, and that the notion of woman as chattel who belonged to a man was part of the old order they were plotting to escape. Then Jack would counterattack, arguing that, with its infantile and undisciplined need for gratification, there was no notion more bourgeois than that of free love.

Jack did more than counterattack with words. He acted. He was willing to go a long way to defeat his competition, real and imaginary. All the way, in fact, to Moscow.

The farewell party had gathered by the entrance to their sleeping car. As the Poklub matriarch stood by, wringing her hands as if they were sheets from the washing, Old Man Poklub stepped forward. He went first, to get the goodbyes over with, and get on to something else.

"So. Give my regards to the Revolution." He thrust out his arthritic hand with its yellow fingertips. "Tell them to carry on without me. Tell them I was sorry I couldn't join in. I did try. I was too early, though. Or too late. Time will tell which one."

He and Gesser embraced. Gesser felt the old man's arms clamp around his sides with the sudden violence of rigor mortis. His hands, two blocks of ice, were as cold as the ground he tended. A roll-your-own burned between his useless fingers.

Abruptly, Old Man Poklub released Gesser from his dead man's embrace. He looked up at the cupola of the LaSalle Street Station, where all voices rose into a single farewell.

"Grand . . . Very grand. Everybody going every which way. I like that, don't you?"

"But we're not going every which way," Sonya reminded him. "We're going somewhere in particular."

She stepped around her baggage cart where the girls still sat and took his hands in hers. "You should take care of those hands of yours. Think of another job. Or retire."

"Retire?" he asked mockingly. "Retire? But I already am retired." He brought the rollie to his lips. "Retired from life!"

He laughed richly at his own joke, then went back to admiring the cupola, a sign that he had had the last word, and was taking leave of the proceedings.

"You're going to Moscow," the Poklub matriarch said a little dreamily, the first time anything approaching wistfulness had crept into her voice. "I've never been there—we weren't allowed, of course. But I have seen pictures of it. Well, very nice for you."

She wrung her hands, a stranger to sentiment. Then she stepped forward, grabbed Sonya and kissed her on both cheeks so roughly Sonya thought it would leave lacerations.

"You were nice borders. Quiet, if a little . . . irregular. Now, girls, it's our turn."

The three Poklub daughters jumped off the baggage cart and lined up in front of their mother, as if forming a line of defense. *Ein, tsvei, drei,* counted the eldest, the wisest, the revisor of the paternal lunacy, and the girls burst into ragged song:

> *For they are jolly good fellows*
> *For they are jolly good fellows*
> *For they are jolly good fellows*
> *Which nobody can deny!*

When they finished that salute, the oldest began to sing:

> *The bear went over the mountain*
> *The bear went over the mountain*
> *The bear went over the mountain*
> *To see what he could see!*

In all their years in America, Jack and Sonya never did learn what the bear had seen once he'd taken the trouble to climb over to the other side of the mountain. Now, finally, they were going to find out.

> *The other side of the mountain*
> *The other side of the mountain*
> *The other side of the mountain*
> *Was all that he could see!*

Then came the turn of the Leisure Palace gang. The traffic on the platform was thickening, the trainmen urging the passengers into the cars. It would not be long now.

Steinstein stepped forward.

"Good luck, the both of you. And Gesser, take care of the little lady. We'll miss you in our way. You were never worth a shit with a cue, Gesser, but you're cracked in the best way, and we need more like you. A dreamer, a guy that doesn't want to hurt nobody, a real studier with that notebook of yours. I'd like to read it some day, though I doubt I could understand it."

Jake and Abe and Hy, that faithful trio of pool-playing Hebes, each gave Gesser a comradely handshake and Sonya a quick kiss that smelled of pomade and oak barrels.

"We gotta tell you, we don't agree among ourselves about this returning business," said Abe, self-appointed spokesman for the group. "The way we figure it, you're either a coward, or crazy, or a hero. So take your pick. And remember, write when you get work!"

"My turn to kiss the lovely lady," Steinstein insisted.

And when he was close to her, much closer than she would have liked—this must be what it's like to kiss a well-groomed pig, it occurred to her—he slipped a handsome, worn silver flask into the pocket of her wool jacket.

"Take it, use it on the train. Or some other time when you need it. It's a little mitzvah from Steinstein, the Jew bootlegger."

Then Jake, Sonya's pool instructor, eased her away from the little gang.

"Make sure you spread the good word about eight-ball in the Workers' Paradise!"

"Sorry we couldn't play more," Sonya smiled, "but those cigars got to me."

"We'll play again, some other day . . . when you come back."

Gesser overheard and stiffened.

"Come back? We're doing all this just to come back? But I'm telling you, we're not coming back!"

Gesser's declaration was so categorical that it put a freeze on the farewell party.

"Sorry, comrades. Sorry you took it the wrong way."

Jake apologized and turned away. Steinstein went to follow him, with Abe and Hy on his heels, the three of them funhouse reflections of the Poklub virgins. Then, suddenly, Steinstein had a thought. It nearly knocked him down. He stopped and slapped his forehead as if a mosquito had landed there.

"Hey, why don't you folks wait till this new President Rosenvelt starts making these changes he says he's going to make? There's big things coming our way. They say he's even going to let us roll out the barrel so he can skim off taxes on the booze to pay for the poor. Why don't you stick around and see what happens? If things don't get better, you can always leave with a satisfied mind."

"But I do have a satisfied mind," Gesser said, "and I'm impatient to use it."

Steinstein shrugged. "Impatient? Impatient in a world of waiting? So be it. Gotta go. Big ajustments in the order of things to ajust to."

Sonya and Jack watched him lumber down the platform, the three shooters following behind. Of all the farewells, Jake's echoed loudest in the busy air.

And when they had faded into the throng of travellers, one of the Lord's own scarecrows came flapping along from the far end of the platform, his unformed, tentative, pale face bobbing above the collar of his black frock coat. It was Maxie Poklub. Onanist, mystic, mama's boy, eternal job-hunter. As he came closer, he took off his hat and waved it wildly, as if he actually needed to attract attention to himself.

"I got a job! I got a job!"

He drew up in front of the leaving party, panting hard. His

sprint down the platform through the station's thick air had awakened old odors from the fabric of his coat.

"You see," said Gesser, turning to the Poklub matriarch. "You won't miss our share of the rent after all. Mazel tov, Maxie."

"There's only one problem," Maxie began, then faltered into silence.

"What's that?" the matriarch asked anxiously.

"It's not the kind of thing a man can admit . . ."

"Come on, don't leave us in suspense," Jack cajoled. "We're about to go. The whole trip we'll be wondering what was wrong with Maxie Poklub's job. Was it in a cathouse or something?"

Maxie took a dramatic backwards step and confessed to what passed for shame in his life.

"I had to change my name!"

Gesser and Freedman waited for the rest. But there was no more.

"Is that all?"

Maxie nodded.

"I hope you got a good one, at least," Sonya said. "An American-sounding one."

"Kade, I got."

"Kade?" Jack and Sonya repeated in unison. "Kade the haberdasher on Roosevelt Road?"

"I can't believe it," said Sonya. "That dried-up little *kommerzant* can't find a woman to have kids by, so he had to find another way to spread his name. Clever bastard!"

"You don't understand," Maxie Poklub wailed. "I had to take the owner's name. Otherwise I don't get the job."

"You took another man's name?" the Poklub matriarch asked worriedly, as if her darling son had committed grand larceny.

Old Man Poklub waved his hand derisively. "Every name is another man's name. So where is the consecration? Anyway, do you really think Poklub's your real name? So what's the difference? Are you any less you?"

"It's a nice name, after all," Sonya tried to comfort the boy. "A little short, maybe."

"It's not your fault, everybody knows that," Gesser added. "You can't have a job and keep your name at the same time. Changing your name is a small price to pay. Can you imagine how a Jewish name would sound on the squawk box down at Kade's store?" Gesser made a trumpet with his hands. "*Maxie Poklub, Maxie Poklub, you're wanted in Junior Miss!* Unthinkable!"

"But it's a Jewish store," Maxie protested. "That's what I don't understand."

"Don't be naive," Gesser told the boy. "How can you expect a man like Kade, who changed his name, to let other people keep theirs? Which is one of the reasons, by the way, why we're getting on this train."

"I wish I could go with you. I wish I could go where you don't have to take the boss's name to get the job."

But Maxie's protests were futile. He turned and joined the Poklub procession as it headed homeward. Jack and Sonya watched him and his family trudge along the platform, against the current of passengers, the very heart and soul and sad body of immigrant self-loathing. Then, to their horror, they saw Maxie peel away from the Poklub family and climb into their Pullman car, a stowaway from his destiny as an insignificant, pale, mother-loving piece of Depression flotsam. *Spare me*, Gesser thought. He's actually going to come with us, this onanist, this voyeur, this clerk, this handkerchief-man. But Maxie's revolt was short-lived. A few seconds later, he stepped out of the next car and reappeared at the rear of the family procession. Neither parents nor sisters had noticed his absence.

That's when they heard the music. Smoky Sam and his Red-Hot Band. They heard it before they saw it because of the hissing clouds of steam between them and the band. First to burst through the cloud was the lovely Miss Pearl, magnificent in her tiara of glittering rhinestones, her expressive, maroon hands gliding between her ample bosom and her generous hips, where her palms opened out in the universal appeal for love. Then came Spielerman, every inch the wiry Yid gangster in spats and wide lapels, clarinet pointed towards the cupola, above which the Almighty of jazz had his headquarters. The other horns followed, and behind them, a man beating a drum strapped to his chest.

The band lurched and squealed and moved down the platform where Jack and Sonya stood, their luggage already aboard the train. The Red-Hot Band carried out a pitched battle for control of the song, with the horns, Miss Pearl, even the drummer making a play for the lead. The musicians enjoyed the battle, apparently, the music was meant to work that way. But by the time the Red-Hot Band gathered in front of the footstool that would boost Jack and Sonya into their Pullman car, it had coalesced and allowed Miss Pearl the lead. Spielerman's clarinet made the anarchic horns behave as he dipped in and out of Miss Pearl's vocals like a flirtatious lover, as she sang about Madam Bucks.

"Ever notice that the less money there is, the more people sing about it?" Spielerman asked rhetorically, once he'd quieted the accompaniment. "We don't have much scratch, but we got big hearts, and we wanted to let you know we won't forget you, even if you're going to the land where they don't allow jazz. Not yet, anyway. But they do have klezmer, or at least they used to, and that's the next best thing. When klezmer and blues united, as Miss Pearl and I have, they made jazz. A great musical copulation, if you get my meaning."

"I'll miss you so," Miss Pearl promised. "When one of the people of the Book goes out of my life, it leaves a hole there."

"You take care of the little lady," Spielerman thrust his chin in Sonya's direction.

"Little lady, my ass!" she said gaily. "The little lady can take care of herself. This isn't my first crossing."

"Of course not, of course not. Do you think you were born here or something?" Spielerman paused. "Reborn, maybe. Like me. Hallelujah for rebirth!"

Spielerman gave Gesser a little wink of connivance, about as welcome as a red dress at a funeral. Cousin, betrothed, husband, lover, travelling companion—whatever he was to her, Gesser would not miss him. Sonya had said it best. The most intolerable thing about the man was his innate ability to fit in.

The trainman approached them.

"Time to make up your minds, folks. All aboard, all of youse that's wanting New York!"

"We're going to give you a real New Orleans send-off," Spielerman told Jack and Sonya.

He pointed his instrument skyward to signal the band, then realized his indiscretion, for hadn't jazz begun as music to accompany the coffin and its bearers to the burying ground? It was too late to take it back. *Hush now, don't explain*, like the song advised. Spielerman put his clarinet to his lips and sobbed out the piece that any good *shtetl* boy starved for joy and release knows: the excruciatingly long prelude to the "Rebbe Elimelekhe." Spielerman played a mighty storm of dissonance and indecision as the New Orleans funeral march and the schnapps-loving rabbi fought it out. The band watched, the lovely Miss Pearl watched, even the trainmen waited to see towards which side of the ocean the music would tilt, the old world schmaltz or the New World cakewalk.

And just when the tension got too much, Spielerman pulled out a riff everybody knew, and the Red-Hot Band, fronted by Miss Pearl, swung into the American national anthem, revised for the cold early spring of 1933: "Nobody Knows You When You're Down and Out."

"What showmen those kikes can be," a trainman said admiringly as the band did a mock, mournful cakewalk down the platform. Then he shouted, "All aboard!"

This time, he meant it.

Smoky Sam and his Red-Hot Band marched off to their next engagement, out of the LaSalle Street Station, into the raw winter air that smelled of burned iron, alewives and despair, the very ingredients of their music. They fervently followed Miss Pearl, Queen of the Jews, as she clasped her hands nobly upon her dizzying cleavage.

Sonya Freedman and Jack Gesser climbed into the Pullman and found their berth. The train was moving by the time they'd stowed their luggage. Later, the colored gentleman would come and pull out the beds. For the man and the woman who love travelling, there is nothing better than a late-night departure: you can't always see where you're going in the dark.

BOOK II

SONYA & JACK'S BOOK OF WISHES

6

AN ICED-OVER PORT

If we are so destitute, if we are so embittered by the fate America handed us, what of this lovely chocolate sampler on the impeccable, folded-down sheet of our bunk? Sonya Freedman glanced cursorily in the oval mirror. Her chignon was properly dishevelled, the very picture of beauteous rebellion. But there was no time to reflect on the luxury of their berth on the *Île-de-France*. Sonya would not have missed the departure from New York for anything.

She hurried back to the deck and found Gesser where she had left him: both hands gripping the rail, transfixed by the sight of the port slowly sliding away. From the deck above them, the band played on.

Streamers rained down from above. Roses flew over the rail like so many distraught Wall Street stockbrokers into the churning, inky water that grew wider as their ship pulled away from the Promised Land.

"Goodbye, Depression, and good riddance to bad rubbish!" a traveller shouted nearby. For him, the Depression was no more than a passing cloud out of whose shadow you could drive, if you only had a vehicle fast enough.

Sonya turned to Gesser.

"So, husband, are we making the right decision?"

He answered by gazing down at the growing expanse of cold black water that stretched between them and the continent. That water, in any case, was making the only decision it could.

"I remember this harbor," he began grandly, pronouncing an elegy for twenty-five years of his life. "I was a scared, silent kid back then, and all of us were penned in together like cattle. I had a scrap of paper with an address in Chicago on it, and I was hanging on to it like it was the word of God."

"You came in on steerage, and you're going out standing on the deck, with a private cabin waiting for you down below. That's progress!"

"Progress? Can you really say that? Where did the money for all these things come from? I hit a Chinaman on the head with a brick, then we took a payment for recovering the property of the proletariat and keeping our mouths shut about it."

"That's the way money works," Sonya reminded him.

"Yes, I do recall," he said dryly, and spit over the railing.

"I can't believe we're standing here on this deck, still talking about money, and you sounding so bitter about everything, at a time like this. It's a waste of a great occasion!"

Jack didn't answer. He returned to studying how the New World forgets itself, and others in the process. The streamers, the flowers, the waving white handkerchiefs of the well-wishers, the grandness of departure, the shipboard band that, he feared, would dog them all the way to Moscow, blaring out the cheerful, thoughtless tunes of democracy.

"Look, there she is!" Sonya shouted.

Against the low grey cloud cover, the backside of the Statue of Liberty was sliding by them impassively, the lady's munificence reserved for those arriving from the other direction.

"I've never seen it from this side before. Tell the truth, I've never seen it at all, except for pictures. The first time, we arrived at night."

The *Île-de-France* bellowed a salute to the lady of liberty. Soot shot into the air, spreading a fine layer of ash over all who stood on the deck.

"A historical moment," Gesser declared with proper glum ceremony as the statue paraded by. "It's always a historical moment when you see the backside of something that everybody else sees from the front."

"Oh, would you laugh a little for once?" Sonya gave her fellow traveller a shake and a hug. "Laugh and the world laughs with you, cry and you cry alone. Anyway, I can't take the cold any more. Do we have to freeze to admire your historical moment?"

"Freezing *is* a historical moment," Gesser declared sententiously.

Sonya moaned dramatically. Would this man ever stop complaining? She put up her collar against the wind that whipped at them, as it whipped at the spectators further down the seaboard, where Roosevelt would be sworn in later that very day, and go on to steal a march or two from the socialists, just as Steinstein the bootlegger had predicted. Jack and Sonya fought with the wind to pull open the heavy iron door to the ship's salon. Once he had wrestled it open, he turned and gave the New World one last look. The Statue of Liberty was growing vague in the mist, its lamp stabbing at the low clouds. *Farewell, luftmensch*, he addressed the man he had been. *Farewell, you useless peddler. Farewell, former self!*

The wind slammed the door unceremoniously behind them, ushering them into the salon.

And into view of a glittering buffet. The food positively glistened and winked at them, as if it had been sprayed with lacquer. The spread was much choicer than the sandwiches at Berg's College of Trades and Vocations, but the two buffets did have something in common. A speech had to be endured before the hungry and the parched were allowed to get their hands on the grub. On the *Île-de-France*, instead of a grim, heroic socialist of the Berg model, the speech was delivered by a character dressed in a white uniform and white officer's hat of indeterminate rank, who served in the army of pleasure.

He raised his eyebrows in mock surprise as Jack and Sonya blew in, then continued his patter.

"We're delighted to have all of you aboard the *Île-de-France*." He gestured with his right hand; in his left was a champagne glass. "A mile long she is, the sleekest ship on the North Atlantic run. And the poshest, too, I might add, if you'll forgive me for boasting."

"Poshest?" Sonya whispered loudly. "What's a poshest?"

"An excellent choice to escape the current . . . misfortunes in our beloved country. And, after all, what better day to choose to sail than Inauguration Day? The thought of all those wretches gawking as the presidential buggy glides by. But here, on board the *Île-de-France*, we're in a country of our own."

The ersatz officer of the pleasure brigade paused to fill his glass.

"The finest Canadian champagne, now that we're out of the temperate old eyes of the liquor police." He made a show of wetting his lips. "But those coppers aren't long for this world. I drink to Roosevelt, even if he's a Dem! Still, with everything out in the open, we'll lose our fine Yankee tradition of ingenuity. So, whoever you are, fore or aft, port or starboard, first class or steerage—not that we have that!—enjoy your passage, and don't forget to avail yourselves of the bubbly!"

The passengers applauded, then stormed the buffet. With a practiced move, Sonya twisted past a lady almost thrice her age and took up position at the table. "I wish to avail myself," she said to no one in particular, then drank off a glass. The champagne was a bit sour, as if hurried into existence, but the bubbles tickled her lips in a pleasant enough way. She chose another. Tiny glasses, containing no more than a lady's tear. From the corner of her eye, she spotted Jack behind the crowd, gesticulating with hand and mouth, signalling her to bring him back some of the spoils. It was a shame to surrender her hard-fought position, but she did after a time, regretfully, pushing back through the crowd of passengers in a shower of spilling champagne and flying *millefeuille* crumbs.

"Here, have a glass, you gloomy old thing. After all, you paid for it."

She thrust a flute into Jack's hand.

"Imagine that! A woman, leading me to drink."

"And not just any woman! Your concubine, your without-bene-fit-of-clergy, your illicit, your tramp, your *whore*."

"Sonya, please!" Jack hissed.

Sonya smiled sweetly, unfocusedly, complacently.

"Champagne at noon. Happens every time. Not that I've ever tried it." She paused, remembering the excesses of her Budapest period. "Well, not in recent memory, in any case."

And she let herself collapse against him in a parody of the drunken slattern. Gesser enveloped her in his arms, awkwardly, embarrassed in the crowd, but protective, too—protecting her from herself, or so he thought. He cast his eyes across the ship's salon, its air growing steel-blue with cigar smoke.

"Full of class enemies," he concluded. "If they only knew where we're going."

"That's what's so charming about this democracy we're leaving. You can slip up and down the wrungs of the ladder in the most curious of ways, and no one cares as long as your shoes are shined."

To prove her point, she hailed a waiter hurrying by with champagne and little cakes as lustily as if he were the Halstead Street trolleycar on a cold Chicago night.

"A sweet, please, and another glass."

She grasped a flute by the stem and steered a train of hors d'œuvres into the palm of her free hand. Poor Gesser, who couldn't believe that something could be had for nothing, was afraid to take a glass. Why waste? Sonya thought, and collected his share.

"Come, dear," Jack said into her hair, "this isn't our world."

Our world? she asked herself, then laughed at the formulation. Such a quaint notion, one's own world; she had never known such a place, doubted it could even exist. But she let Jack steer her towards the exit and she went without protest, willing to leave Babylon as long as she had a good supply of food and drink.

Leaving the salon turned out to be a bad idea. Outside, a gale was blowing. The *Île-de-France* was lumbering through the heaving, grey, impassive waves.

"What have you done to us? We'll freeze out here!" Sonya complained, the wind tearing at her chignon.

They stumbled towards the back of the bulkhead in search of shelter, two misguided travellers in the storm, but there, the wind lashed just as fiercely. There was a tidal wave in Sonya's glass, and the gale threatened to pull apart the thousand superimposed leaves of the pastry she held in her hand. Her eyes burning with soot and wind, she chose to protect the most precious cargo first by consuming it. She drained her glass neatly, in itself a feat in this wind.

"And now for dessert," she announced to the gale, and bit into a flaky pastry.

It nearly made her choke. Its contents were soft, viscous, salty. Fish eggs! How could the world do that to her? It had stuffed her sweets with fish eggs! Betrayed, she tossed the hors d'oeuvres into the air and the wind did the rest, sweeping them away neatly, high over the rail, fish eggs returning to their chaotic element.

Gesser yanked on the steel door that led back to the salon, but he was no match for the wind. All because he didn't feel comfortable in *those* people's world, Sonya thought as she watched him struggle with mild interest, as though he were operating on another plane. The pitch and roll of the ship, the champagne buzz at this early hour after a near-sleepless night in the Century Limited and a morning without breakfast, the uniform grey of the sky and water—all this put her at some remove from the proceedings.

Gesser moved along the bulkhead to the next door. He gave the metal handle a yank and, miraculously, the steel hatch sprung open like the enchanted entrance to a cave. Sonya dashed for it with visions of glasses of champagne to wash the fish taste from her mouth, and Gesser on her heels. Behind him, the door slammed with a cavernous iron crash. But this door did not lead back to the pleasure dome. Above them, a ceiling bulb in a cage of mesh swung crazily and they gazed down a painted metal stairway only slightly less steep than a fireman's pole.

"This way to steerage," Sonya called out.

With one hand on the rail, she launched herself down the stairs, protected by the gods that look after fools and the intoxicated in such situations. How much did I really have? she wondered as she descended. Three glasses? Five? Seven? I'm out of practice, that's the problem, in Budapest I would take a bottle of Tokay all for myself, thick and sweet at that, and be no worse for wear. She felt

Gesser scuffling behind her, eager to slip past her and catch her should her salt-slick hands let go of the rail. But she wouldn't let him by. She didn't need any help; protection of his sort would only make her nervous. Hands on the rail, she swung out over the steep stairwell just to prove to herself and the rest of the world that she was in complete control of the moment.

"Son-ya!" Jack pleaded.

"To the steerage! To the boiler-room! Two poverty-stricken members of the intelligentsia retiring to their luxury berth! Ah, the mysteries of democracy!"

Then she leaped from the fourth step, hit the floor and sprung upright, as splendid as a young tumbler on a mat.

"Let's see now." She took a few steps down one hallway, reversed, tried another, patting her pockets for the key. "These doors all look the same, that's the problem. They all open into rooms, but such rooms, we don't know!"

Jack was prisoner of her wanderings as Sonya explored the ship's corridors, empty now, with everyone above celebrating their passage into international waters. By some miracle, Sonya found a lock into which her key would go, and inside the room were their unpacked bags, the rope still wound around them, the knots tied so tight it looked as though they'd never get them loose.

"Home sweet home!"

She threw herself face down on the bed.

"Forgive me, dear husband," she said into the pillow, "it is all too much adventure for me."

Jack sat down beside her. With painstaking pleasure, he set about removing the many pins and clips and fasteners from her hair. He hummed a little tune as he worked on her layers of scarves and sweaters and woollens and underthings. The tune, to his surprise, was "The Bear Went over the Mountain." How sweet it is when the predatrix, spent in foolish play, finally surrenders. She who has had her bridle up, now assumes the bit. I will clutch this long red mane and ride. He did not bother turning her over. He reached for a pillow and slipped it under her belly, then blessed the fruit of the vine that upon these splendid occasions can give such pliant, glistening forgiveness.

The treachery of desserts stuffed with fish eggs. That was the problem. Their perfidious nature. The confusion of the sweet and the briny. Sonya Freedman gulped down the bad taste in her throat and wished herself back to sleep. That never works. Not when the bed is rising and falling, the entire structure that kept them atop the waters creaking to its very core. Her head lifted higher than her feet; that, she could accept. But when her feet rose above her head, that went beyond the tolerable.

In the parsimonious glow of the nightlight, she considered the possibility that she was still drunk, hoped it was so. But no. She remembered everything with too much clarity, excessive clarity even, the cool air on her backside after Jack had finally succeeded in freeing the lower half of her body from her clothes, the exaggerated care with which he parted the lips of her sex and dared to enter her first with his fingertip, then with his tongue, and how, afterwards, he had plunged into her and began swimming inside her like a dark fish.

A dark fish in the sea beneath her bed.

The sea.

She made a dash for the head.

In the toilet bowl the water rocked and slid as the *Île-de-France* took the waves. God, spare me. I've changed my mind, I want to go home. And with that futile resolution on her lips, she vomited up the hors d'œuvres, the sweet and the briny alike.

After a time in the chamber, she struggled up the sliding wood panel that gave the toilet an excuse for privacy, and found Jack Gesser sitting in a chair by the light of the bedside lamp. He wore a sheet wrapped around his shoulders like a shawl.

"Why do *you* look so bad? I'm the one who's sick."

"For a minute, I thought you were pregnant."

"Don't you wish!"

He turned his head quizzically. "If you must know, right now, no, I don't wish it. You're seasick. The best thing is to go up on deck."

"It's too cold up there. Anyway, I'd never make it up all those flights of stairs. And I don't even remember where up is!"

She wailed and grasped her stomach, as if the ship's lumbering progress were being made over her belly. She stripped a blanket off the bed and wrapped herself in it. Then stood up, paced, watched hypnotized as the water shifted in the pitcher on the bureau.

"If there were only a porthole or something, some air . . . No, that would be worse, all those waves, all that water."

She took to her bed and grabbed the pillow, a stable island in a trackless, tilting world.

"I'm not moving. Ever again. I'm just going to wait right here until it goes away."

Gesser watched her stubborn, hunched shoulders. The worst way to fight the malady, he thought. Then he did what most men do at times of moral quandary: he tiptoed out of the room in discreet abandonment, hoping that was what she would have wanted, to be alone, had she had the power and the inclination to speak.

Gesser worked his way upward through the man-made labyrinth of the ship, towards the deck and fresh air, where Sonya should have been. Poor Sonya, he thought, always so light and gay and free, while I'm the twisted, nervous bird of gloom. Which one of us, he wondered, will fare best on this journey? The one who travels best, Gesser decided, is the one who knows endurance.

It was too early to say which of them that might be.

Gesser found his way into the dining room. It was vast and lit by swaying chandeliers. The settings were many, the diners few. Evidently others were suffering as Sonya was on their first night.

"Sir?" the maître d' inquired. He wore an anxious look at the prospect of a solitary guest. "Will this be for one?"

To his shame, Gesser realized he was ravenous.

"Dinner," he said. "For my wife and I."

Jack Gesser happily ate two suppers that evening. Each time a waiter came by with a different course, Gesser indicated the empty setting.

"I am expecting her. I can't imagine why she is so late. You know women . . ."

He gestured vaguely, indulgently, at the empty chair. The waiter set down the plates. Jack Gesser cleaned them both, eating quickly, eyes down as if analyzing the rich sauces of the *Île-de-France's* cuisine. As the ship made its difficult progress across the North Atlantic through the late winter storms, the waiters stopped arching their eyebrows every time Gesser requested dinner for his wife, who would be making an appearance any minute now. He paid no attention to their irony; besides, it was no skin off their noses whether he ate one, two or a dozen dinners.

He was happy to dine alone, without conversation to distract him from his intake of food. But one evening, a tobacco-colored man with mustaches waxed to the keenness of saber points stood before him and considered the collection of dishes that Gesser had scoured to a mirror-shine with slabs of pearly white bread.

"Stocking up, friend?" the man asked.

Gesser bit deeply into a slice of orange melon. Too deeply, it turned out, for he felt the rind against his teeth.

"Not stocking up, brother," Gesser corrected him. "Catching up."

He followed the melon with a slice of delicious, dried pork meat, so thin the light from the swaying chandeliers shone through it and cast a rose-colored glow on his porcelain.

"Very cleverly said," the man congratulated him. "But clever words don't matter. They won't change anything. Eat now if you wish—it will do no good. It will only stretch the stomach, and make it more hungry when you reach the famine land."

Gesser chewed, swallowed.

"If words don't matter," he said to the man who hovered over him, then paused to pull a line of pig fat off the edge of his ham, "then why lecture me, comrade?"

"I am not your comrade."

The man's offended tone was comic. Gesser decided to take richest advantage of it.

"You certainly are, comrade. I'm willing to bet we have the same destination."

Gesser went back to his sweet, salty pork. When he next looked up, the tobacco-colored man was gone. But he would return, Gesser felt sure, so after his meal he went to the ship's library and pulled the thickest book he could find off the shelf. A book that would protect him from interruptions, for who would dare intrude on someone engaged in the sacred act of reading? The book's author was a man called Sterne. A promising name, but it turned out, as he discovered next mealtime, that this Sterne did not write his kind of book. After the first few pages, it became apparent that a gentleman who was not even born yet had undertaken to tell the story. Gesser was not a good audience for this kind of self-conscious sporting; reading was too noble a pursuit to be wasted on trivial fictions. But during mealtimes, he kept the book open on his table by means of judiciously placed salt and pepper shakers, warding off prospective conversationalists who might interfere with his appetite.

The cabin had begun to take on the stuffy odor of a sickroom. The berth was hellish for Sonya, but she would not go up on deck, too afraid to leave her bed and assume the upright position. She would retch, hug her pillow, then fix her eyes on the water pitcher on the bureau as the liquid inside pitched fore and aft.

Once, Gesser made the mistake of showing up with a plate of food.

"If this joint had a window, I'd throw that stuff out," Sonya stormed, "and you with it! You're so cruel!"

Gesser retreated with the tray, banging into the door frame as the *Île-de-France* plunged into a trough, upsetting the dishes like a bad waiter in a vaudeville routine. From then on, Jack kept his visits to a minimum, descending only to sleep and, later, when he discovered that the leather couches in the salon were infinitely more airy and comfortable than his bunk down below, not even for that purpose.

She's not a good sufferer. He shook his head sadly.

Early one morning, Gesser stood leaning over the stern rail. His mood was foggy, as foggy as the haze slowly burning off under a timorous sun, revealing the wide entrance to the Channel. He had been woken that night by a solicitous barman reminding him that he'd rented a cabin below, and did not have to resort to the couch. *Does it matter where I sleep, as long as I sleep?* Gesser grumbled in Yiddish, the language of his dreams, but one that the barman did not understand. Then he returned to his version of comfort, curled on the smooth leather couch, without blankets.

The morning's vista cheered him slightly. The clouds were high, thin and fleecy, the water flat and unhostile for the first time since the New York harbor. His weary eyes took in landfall on the northeast horizon. England, he supposed. Another station on his way. He thought back to the farewell party at the LaSalle Street Station, and Spielerman's sense of timing and charm. Even the conductors had loved him. Though an ocean separated them, Gesser had still not wrestled Spielerman out of his mind. Spielerman in spats. Spielerman, the king of cathouse jazz. Spielerman, his face buried in Miss Pearl's vast, burning brown cleavage. Spielerman, Sonya's lover. Spielerman, the chameleon Jew. Is that the only way for the Jew to prosper—to lose himself?

Jack Gesser felt a presence and looked up. Sonya Freedman was leaning on the rail by him, smiling, in her best—her one and only—travelling dress. She pointed towards the distant land mass, a green-grey rump on the horizon.

"Is that Russia?"

"That? No, it must be England." Gesser laughed. "You haven't been down below that long. Anyway, Russia's not that green this time of the year."

She stared at the coast in some disappointment.

"Feel better?"

She pointed to the smooth waters.

"That's why," she said. "I swear, I'm never going to make this crossing again."

In Southampton, they marvelled at the cheerful yellow jonquils of the precocious English spring, planted along a promenade that afforded them a view of their next ship being prepared for travel. A dank, creaky, herring-smelling freighter that put Sonya and Jack more at ease than the luxury of the Île-de-France. They never learned the ship's name; Jack called her the S.S. Pickled Herring. No one welcomed them on board with dainties stuffed with fish-eggs.

But the reeking old freighter provided an odd sense of comfort, as if it were at ease on these waters, and with its destination, the port of Leningrad.

Jack and Sonya discovered they were not alone on this voyage. They found themselves playing the shipboard comedy of idle travellers confined to a slow-moving vessel, with all the time in the world before them, and not even a pack of cards to pass the days. As they moved through the Cat's Gut into Baltic waters, a couple with a worn atlas in their hands approached them, wondering about the hazy land masses that slowly paraded by. They were dressed in thick tweeds, as if ready to go golfing or shoot pheasant on a foggy moor somewhere.

"Do you know this route?" the male half of the couple asked Jack in a well-manicured British accent.

"Not from this angle."

"Then I suppose you wouldn't know if that's the Soviet Union yet?"

Gesser looked out across the choppy waters with their medium swell. In the failing afternoon light, the coastline they saw could have been Sweden or Finland, Russia or the Illinois side of Lake Michigan.

He shrugged. "It's too soon."

"We're so thrilled to be going there," the man's wife piped up.

The Englishman stuck out his hand and grasped Gesser's. "White," he announced. "British. Foreign specialist."

The couple's good will and bald naivety inspired the worst sort of mischief in Jack Gesser. He shook the hand offered him.

"Gesser. *Luftmensch*." He nodded towards Sonya. "Freedman. Raving red beauty."

Mr. White cocked his head quizzically, too polite to admit he didn't know what the hell Gesser was talking about, or even what his words meant. Like the city of Chicago, the English language was a big place. You could live there forever and never run into certain people.

"I take it you're a foreign specialist yourself," Mr. White pursued. "I'm in engineering. The missus is a schoolteacher."

"Foreign specialist?" Gesser considered the classification. "Foreign, yes. Wherever I go. It is a vocation. But specialist, no, not much of a specialist. I was a peddler in the New World."

He stepped back from the rail, cupped his hands around his mouth and let fly the sad, eternal call of the Sangamon Street fruitman. *"Vah-ter-mee-loans!"*

"Don't let him josh you," Sonya warned, laughing. "He did more than sell melons. He was a *goniff*—a first-class thief, even if his career was cut short by success. He used a brick of all things. He stole from the poor, and kept it. Then he was a spy, a secret agent, working in the hot countries, for the cause of the proletariat. It turned out he was a double agent of sorts. He may not look like it, but he is a man of resources. He can live off air, like those plants that hang from trees."

"A quality you could not do without in the world we knew," Gesser added.

"The important thing," Mrs. White said, hoping to put a stop to all this play, "is that we're all going to Russia—"

"The Soviet Union, dear," Mr. White corrected her.

"The Soviet Union," she acknowledged. "The Soviet Union, together, to build a more humane society, based on equality and respect for individual beliefs."

"You see, we're Unitarians," Mr. White confided to Jack and Sonya, as if confessing to something shameful, the practice of sodomy, for example. "Our beliefs were never accepted in England."

Sonya shot Jack a brief glance. "Who are these crazy people?" she wondered out loud in Yiddish. "And who cares if other people don't accept your beliefs, as long as they don't kill you for them?"

"Unitarian means they believe in one God," Jack informed her in the same language, displaying his learning.

Sonya turned to the Whites. "Ah, one God, I understand! We have one God, too. That is, when we have him."

Mrs. White clasped her hands together tightly, as if afraid they might fly off her wrists. "We have so much in common," she declared.

Jack and Sonya inched along the ship's rail, and away from Mr. and Mrs. White and their elastic, murky God.

"I'm sure we'll be seeing you around," said Jack, once the distance between them had grown large enough to notice.

"Yes, well, why would a young couple want to waste time with stodgy old folks like us?" Mr. White chuckled indulgently.

Sonya smiled a winning smile. "We're newlyweds," she said.

"How lovely! And you're going to the Soviet Union for your honeymoon! Isn't that devotion, then, to spend that precious time serving a good greater than yourselves?"

"A good greater than yourselves? Is that what you call Stalin? Such fine talk—poetry wasted on a murderer!"

Everyone turned to gaze at the intruder, the spoilsport. The waxed, saber-pointed mustaches were drooping, and the swarthy skin was a slight greenish hue from his days at sea. But the man was the same who had bedeviled Gesser on the *Île-de-France*.

He extended a hand no one shook.

"Koshgarian," he introduced himself. "Such good intentions you have. To be thrown to the dogs." He gave a bark of greasy laughter, as if relishing the prospect. "Into the sausage grinder, more like it! And such tender meat, too!"

"I wouldn't count on it being that tender," Sonya told him.

"Would you be bitter about something?" Mrs. White inquired innocently.

"Bitter? Bitter? How can you talk about bitter?" Koshgarian demanded of the poor Englishwoman, who looked genuinely pained. "My people are being destroyed by Stalin, and I am asked whether or not I am bitter!"

"If your people are being destroyed," Sonya countered, "then why go there? To march into the jaws of destruction—since when was that the point of immigration?"

"I am going there to destroy the destroyer," Koshgarian said boldly.

"All by yourself?" Gesser asked.

"I had a barbershop in New York. I sold it. I sold my furniture, my Victrola, all the clothes that a barber must have to make himself presentable to his customers. With that I made myself a nice pile of money. And now, those American dollars in my pocket will help gain freedom for my nation."

"Only a fool would boast about how much money he is carrying," Gesser told him, "especially when he's surrounded by strangers."

"But you are not strangers to me."

"I suppose you know us?" Sonya said incredulously.

"I know your kind."

"Is this a comfort to you, to know someone's *kind*?"

A red flush of anger came up under Koshgarian's tobacco-colored skin.

"Words!" he thundered, then stalked off along the ship's rail, and turned behind the bulkhead.

"He certainly is obsessed with this Stalin fellow," the Englishwoman commented. "I do wonder why."

"Age-old national hatreds," Jack told her. "They never go away."

He and Sonya disentangled themselves from the Whites, then retreated to their honeymoon intimacy deep within the S.S. *Pickled Herring*. Later, as they clung together in the overheated cabin, in the stink of diesel oil, Jack tried to dismiss Koshgarian. "A malcontent," he called him, using the word that had so often been used against him. "There are malcontents everywhere. The way we were on Sangamon Street. We don't care about one man. We care about the new man. And woman, of course."

The freighter sailed on through the frigid currents, in the darkness through which blocks of ice floated. Some were as big as synagogues, others as big as poolrooms. But all were much less welcoming.

Decades afterwards, when she recalled her arrival in Leningrad, Sonya Freedman would begin to hum "The Bear Went over the Mountain," and remember her greatest disappointment. She never did get to see the Hermitage, that captured palace presented to the people as a gift from the Revolution. Neither did she see the cathedral of the saints Peter and Paul. Or the Italianate fantasies that Peter the Great had imposed on this raw-aired, northern city. Or the busy Nevsky Prospekt, full of elegance and intrigue. They arrived at night through a mute, black seascape. The harbor was in an industrial section far from the center of the city. Sonya glimpsed a tower rising resolutely into the air, but it turned out to be a factory smokestack, not a church spire. The ship made agonizingly slow progress, as if the Gulf of Finland were made of molasses—frozen molasses at that. The freighter felt its way forward through the chunks of ice towards a port that seemed blacked-out, as if in wartime. A conservation measure, no doubt. She and Jack stood expectantly at the rail until it became apparent that nothing was going to happen, at least not yet, except that they would freeze to death. Finally, they retreated to their cabin, where they sat under the feeble yellow glow of the ceiling light, in their coats, exhausted and disappointed by the wait. Their eyes met, then strayed. Sonya fiddled with the clasps on her bag.

Departure always rides lighter on the soul than arrival. Especially arrival in an icy port, in darkness, in winter.

Then there was the issue of the jewel. The single red stone that Jack carried. True, he was carrying it home, but if he were questioned, how could he explain why he, an insignificant foreign specialist without specialization, had in his possession a rock from the Czar's crown jewels? Jack thrust his hand into his pocket and touched the jewel. Then realized he was calling attention to just the thing he wanted to conceal, and he snatched his hand away.

The night wore on. Sonya reclined on her bunk, her jacket buttoned and her boots laced up, waiting for something momentous to happen. Finally, she closed her eyes and was quickly visited by a traveller's dream. She was aboard the great ship of the self, thrusting, running, pushing through unyielding water. The harder she worked the more slowly she advanced, until she understood that she herself was the water, that great, suffering, impassive blanket that covers the earth, and that she must endure. And since in most traveller's dreams there is death, Sonya dimly understood that to arrive at her destination would signify the end. The end of what? The dream or the dreamer? The end would come in catastrophic fashion, she felt sure, judging from the hollow, echoing explosions in her ears. She awoke to the sounds of a commotion in the corridor outside. A sailor was banging on the doors of the empty cabins with unconcealed joy, as if they were the heads of the passengers, or of his commanding officer.

"Maritime Station, everybody out!" the sailor shouted, bouncing drunkenly off the narrow corridor walls as he came. "Maritime Station!"

Then came their turn. He hammered at their door. It suddenly gave way and he flew into their berth, a giant with a sweaty, coal-streaked face and a mouthful of teeth that looked like boulders at the foot of a cliff, stinking of drink, the very reckless incarnation of all they had undertaken.

He beheld the two passengers and their modest bags, and felt the privacy of the cabin he had barged into. Then he belched a cloud of gaseous vodka into the stuffy air.

"Everybody out. Maritime Station," he said in a curiously gentle voice.

"I know. We heard you," Gesser told him.

A motor launch bobbed in the frigid water beneath the freighter's flank. Sonya Freedman stood on the deck in the salty, biting wind, in the darkness, still not awake, not yet grasping the fact that they were finally at their destination. It was her dream's fault, the giant sailor's fault, too. She scanned the horizon and saw darker shapes against a dark sky that could have been anything: the Venetian facades of the old order's palaces, or museums, power plants, factories, the port—she did not know which way to look to see beauty in this night. A rope ladder, unrolled down the side of the ship, dangled over the launch. She did not want to descend that way, she wanted to complain, then realized there was no one to complain to.

Jack's voice was in her ear.

"One last step," he urged, "then we're there."

Sonya started down the rope ladder that swung out over oblivion, her face pressed close to the side of the freighter, whose pitted paint and rusty flanks could have stood for the map of her soul at that moment. The descent seemed to take hours, and when her foot finally touched the wooden edge of the launch and a pair of male hands grasped her hips from below as if she were a sack of merchandise, it startled her. From above, carrying both their bags, one hand on the rope ladder crackling with ice, Jack descended towards her. He looked happy, as if he thrived on this kind of ordeal.

The launch pulled away from the freighter. The boatman used one oar as a gaff to push off from the mothership, then fight the chunks of ice that floated between them and the wharf. Sonya was dimly aware of the other passengers: the talkative Whites, frightened into silence, and Koshgarian, the man who hated Stalin, who nodded smugly to himself, as if this rough final crossing was a confirmation of all his beliefs. Sonya found herself staring at the boatman's boots. From one boot-top straw peeked out; from the other, newspaper. She stared at that newspaper, wanted to read it, then realized she could not. She was entering an illiterate, dependent state, a kind of second infancy. It was called being a foreigner.

The choppy waters of the Gulf of Finland pitched the launch against the wharf. The timbers squealed.

"Maritime Station," the boatman muttered.

They tied up. Jack and Sonya scrambled out of the launch, their legs wobbly after days at sea. *Thank God, dry land*, she thought. She wanted to kiss the dock but decided against it, and that was just as well. Her lips would have frozen to the pavement.

"Well now, where's the welcome wagon?" she tried to joke, then shivered under the string of lights that marked the customs house. *How could there be a welcome?* she asked herself. *How could there be when no one knows we're here?*

The door to the Maritime Station opened and a customs man emerged, hiking up his pants and wrapping his tunic around his middle, as if he had just finished pissing against a wall. His uniform was a patchwork of grades and services, with a different number of stripes on each shoulder. He called out something into the wind. Sonya didn't understand, but she picked up the bag that the boatman had tossed at her feet and, among the pilgrim passengers, filed into the building next to the Whites, who glared suspiciously, fearfully at the heaps of snow around the building, foot soldiers in General Winter's army, as if they were polar bears about to devour them.

Inside, a coal stove dispensed its heat over a scene of masculine boredom. The chairs arranged in a circle around the stove, a newspaper upon which a half-consumed salt fish lay, and peeking out from under the paper, a deck of cards. A half-dozen rifles, some with salt-stained barrels. Onion, black bread, from a hidden cache, vodka. The smell of this elemental food brought tears of nostalgia to Jack's eyes.

Freedman and Gesser. Koshgarian. The White couple. The workers' paradise would be enriched by an odd assortment of comrades tonight. Spontaneously, they formed a line in front of the customs desk. But at that critical moment, the light bulbs in the ceiling fixtures flared an angry yellow, then died. The inside of the Maritime Station turned as black as the Gulf of Finland.

Mrs. White let out a high-pitched gasp, as if some rodent had used the cover of darkness to climb up her skirt.

"Capitalist sabotage," the customs man said with a certain mechanical insistence. "There can never be vigilance enough in this country."

Gesser sensed Koshgarian's presence behind him in the dark.

"The greater good needs you, honeymooner. To fix the lights. Though I suppose you prefer the dark."

The man cackled and broke the darkness with a match. In its flare, Gesser saw his self-satisfied face bent over his cigarette. Then Koshgarian held up the match that cast a weak glow over the customs men feeling their way through the dark hall.

"Stalin's irregulars. Boots stuffed with straw. Heads, too."

Gesser was about to tell him to shut up for his own good, that the English language was everybody's property. He changed his mind. Let the man talk, it was his right.

The customs men blundered around the table, found their jackets, tripped over the chairs like the Keystone Kops, then disappeared out the door in search of the cause of darkness. On the other side of the barrier, smokestacks rose into the sky. Beneath them, in convenient proximity to the means of production, giant apartment blocks huddled.

There were shouts and arguments from around the back of the customs shed. The problem had been found, but no one knew who to blame yet. Jack and Sonya stood close to each other, but not touching, in the darkness. Behind them loomed something pale and disquieting: the faces of the Whites, who were manifestly afraid of the dark. No one spoke. The no-man's-land between a departed freighter and a barred customs barrier is not a fertile field for conversation.

Koshgarian's cigarette flared and the rich smell of Latakia tobacco filled the hall. In this place of deprivation and respect for authority, the luxuriant scent was like blasphemy.

Mr. White breathed in the smoke and nodded with satisfaction.

"What I wouldn't do," he said in his clipped, precise voice, "for a cup of tea."

Jack and Sonya said nothing. What answer could there be in a darkened customs post, in the middle of the night, at the stale end of a Russian winter, in the workers' paradise, waiting for the lights to come back? Not only was there no answer; the very suggestion was an absurd insult, a manifestation of instability. Which is why no one answered. At a time like this, anything but instability is called for.

The man irritated Gesser. He would bring down bad luck on all their heads. Bad luck, Jack knew, was contagious. It thrived in dark, enclosed, sour spaces like this. Gesser moved his hand into his pocket and touched the stone. What would he say if it ever came to light? That it was all history's fault, history's idea of a joke, involving a little man in big circumstances?

Mr. White spoke up again, calling for his impossible cup of tea.

"Please, dear," Mrs. White whispered to her husband.

"A cup of tea," Mr. White repeated. The sound of the words must have pleased and amused him.

"Please," Mrs. White whispered again.

"Yes. A cup of tea."

The request was made politely, as if civility could procure him something that did not exist. An edge of hysteria crept into his voice.

"Dear," his wife reminded him.

"*I'm just having a bit of fun,*" Mr. White protested to his wife.

Koshgarian laughed. A cruel, mocking laugh, rich in contempt for the Whites. At that moment, Gesser hated the man and his self-assurance. *Go ahead,* Gesser addressed him silently, *say something else about Russia.*

Koshgarian obliged.

"You don't have any more chance of getting a cup of tea here than you do finding diamonds up a pig's ass." He emitted a cloud of smoke from both nostrils. "Your chances of getting a cup of tea are about as good as them fixing the generator before the sun comes up."

Koshgarian was wrong, as it turned out.

The lights flared into existence again, yellow and uncertain, but bright enough for the customs men to proceed with the duties of state. Certainly bright enough for anyone to have seen Gesser furtively, guiltily, conspicuously pull his hand out of his pocket.

The customs men, their patchwork uniforms smelling of smoked fish, argued their way back into the building. The generator had run dry, and though they did not yet know who to blame, at least they had agreed on the solution. At his bureau, an official rapped on his desk with a paper punch. Normalcy returned to the Maritime Station. The passengers shuffled forward. Mr. White, with an edgy smile. Mrs. White, chewing on her muff. Gesser and Freedman, unnerved by their fear of authority, Gesser with his hand playing at his pocket edge. Koshgarian in a cloud of luxurious tobacco smoke.

The Whites presented their documents.

"Foreign specialists," Mr. White said crisply. "Me and the missus."

The customs man gazed at their photographs, then at them, then laconically motioned them forward. Gesser and Freedman were next. Their American passports were examined carefully, but with some loathing.

"You speak Russian?" the customs man asked Gesser.

"Yes."

The customs man frowned. The senselessly complicated Russian language could be counted on to keep foreigners on the outside. Here was one who would understand everything around him—at least as far as words were concerned. A drawback, yes, but there was nothing to be done about that. The man's papers were in order.

The customs man waved Gesser and Freedman through. And so the last of the Czar's crown jewels returned home. The return was remarkably banal, for Gesser and for his jewel. Momentous occasions are usually experienced that way. You're cold, too deadened by fatigue to be hungry, you're haggard and accepting. It's better that way.

Then it was Koshgarian's turn. He took a last puff on his cigarette and stepped up to the customs man's desk.

"Foreign specialist, too?" he asked in Russian.

"Yes."

"Born in Russia?"

"That, too."

The customs man flipped through his American passport, saw nothing that interested him and waved him through.

The Whites and Jack and Sonya waited by the exit. Outside, a truck stood, its engine idling, a plume of exhaust rising in the cold air. As Koshgarian crossed the stone floor towards them, two militia men, who had been displaying remarkable attention to half a salted fish, rose and surrounded him. They turned and frog-marched him past the customs man's desk to a side room where the lights burned brightly.

Koshgarian tried to free himself from their grasp.

"What are you doing? You can't do this! Where are we going?"

"To look for diamonds up a pig's ass, comrade," the customs man told him in very good English.

"You can't do that!"

He tried to wave his American passport but the militia men had his arms pinned.

"You are also a Soviet citizen, on Soviet territory," the customs man pointed out. "So don't try to wave your passport in my face."

The door to the brightly lit room slammed, the shades went down. There was no sense dwelling on Koshgarian's misfortune. Gesser and Freedman and the Whites walked to the truck waiting to take them to the Moscow Station and the overnight trip to the capital.

"I can only assume he'll be treated fairly," Mr. White said as they boarded the trunk.

And that, though he did not know it, was Koshgarian's epitaph.

They sat freezing in the heatless cab of the idling truck. The mute, smoking driver checked a scrap of paper, then counted Jack and Sonya and the Whites, to make sure he hadn't made any mistakes in his arithmetic.

"We're all that's coming," Jack told the driver when the cold became intolerable. "The last one . . . the last one was detained."

The driver grunted and ground his truck into gear. As they left the harbor and drove towards the train station, their bags sliding in back with every turn, Jack realized he had done something absolutely new and thrilling.

He had spoken for the regime. Worse yet. He had apologized for it. As of now, he was part of it.

7

THE INTRIGUES OF THE CLASSLESS SOCIETY

That night, on the Leningrad–Moscow express, Sonya Freedman was awakened by the smell of hard-boiled egg, heavy, nourishing and sulphurous. She opened her eyes. To her right, Jack, neither awake nor asleep, was staring through the window glass at the emaciated lines of leafless birches, and the heavy, snow-laden spruce.

The egg-eater was seated on the bench across from Sonya. Mechanically, in the darkness, he finished peeling his egg, wrapped the shells neatly in his handkerchief and bit off the top of it. The smell rose up from the yolk and suddenly nauseated her. She had heard of such reactions. Pregnant women suffered from them, owing to their sensitive state. This, she knew, could not happen to her, so she draped her headscarf across her nose and settled back to sleep.

When it came to the fact of her barrenness, Sonya Freedman had picked selectively from the treasure-chest of science and mythology of the good doctors of Budapest. She had rejected their diagnosis that she possessed a hysterical condition, since she understood that to mean she had an illness of the mind, and she was sure she did not. They had told her this hysteria was manifest in her barrenness, and she had believed them when they told her she could not conceive, because the condition suited her. It gave her a tremendous, unspeakable freedom. It freed her from becoming wife and mother, and let her lay claim to her own extraordinary origin: that of the child who kills her mother, and is punished for it in her womanhood.

Sometime later, during that endless, promiscuous night in the train coach, Sonya was awakened again. The air was searing the insides of her nostrils with a gaseous, corrosive essence. The coal stove in the car had backed up and was sending its fumes into her compartment, or so she believed. She pressed her scarf to her nose and eyes. Through its weave she clearly felt the egg-eater's stare, frank, evaluating, but devoid of desire. That stare frightened her more than the male leers she was accustomed to; there was something inhuman to it. She closed her eyes again and tried not to breathe. She felt every single body, male or female, that slumped restlessly in the coach that night. It was true: there was no word in the local language for *privacy*.

Gesser slept on beside her. The worse the conditions, the better he slept; on this train ride, he was lost in deep slumber. He maintained that state of grace all the way to Moscow, and she hated him for it.

*   *   *

My God, this place is no more than an overgrown village, was Sonya Freedman's first thought when the crowds carried her out of Leningrad Station into Moscow the next day, and onto a semicircular square. The sun burned brilliantly in a swept sky. It was probably better that they didn't know just how cold it was.

Together, like two sleepwalkers, Jack and Sonya moved away from the station, past the kiosks and vendors selling State goods. Fires burned in barrels in the station square just as they did along Sangamon Street, and everywhere people strove for warmth. Jack and Sonya stood poised at the lip of the square and considered the scene of frozen chaos, one they were hardly ready for, their nerves tattered from the ride in that barracks on wheels that passed for a train.

"So it's true what they say," Gesser mused.

"What's true? After last night, I don't think I can tell true from false."

"It's true that everybody works here."

In the square, the snow-sweepers, sex indeterminate under their shawls and scarves and sheepskin hats, were universally occupied. Inches from their feet, horse-carts passed.

"Not an apple-seller in sight. When was the last time you saw that?"

Amid the shovellers, like cats among the pigeons, cars driven by the *apparatchiks* careened across the ice. The drivers were all learning on the job, and had discovered the horn but not the brake pedal yet. Their recklessness recalled Cape Haitian, but a frozen kind of Cape Haitian, where no mambos were played.

Sonya wiped her forehead and inspected the streak of soot on her hand.

"I feel like I've been in the coal mines."

In answer, Gesser turned and spat discreetly in the snow. His spittle made a black indent on the white crust. A cart approached, the long-suffering horse's nostrils decorated with icicles. The driver slowed and stopped. He could not offer his services for cash, for that would constitute profiteering, so the exchange with this delivery man on some State errand, who was doubling as a gypsy cab, had to be wordless. Gesser gave the driver the address of the Kosmos Hotel on Kuznetsky Most and he and Sonya climbed onto the back of the wagon, atop the sacks of coal and potatoes. Then they were off again. Sonya gave the potatoes a squeeze through their burlap sack. They were frozen, as hard as the coal.

And so they clattered towards the center of the overgrown village, Jack Gesser and Sonya Freedman, king and queen of potatoes and coal.

On the boulevards, the long curving apartment blocks of the Moscow baroque paraded by, soldiers of the old regime, what the czars had had time and inclination to rebuild after Napoleon had torched the place. Those buildings made Moscow look almost like a European city. The colors were wonderful, all the more so because they were unexpected: dark mustard, a pale lime hue, a red verging on orange, like fine smoked salmon. The pastel shades softened the harsh winter sunlight, and briefly gave a gentle light to the overgrown village, the kind of sheen and wisdom an old piece of jewelry might give off. Then the cart crossed a strip of dejected parkland and the city reverted to its origins: a collection of crude cottages. The driver slowed and pulled up before a group of low, stout, stunted, stuccoed cabins, as tough as nuts. The huts were scattered like dice around a central courtyard, snow piled up nearly to their wide eaves. The driver stepped down, and with grunts and gestures, as if he were mute, made them understand that, no, this was not Kuznetsky Most, mercifully enough, and that, yes, they were to hand down the sacks to him, that would make his life easier.

A delivery man supplementing his income with the odd passenger. The practice was universal apparently, Gesser thought as he and Sonya sat shivering on their hill of potatoes and coal, their privilege as passengers exposing them to the winds and making them feel foolish.

"I wonder why he didn't ask us to help him," Jack said.

"Each according to his means," Sonya answered. "Maybe he could tell that after a night sitting on a wooden bench, breathing coal gas, we didn't have the means to help. I couldn't sleep on that train. Amazing that you could."

"It takes practice. And endurance."

"I studied your method. I watched how you did it. It must have worked, because I drifted off after a while. Too bad the smell of eggs woke me up. I started thinking about that British man and his cup of tea. Do you think he was really joking? I mean, a cup of tea at a border post . . ."

"Some people don't know how to do without."

"I think he was . . . disturbed."

"Such a luxury, being disturbed. To have imaginary problems."

Sonya said nothing. She knew enough about imaginary problems to understand how useless it is to debate them with people who don't believe that they constitute life itself. She pictured Mr. White in the customs hall and trailing behind him, Mrs. White, gnawing on her muff, dragging her suitcase as if it were filled with lead. That image bothered Sonya more than Koshgarian's fate. His, at least, was rational. It obeyed a certain logic.

Sonya turned her back to the wind and toyed with the uneven shapes of the potatoes under their burlap cover. Her eyes stung from the cold, and when she closed them she saw the railway carriage and the egg-eater again. The delivery wagon jerked and her head slumped forward. She would have fallen off had Jack not caught her. Then they were riding through the Moscow streets again and Jack was whispering to her, *Sleep, sleep*, and she did, finally, in the cold and discomfort, just the way Jack could, all the way to the Kosmos Hotel on Kuznetsky Most. In her fitful sleep she felt a perverse pride. *I, too, am capable of brutish endurance*, she thought.

"We're lucky to be here," Jack said, dropping their suitcases in their hotel room.

Sonya answered by breathing out a plume of steam that slowly dispersed towards the ceiling of the room, where a chandelier had once hung.

"Okay, lucky to find a room." He pulled her closer. "When two lie together, there will be warmth."

"Especially if the two are like sardines in a tin."

She lay down on the single cot with her feet hanging over the edge. Jack knelt before her and neatly unlaced and pulled off her boots. In the hallway outside their room, a coal stove rumbled and glowed, heating the common hallway, giving a ration of warmth to those guests willing to keep their doors open. Gesser, unwilling to share in that bargain, closed theirs and slipped the latch into the eye.

They kissed under the cold blankets. He tasted something metallic on Sonya's breath, as if the ocean liner and the freighter and the railroad train that had brought them to this room had each left an essence of iron in her, which she now expelled in short, sharp bursts of awakened passion. Her cold hands ran under his wool tunic and shirt and undershirt, and pinched his nipples in the lovers' mixture of pleasure and punishment.

"We'll have to be careful," he whispered.

"Careful? You know there's no careful with me."

"Quiet, I mean."

She followed his gaze upward. The wall partition did not meet the ceiling. A couple feet of board were missing from their intimacy.

Sonya sighed heavily, fell back.

"I think I'm too tired to be careful."

In the late afternoon light they ventured out to wander in the cold air, following curving Kuznetsky Most to Hertzina. "The Street of the Heart," commemorating a nobleman's love affair, and the *fils naturel* his passion had produced. It was a rare trace of sentiment in the capital. Amazing that, after the Revolution, no one had thought to change it to something more heroic.

The name survived because it was German, a language no one would admit to understanding. *Du bist mein hertz, hertzela,* Gesser told Sonya as they walked in close embrace along that street, and she smiled at his naive compliment.

In a tiny, snow-packed square, they came upon a statue of Gogol. A man with a wooden coal-shovel was carving a path through the snow to the statue's base. Jack and Sonya took that path, easing past the shoveller who glared at them for having tracked snow onto his clean walkway. Then he turned and glared at the statue for having inspired these idlers to commit the act, as if it were the statue's fault, though he had no idea who the great green-bronze mass molded into a man's form was. Jack and Sonya stood before Gogol's powerful features and beheld his heroic furrowed brow.

"Can you imagine," said Sonya, "the city of Chicago ever putting up a statue for a writer? Impossible!"

"I can see it now: Upton Sinclair in the stockyards—fat chance! Here, at least, they revere culture."

They circled the statue. Around its granite base were carved bas-relief figures from Gogol's fictions and plays. Gesser recognized the

Inspector-General, Taras Bulba, some old landowners, a folkloric gnome or two, Cossacks, the actors from the village tales, and a handful of comical, superfluous female members of the bourgeois society, now evolved into new beings, or evolved out of existence.

"Someone's missing," Gesser pointed out. He struck an actorly pose. "'Gentlemen, let us save the moon, for the earth is trying to sit on it!'"

"That doesn't sound like Gogol."

"It is. It's the Madman himself, in person, the Madman and his famous Diary. Nowhere to be found on this statue. My favorite character."

Gesser grasped his head in mock agony, in imitation of the Madman who, in turn, imitated the shaved ecclesiastical heads of the soldiers and grandees. "If you persist in calling yourself King Ferdinand," he threatened, his portrayal of mental anguish surprisingly persuasive for an amateur, "I'll knock the inclination out of you."

"*Feh*," Sonya exclaimed. "No wonder he's not on the statue. What good is yesterday's madman to this society, no matter how convincingly he speaks?"

"I suppose you're right. He's not very . . . optimistic. Still, once I memorized most of that play. I can't help it if I still remember the lines. It seems a shame to have to forget all that learning."

They slipped past the shoveller and left the green-bronze Gogol to its private agony. True, it would have been senseless, even counterrevolutionary, to expose the Madman to public view in a country struggling to join the century that the West had entered over thirty years ago. Gogol had to be heroic. Not only heroic: well muscled.

Jack and Sonya continued along Hertzina Street, bordered on both sides by the rare and lovely facades of the Moscow baroque. Pillars, cherubim with eye sockets filled with snow, curlicues, every Italianate fantasy in stone, all painted in the colors of mustard, light sienna, salmon, the blue of robins' eggs, astonishing for a winter city. Between the sidewalk and the street rose tall snowbanks, which was just as well, since the street was running with muddy water.

Then Hertzina opened abruptly and they found themselves before the vastness of Red Square, vaster still because it had been entirely swept clean of snow. On all sides the old monuments were turned to new uses. To the left was the Metropol Hotel where the Party elite now lodged; to the right, a temple in the Greek style had been transformed into a giant repository for the manuscripts of the Motherland. The square was much bigger than necessary, but it was not the Revolution's fault; the Revolution had only inherited it. Gesser's native village, an entire *shtetl*, maybe even two, could have easily fit into it. The other side, where the Kremlin walls ran, seemed miles away, and the Kremlin itself floated like a distant island on the horizon. Before such enormity, Jack and Sonya clung more tightly to each other.

The winds rose, announcing the coldness of the night. From a tall flagpole in the center of the Square, a red flag as big as the Poklub flat lifted, then opened, revealing its insignia.

Sonya put her head on Jack's shoulder.

"It's such a thrill, it's so grand. I feel like I'm drunk."

"It's like being at the very center of an idea, the exact center of history."

Their chapped lips hurt when they touched, but who could resist a kiss before the inhuman grandeur of Red Square, as a cortege of black ZIV limousines came slanting across the bricks of the Square to be gobbled up by the Kremlin gates? In Moscow, in winter, a public kiss was as rare as orange juice, and just as foreign.

*   *   *

It was a relief to get back to Kuznetsky Most. The street described a gentle crescent and was lined with stalls and kiosks, with the murmur of petty commerce that reminded them of Sangamon Street. But here, there was a sense of order, an air of patience, endurance, you might call it. No one was diving for a half-frozen head of cabbage that had rolled off the top of a fast-moving wagon. No sandwich men stood with roughly lettered signs proclaiming their desire to work. Here, everyone worked. To work, to have a reason to work, was an ideal in itself.

On the sidewalk, a woman was selling sunflower seeds from a massive burlap sack that wore a light dusting of snow. The seeds were probably frozen inside, but Gesser wanted some, just a handful, to have the taste of the stolid, boggy Russian earth in his mouth. He extracted the last of the rubles he'd been able to acquire at the Maritime Station.

He broke open the frozen hull with his teeth, spat out the two halves and held the precious seed between his teeth. Who was it who said the Russians would never figure out their destiny because they were too busy chewing on sunflower seeds? Jack cracked a second shell and offered the meat to Sonya. She nibbled it off his little finger, for her hunger had returned. This nut, at least, knew its destiny: to be pulverized and ingested for the greater good of Sonya the Red.

Jack and Sonya moved along the street, chewing the seeds, hand in hand through the stolid, dignified, ever-moving crowd. Everyone was in constant movement, like ants on an anthill, as if every man and woman were being called to an urgent rendezvous. The truth was elsewhere, of course. If you did not move, you'd be committing idleness, and committing idleness was to be avoided when the militia was near. And the militia was always near.

In a knot on the sidewalk was a group of men who were not moving. But they were musicians performing a job of sorts, and they were tolerated despite the frivolity of their task. A trumpeter, an accordionist, a gloveless guitarist, a singer with ground glass in his throat. The hat on the sidewalk before him was heavy with kopeck coins. The crowd passed, someone would bend quickly and drop a coin into the hat. The charity of the poor, their eagerness to bestow it, the quick and almost furtive pleasure they took in the act, was moving to Jack and Sonya. She understood nothing of the song, but unknowing made the tune all the more charming.

It was not the same for Gesser. The melody froze him in time. It took him back to his village childhood, his apprenticeship to the printer, when he would run the bundles of papers from one village to the next, and in between learn to set type under the eye of his mentor, who doubled as the town slaughterer. Between the villages, young Gesser would pass the taverns where the Russians drank and ate what they were allowed to eat, which was anything dead or alive, and plotted the brutish violence that would be permitted them once the vodka had done its work and freed the man inside. Gesser would find the strength in his tired body to run twice as fast as the music rolled out the open tavern doors, mocking him and his careful beliefs that forbade him so many of life's pleasures. He would not slow down until he was out of earshot and the music's spell was broken.

Now he had returned. *Plotted* to return. A victim journeying back to the scene of the crime, not to relive the hurts but to remake his life, and in the middle of winter, no less. The more impossible the task the better—let us rewrite the humiliations out of our past with the help of the Revolution!

Then, from the slow, shuffling crowd a man appeared, wearing no gloves, his hands folded inside his sleeves for warmth. Something was hanging from his overcoat sleeves: it was a dried smoked fish, a particularly practical kind of nourishment, since it demanded no refrigeration or cooking. Moved by the music, the man began to sway awkwardly, a heavy bulky mass of defeated, sentimental flesh who had only these few bear-like steps to express what he felt.

"Do not laugh at me!" he addressed the crowd, though no one was wearing even a hint of a smile. "I am a partisan of the civil war. Thanks to us we preserved the Revolution!"

Each to his excuse, each to his state of grace. One is a drunkard, the other a veteran. Some are both, so much the better. The man executed his dance on the sidewalk in front of the musicians. His fish danced with him, not that it had the choice, for the deserted white globules where its eyes had been showed it had long ago lost its will. The fish's owner was a drunk, and as a drunk, all was forgiven him. In Russia, drunks inhabit a state of grace, like little children. Jack and Sonya watched as the man swayed and the fish imitated him. The man's sad humanity charmed them, though Jack was aware that his sense of resignation was vaguely counterrevolutionary.

The musicians accelerated the rhythm of their languorous tune, and coins rained into the singer's hat. When the sentimentality of the music became too rich for this hard-bitten people, the guitarist played a final sequence of chords, then raised his instrument to signal the end of the song. A little cry of pain escaped Sonya's lips: the guitarist's frostbitten fingers were running with blood. Pride showed in his eyes. *Observe my devotion to my art*, his battered, frozen fingers said.

Gesser dug into his pockets and found a coin. It felt particularly heavy compared to the kopecks, and no wonder. It was an American quarter. *Goodbye, two bits*, he wished his last bourgeois change farewell and dropped it into the singer's astrahkan hat, where it made a decidedly solid sound among the tinny Russian coins.

They moved through the carnival of Kuznetsky Most. Between two fish stalls, they came upon a woman in a massive sheepskin coat, rocking back and forth like a Jew in prayer. *Abizian, abizian,* she was calling in her plaintive street-vendor's voice. Gesser knew the word. It came from fairy tales. The small, unnaturally wise, nearly human face peeked out of the fur of the woman's coat, like a precociously wizened child in swaddling clothes.

It was a monkey. There was something perplexed in its expression, as if it could not quite comprehend how it had ended up in this cold climate, offered up for sale. That lost quality in its eyes made it absolutely irresistible.

"Look at the little darling, he must be cold!" Sonya cried. "I wonder what he's doing here?"

The vendor extracted the animal from her coat.

"Buy this monkey," she ordered Sonya.

The monkey squealed in protest over the cold and batted its paw ineffectually at the hairs on the woman's chin.

"Buy him," the woman commanded. "Or he'll freeze to death. Monkeys aren't made for this climate, you know."

"I know," Jack said. "But we really can't. We're in a hotel. There's no room for a monkey. There's nothing for a monkey to eat."

"They eat what we do: anything. Except maybe a little less."

Jack shook his head. The monkey was whisked back inside the woman's coat.

"I want him," Sonya said. "We *have* to have him."

Jack edged her away from the monkey vendor.

"A monkey, when we don't even have a place of our own? I'll get you one sometime later. When we have more than a hotel room to live in."

They moved down the snow-packed sidewalk, past the fish stalls, with Sonya still wanting the monkey.

"I wonder what he's doing here. How does a monkey get to Russia, in winter? He knew he was in the wrong place, I could tell. He had that look about him."

Gesser shrugged. Where does a monkey in Russia come from? And what does it eat? Does it really eat anything, including these frozen, salted, smoked, mummified, reduced fish?

At the last fish stall Gesser stocked up. He took two. But when he went to pay, he realized he had no rubles left. Instead of the Byzantine scroll of the local money, to his embarrassment he produced an American dollar bill from his pocket.

"I'm afraid I don't have anything else. We've just arrived."

He went to put the fish back on the paper as a little hollow of hunger burrowed into his stomach. The fish vendor held out her hand.

"What kind of money is that? Show me, I've never seen anything like it before."

"It's American."

She inspected it, saw how drab and green it was, with so little in its design or color to recommend it. She handed it back to Gesser with a look of distaste.

"You're a foreign specialist," she told him. "You don't have to pay."

"That's impossible."

"Is it? You've come here to work with us. You'll pay me later. When you can." She thrust the fish at Jack. "I can give these to you, you know," she said proudly.

With the door to the hallway open, Jack Gesser and Sonya Freedman contrived to dine in some measure of warmth. He took his penknife and separated the skin from the bone, then laid the fish open on the paper. Jack Gesser, provider, carving the roast.

"A fish like this I've never seen."

"Maybe it's carp."

"I know carp."

"Maybe it's Russian carp. Different."

"Soviet carp."

"It looks like a bomb went off inside it."

Needle-thin bones flew every which way through the flesh, as if it had been fished with a depth charge. But there was enough birch—smoke taste, and they were hungry enough to find it edible, if not appealing.

"Not only did she give us the fish. She gave horseradish to go with it."

The horseradish was virulently sharp. It made Sonya's eyes water, but at least it chased away the cold.

"Now, if only we had some bread, we would be rich!" Jack sighed.

"I don't have bread, but I have starch. That's just as good."

Sonya produced two potatoes from the sagging pocket of her coat.

"Where did you get these?"

She shrugged. "They fell off a truck."

She squeezed them. It was as she had suspected. They had frozen, then thawed, perhaps more than once. But they were real Russian potatoes, Soviet potatoes at that, brown and burly and tasting like earth, and they had something magical about them. Jack took his penknife and sliced off paper-thin sections. He held one up before the lamp. Its yellow light was blurry through it, as through a frosted window. A meal they would have spat on back on Sangamon Street was a feast now, and not only because of hunger. Hunger they had known on two continents. It was a feast because of the romance, the harmony of the elements, all sprung from the same soil and water, all having weathered the same winter. They were eating the stubborn, tough fruit of their dream. And with it the last of the bread vodka they had procured on the freighter S.S. *Pickled Herring*. The vodka, drunk without the benefit of glasses, conferred an air of ceremony on their supper and a sense of ritual, the way alcohol always does, which is one of its many virtues, along with intoxication that dangerously loosens the tongue. This is potato; it comes from the earth. This is fish; it comes from the water, a realm we cannot inhabit, that is hostile to us, that we crossed to be here. This is horseradish. It stands for bitterness. This is drink, made with man's ingenuity from whatever he has on hand. It makes us laugh, it makes us cry, it brings whatever is on the chest to the tongue, it allows us to endure, and God knows that's the virtue of the century.

Sonya brushed away the tear that hesitated at the edge of Jack's eye.

"Weeping, husband?"

"Just the horseradish," he said. "The horseradish of my youth."

He folded up the paper where the chaotic fishbones lay, stripped bare. He went to dispose of the carcass, but saw no trash basket in the room. Why would there be one? There was nothing to throw away in this country.

He ventured into the hallway, oily fish bones in hand. There wasn't even a collective trashcan. A solution came to him, the product of bread vodka, no doubt. With his sock-clad foot, he flipped open the door to the coal stove. A smell of well-travelled boot and singed mutton rose up on contact with the hot iron. He cast the bones into the fire, slammed the door shut and made it back into their room. In the flame-box, the oil and fish grease and newspaper sizzled and sparked, and the bones were consumed. That which you can't use, someone else always can, even when that someone is fire.

The odor of charred fish spread from room to room through the Kosmos Hotel in equal measure over the top of each partition.

There were no complaints from the guests. On the contrary. The smell gave the sleepers at the Kosmos a chance to dream of a miraculous meal from the sea, the way the poor dream of winning the lottery. The next day, refreshed by their fantasy, they would awake to discover that the brave, stubborn Moscow sun had worked the first layers of ice off the windows of their rooms.

8

THE GREATER GOOD

It seemed as though everything important was located on Hertzina Street, the street of the heart. In their first days in the overgrown village, Jack and Sonya took that as a favorable sign, as if
everything that came from the human heart was good. Hertzina
emptied into Red Square, but its inexplicable curves in this otherwise grid-like city shut out the view of the Kremlin walls at the
end of the thoroughfare. Its modest length housed the highest
summits of socialist cultural life. The Moscow Conservatory,
founded by a Jew named Rubinstein. The Mayakovsky Theater,
with its facade of pale salmon and burnt mustard. As the spring
took over, the sun warmed the snow into water, and great streams
flowed in the uneven ditches that bordered the bricked-over
street. Jack and Sonya passed all those things and more on that

hopeful, sunny morning on their way to the offices of the *Moscow Daily News*, which were tucked away in an inner courtyard behind a protective *porte-cochère*.

In the second courtyard, a careful sign admitted that the *Moscow Daily News* had its offices upstairs. The sign was modest, but once inside the door, as they stamped their feet to rid their boots of mud and melting snow, they saw they were doing so on a slab of solid pink marble. The building that housed the newspaper, which was the English voice of the workers of the world, had once belonged to a Swedish captain of industry. Now the *Moscow Daily News* shared the building with a few irregular correspondents from the American bourgeois press. In the overgrown village, the dearth of privacy extended even to office space.

Everyone in the Sangamon Street ghetto, and in all the ghettoes like it, naturally knew about the *Moscow Daily News*. The mecca for all the rebels passing through Moscow, where they could play out their revolt on an international scale, it was a kind of social club, though much grander than Berg's old College of Trades because here, according to the rumor, Berg actually ran things. The word that filtered back to Sangamon Street was that the old Messiah of Division Street was publishing his own paper. Imagine that! One of our boys controlling the means of production! Comrade Berg, the Proteus of the Revolution, who had returned home so precipitously after the jewels had been converted into cash in Chicago.

Jack and Sonya began to climb the curving, worn wooden stairway to the paper's offices. Who knows what Czar Nikolai's jewels eventually paid for? Both the Czar and his stones would have been astonished. But one was dead, the other insensate; both had been swallowed up by history. Perhaps tool and die machinery. Purloined industrial designs. Small arms. Replacement bulbs for the footlights of the Bolshoi. Crates of blood oranges from Sicily for the elite. Gesser and Freedman had played their part in each of those purchases—and in saving Berg's skin, too, no doubt, after the rocks had gone astray on the Haitian coast. Never mind the matter of the missing stone. It was a detail they could easily set right, a minor indiscretion compared to their accomplishment. For their services, Jack and Sonya supposed, Berg would at least remember them—if they could find him.

After all, hadn't he promised them, his almost-faithful messengers, that their names would be mentioned inside the Kremlin walls?

The *Moscow Daily News*, said the opaque glass panel in English. Jack pushed open the door. The face at the reception desk was decidedly Muscovite. In a bulky coat she probably never took off, wearing gloves with the fingertips snipped off, a starchy woman sat punishing an ancient Remington typewriter with a Cyrillic keyboard.

"We are looking for Mr. Berg," Gesser ventured as the woman banged away at her keyboard. "Mr. Mitchell Berg."

"Comrade Berg?" the woman corrected Gesser over the clatter of her typewriter.

"Yes, of course. Comrade Berg."

"Berg? Berg? Is that what you said?"

"Yes."

"We have no Berg here."

"Isn't this the *Moscow Daily News*?"

"You saw the sign on the door," the woman accused him. "But there's no Berg in this place."

"The Berg we know," said Sonya, "was in Chicago, not so long ago. A big dark man with a mustache. He talks like Shakespeare. At least in English he does."

The woman suddenly remembered an urgent errand—filing a fingernail broken by a Remington key, perhaps, after the machine she had been punishing rose up and smote her back. She got to her feet and disappeared behind an oak partition. Gesser took this as an invitation and motioned to Sonya to follow him. Together, they ventured unescorted into the offices. As they went, he breathed deeply of the smells that came from the press room in back, the ink, the smudgy odor of lead type, the solvent-soaked rags, mixing nostalgia and nightmare as they conjured up the little village printing press in Soukenai. For Gesser, the smell of print was inseparable from that of butchery, animal and human alike.

It was then they spotted the Messiah of Division Street.

He was standing in the only office that had a door, and a window to go with it, which overlooked the courtyard with its heaps of snow and splayed wagons awaiting repair. Berg was looking out the window into the courtyard, contemplating God-knows-what, but there was no mistaking his broad back, white peasant blouse and dark, slick hair.

Jack Gesser strode into the office, hand extended.

"Comrade Berg!" he greeted him lustily.

Berg wheeled around, a look of pure panic on his face, as if he had seen a ghost. He did not return the greeting or shake Gesser's hand. He would not admit to the possible liability of being Berg. Then again, neither did he deny it.

Sonya laughed at Berg's discomfort. A man in discomfort, especially a great and powerful man with a great and powerful cluttered desk, was a heartwarming sight that lifted her spirits.

"I've got a hunch Comrade Berg isn't called that any more," Sonya said. "If that ever was his real name."

Berg positioned himself behind the barrier of his massive desk. Here was provocation entering his office, from what quarter and to what end he did not yet know. That these people might have shown up by sheer chance did not enter his mind. In his imagination, there was no cubbyhole for the fantastic commodity called chance.

With a military attitude, he thrust out his chest and extended a hand.

"Comrade Mikhail Borodin," he announced in a very loud voice.

Gesser took the hand and felt his knuckles crumble.

"I can't believe it, he doesn't remember us!" Sonya exclaimed. "It's obvious he doesn't know who we are. But who can blame him? We're nobodies. Nobodies in the service of the Revolution!"

"Of course I know who you are," Borodin insisted in an offended tone. "But as for your names . . . I am sorry. I have no retention of names. When the pressure grows, you have to get a new one, so it's no use getting attached to them. I've had several, including Berg, which is a thing of the past, may I point out to you. I am Borodin now, and I hope to stick with him. But you, who *you* are, of course I remember."

"You should, comrade. We're the ones who recovered the property of the proletariat."

Borodin interrupted her with a cautionary finger.

"The *plans*," he reminded Sonya.

"And now we've made our return," Gesser said grandly. "All those lectures at the People's College of Trades must have had their effect. We ended up choosing, and here we are."

"Well, I am . . ."—Borodin sought the right word, which in turn sought to avoid him, and succeeded—"honored," he tried out. "Not everybody is willing to go so far from home."

"Home . . ." Gesser shrugged.

"Perhaps it was your persuasive powers," Sonya teased.

"And the need for something greater," Jack put in.

"The desperation of the place didn't hurt either."

"Desperation?" Borodin echoed Sonya. "Chicago has no monopoly on desperation . . . but what of it? How long have you been in Moscow?"

"Since yesterday."

"And here you are already, reporting for your orders. You did not want to take time to see the sights?"

"We saw Red Square. Last night," said Sonya.

"Yes? And how was it?"

Sonya smelled a trap set by Borodin's intellect.

"Certainly you know it better than we do," she replied.

"It is said that Red Square looks different, depending on the angle from which it is viewed."

"We saw it from the sidewalk. Street level. The way most see it, I would imagine."

"Except that we were kissing, which nobody else was doing," Sonya reminded both men gaily.

"Yes, now I remember you," Borodin told her. "You are the kind of woman that is sometimes found in America."

"And now in Moscow."

"Yes, apparently so, since you are here . . . Well, I suppose you have not come as tourists. You have come here to help. Help is what we need. I, for one, do not spurn foreign help, as some do. How could I? Is this not the *Moscow Daily News*, a paper committed to the brotherhood of workers around the world?"

Borodin launched into a defense of his association with foreigners. Though the charge was unspoken, at least in this room, it seemed to be loud enough in his head. Jack and Sonya stood uncomfortably, expectantly, in front of his desk, waiting for him to finish up and remember that they were there, with their own particular pressing needs: a roof, a job, a handful of rubles in exchange for the few dollars that remained, not to mention a desire for a useful life.

"The word *foreign* is on everyone's lips here," Gesser interrupted Borodin's plea. "We've been called *foreign specialists* I don't know how many times. I've been away from here too long; I can't remember if the word's an insult or not."

"A call went out to the West, to workers and members of the intelligentsia, to come and help build socialism. You heard that call, and you weren't the only ones, as you'll soon see. So how can it be an insult?"

"I don't know," Sonya said. "There's just something in the way they say *foreign*. Even when they want to mean good by it."

"Don't take it personal," Borodin advised her, in an accent that showed he hadn't forgotten Division Street. "People are superstitious everywhere. In Chicago, they're afraid of the boogeyman. Here, they're afraid of foreigners."

"And I'm not even a foreigner. I'm from somewhere in between," Gesser said wistfully.

Borodin gave Gesser a long look and wondered just how suitable a worker he would be. The *Moscow Daily News* was rife with loose cannons, and he did not need any more undisciplinable cases or ladies from suspicious class backgrounds who had come here to express their bourgeois sense of personal revolt. True, he'd exhorted Gesser and Freedman to follow him to the New Jerusalem, but he had invited plenty of others, too—the entire Yiddish-speaking population of Chicago, in fact. That didn't mean he'd ever thought they would actually track him down and show up at his doorstep, so enthusiastic and so totally lost.

"Refresh my memory. What are your trades that might prove useful here?" he asked Gesser.

"Useful?" Gesser mused. "Let's see, once I tried my hand at turning metal, before the factory went bust. And back when I lived here," he added with a longing look towards the back rooms, where the printing presses rattled and hummed, "I was a printer's apprentice."

Borodin decided to put Gesser's discipline and revolutionary will to the test. There were two telephones on his desk. He picked up the one with the dial and rang the same number, over and over again, until the line agreed to work. There followed a hasty conversation, the rule in Moscow, for no one knew when the telephone lines would stop working.

A minute later Borodin hung up.

"There's a lathing job at the Loputchkha auto plant. Since you're in a hurry, you can start next Monday. You will have the weekend to see the rest of the sights. That will probably be sufficient. There are already foreigners working at Loputchkha. And there is a workers' residence for them, and a tramline that runs between the two. Very convenient."

"A foreigners' residence?" Gesser questioned.

"That is the organization here. It is thought that foreigners will feel more comfortable that way, being with their own kind."

"But you know that isn't true."

"Do I know that?" Borodin countered. "This idea, this touristic idea, according to which an individual will want to identify with a foreign place and people, this colorful ideal has no currency here. I understand it, but I do not run the show. To merge with another people is the domain of spies—that is what is thought here."

He turned to Sonya. "Your Russian is a problem."

"I don't have any," she volunteered.

"But you have English, and it sounds adequate to me. You will work here, at the paper."

"Jack was a printer. He should work here, too."

"Yes. But he was a printer at another time, under the *ancien régime*. That experience is obliterated. It is—how can I say?—worse than obliterated."

Borodin stood up.

"So, all is settled. Welcome to Moscow."

Jack Gesser and Sonya Freedman left the *Moscow Daily News* with their marching orders, but without peace of mind. They were still on the wooden stairway that led down from the office when Sonya said, "This Borodin is not the same man Berg was, and it's not just the change of name. He doesn't have the same fire, that's for sure."

"He's not preaching any more. He's not leading, he's . . . administering. He was running the show in Chicago. He's not the Messiah of Division Street any more."

"It must be a disappointment."

"Well, he's still carrying on his work. And he does have his own newspaper. Not every man can boast of that."

"I don't know what it is," Sonya speculated, "I get the feeling he's always looking over his shoulder. Only I don't know at what."

"Don't ask me. I don't have much experience as a leader of world revolution."

But Sonya would not let up. She wanted to understand the transformation of the man. Borodin had two telephones on his desk. That in itself was a sign of importance. But only one had a dial. That one put him in touch with the city of Moscow, its factories, the places where foreign specialists could be most useful. The other was connected to the Kremlin. It had no dial; he could only wait for it to ring.

They splashed through the melting snow in the double courtyards and lingered on Hertzina Street.

"What's funny is that Borodin doesn't seem like a Jew at all," Jack said. "He doesn't even *look* like a Jew any more. He doesn't talk like one. He has remade himself. Recreated himself. The Lord makes;

man can remake. Or so it seems . . . I guess that's what history is about: changing who you are. Still, I wonder how he did it."

"They don't call the Soviet citizen the new man for nothing."

"It can't be that easy. Otherwise, more people would have done it. I would have done it, and a long time ago."

Sonya grasped his arm and pulled him closer.

"I don't want you to turn yourself into someone else. Don't you see that?"

No, Jack Gesser did not see that. Nor did he believe it. He didn't especially want to be himself; why would anyone else want that? In flight from himself, he was not so different from Mikhail Borodin, his new comrade. Like Borodin, he had changed countries in search of a new and more attractive self. A useful one, one in tune with the romance of the century. On Monday he would join the industrial proletariat in the giant yet feasible task of building socialism in the country where once the bread had fallen butter-side down.

Just as well they had only the weekend to wait, for there were precious few sights to see in the overgrown village. Avoiding the vastness of Red Square, Jack and Sonya stopped to marvel at the Mayakovsky Theater, its irregular red-brick copingstones and turrets, Arabic arches grafted onto solid Russian flanks, a battleground of architecture, and the very image of the poet who, three years earlier, had given himself the gift of death. Jack and Sonya knew nothing of Mayakovsky. There were so many poets of his type, it was hard to memorize the fate of them all, whether they had died martyrs or disgraced, whether they had fallen, or been pushed, or both.

In Moscow, the equation was simple. With a job came a room. The two were inextricably wed. Two days later, on Sunday afternoon, Jack Gesser stood in the room at the Foreign Specialists'

Residence on Zabatskaya Street, scanning the walls. The partitions reached all the way up to the ceiling, a welcome luxury after the Kos-mos Hotel and a rare Soviet concession to Western needs, for Zabatskaya had been built for foreigners, according to foreign plans. Western-style privacy had been at the center of the design. Here, Jack and Sonya would have more than the traditional Russian nook wherein the individual might entertain his square meter of thoughts.

He set down their bags on the parquet floor and took inventory of the room. Two cots, two desks and two chairs, a reading lamp, something of the scholar's cell to the room that pleased him, as if factory work did not disqualify the worker from the life of the mind. The standard Muscovite window, double-paned, with glass so thick it seemed beveled, each square opening separately on miniature brass hinges, with enough space between the panes to serve as an icebox.

Best of all, the lodgings were free. There'd be no sourpuss land-lady to appease now. Instead, the State was their landlord. In return for the room, they would do their part as citizens, accord-ing to their means, which would turn out to be ever-expanding, for so were the State's needs.

"We're actually here!" Sonya said, as giddy as if she'd been drinking champagne. "I can't believe it, our own room in Moscow."

She and Jack embraced and gazed fondly at the room, arms around each other's shoulders, as if contemplating a child they had produced. The room was plain, of course, spartan and graceless, a cell in a residence put up in a hurry by underpaid workers accord-ing to plans they could not fathom. But it was a Moscow room, in the very heart of history.

Not to mention that the walls rose to form a hermetic bond with the ceiling.

"Let us solemnize this room," Jack told Sonya. "This bed."

He gave the blankets a shake to see what would hop off them. Nothing did.

On that afternoon of all hopes, the two cots they had pushed together in the room at the Zabatskaya Foreign Specialists' Residence became the center of the world. Their lovemaking, like drunkenness for the Russians, was their state of grace. Gesser remembered the peasant woman of Soukenai, for whom the act of love was a simple occurrence, like knocking the mud off one's boots, and not a sacrament, as he considered it to be with Sonya. Sonya thought of Borodin, the king of returnees, to whose intercession they owed their jobs. Not because she would have preferred him in her bed, but because of the transformation he had suffered since Division Street, the way he'd changed since his days as the Messiah of the Ghetto.

They went to work the next day, something they hadn't done in months, years even. A new life began. It was a life of many things, but mostly of tramlines. On those cold spring mornings, the sky still resolutely black, Jack took his tram to the Loputchkha plant on the northern edge of the ever-growing overgrown village. Sonya had the privilege of leaving later and working in the center of the city, with paper and printed word, which made her, willy-nilly, a member of the intelligentsia. She had taken Jack's old trade, while he had been sent to the edge of the city to turn metal parts on a lathe. But it wasn't in the spirit of the time to complain, for wasn't everybody making sacrifices, and wasn't deprivation shared equally? There were rewards, too, like those Sundays when, on another tram, they travelled to the Conservatory to hear the best interpretations of classical music for the equivalent of a few pennies.

The first Sunday morning at the residence Jack and Sonya found their ears unexpectedly assaulted by the sound of Mr. and

Mrs. White in the hall, arguing without much conviction over who had misplaced the precious bar of soap. The Whites greeted them in their jolly voices, acted as though they were long-lost friends and introduced them to their comrades. The kitchen of the Zabatskaya residence for Foreign Specialists resembled a branch of the Fabian Society. The good-natured enthusiasm of the Whites and their kind, more suitable to a Boy Scout jamboree than to the building of socialism, irritated Jack and Sonya no end. But like it or not, those pale-skinned, thinning-haired specialists in flight from the great universities of England were actually physically building socialism. They had come to design and oversee the construction of the canal between the Volga and the Moscow rivers, through the mosquito-ridden bogs north of the city. Their jollity was matched by their chronic complaining. There was too much cabbage, not enough meat, the tinned foods were botulistic, the Soviet masses did not seem to appreciate their sacrifice: that the pride of the Cambridge engineering faculty had given up its entitlement of afternoon sherry to come and design the canal. Jack and Sonya considered them selfish, bourgeois and contemptible.

Jack spent half his life on the trams. He became expert in sleeping on them, falling asleep effortlessly and knowing, in his sleep, when his stop was approaching. He had even taught himself to sleep while waiting for the tram, half standing, half leaning against a post, and awaken before the creaky yellow wood-and-metal coaches arrived, sounding as though they would expire at the very next stop. With the others, he would push towards the front of the line. Being wiry and determined and having no patience with the sheeplike stolidity of the crowd, Gesser would usually be among the first to board the tram. But it made little difference. Inevitably, the car was full.

It took Sonya longer to learn how to sleep on the tram. Asleep, she felt vulnerable, and would not let herself go. Sometimes she would drop her eyelids and toss on a sea of uneasy sleep for half a minute, practically nauseous with fatigue. Then she would spring awake, convinced that someone was watching her. Violating her.

When the *Moscow Daily News* had its printing press requisitioned for some more urgent State enterprise, and Sonya had to accompany the paper to a print shop, sometimes in the middle of the night, she learned to sleep in public. Even in the small hours, the city was alive with moving people, with the perpetual, aimless motion of a disturbed anthill. Men and women, manifestly going nowhere, impatiently waited for their tram at two o'clock in the morning, tapping their feet, masking their vodka-soaked breath behind their hands, chewing an apple or a bit of fish, consulting their nonexistent watches, as though they were intent on some official assignment, instead of being guilty of punishable idleness. Here, finally, the sexes were equal, for women waited alongside men. As a worker authentically in the commission of her duties, Sonya had the privilege of a place at the front of the line. But this did not guarantee her a seat, since the trams were crowded whatever the hour, and many people had similar or greater privileges. In those trams, lit just enough to be visible in the darkness out of which they loomed, Sonya would achieve a deep if fleeting sleep, using her bundle of proofs as a buffer against the frigid window.

She had her best sleeps at the Conservatory, at afternoon's end, as dusk prepared the curtain of night it would soon cast over the city. Sometimes in the great hall, they would catch a glimpse of Borodin in one of the front-row seats reserved for him and his caste. He would be locked in conversation with men in drab blue suits, shiny imitations of the Western model, though he himself held to the loose white embroidered peasant blouse that both spoke of his attachment to the old values of the Revolution and showed off his physique. By the way he made his point with the suited men, it was clear that they were his superiors, and, unlike him, profoundly uninterested in the process of debate.

All voices would fall silent when the lights dimmed. As the piano and strings filled the hall, Jack and Sonya would lean back against the hard, clean, polished wood of the upper balcony seats and go where the music went—into a realm of pure abstraction where no trams rumbled. They considered that falling asleep in such perfect peace was a tribute to the music, and they were not the only ones who thought that way. How luxurious, how deep the seats at the Conservatory were! To take your seat there was like settling into a kind of vessel, safe from all eyes, upon a sea of gentle forgetfulness, on Hertzina Street, the street of the heart. In that vessel they would be gently rocked to slumber, buoyed by spirited yet flawless interpretations of the classics, which constituted culture in their new land.

Jack and Sonya spurned the steamy, cabbage-smelling kitchen of the Cambridge Fabians on Zabatskaya and recreated their world of high ideals and low comedy at the Anglo-American Club. It was a curious institution, the only duly constituted social club in the capital of socialism. The Club was presided over by, who else, that noted Anglophile Mikhail Borodin, and it had its headquarters in the common room above the *Moscow Daily News*. Though none of its members clung to the old Covenant with the old God, still, traditions were traditions, so it convened on Saturday evenings, after the Sabbath. Once a week, the common room was transformed into a kind of Hebrew social club wherein even Gentiles were made to feel Jewish. It was a home away from home, a kind of Steinstein's Leisure Palace without the pool tables, where Borodin reigned over his foreign legion in tones Shakespearian, where former peddlers and piece-workers from New York and Chicago and Montreal, and every other center where disillusionment was manufactured, would crack the vaudeville jokes that everyone knew by heart. There were miniature sandwiches, sweets and tea and, on good days, vodka, with Borodin the perpetual host, since he was the only one with the connections to procure these little treats.

As it was in the days of the People's College of Trades and Vocations, the buffet would not be opened until the speeches had been made and the entertainments concluded. Borodin then stepped onto the stage in the common room and considered the gathered workers, loose cannons and half-cocked idealists all of them, all casting longing looks at the buffet.

"Allow me to remind you why you are here," he began grandly.

"For the grub," Pinsky the waggish choir leader said in a stage whisper.

"Yes, for the grub, as you say," Borodin admitted. "And because you answered the call to build socialism and the classless society, because you believe in the new man and woman and the international proletariat . . ."

The crowd, Borodin knew, was only half listening. Which was to be expected, because he was only half speaking. Not that he didn't believe in what he was saying; he did. But he did not believe in having to recite your beliefs by rote, like the church fathers with their obscure, obsolete credo. Standing before the happy, unruly, carefree little group, Borodin knew whom he was really talking to: the invisible but omnipresent, attentive audience called the State. His old comrades down the street in the walled fortress of the Kremlin, who looked upon his career with disapproval. Some were opposed to the idea of bringing in foreigners to help industrialize the country, for in it they saw a confession of inadequacy. Others sensed the taint of failure that clung to him like a bad smell, because of his bungled mission in China, and the fiasco with the jewels. For those failures and near-failures, he would never be forgiven, even if they weren't his fault.

He concluded his speech and the crowd surged forward to descend upon the buffet like locusts, with every intention of sweeping the tabletop clean like the avenging mandibles of a biblical plague.

Borodin held up an imperious hand.

"The entertainments have not yet been concluded," he scolded the crowd. Then he smiled. "I'm sure the songs that are to follow will stimulate your appetite, since they are about hunger in the capitalist countries."

The pride of the Anglo-American Club shuffled towards the stage. The choir, led by Marcus Pinsky. The very appearance of that wiry, rubber-faced scrap of a man at Borodin's side made a mockery of the serious-minded Soviet. Pinsky was court jester, Borodin's own personal monkey.

"Steamboat Willie!" a voice from the crowd shouted.

"Maybe if you're good boys and girls, I'll give you a nickel so's you can go to the show."

Before he let his ideals get the better of him, Pinsky had drawn a certain animated mouse for a cartoon studio in California. Now his pen was harnessed to work on industrial design projects for a plant that made agricultural machinery; the mouse had been displaced by nobler pursuits. But something of the talking rodent remained in Pinsky, for he had inhabited it so long that he had become part mouse himself, and could imitate the animal's voice perfectly.

Which is what he did to entertain the crowd at the Anglo-American Club. He put both hands in front of his mouth to make a trumpet and squeaked out a throat-searing falsetto.

"If you don't sing, you don't eat! I know some of you choir members aren't up here, so get your tushes on stage on the double! We

didn't spend all those minutes practicing for nothing! And since
this is a people's choir, singing people's songs, those of you who
aren't part of the choir shouldn't take it personal-like. Come up
and join us if you dare!"

To be invited on stage to sing songs of the Great Depression by
a man with the voice of a cartoon mouse was irresistible. Half the
members of the Anglo-American Club moved towards the stage.
Some vaulted easily onto the raised planks while others scrambled
up as if they'd never had to jump a wall in their lives. Jack and
Sonya were among them. Pinsky's cohort, the big Finn Lehto,
reached down to help Sonya up. He gave her such a swift ride up
that those people behind her were treated to a brilliant flash of
pale knee and thigh, the tender part where the knee bends. Half
the Club was on the stage by now. All artists, no audience. But
wasn't that the ideal?

With the choristers still jockeying for position, Pinsky called
for the song to begin. Lehto sang lead. The big Finn's bass voice
boomed out, and the others followed, and what they lacked in
musicianship they made up in feeling.

> *Once I built a railroad, made it run*
> *Made it race against time*
> *Once I built a railroad*
> *Now it's done*
> *Brother, can you spare a dime?*

That Saturday evening, the comrades of the Anglo-American
Club were transported by pure nostalgic joy, the pleasure of rec-
ollecting past miseries. They had not chosen that song because it
illustrated why they'd left the seat of capitalism, as Borodin liked
to believe. They sang out of homesickness, pure and simple. If you

had come all this way, through the winter, to this unlikely country, you certainly wouldn't stand up and admit to being homesick. So instead, you sang. You didn't have to admit anything. The song took care of it for you.

A 500-gram bottle of vodka moved slowly down the chorus line. The song called for a drink; a drink called for a song. When the bottle came to Gesser, he raised it in a toast to Sonya.

"To brotherhood, and sad songs, and to you."

Sonya leaned over and flicked a tear off his cheek.

"It must be that horseradish again," Jack apologized.

She accepted the bottle from him. As she raised it to drink, she looked out into the crowd, and behind the swaying faces she met Borodin's eyes. He closed them slowly, as if to shut out the scene. Public inebriation, even the intent to inebriate, was in gross and direct contradiction to the building of socialism. Besides, the songs were foreign, certainly nostalgic, and nostalgia by its very nature was as counterrevolutionary as public inebriation.

When Borodin reopened his eyes, he found himself staring across the room again into Sonya Freedman's face. Deliberately, she placed the bottle at her feet, behind her, as if to hide it from view.

From the back of the hall, Borodin smiled gratefully.

"Brother, can you spare a dime?" the choir appealed.

Borodin stepped forward, clapping his hands briskly to signal the end of the concert.

"Very good! Excellent! Now, let us pass to the refreshments. We have all earned it."

The choir had plenty more songs to sing. And they wanted to hear Lehto the Finn harness his enormous bass voice to some sad melody from his country. They wanted to be transported; they didn't mind not understanding a word of the song. They knew what the sob in his voice and the vengeful swing of his fist meant.

But it was not to be. Borodin could not afford to have a man on his stage singing words he could not understand.

The choir members began to drift off stage, recognizing they had been given the equivalent of the hook. Besides, who could argue against the sandwich buffet and the waving, collectivized fields of wheat on the labels of the bottles that promised good grain spirit?

Another typical Saturday evening at the Anglo-American Club. Gesser, Pinsky, Lehto, Borodin and all the other hopers and wishers. And beautiful Sonya the Red.

After one of those nights during which Borodin had struggled to keep control over his undisciplined troops, Jack Gesser caught him in an unguarded moment. That in itself was something of an accomplishment. Borodin was open to everyone, equally, as long as they approached him in groups. There was safety in numbers— for him. He shunned private interviews where demands might be made on him.

But Gesser knew how to capture and hold his attention.

"I want to talk about the jewels," he said to Borodin in Russian.

"I'm listening."

"When we recovered the . . . property of the proletariat, I got a bit curious. I wanted to see what was inside the lining. I felt the bumps. I opened it up. When I saw, I put everything back in. Except one. One, I forgot." He pretended to shake hands with Borodin. "This one."

Borodin opened his palm and considered the red stone. His expression, it occurred to Gesser, was too serene, almost unconcerned. He did little to conceal the jewel.

"How did you close up the lining?"

"I sewed it," Gesser answered apologetically.

"You did very well. I noticed nothing."

"You know the saying: the best turner in the village is the tailor."

Borodin closed his hand again and slipped the stone into his pocket.

"It is very curious. No one noticed anything at the time. There was no inventory. You could have taken five of them! We were so eager to . . . liquidate the jewels and change them into something else useful to us that we didn't pay any attention. But I appreciate your honesty. It creates a bond between us. But in a way, comrade, it is too late."

"Too late?" Gesser felt as though the floor was dropping away from beneath his feet; this was worse than any threat of proletarian justice. "Too late to liquidate? Too late to be useful?"

Borodin smiled thinly. "I don't know exactly how to explain it, here, in this place . . . That era in our relations with the world is over. That heroic era of travelling."

Before he could explain, Borodin was swarmed by a group of inebriated choir members. Gesser was forgotten, and so was his jewel. For the time being, at least.

At the Loputchkha auto plant, Jack found himself in a place where, as a peddler, a studier, a *luftmensch*, he had always longed to be. The world of things. Resolute metal. Hard objects forged from something other than words. After the world of ideas and yearning, of promising oneself the future, the Loputchkha factory felt positively real. At the start, in any case.

Gesser was lousy at metal-turning. In another plant, in another system, he would have been shown the door, or not hired in the first place. But at Loputchkha he had a role to play beyond what he could manage to grind out on his machine. He was the foreign specialist, proof that the West, or parts of it, supported socialism.

A walking example to the Soviet workers, who responded by patiently teaching him how to wrestle his recalcitrant machine into submission. A machine that had been built in Michigan City, Indiana, he discovered when he bent down to pick up a dropped wrench. He knew the place. It was the next stop past Chesterton on the Illinois Central electric line.

Loputchkha provided him with a steady diet of iron filings, a sense of participation in the great twentieth-century romance and lunch. On the first day in the canteen, he was presented with cabbage soup in which a chunk of flesh floated—from a mammal, most likely. *Sometimes, is nothing better than cabbage?* he philosophized briefly, then tucked into the broth. In accordance with the Soviet people's love of sugar, soup was followed by desert, something called *k'sai*, a dish of potato flour moistened with a kind of berry purée. The texture is what stopped Gesser. The way the skin of the sweetened porridge resisted his blunt, soup-stained spoon. The way, when he finally broke through it, the stuff made an odd sucking noise, like a dead man passing gas.

"You don't want it?" one of Gesser's Loputchkha comrades suggested to him.

Gesser shook his head and the man seized his metal bowl. The comrades at the mess table looked on disapprovingly. A man didn't surrender his grub so willingly, without a fight, unless the comrade really needed it. The whole thing stank of luxury.

"*Innostranyetz.* Foreign specialist," the comrades agreed among themselves, as if the label explained every deviance.

On the tram back and forth from Loputchkha, Gesser sat memorizing Russian words. Differential. Universal joint. Bearing. Words he had had no call to know in Soukenai. Words that had not needed to be invented. After the first week, he opened his little pay packet. My first Moscow wages, he thought proudly.

What he saw amazed him. In the packet was a lineup of green American dollar bills. Gesser was dismayed. A mistake, surely. But it came to him that everything did follow a kind of logic. A foreign specialist living in a foreign specialists' residence would naturally be paid in foreign money.

Would he ever fit in?

At the Zabatskaya residence that evening, he came into their room and found Sonya sitting on a chair, still in her coat, considering the raw Moscow spring through the double window. The slump of her shoulders was not that of a woman in the midst of adventure.

He bent and kissed her hair. It smelled of lead. Hers of lead, his of steel. The new iron age. He considered telling her of the foreign cash in his pay packet, then decided against it. Why worry her? And why admit this tiny failure, even when it was not his fault?

She looked up after his perfunctory, defeated kiss.

"So, are we building socialism yet?"

"I don't know. I think it's a little too much for one person to build."

That evening, by some synchronicity in their respective swing shifts, Jack and Sonya found themselves spending the evening together. They had lost the habit of togetherness. He read the papers; she, a book from Borodin's library. Outside, the evening was black and inhospitable, the temperature seasonless, like so much Moscow weather when it is not brutal winter. They turned on the radio. It was the oddest instrument they had ever encountered. It had no dial with which to select a station. Instead, there were four buttons that corresponded to the four stations offered, each button tuned to the correct frequency. Jack made his choice and lowered the paper as Tchaikovsky, tinny yet moving, filled the room. Sonya rose and went down the hallway to the bathroom to wash.

When Jack next opened his eyes, the light still burned in the room, but a buzz of static had replaced Tchaikovsky on the radio. He turned his head back and saw Sonya's form hunched protectively under the blankets. She was asleep. Jack closed his eyes again, but they would not stay closed. He found himself staring at that point where the ceiling met the wall, and it was some time before he realized what his eyes had fastened on. He was gazing at the seal the partitions made with the ceiling, an architectural detail that had once seemed so significant.

Later, Jack opened his eyes to a sky that was smudgy grey with pre-dawn light. The electric bulb was as wan as a dream. Abruptly, its yellow filament flared and wavered as a surge of power ran through the residence, and the filament snapped. Now, where will I find another one of those? Gesser wondered in the dark. Under the blankets and covers, Sonya slept a deep, motionless sleep. That was the trouble with building socialism: it was so exhausting. Bone-weary fatigue replaced the habit of togetherness and made the lovers subservient to the great adventure of the State. How could a man and woman's lust for each other be stronger than swing shifts?

Their life did have its interludes of pleasure, even as they sacrificed for a system that kept them on the outside. There were the Saturday evening parties when Pinsky did his "Steamboat Willie," and Lehto shook the rafters with his voice, the nostalgia of his songs as sweet as the sugary mush at the bottom of a teacup. On Sundays they would walk along the Garden Ring amid the rattle of diesel trucks, then take refuge at the Conservatory. When rubles replaced American dollars in his pay packet, Gesser considered the change a good sign, though not everyone agreed with him. Here was a mark of acceptance, he maintained, not just proof that the State was running out of foreign currency, as some claimed. Meanwhile, on the western border, the German nightmare was taking form, according to the Kremlin's predictions.

Though the newness had long since worn off their Moscow adventure, Gesser did not regret it. He did not believe the duty of the State was to entertain its citizens. Had they been asked, they would have said they were happy. But as no one asked them, they said nothing. Such questions were not in the order of things. They were living, he and his Sonya and their kind, in accordance to a plan, a desire, a law. And that was accomplishment enough in those days for people of their ambitions.

It was a life of sorts. In some ways, it was one of luxury compared to what they had known on Sangamon Street. There was steady work, and a sense of having chosen their lives, of being part of something greater than themselves. They had ceased being victims of circumstance. And then, there were those small victories over the system, as when they found a seat on the tram. That counted for something, too.

And if any of those adventurers had doubts, they were too proud to admit it.

One year, a Passover supper was organized at the Anglo-American Club. Borodin agreed to look the other way, even though the name of the Almighty was in increasingly ill repute. "If anybody asks, I will say it is folklore," he replied to those who asked permission to use the Club for the supper. "The custom of one of the many Soviet peoples in our great nation."

There was no trouble finding the necessary ritual foods in Moscow. There was shank bone. There was an egg for everyone. There were bitter herbs and salt water. Onion, plenty. They manufactured a semblance of unleavened bread. Such is the advantage of a feast of poverty: it can be served in any country, under any conditions. Prescient of the Almighty to have chosen such symbols, wouldn't you say?

There were no books to read from to make the service, but the celebrants knew the slavery-to-freedom story by heart. "Once we were bondsmen, now we are free men," boasted the sacred fable. Towards the end, when most of the story was told, as the hopeful have always done the celebrants joined in to proclaim in unison, "Next year in Jerusalem!"

"Next year? But we're already there."

It was Pinsky who spoke. The leader of the choir. A silence as great as all Siberia came over the table. That silence said so many things the effect was deafening.

Some scoffed at him. Others applauded. Still others—and they were the majority—were too stunned by Pinsky's outrageous claim to argue with him.

How could anyone live, how were Jack and Sonya to live, if they had already achieved Jerusalem?

And if they had, then what? What was there to live for?

BOOK III

AN ENEMY OF THE PEOPLE
SENDS HIS REGARDS

9

THE FORTRESS BORODIN

In the spring of 1938, after some five years of faithful service and the production of thousands of approximately fitting parts at the Loputchkha auto plant, Jack Gesser lost his job. When the factory commissar informed him of this, Gesser could not fathom the announcement, as if he had temporarily lost his mastery of the Russian language. But it wasn't the language's fault, and the commissar was clear enough. Gesser had simply forgotten what it was like to get the sack; he did not believe it was possible to lose your job in Moscow. Those disasters happened only in his former world, whose logic he had slowly started to forget.

Losing a job in Moscow, Gesser soon discovered, entailed more than just a job. When he was terminated at Loputchkha, simultaneously, by malevolent coincidence, his claim on his room at the Zabatskaya Residence for Foreign Workers ran out.

How could it not run out? Was he still a foreign specialist? No, he was not. How could one be a foreign specialist without a job? And if one were no longer a foreign specialist, how could one live at a residence for those sorts of people? It was the kind of logic you could not argue against. And not only was the process inescapably logical, it was also terribly rapid. As quick as dropping into a hole in the sidewalk that some negligent local worker had left uncovered.

This wasn't the first time Jack Gesser had lost a job. Back on Sangamon Street he had lost many of them. Sometimes he lost more than one in the same day. Other times, he lost a job before he'd even had it. When that happened, he simply changed status, from temporarily employed to temporarily unemployed.

But in Moscow that possibility was not open, since, officially, everyone worked. Not working was a crime that was simply not tolerated. Gesser glanced down and consulted his imaginary wrist-watch as he rode the tram in the middle of the day, when everyone else was busy producing something. Now, finally, he understood the meaning of that nervous habit he'd observed in others.

He hadn't lost his job because of what he had done. It was because of what he was. In those days, reasoning in Russia was becoming ever more ontological. It worked this way. One day, the Loputchkha plant received a new commission to build military vehicles. Appeasement may have been national policy in Western capitals, but the Soviet commanders knew war with Germany was inevitable. Military vehicles were sensitive material to which foreigners could not have access; *foreigner* was synonymous with *spy*. The foreign specialists at the plant, and there were many, were all released.

Why were the foreigners forbidden access, even though they would have been making the same differentials and the same axles

and bearings they had always made? Because they were foreigners.
As such, they belonged to the category of the not-completely-
trusted. And to be not completely trusted was to be utterly dis-
trusted. It was one or the other. It turned out there was really no
room for dialectical thought in the current State system.

Gesser took the tram downtown to tell Sonya the bad news.
They had lost their room at Zabatskaya because of him.

He found Sonya and Borodin together, standing over a page layout on a table. He glanced at the story. In it, the Depression raged
in capitalism's great cities as Germany rearmed. Meanwhile, the
armies of the unemployed swelled. Well, Gesser thought briefly, at
least I have company. Too bad they're in all the wrong countries.

"I lost . . . ," he began.

He found he didn't have the strength to confess his failure to
Sonya.

Borodin spoke first. "I know," he said. "Come into my office."

Jack followed Sonya into their guardian angel's lair. Borodin
closed the door. His voice was toneless as he stared down into the
courtyard, at the oaks and birches that grew there, and under them,
his motorcycle with its sidecar painted that odd, shiny turquoise
color—or was it chartreuse—he couldn't think of the right word for
it just now; it was the color of the veins in a cheese that had gone off.
Even as he put together the speech in his head, he had to fight off a
fascination with that color, and with what it might have signified to
have received a motorcycle painted that way, instead of dignified
black. He, once Lenin's confidant—better, his translator—courier of
the Czar's crown jewels, now reduced to driving a chartreuse motorcycle with a comical, toy sidecar! He tore himself away from the
window and considered the tactics open to him. If one is threatened,
he postulated, for he rightfully saw the exclusion of the foreigners
as an attack on himself, is it best to concentrate one's forces, or does

bringing them together only render them more vulnerable to anni-hilation? In which case, is it better to disperse them and risk isolation, not to mention loneliness and solitude? At this late stage in the game, the second outcome was intolerable.

He turned and gazed upon his charges. Their expectant, trusting look was a dreadful burden upon him.

"I can offer you a job here," Borodin heard himself say to Gesser. "As I recall, you were a printer at one time."

"Under the *ancien régime*."

"Yes. The *ancien régime*." Borodin laughed softly. "I do remember saying that. Some time ago, that was. With a job, you'll be able to stay here. So, two problems will be solved."

"You have rooms here?" asked Sonya.

"We have . . ." Borodin gestured vaguely. "We have a hostel of sorts, on the upper floor. Right now we have more rooms than guests, an unusual occurrence in Moscow. I've been able to keep this hostel . . . out of general knowledge. It's been a secret of sorts."

That very evening, Jack and Sonya moved to the top floor of the *Moscow Daily News* on Hertzina Street. The fortress Borodin. A room in the city center, within the Boulevard Ring and the Garden Ring both. Prized real estate, a stone's throw from the Kremlin, not that anyone would throw a stone at it. Gesser crept back to Zabatskaya to retrieve their bags, feeling like a thief, or worse. Losing your job for reasons of state security was a crime in itself.

He shouldn't have bothered feeling ashamed. At Zabatskaya, when he walked in the front door, his ears were filled with crisp British oaths and the slamming of steamer trunks. In the eternal odor of cabbage soup, he came upon Mr. and Mrs. White in the hallway, busy over a gaping suitcase.

"I suppose you got the sack, too?" Mr. White said.

Gesser nodded.

"Because you're a damned foreigner, and not to be trusted?"

"I suppose so."

"You suppose? Do you remember how they begged us to come and lend them our expertise? All those years we spent mucking about in those bloody bogs, trying to convince the water to run uphill. And now do you know what I found out? The workers building the canal were political prisoners! Slave labor! Do you think I'm going to co-operate with that? So, what about you? I suppose you're here to pack your kit, too?"

"Not exactly, no."

"You're not leaving Zabatskaya? You have to, you know. Or didn't you know that?"

White's outraged bellowing was beginning to give Gesser a headache.

"Yes, I do know, Mr. White. But I'm not running away. I got another job. It's different for me. I *wanted* to come here. I came back."

White straightened up painfully from his open trunk, a foot on either side of it.

"Well then, I don't know what to say. Bully for you. You can have your revolution. And you know what they can do with that canal of theirs!"

Mrs. Barnaby came into the hallway, holding a light bulb.

"We bought this ourselves," she said. "Should we take it with us, or leave it for them?"

Mr. White took it roughly from her hand and stared at it.

"It won't fit any of our sockets, that's for sure. But I hate to leave it for them."

Then he got an idea. He raised the bulb over his head and brought it down on the parquet hallway. The bulb exploded in a great mist of glass fragments. *You lousy bastard*, Gesser thought. *I could have used that.*

Gesser let himself into their room. Their home for the last five years. It did not take him long to fold their clothes into the two suitcases and collect the knickknacks they had acquired. The brass monkey that held salt and pepper shakers, which he had gotten for Sonya on their first anniversary in Moscow. The blood-red scarf with the deep maroon roses and other flowers that sprang from the spinner's imagination, for their electric blue petals were so intense they brought light to a room on a midwinter's day.

Gesser rubbed the cloth of the scarf between his fingers. It hit him how much he loved this place. He did not understand how the mistake had been made at the plant. How any commissar at Loputchkha could have imagined he was untrustworthy. True, the country was preparing for war, vigilance was required. This Gesser believed. Still, the idea that he, Jack Gesser, could be a German spy was ludicrous, and anyone who bothered to get to know him would laugh at the notion. But what government had the time to know all its citizens, especially its newest members? If a man was suspect because he was a foreigner, the solution was simple. He could cease being a foreigner. Gesser was lucky—unlike White, he had that chance. He was born a Russian. He would request his citizenship back and no longer be an *innostranyetz*. It was his right, the final step in his return. Isn't that what separated him from the Whites of this world? He was ready to tie his fate to this place. It was his country.

By the time he caught the tram back to Hertzina Street, Gesser had begun to see that losing his job at Loputchkha was an opportunity. There are times when history challenges a person. The way he responds determines whether he is with, or against, history. Jack Gesser intended to keep faith with history.

Anyone who thinks of Moscow as a place of eternal winter has never spent a summer in an attic on Hertzina Street. That summer, the heat of the Caspian deserts visited the city and was joined by the northern smell of smoke from burning peat. The lowlands around Moscow, those miles and miles of peat bogs where useless scrubby birch grows, began drying out in the unaccustomed southern heat. A lightning flash, a careless or vengeful peasant tapping out his pipe, and the fire was on. When a peat bog catches fire, it will burn until the next winter's snowfall puts it out.

Jack Gesser and Sonya Freedman sat and sweated on the top floor of the fortress Borodin, which their benefactor had called his hostel. The attic was as wide as a baseball field and without partitions, but that did not matter. They were the only tenants, free to wander through the vast room, their bare feet leaving moist tracks in the dust. They found a bed among the furniture that had once belonged to the old, exiled bourgeois owners of the place. The bed was an enormous fantasy constructed from brass and carved wood, with a straw mattress in place of its original one. They pushed and tugged it to the base of one of the round windows that looked down over Hertzina, windows like the portholes of the Île-de-France, only in Moscow the ocean was hot and grimy and deceptively drowsy. They bobbed carelessly upon its surface, employed, lodged, fed and maintained by Mikhail Borodin. Their trust in him was greater and more perilous than it had been the time they'd set out for the jungles of Cape Haitian.

But this they did not know.

What did they know? Heat and, at night, the meager, sooty breeze they could feel if they stood naked before the little round attic windows. That breeze brushed their skin and awoke in them the early passions of Sangamon Street. Their passion was more than the work of the breeze. It arose from the strangeness of that giant attic, the remnants of nineteenth-century furniture among which they camped like orphans, overlooking the city, its secret courtyards, its *porte-cochères*, its struggles for power about which they were so strikingly naive. In one corner of the attic they discovered a couch that would have been at home in Freud's study, and might well have served one of Sonya's predatory Budapest therapists. They wrestled it into the center of the giant room. Sonya stood silently and contemplated the piece of furniture, as if it were a species of terrible, carnivorous animal long forgotten, a prop from a nightmare. What was it that made her take to the couch, recline naked upon it, then spread her legs on either side of it? She closed her eyes in the heat. Perhaps she did not realize the movements she was repeating. Gesser knelt before her on his bony knees. Her splendid red bush was crusted over with sweat and the sperm he'd given her that morning, and he separated those fiery strands one by one with exaggerated, loving care. Decades of dust rose up and surrounded them as they beat that couch with their bodies until it gave up every memory.

Life at Zabatskaya, the stable, fatigued life of the worker in the workers' state, was just a dull memory replaced by the intimate madness of the fortress Borodin. They had been safest in the days when Gesser toiled anonymously at the plant, serving a metal lathe manufactured in Michigan City. Now the earth had fallen away from beneath their feet, orphaning them from the State, but making them lovers again. As Gesser lay on the couch, feeling the sheen of sweat on their joined bodies separate into beads and run down into the stuffing of the couch, he wondered why this madness was visiting them now, when their position was most precarious.

The answer, of course, was in the erotics of the century.

Gesser did not like being orphaned from the State. If I reclaim my Russian citizenship, he reasoned to himself as Sonya's grip on his back loosened and she surrendered to a hot, grimy and perfumed sleep, perhaps I'll be able to escape the stain of being a foreigner. A few days later, saying nothing to Sonya, he presented himself at the appropriate offices, declared himself a returnee and undertook the process of applying for a Soviet passport. While others like Mr. and Mrs. White were casting for a way out, he was struggling to bull his way in. Doing that required days and weeks of waiting and painful justifications at a wicket behind which a sausage-smelling bureaucrat hovered. But Gesser persevered, and was rewarded. Armed with his new documents, he petitioned Loputchkha for reinstatement. Proudly, he displayed his Soviet bona fides. "I have taken my stand," he told the commissar proudly at his hearing. "This is my gesture of faith." The vocabulary of sentiment and belief befuddled the commissar, who referred the case to the factory committee.

Strangely, after deliberation, the committee remained unmoved by Gesser's *beau geste*. His job had already been taken, he was informed. It was too late to reverse the process. What did he expect them to do with his replacement? Discharge him? "Especially now," the committee added, "now that you have taken another position in an area no doubt better suited to you."

What objections could he possibly raise? After all, the committee was right.

Now came the full fruit of paradox. He was a Soviet man, yet without the security the State was supposed to confer on its citizens, especially the most zealous, selfless ones like himself. The oddity of his position struck him through those hot days and nights as he pondered the mistakes that had been made at the plant and elsewhere, mistakes without appeal. Blue-brown peat smoke drifting in from the burning countryside broke up the rays of the setting sun into a thousand unnatural colors. In the Russian midsummer, sunset did not come until close to midnight, as if the sky took pleasure in tormenting the earth with its heat. The wonder of those midnight sunsets soon turned to nervous exhaustion.

Jack and Sonya sat watching the unearthly glow of the sky, and soon began praying for darkness to come at its former hour and bring them relief. At times she would leave her chair by the western window, clothed in an unfastened dress, or wearing nothing at all, and lie upon the analysis couch. She spoke not a word to him. He would rise in the same kind of trance and come to her. When they made love, she would beat upon his back and his chest with rage and fury, as if blaming him for the heat.

Once, as they lay in the thrall of midsummer, their skin and hair and clothing greasy with peat-soot, they heard a lusty chant from the street below. *"Peevah! Pee-vah!"* a vendor was shouting. In the humid air a horse whinnied, and there was the sound of crates being stacked as the beer wagon was unloaded in the little park across from their building, where on Sundays such commerce was tolerated.

"I'd love a beer," Sonya said dreamily. "I'm so thirsty. You've taken everything out of me."

She wriggled out from underneath him and stood up, lifting her breasts to wipe away the sweat.

Jack threw on his pants and undershirt and trudged down the stairway, passing the door to the *Moscow Daily News* on the way. Though it was Sunday, work was being done in the office. A typewriter clattered away, as if arguing fruitlessly with itself, or with some other machine that refused to respond. Through the translucent glass door, Gesser saw a bulky, pacing form that could only be Borodin. Gesser stood and watched the dark form. Borodin on a Sunday. Borodin who seemed to live in his offices, or in hurried transit, a man who never came to rest, who never alit. Like the hawk that learns to glide on the wind currents in effortless flight. But Borodin was no bird of prey now. If he stayed in the air, it was because he was afraid to land.

Inside the office, the phone rang. The one without the dial, whose alarm Borodin awaited. He grabbed for the receiver, and as he did so Gesser turned and continued down the stairway and into the street.

A line had formed by the time he made it into the park. In Moscow, lines had a life and logic of their own. A person might join a line without knowing what he was waiting for. That didn't matter; if other people were waiting, he should, too. Other times, a line might spring up spontaneously without there being anything to wait for. But it only appeared that way; usually the waiters would be vindicated by the appearance of a cart of cabbages or beets. This time, with the beer wagon and the stacked crates, the heat and the catch of peat smoke in their throats, people knew why they were there.

Most had spent the day in pursuit of beer wagons, going from park to park, corner to corner, loitering around the subway entrances, wherever there might be hope of refreshment, sweating off one beer in search of the next. Out of thirst, out of boredom, because it was Sunday, because the heat had never been this thick—as thick as a Kremlin plot—and the smoke this choking. The beer was rarely cooler than tapwater, but it had that pleasing bitterness, and a few points of alcohol in it to lull you to sleep in the shade of some tree, if you could get enough, which meant standing in several lines at once.

Men were literally rising from the earth beneath the park. They were sandhogs, thrusting the subway lines in all directions, twenty-four hours a day, digging tunnels as deep as bomb shelters. Just as Gesser reached the head of the line, a pair of subway workers pushed in front of him.

"End of the line," Gesser told them.

"We're drunk," one of them boasted.

"All the more reason you can wait," Gesser retorted, "and let us catch up."

The man displayed the shovel he carried.

"We're working. We're in the commission of our duties."

"Either you're drunk or you're working," Gesser joked. "You can't have both excuses."

The crowd laughed. Behind him, a few men shouted at the subway workers to go to the back of the line.

The first worker turned his dull eyes slowly towards Gesser. Laboriously, he searched for a riposte. Finally, he found it.

"Here's a little Jew that's got to have the last word. You think that's how you win a fight?" The man sniffed the air. "Here's a little Jew that smells like he's just had a piece of tail. It better not have been Christian tail!"

"How can I tell," said Gesser coolly, "since the Revolution put an end to those medieval superstitions?"

"I don't care—"

Before the worker could finish the sentence that might have proved fatal, his friend clapped a hand over his mouth.

"You won this round, little Jew," he hissed at Gesser through his wiser comrade's hand. "But your day'll come."

"You won the round, comrade, not me," Gesser told him. "You got your beer before anybody else."

Gesser crossed through the park, holding four beer bottles between the fingers of both hands. As he toiled up the stairway, he decided against mentioning the incident to Sonya. Why worry her? And considering what the past had already brought him, and her, too, a few unkind words in a park were not worth lingering over.

When Sonya began to jerk awake in the middle of the night, gasping for breath and spitting hard little knots of peat soot onto the back of her hand, they decided to leave Moscow. Borodin granted them a few days' leave. Their absence would be no hardship for the paper. Gesser's job was mostly a fiction, a general assistant's post, and even in 1938 there was no shortage of people with reasonable skills in English to read proofs of the *Moscow Daily News*.

They took the electric line that ran out of the city to the north, into a landscape of low fields and lines of birches. Sonya's much-travelled bag rode at their feet, packed for an excursion to the country—sandwiches, blanket, change of foot-rags. Jack had no name for Sonya's disorder. He decided it was asthma. With the heat, the smoke, the disorder of city life and their strange tenancy in the fortress Borodin, no wonder she was affected.

They disembarked at the Novinki stop and waited for the train to pull away and the other passengers to disperse. Then they crossed the tracks and took a dirt and clay road that sloped softly into a valley that bottomed out in a peat bog. Mercifully, it was not yet on fire. A kilometer or two along that road stood the Loputchkha plant dachas, cottages sinking into the bogland, set aside for the most zealous workers as weekend rewards. In the hollow ahead of them lay the scattered houses of the hamlet of Novinki, the pond, the well, the muddy main track.

Sonya stopped on the road, turned around, listened.

"Did you lose something?" Jack asked her.

"No. Yes."

In the ditch, tough weedy daffodils grew, and Queen Anne's lace, and northern poppies. Around them bees hummed. The flowers bent from their weight as they alighted. From the distance came the crack of a whip and the sound of cattle lowing.

"We're not supposed to be here."

"The place belongs to Loputchkha," Jack countered.

"Yes. But you don't. And you know it."

"It's a weekday, the dachas will be empty. The ends justify the means. You needed to get out of the city. If we're going to sweat, we might as well do it out in the fresh air. Now, come on. If you don't want to attract attention, don't stand like a post in the middle of the road."

They moved down the slope to Novinki. As she walked, Sonya could not keep her head from turning, as if it obeyed a will of its own. But there was nothing to see. The road behind them was empty, without even a clod of manure.

"Do you really think they care about a couple of nobodies going for a stroll in the country?" Jack asked her.

"They? They? Who's they?"

They walked under a sky leaden with humidity. The hay in the fields, still uncut, was bent and heavy and yellowing. The village houses were low, their slanting roofs all but covering their windows, keeping out the wind and weather, and the light, too. Along the roof lines and shutters were traces of the old individualism: intricate, sculpted gingerbread patterns from which the paint had faded.

There was no paved street in Novinki, just a wide grassy common with a track cut through it. Those who had flattened the path were nowhere to be seen. Jack and Sonya came to the well and stopped to fill their water bottles. The pump protested, squealed, ground its badly neglected gears. The sound was as loud as an air-raid siren to Sonya's ears.

The only reaction came from a flock of geese at the edge of the village pond. As Jack and Sonya passed them, the birds left off haggling over whatever obscure issue had been occupying them to hiss at the two lovers.

"Do you think they're spies?" Jack joked.

"No. But their owners are."

"Then let's give them something to report us for. Misappropria-
tion of State property. The Soviet strawberry, as rare as geese teeth."

Jack bent down at the lip of the pond. The grass was full of wild
strawberries, so red they were almost black, with all the heat of the
intolerable summer of 1938 concentrated in their sugars.

Jack gathered a handful and fed them to Sonya, one by one.

"I knew you were going to do that," Sonya told him.

"Yes? And was it unpleasant?"

"No."

With the tip of her tongue, Sonya pursued a tiny strawberry
seed stuck between her teeth.

"Sometimes love is not very original," he said.

Love, Sonya repeated to herself. *I almost forgot I'm in love.* She
stared down into the pond. In the green-black water, her face was
a darker plane surrounded by the halo of her hair. She made a half-
hearted attempt at brushing it away from her face, then gave up.
Examining yourself in a mirror of any sort—what a dreary propo-
sition that was.

"This place is so gloomy. It looks like a ghost town."

Jack tilted the handful of berries he had gathered into his mouth.

"Everybody's out working somewhere else. That's the way it is
in the country."

Sonya didn't believe it. She sensed abandonment here. She let
herself be led along, out of Novinki with its geese cackling behind
them, through the dried fields towards a line of birch trees whose
leaves hung motionless in the still air. The outline of the trees was
blurred; here, too, there was peat smoke in the air. Past them lay
the orderly dachas of the Loputchkha plant. The land the factory
had been allotted was too acidic for anything but the toughest,
bitterest grasses. The plant workers' Sunday project was to reclaim
that land. Here and there, around the cabins, were piles of sand to

be mixed with the bogland to reduce its acidity. Perhaps then the land could be persuaded to grow potatoes, cucumbers, perhaps even a few tomatoes. But it would take more than one day a week to change the nature of the Russian earth. Like the nearby village, the deacidification project looked abandoned. Some of the sand had been carted away to serve private projects.

It was easy to break into the dacha. A simple hook-and-eye latch held the door fast. Like children in a fairy tale, Jack and Sonya slipped into the little cabin.

Inside, Sonya unlaced her boots. Jack did the same. Sonya unbuttoned the wool sweater she wore despite the temperature. It was a kind of fetish object, to be used as a pillow or a wrap. Jack hung it up for her on a wooden peg on the back of the door. Sonya pulled her dress over her head. Jack received it. He spread their blanket over the bare pine slats of a bunk. Outside, insects raged in the heat. Sonya went exploring and discovered a water barrel, a steel tub and naptha soap. She filled the tub and set about scrubbing her dress and underthings. There is nothing more glorious than a naked woman in the summer heat washing her clothes, but what was missing from this vision was innocence. The water turned black with Moscow grime as on and on Sonya scrubbed. There was so much not to think about, and it was easy to do just that when you were scrubbing clothes. She rinsed her things, went to the door, then hesitated a moment on the threshold. "The hell with them," she said out loud, and marched into the hazy sunlight, naked and shining. A pitchfork jutted out of a sandpile. It made no sense; how was anyone supposed to shovel sand with a pitchfork? Sonya draped her dress over the handle of the pitchfork in the sun.

Red-haired, freckled, soaking with sweat and wash-water, hair streaming down, mad with heat, she came back to the dacha humming "The Bear Went over the Mountain."

*   *   *

They awoke in the evening, starved. Jack sat up, picked a few splinters out of his backside.

"Only with you, my love, could I sleep naked on a board."

While they slept, Novinki had come back to life. Jack was right. The inhabitants had returned from whatever State fields they had been assigned to. He went to the window. Across the prairie, under the luminous midsummer sky, smoky fires were burning to keep down the mosquitoes. Someone had set a ladder against a house and was busy on the roof, nailing down shingles. A woman was cutting back thistles on the common with a hand scythe that glinted dully as it cut through the air. The village had become industrious again. The villagers were doing real work. Their work.

Sonya spread the supper on the table. Smoked fish, radishes, two apples, bread. And a bottle of lemon vodka with a pair of large thimbles they used for glasses.

Sonya poured herself a shot.

"I want to get drunk," she announced.

Jack smiled indulgently. Before he filled his glass, Sonya had polished off two shots. Their glasses met with a distinctly tinny clink.

"May the bastards croak," Jack toasted.

"May they all croak," Sonya insisted.

They drank. She poured.

"May onions grow from their navels," Sonya toasted.

"May roots sprout from their balls and grow into their mattresses, and keep them bedridden," Jack replied.

"And may lice copulate unnaturally in their bedsores."

They clinked their glasses together and drank. No one had to ask who *they* were. An all-purpose *they*, it included all those Jack and Sonya hadn't encountered yet. Jack's *they* and Sonya's didn't necessarily match, but that didn't stop them from drinking.

With whetted appetites, they consumed their feast. The anatomical eccentricities of the exploded Soviet fish had long since ceased to bother them. As long as it did not have two heads, a fish was good to eat. And if it did, you just whacked off one of them and dug in.

From across the prairie, in Novinki, someone was strumming a guitar and singing a gravelly complaint. For a moment Gesser wished he were there in the fields with the rough grub and rougher drink and the lying stories of bravery, the camaraderie men turn to when they're sated by the overrich love of a woman. But that could not be. A Jew had no place in those circles.

He filled his thimble again and sadly eyed the lowering level of the bottle. He raised the tinny thimble to make a toast, but found he had nothing to say.

"To our trip to the country," Sonya rescued him.

"Yes. And to Loputchkha, whose dacha this is, and who fired me."

"You and every other *innostranyetz*."

"Yes, of course. I applied for reinstatement, you know."

"And?"

"My position had already been filled. I guess they got tired of waiting for me."

Sonya blew out a mouthful of air in disgust. Jack reached for her but she spun away.

"Let me get my dress before the dew falls. While I'm at it I'm going to make a contribution to the Soviet economy."

She went outside, grabbed her dress from the pitchfork and put it on, then went in search of the outhouse. Gesser picked up the last bit of food from their supper, a bitingly sharp radish, and dipped it in the fish oil. The sound of hammering drifted through the heavy air. He envied the man who could work on his own roof, though there was plenty to do here at the Loputchkha dachas. The bog-grass should be broken, the roots turned and mixed with sand. The outhouse waste should be composted under a tarp so it could be used for fertilizing the young apple trees next year. Gesser was always ready to work, even for the plant that had fired him.

He stepped onto the porch. Immediately, mosquitoes the size of bullets rose up. He walked across the boggy yard, the sucking wound of the Russian earth, the soil of childhood disaster. Smoke floated over from Novinki, but not nearly enough to keep the bugs down. With the buzzing of mosquitoes in his ears, echoed by the buzzing of lemon vodka, he considered his attraction to this worthless, cruel ground. And to those who lived so poorly on it, so defeated that superstition had replaced any sense of ideals.

The outhouse door slammed on its spring and Sonya stepped out, oblivious to the mosquitoes.

"I hope you remembered to flush," Gesser said.

His joking had become a compulsion.

In the middle of the night, Gesser opened his eyes and saw Sonya's strange posture. She was on her elbows and hips on the rough pine slats, as if crawling under sniper fire. Her breath was sour with fear.

"Is the door locked?" Her hiss was a whispered scream.

Gesser thought of the flimsy latch.

"Locked? Yes, for what it's worth."

"For God's sake, for once give me a straight answer!"

He groped for the matches, his hand made contact with the glass chimney of the lamp.

"No, not the light!"

"Then I'll go and see—"

"No!"

Sonya clamped onto his hand with desperate strength. Gesser lay on the boards, aware of how intolerably uncomfortable he was as they waited for Sonya's nightmare to materialize at the flimsy door. As her fear passed into him through the embrace of her fingers, he realized that no one was there. Eventually her grip relaxed, and after a time she fell asleep. A bad dream, he thought. Another one. Now he was imprisoned in that dream, and she was free of it. Well, isn't that what love is for?

He unpried his fingers from hers and went to the window. The fields were wrapped in thin fog. Dew sparkled in the moonlight. Trails of smoke drifted among the dachas, and by a campfire near the Novinki pond a man was shouting out a song in a drunken, atonal rage. Tomorrow, the owner of that voice would blunder through the day at the collective farm, pull out crops instead of weeds, damage the worn machinery, mix sugar with the diesel fuel. Purposely or not, he would generate the kind of sabotage for which the unseen but omnipresent enemies of the people would be blamed. At the end of the day, he would return to Novinki to labor away industriously at his little garden plot.

The next morning Sonya recalled nothing of her dream. That was just as well. The job of dreams is to be forgotten. By mutual consent, they agreed to return to Moscow. The country had not fulfilled its promise. The breathing was no better there.

Though the heat wave had moderated, the smoke from the bog fires still hung in a purplish-brown pall over the overgrown village when the tenants began arriving at Jack and Sonya's love nest. A shared love nest quickly becomes no love nest at all, but they had no choice but to welcome them. In one way or another, they had all encountered the same misfortune Jack had met at Loputchkha.

It was worse for the new tenants than it had been for Jack and Sonya. The new ones had no replacement jobs, and they were so numerous that they elicited no further concern from Borodin once he had shown them where the stairs were. Borodin himself never set foot in the attic. Why would he want to gaze upon the spectacle of this small but fast-growing community, the very mirror of his failure?

The first tenant made the usual Muscovite entrance: chaotically, in the middle of the night, in a slapstick manner that didn't give you time to realize it wasn't funny until after you'd laughed. Lying on the straw mattress that had given him a permanent itch, Jack awoke to the sound of footsteps in the attic. *The construction workers*, was his first thought. He opened his eyes to the eerie, unnatural grey light of the summer sky revealed in dusty shafts through the round attic windows. Hertzina Street lay in relative peace; it must have been four or five in the morning. Sonya was sleeping in what had become her usual spot—the analysis couch, her legs spread and her sex open and glistening, her fiery red bush swept up as by a whirlwind.

"Squeezed, squeezed, always getting the squeeze. Well, here at least it looks like there's not another living soul to have to share with."

That optimistic prognostication was followed by a sound recognized the world over: that of a suitcase being dropped by an exhausted man. Gesser knew that vaudeville voice, the nasal New Jersey accent that could imitate a squeaking mouse with uncanny accuracy. It was Marcus Pinsky. Gesser knew him not only from his accent, but from that compulsion of his to add a few extra words when he should have kept his mouth shut, even when he was alone.

Or thought he was alone.

Gesser rose from the bed and dropped his shirt over Sonya. She stirred but slept on.

Pinsky stood in the dim attic, stripping off his layers of clothing. Whoever had shown him upstairs had departed. It must have been Borodin, but what was the man doing, taking in the social dregs at this odd hour, committing ideological suicide?

Naked and barefoot, acquainted with the topography of the attic, Gesser was on top of Pinsky before he even knew he wasn't alone.

"Good evening, comrade," Gesser said in a low voice.

Pinsky jumped a foot into the air, as if Uncle Joe Stalin himself had materialized beside him.

"Gesser! What in the hell are you doing here, buck-assed naked in the middle of the night, with your schmuck hanging out? Not a bad schmuck for a little guy."

"Keep your voice down, Pinsky, people are trying to sleep."

"People? Here?"

"My wife, Pinsky. Remember her?"

Pinsky slapped himself in the forehead, then sank onto his suitcase.

"How could I forget? She haunts my dreams. Gesser, what the hell is going on here?"

"*Here?* Here, people were enjoying their sleep, before you squeezed in."

"No, you putz, I don't mean here. I mean *everywhere*. This whole place."

"Pinsky, you're not making any sense."

"Why should I be making sense, when nothing else is?"

"Look, Pinsky, you're drunk or something. If you're not, you should be. Sack out here and we'll talk about it in the morning. Which is going to come pretty soon, by the looks of it."

Pinsky's rubber clown face was mournful in the pre-dawn light. It's terrible to be a clown when you have something to say, and no one will believe you.

Then his face lit up. "Hey, Comrade Gesser, remember Lehto, that Finn who used to sing bass in the choir?"

"What do you mean, used to? I saw him . . . I don't know, a while ago."

"Yeah. Well, he sends his regards."

"He sends his regards," Gesser repeated.

"Yeah. He sends his regards."

"That's nice."

Pinsky stared at Gesser, outraged.

"You mean you really don't know what I'm talking about?"

"Pinksy, I told you to keep your voice down. This is my flat."

"He was arrested by the NKVD."

"What for?"

"I can't believe you'd ask that question!" Pinsky was scandalized. "Does it matter what for? They say he's a spy. That he sabotaged some plant or other. Lehto, our Lehto, the best bass in the choir, my choir, a goddamned enemy of the people! Ridiculous! He came here to work for this country, not tear it down."

Gesser sat down in the gloom. His belly churned and groaned. He thought of what he had put in his stomach the evening before. A glass of water with a little sugar in it, the usual nightly concoction for warding off hunger.

"Why would they arrest him if he didn't do anything? Do they really have time to go around arresting nobodies like Lehto, if they never did anything? It doesn't make sense."

"I agree, Comrade Gesser. It doesn't make sense."

They sat in silence for a minute, naked Gesser, clothed Pinsky, in the dusty attic of the *Moscow Daily News*. The breeze from the open window should have been welcome; instead, it gave Gesser gooseflesh. He thought of fascist Germany across their western border, builder of fifth columns, enemy of socialism, perpetrator of *Kristallnacht* and worse. If you believe in the existence of the enemy, and Gesser did, then you must believe in his spies. But how could their Lehto be a spy? How could any spy seem to be a spy? Was it not the nature of spies to appear as one of us?

Gesser stood up, gave his balls a hitch, brushed the dust off his butt.

"I know one thing: I'm not a spy. I'm even a Russian citizen now. I've got the passport to prove it."

"Good for you," said Pinsky. "Now you belong to them, right down to the last hair on your ass. I just hope you got your hankie pack ready."

"What are you talking about?"

"Your arrest pack, you simpleton, for when they come calling."

Gesser listened with sudden interest. Someone had something he didn't have.

"A hankie. Sheets. A pillowcase, socks, underwear. And whatever rubles you can find. It sounds like chickenfeed, but it could save your life. You got a bed?"

"I've got two."

"Then stow yours under one of your beds, you lucky Jew, just in case your luck runs out."

"Whatever we're doing in this country," Gesser said, offended, "it doesn't have anything to do with luck."

Pinsky shrugged. "You're the philosopher, not me. I always said so. I'm just a happy-go-lucky mouse that tells jokes."

"It's my lot in life," Gesser said, "to share my flat with a singing mouse."

Pinsky shrugged sadly as Gesser disappeared into the darkness of the attic towards his corner. Those were the wages of being a clown: no one believed you. But weren't clowns more in demand in times of hardship? Maybe people didn't know how bad times were yet. Maybe they didn't know they needed a clown.

Pinsky bunched his coat into a pillow, sneezed the dust out of his nostrils and lay down on the floor. It was not a comfortable floor as floors went, but being comfortable was not the vocation of floors. It was smooth and dry, and quiet, and as a result of those not inconsiderable virtues Pinsky lapsed into a shallow sleep—the only kind that had been available to him since he was abruptly found unfit to participate in the new society. Without a Sonya Freedman, without the shaky patronage of Borodin, he felt terribly exposed. Perhaps a Russian passport would have provided some cover.

Pinsky turned and shifted on the cool floor. In his sleep, with his little finger he removed the residue that the grimy Moscow air had left in his nostrils. Pinsky from Pinsk. He had as much right to a Soviet passport as Gesser. He could probably still get one, if he hadn't been too disgraced.

Pinsky laughed himself awake with that thought. What an idea, that you should belong to a system in order to be spared its punishment! He'd get the hell out instead.

On the other side of the attic, Gesser bent over Sonya and touched her shoulder. She opened her eyes.

"I heard voices," she said.

"It was nothing." He offered her his hand. "Come into my bed."

"You know that straw makes me itch."

"So what. Whatever I have, you have by now. I'm cold."

"Cold? In this heat?"

She was too sleepy to argue. She accepted his hand, then settled in next to him on the straw mattress. He climbed between her legs and a minute later, automatically, they were going at it. Sonya was loud; the bed, louder. Jack did not have the heart to tell her they were no longer alone. One last free night is all he asked for.

The experience was shattering for poor Pinsky. He never imagined a woman could produce such cries and howls and be alive at the end of it. Fucking, he thought. They are fucking. Is this any time for fucking?

*   *   *

Pinsky, it turned out, was just the advance guard of the internal exiles who began to set up house in the attic of the *Moscow Daily News*. Just as Jack and Sonya were reconciling themselves to having to share their privacy with Pinsky, another man showed up, one they'd never seen before. They had just finished devising a way of living with him when another appeared. Then a couple with children of an age that did not respect the complex network of old furniture, sheets and crates that stood for walls in this new collective flat. Some called the process squeezing. Others, more ironic, called it sharing. By the time a dozen or more people had moved into the wide attic where once Jack and Sonya had roamed, naked, they understood what it meant to be squeezed.

With the tenants came domestic help. Spontaneously, uninvited, but entirely useful, by the same process of nature that makes plants grow on bare rock. A creature of indeterminate age and sex who worked for no salary, only the roof over her head and the assumption that she would receive her share of whatever soup was on the fire. She never introduced herself. Jack and Sonya called her Mother Russia.

"What business does a domestic have here?" Sonya asked Jack. "What are we, landowners? What is this?" She pointed to the giant, dusty attic room, artfully divided by the clutter. "A mansion? A chateau?"

"To her, we're as wealthy as landowners," Jack told her.

Just as the smallest, most primitive organism can support its share of parasites, no one who had a room, or even part of one, was so bereft that they didn't have a little corner for someone else. And Mother Russia, whose real name was Mafili, was no parasite. She ended up teaching them a lot about the ways of the overgrown village.

10

MAFILI'S LAW

The human heart's ability to adapt is prodigious. Equally astounding is the body's capacity to accept discipline and fall into line. Through the end of that summer and fall, the tenants of the fortress Borodin set about proving those truths. Excluded by the State, they simply found other occupations. Some were even paying occupations. They taught basketball, they gave singing lessons, they went into private distilling. Not very different from their lives in America. Those who remained after the first warnings had sent the Whites and their kind scurrying home stayed on out of prideful stubbornness, which they called idealism; besides, where else would they go now?

None of the attic-dwellers was willing to admit he might have taken a wrong turn somewhere. All believed that their exclusion was the result of some terrible mistake, and given time enough and their stubborn resources, someone would eventually set that mistake right. Perhaps some stayed out of sheer inertia—paralysis, if you like. They waited: for the engine idling in the street below, the footfalls on the stairs, the doorknob rattling in the middle of the night. In the meantime, the population of the fortress Borodin went about the business of living. That was, after all, their duty as human beings.

Mother Russia steered a wet rag impaled on a pointed stick down the thoroughfares between the furniture, partitions and hanging sheets of the fortress Borodin. Where once Jack and Sonya had howled and sported and wrestled naked in the dust, on beds and couches invested with all manner of bloodsucking insects, two dozen people now lived. They generated plenty of tasks for a housekeeper. Mafili was dressed in her inevitable Mother Hubbard and pinned-up wool sweater. By now, the peat smoke had become an enduring fact of life, an irritation with which you lived, like a physical infirmity that at first is intolerable, then becomes part of you. The pall of smoke seemed to have settled permanently around the top floors of the buildings of the Moscow baroque, darkening the mustard- and salmon-colored facades, bringing a steady supply of grit for Mother Russia to chase down. The word in *Pravda* was that the fires had been tamed, but extinguished flames were still sending out smoke.

It was a tough time for anyone afflicted with an imagination. Fortunately, Jack Gesser was not overly burdened. Sonya was the one who suffered most. She'd become asthmatic again and wondered through her breathlessness why Old Joe Stalin didn't just order the fires to go out, since he could accomplish so many wonders with mere words. As for the other inhabitants of the attic fortress, and the great body of Muscovites on the streets below, they learned the art of shallow breathing.

Mafili reached Jack and Sonya's quarters with her damp rag, black by now. Jack lay on his straw pallet, scratching himself desultorily, reading a Dostoevsky novel he had lifted from the *Moscow Daily News* library. There was less work at the paper, now that it had been demoted to a weekly. "The *Moscow Daily News*," ran the joke at the Anglo-American Club, "the only daily to come out once a week."

But who could complain? they reasoned. The paper was still coming out, wasn't it?

Gesser was not particularly happy to have Mother Russia in his quarters. He read a kind of silent admonishment under her studied, blank expression. Mafili circled his bed, staring malevolently at the constellation of stains on the analysis couch that he and Sonya had managed to keep for themselves, even though some of the tenants were sleeping on the floor. Mafili chewed her gums noisily, then spoke so abruptly that Gesser was startled into dropping his book.

"Dostoevsky? The underground? This negative hero?"

Gesser was astonished. He didn't expect a cleaning woman to challenge his choice of reading material.

"A precursor of the Revolution," he defended himself. "He was sentenced to death by the Czar. Only a miracle saved his life. Ruined it, too, of course."

Mother Russia raised her eyebrows skeptically at the word *miracle*.

"I wouldn't read such negativity. A man brooding over his body, his mind . . . his weaknesses."

"And why not?" Gesser teased her, discovering to his surprise that he liked the sour old woman after all. "Is it not a worthy subject for art?"

"Art? I wouldn't know."

She paused to lean on her stick, considered the rag and what it knew about the floor. Then she pronounced Mafili's Law.

"It's best not to talk about something if you don't want it to happen to you."

"You mean if I read Dostoevsky, I'll end up being sentenced to death, or with a diseased liver?" Gesser asked incredulously.

"Yes. In a manner of speaking, that is true . . . Anyway, that's my advice, in case anyone's listening. But I don't think they are, do you?"

Then Mafili returned to her rag and stick, shepherding the dust and grime from one end of the giant room to the other in the timeless Russian tradition. Mafili and her wisdom of the ages. She was right: it was wasted on the attic inhabitants. They enjoyed complaining. It was their art form, part of what it meant to be alive. To criticize something was to participate in it, albeit at a distance.

The door slammed as she headed for the pump in the courtyard below. Gesser slipped the old negativist Dostoevsky under the mattress. And wondered, too late, how it was that Mother Russia, who claimed never to have read his books, knew that Dostoevsky enjoyed brooding over his diseased liver and spiteful heart.

He threw a shirt over his undershirt and set out down the stairs to put in an appearance at the paper, and discharge his duties, which were, in truth, nonexistent. Somewhere on the stairway he changed his mind. The next thing he knew he was on Hertzina Street, where he noticed the air had freshened. Up in the attic it was still summer. On the street, a change of season was underway.

Once again he marvelled at the emptiness of Red Square. Not a bench, a fountain or a flowerpot. Across the vast expanse was the disquiet facade of the Metropol Hotel, where the cadres came and went with eyes in the backs of their heads. Gesser crossed the Square and on the far side, under the Kremlin walls, he sat on a bench shaded by a maple that showered red leaves on him. The crowds that wheeled by belonged to the circle of hell reserved for the restless, the squeezed, the room-sharers, those who spoke a language that did not include the concept *privacy*. Gesser observed the ingrained stiffness between husband and wife, the men having little use for the women except on Saturday nights, and the women for the men, not even then. The children, alternately slapped and coddled, burdened with everyone's foolish hopes, which accounted for their prematurely aged, sallow features. Russia. Country of children. Gesser wondered what he would do with a child at a time like this. It was better to leave new life where it was: waiting in the ether. But what with Saturday night, and vodka, and rage, every year you ended up with another one of these future tyrants in their stained sailor suits, clutching their packets of sweetened, colored water, their faces grey, their teeth already decaying stubs in their mouths.

Gesser wandered along the walls and passed by a lunch kiosk. He stopped for a snack of sausage and bread, but the looks he received told him not to linger. There is an age-old riddle among the Chosen, which is simpler to resolve than the question of the dropped onion sandwich. Question: *When do we discover who we are?* Answer: *The first time someone hates us.*

The air was more temperate along the river, behind the Kremlin, and the smoke less cloying because of the freshness of the water. Two old men, their chests heavy with medals, were fishing with birch poles on the concrete embankment. A squadron of bodies hit the surface of the water, scaring away what fish there were: members of the Dynamo swim team, practicing their strokes in the oily wake of a sand barge.

Gesser crossed the bridge and took Dimitrov Street into unfamiliar neighborhoods. He felt the vague dissatisfaction that idle wandering always brought him; even now, he feared wasting his time. Enjoy these sights, he chided himself, for didn't you choose this life? And if you are not satisfied in a place you have consciously chosen, where *will* you be satisfied? He walked, and reminded himself he was supposed to be happy. He recalled Pinsky's outrageous claim during that long-ago Seder dinner: they were *already* living in Jerusalem.

That, of course, could not be true. Such a place could not exist on earth, and if it did, it would be uninhabitable. Intolerable. Against man's need to dream and complain and invent. It would have to be destroyed.

Anyway, what did a talking mouse know about Jerusalem?

Gesser came upon the end of a line but did not join it, since it was exclusively female. He passed the shabby creatures who waited on the sidewalk and compared them to Sonya, and thanked his good fortune, then wondered what the State would do about Sonya Freedman. It could not permit her to exist; she was too beautiful. Her freedom and beauty were an affront to the State's domination. The State's revenge, of course, would be to turn her into one of these waiting creatures on the sidewalk. Gesser passed the head of the line. It was a dry goods store. Sheets, pillowcases, handkerchiefs. The makings of the arrest pack, according to Pinsky. Could all these women standing calmly on the sidewalk in front of a State dry goods store be preparing someone else's, or their own, arrest pack?

Could it be happening in this matter-of-fact way, in broad daylight, on Dimitrov Street? Who could he ask about it? No one. The question was in the realm of the unaskable, a realm growing ever larger. Lehto the Finn had fallen into it, and surely others Gesser did not know about. There were many reasons why the question could not be asked; the first was Mafili's Law. How could Gesser ask a stranger on the street, when he could not ask his friends, his lover or, indeed, himself?

He walked on.

At the top of Leninsky Prospekt, he stumbled upon a market in young animals. A woman was holding a squirming puppy; on her jacket was pinned a photo of the full-grown dog, ready for whatever work it would be called upon to do. Then he saw him. Those lonely, knowing, displaced, curious eyes. Gesser could have sworn it was the very same monkey Sonya had begged for, and he'd refused her, on their first day on Kuznetsky Most, when they lived at the Kosmos Hotel. Gesser recalled the romance of those first bitterly cold winter days, years ago, when he and Sonya had walked, bodies locked together, on Kuznetsky Most, with no money, living on love and the hospitality of people who seemed so glad to see them. The drunken dance, the salt fish swinging with the soldier's shuffling dance, the trumpet-player's lips frozen to the mouthpiece and the guitarist's fingers running with blood . . . God, what a country!

Gesser resolved to buy the monkey. It was the only animal for sale that was wholly useless, and that made it irresistible. Maybe it would make Sonya smile, or get her off the analysis couch and into his bed. Maybe it would change their luck. Though whether a monkey has ever changed anyone's luck is hard to say.

The monkey was sitting on a wooden crate, examining its toes, a piece of bread by its side. It was as small as a teddy bear, with a short, sleek brown coat, black eyes and a tail longer than its body. A cord ran around its neck.

"I suppose it's expensive?" Gesser asked the vendor.

"Monkeys don't grow on trees."

"Where did it come from?"

"The jungle," the vendor said impassively. "Where else should monkeys come from?"

Gesser took a step to leave.

"Do you want to sell it or not? Maybe you'd rather keep it. If that's the case, what are you doing here?"

The monkey understood what was a stake. It stood up on the crate like a trained dwarf and stuck out its paw for Gesser to shake. Gesser had no choice but to oblige.

"Some African diplomat came to town. While he was here his country decided it didn't need him any more. It was either stay here, or go back and—" The vendor mimed a throat being cut. "He made the wise choice. But the monkey got the heave-ho." She contemplated the little primate refugee with fondness in her eyes. "He's a diplomatic monkey. That's why he's so well behaved . . . Must be hard for a black African foreigner to live in our country."

"Especially without his monkey."

"I was talking about the monkey. There, I told you the story. You want him or not?"

Gesser did.

What kind of man buys a monkey at the end of the hellish summer of 1938, in Moscow, when he's living in a communal attic?

A man who wishes he had bought one the first time around.

As Jack Gesser climbed the stairs of the *Moscow Daily News* building with the monkey riding gaily on his shoulder, it never occurred to him that the animal might not be welcome. He didn't discover that a monkey was inappropriate for the times until Sonya came into the chateau, which is what the other tenants called their established corner of the attic, and saw it perched on the padded back of the analysis couch.

The monkey was nervously passing a cube of cooked potato from its right paw to its left and back again. Sonya looked at it, then at its larger human reflection, then back at the couch again.

"Remember how you wanted a monkey that time on Kuznetsky Most?" Gesser pleaded.

Sonya wanted to quote Marx: *first time tragedy, second time farce.*

The Eighteenth Brumaire of somebody or other, she was too tired to recall, but Borodin would know.

"I remember," she said dully. "I remember that particular historical moment. So, now we finally have a monkey. Very nice. Does it have a name?"

"I suppose it does. But I forgot to ask."

"I think I'll call it Uncle Joe."

"You can't do that!"

Gesser screwed up his eyes and cocked his head and wondered whether, of the two of them, she wasn't the craziest after all. Naming your monkey after Stalin was equal to suicide.

"When you do that you look just like the monkey," she said, throwing herself onto the couch.

The monkey leaped off his perch in a panic, dropped the cube of potato, caught it in mid-air and managed to land gracefully on his feet. He turned to Sonya and made a clicking sound with his tongue. Not angry, just disapproving, and slightly disappointed. Sonya threw her boot at him.

Harried out of the chateau, the monkey went exploring. He felt right at home in the rest of the attic, with its jungle of cords, wires, beams and rafters, dripping wet with newly washed foot-rags, and shaky mountains of furniture. Uncle Joe—no one but Sonya would have even considered calling him that—turned out to be a naturally judicious monkey, a true diplomat, and he won friends with his discretion. He climbed out an open window to deposit his pellets on a dizzying ledge, then brushed them off into the courtyard below with his paw. He had had time to develop a taste for Russian food, and at supper he good-naturedly begged a tidbit off everyone's plate. Each gave, according to his means, and together, the scraps made a very respectable meal. There is always room for a clown, as there is for domestic help, no matter how straitened the situation.

Mafili recognized this and took to Uncle Joe immediately. She even gave him her feather duster to play with.

At the end of the evening, Sonya surprised Jack by coming into his straw bed.

"I thought the straw gave you an itch."

She took a dusty blanket from the chest of drawers that helped form the outer wall of the chateau and pulled the cover over them.

"Are you cold? The wind changed today."

"Pinsky sends his regards," Sonya said in a toneless voice. "He went out and he didn't come back. They arrested him in the street. He didn't even have his hankie pack. That goes to show you: precautions don't help."

Even under the blanket she was whispering. The air was intolerably stuffy, it imprisoned them. But at least the blanket muffled their voices and gave them some sense of security. Even in that private tent, Gesser could find nothing to say. He lay there breathing in the scent of their bodies, smelling how fear had turned their sweat from sweet to sour, a change that signified the end of love. This was the smoky autumn of 1938: two believers, two builders of socialism were huddled under a blanket so they could speak of the unspeakable without being heard.

"Now it's Pinsky," Gesser said. "What did he do?"

"Nothing, of course. Sabotage, spying, making a joke, I don't know. The usual."

"I can't believe Pinsky is important enough . . . important enough to get arrested. I can't believe anyone would actually be paying attention to us."

"Everyone is important in this society. Even you and me. And if we're not important, then we know someone who is. Like Pinsky."

Gesser took her hand. It felt lifeless. What did Pinsky do to get arrested? He must have done something. A man doesn't become an

Enemy of the People by accident. How much did he, Gesser, actually know about Pinsky? Pinsky was a wise-ass, he talked too much, he had to have the last word, he ran the choir and was good at it, he was a friend of Lehto, who was also an EOP. That was all Gesser knew. Maybe there was a side to Pinsky they didn't know about. Maybe the arrest had been a mistake. Mistakes are made, names are confused sometimes. Anyone from Pinsk can be called Pinsky; there must be tens of thousands of them. If a mistake had been made, it could be rectified. For a second or two, Gesser considered going to the Lubyanka and seeking information about the case. But then there was Mafili's Law. Don't talk about it if you don't want it to happen to you. Gesser had never heard of anyone who voluntarily went to the Lubyanka.

"When Pinksy came here, that first night, he told me about his hankie pack . . . You don't have one, do you?"

"Everyone does," she told him.

"But . . . where?"

"Is *where* the issue? I don't think so." She paused and considered the wisdom of telling him, then decided he might need to know one day. "It's in the bottom drawer of the big chest."

"What does it do?"

"Nothing. It's there. That's its job. To sit there and wait and not be used."

"Well, I'm not going to have one. I'm not going to live like that!"

"That's an individual choice," she told him coolly.

Individual, in the jargon of the day, meant *wrong*. So be it. Gesser had his convictions about the way a man was meant to live. He could not believe that every one of the comrades in the fortress Borodin secretly hoarded a hankie pack under his bed. Especially since half of them slept on the floor. But it wasn't the kind of thing you could inquire about without raising all sorts of intolerable questions. You couldn't ask about a person's secret life. Sonya had kept an arrest pack without telling him. He considered that an infidelity worse than if she'd given herself to Pinsky, Lehto, or any of her other admirers in the attic.

"Well, Pinsky had an arrest pack and it didn't help," Gesser concluded. "Maybe it even hurt, how do we know? He was the first one to come here back when we lived alone. He knew about Lehto. I didn't even know what someone sending their regards meant. He laughed at me. He was the first one to talk about it. And now he gets arrested."

"Yes," said Sonya dryly. "Knowledge is a disease: contagious and deadly. Soon we will even be afraid to tell a story. Soon, even a joke will be risky. Soon, we'll all be walking around with blankets over our heads all the time."

That was the moment when Jack Gesser lost Sonya Freedman, though neither knew it at the time. Jack Gesser, thinking backwards, rationalizing lunatic brutality. Co-operating with the madness of the system by concluding that since Pinsky had been first to see the wave coming, he must possess some guilty knowledge.

Don't blame Gesser; he was only doing what humans do. Trying to make sense of things. Lining up the world with what he believed. Toughing it out till tomorrow when, perhaps, all would change and all mistakes would be set right. Don't blame him; he was the victim of an ideal.

And of scratching. The heat under the blanket made his bites burst into an angry frenzy of itching. He threw the blanket off his head and chest for a breath of air and there was Uncle Joe the monkey on his perch on the back of the analysis couch. Formerly the love couch. Uncle Joe was staring at Gesser with imploring eyes, as if begging his pardon for something he had not meant to do.

"Well, excuse me for living, too," Gesser said to the monkey, and pulled the protective cover back over his head.

"What's it doing?" Sonya asked.

"Nothing. Looking at us. Compassionately, I'd say. God, I'm glad I have a monkey at a time like this, and not a child."

Sonya moved her hand carefully out of his.

With those words, Jack Gesser lost Sonya a second time. Maybe that was all for the best, considering what was to come.

The members of the Anglo-American Club were wary as they returned for their first soirée since Pinsky had sent his regards. The choir had survived the loss of its finest bass voice when Lehto sent his. Now, without a director, it had lost its rhythm. Not suprisingly, no one volunteered to replace Pinsky. The position of choir leader was, let us say, deemed unlucky. Some members even suggested disbanding the choir. But what would Saturday evenings be without those sweet, nostalgic tunes? Finally, by common accord, the members decided that the choir would sing without a director. They hoped that only the director's position was contaminated, and not the entire choir. It seemed safer that way. No one stuck out.

Without a leader, the choir became careless. The members veered away from the defensible union and Depression songs into celebrations of carnal love and drink. And why not, since the former repertoire had not gained them any points with the men in the castle at the bottom of Hertzina Street. It was Sammy Spielerman's theory of the blues all over again: the more the singers needed their hearts uplifted, the deeper the despair contained in their songs.

Instead of stopping the procedures, Borodin looked on with a slight smile, paying little attention to the choir's raucous entertainment. He was too busy totalling up his own losses. They began with the petty: there were now no more sandwiches to embellish the buffet. Fortunately, there was still vodka. Then they moved onto the symbolic, as he informed his proofreader Comrade Freedman once the choir had lurched into silence.

"Our printer has been moved again," he told Sonya. "The sector is virtually impossible to reach by tram. I'm going to have to take you out there. And since we've been pushed to the end of the line, there's a good chance we'll be going there rather late in the evening."

"Whatever's necessary to get the paper out," Sonya said.

"We will not admit defeat," Borodin promised her.

Without the buffet to provide a center of attention, the crowd milled around aimlessly. Those who swore they never drank without eating found they had changed their minds.

Borodin cleared his throat grandly. "Work beckons," he said, and made a quick move for the door.

But Gesser stepped into his path.

"I'm sure you know what happened to Pinsky," he told Borodin. "I can't believe he was a spy. He was too much of a smart-alec. You must have some influence, you've been around a long time. Can't you look into it for us? And while you're at it, can't you find out what happened to Lehto the Finn?"

Borodin smiled at Gesser's naivety.

"It's a delicate matter, dealing with enemies of the people. One must not express too great an interest. To have two enemies of the people is a very bad reflection on the Club, as you can imagine."

"Of course, of course. But if he really is a spy, or a saboteur, or whatever he's supposed to be, don't we have the right to know what he did and how he did it, so we can protect ourselves next time, and make sure it doesn't happen again?"

"Touché, Comrade Gesser. I will attempt to use your logic during my next meeting at the Kremlin."

"Pleased to be of service, Comrade Berg. Just don't say it came from me."

Borodin retreated, his big shoulders slumped.

"Why the hell did you call him Berg, you fool?" Sonya demanded of Gesser. "Pointing out a weak person's weak spot, when he already knows it better than you, is no way to help out."

Gesser watched Borodin close the door carefully and retreat into his quarters, the maze of rooms behind the newspaper office. Into his privacy, Gesser thought enviously. *Comrade Borodin sends his regards.* Gesser tried on the thought. *Mikhail Borodin, Enemy of the People.* The formula appeared senseless, idiotic, lunatic, like claiming that rain was dry, or that Lenin was an agent of capitalism. Borodin in Shanghai, Borodin in Chicago, Borodin organizing socialism in Mexico City, Borodin suffering a beating in the Barlini prison in Glasgow. Borodin, Lenin's translator. All for the Revolution. As far as everyone in this room was concerned, Borodin *was* the Revolution.

Sonya shook his arm. "I spoke to you. Are you not answering me now?"

That's the way Borodin talks, it occurred to Gesser. The exact same inflections, the elegant, slightly stilted forms. But why bother pointing that out?

A few weeks later, Gesser and Freedman were sitting side by side on the analysis couch, bowls of soup on their knees. Uncle Joe was on his usual perch, waiting for them to remember him with a cabbage leaf or a bit of root vegetable. Sonya had declared a truce with Uncle Joe. It wasn't the little primate's fault that Gesser had said he was glad he had a monkey and not a child. Unlike the rest of them, the monkey hadn't asked to come here.

"Borodin wants me to look after the paper tonight. He's going to drive me out there if he can find the gas."

"And if he can't?"

239

Sonya shrugged wearily. "He will."

Their spoons scraped against the bottom of their bowls, signalling meal time for Uncle Joe. The monkey skittered down from his perch and stood before Gesser. He had saved a piece of turnip for him.

"It's a long way to your next banana, buddy," he told the monkey. "This'll have to keep you in the meantime."

Uncle Joe took the tribute and returned to his perch. Like his benefactors, he had learned to eat slowly and deliberately.

"That damned monkey eats as well as we do," Sonya said.

She got to her feet and smoothed her dress. Then stood before Jack, her hands still running the length of the rough fabric of her dress, her mind on the ride she was about to take. It was a historical moment of a kind, but unlike those they had already known and appreciated. Jack opened his mouth to speak—he was about to ask her whether they hadn't had enough, whether she'd consider deserting this great failed experiment. But before he could find the words to admit the defeat of a lifetime, she turned and strode out.

That evening, the wind shifted in Moscow. Sonya Freedman stood on the sidewalk on Hertzina Street, waiting for Borodin to coax his motorcycle to life in the courtyard. She discovered she was shivering. The northern winds had finally beaten back the southern desert heat. Sonya rubbed the gooseflesh on her arms, bare under her light woollen shawl. She hugged herself tightly as Borodin came wheeling up on his chartreuse motorcycle with the gallant chrome stripe running the length of the sidecar.

They rode. In his leather coat and goggles, hair pushed against his skull by the wind, Borodin seemed oblivious to her. His eyes were on the streets of the city, not the city itself but what lay behind it, the hidden connections that others did not suspect until

it was too late. Borodin saw the steel rods that ran under the concrete structure of things. Or at least that's what Sonya imagined.
She figured she'd earned the luxurious escape that this brief wave
of feeling gave her. She felt Borodin through the road a foot
beneath her backside, the bump of the sidecar over the broken
bricks as they crossed Red Square. She felt him through the deafening effort of the motor. And through the kindness of the blanket
he had left folded on the seat, which she now spread over her
knees. She was drunk with the pleasure of speeding through a city
she had seen only from the sidewalk, as a weary walker or a soaked,
impatient tram rider. As they roared down the center of the
deserted quayside promenade, maneuvering around the potholes,
Sonya told herself that this moment justified and excused everything else. The city, briefly, belonged to her and Mikhail Borodin.

It was enough to make her forget where they were going to in
the middle of the night. An obscure State print-shop in an inac-
cessible part of the overgrown village, to which Borodin's interna-
tionalist paper had been demoted. Borodin knew this, even if his
passenger did not. He fed his machine more gas as he considered
his fate. He was going too fast. He glanced briefly at the sidecar
to see if there was fear on Sonya Freedman's face. Nothing but
ecstasy there. Western women! Did she not know she had hitched
her wagon to a falling star, or was it his fall that made him attractive? In his world, the company of women was a corollary to
power, a result of it, and now, at his least powerful point, this one
materializes to accompany him on his ride into . . . into the night.
Up ahead, without warning, the pavement disintegrated and he
dropped his speed. He considered the outcome had he accelerated. An accident, at this point, was as good a way out as any. But
why take this woman down with him?

*   *   *

The sky showed that flat kind of blackness it takes on in the small hours by the time Borodin and Sonya emerged from the print-shop. They had finally gotten the job done, after spending the requisite time haggling over whether it existed in the first place. You know you've lost your status in the State apparatus when its inefficiency takes over. A misplaced requisition order, a message left untransmitted, and you cease to exist. Instead of controlling the bureaucracy, you are its victim. You are sent to the back of the line, and when you finally reach the wicket, the employees have left for the day.

What do you do when this slippage occurs? You endure, you are patient, you never admit you have even noticed anything awry. You have done something to awaken the hostility of the system. You do not admit to it, so you can do nothing to appease it. Nothing but wait and hope that, by some miracle, you will be passed over. Not everyone cast into the sea in a storm will perish. You hope to be one of those left to tell the tale. There is always someone left; if there weren't, if no one was drawn from water, there would be no history, and we would know nothing of the suffering.

Borodin and Sonya Freedman left the printer's with their hefty stack of boxed newspapers. Borodin took a length of rough cord, tied the boxes to the rack on the back of the sidecar, behind Sonya's seat, and fired up the motorcycle again. Moving, he was invulnerable; moving fast was the best kind of invulnerability. And Sonya loved speed, too. The wind whipping at her headscarf and pushing her dress against her breasts, the heat of the engine keeping her warm, the feeling that this was an essential moment of the century, the sensation of being part of something larger than herself, yet intensely personal, which no one else in the world shared. Part of history, but better than it. Better than the drab, quarrelsome, self-justifying idealists of the attic fortress.

There was no surprise, then, when Borodin steered his motorcycle up the Boulevard Ring, and instead of turning into the top of Hertzina Street, cut left past the Foreign Ministry and coasted up to the gates of the Zoopark. A *tête-à-tête*, she thought happily, this is what I want. Not that there was any opportunity for them to negotiate their destination beforehand, and that was just as well; she was demoralized by the constant consensus-building of the attic room. The engine idled unevenly as Borodin fiddled with the Zoopark gates. The noise was deafening to Sonya's ears, as if every apparatchik in the Foreign Ministry could hear the commission of this eccentric crime. In the perilous autumn of 1938, when all indiscretion was to be avoided, Lenin's translator was breaking into the Zoopark in the dead of night, in the company of a foreign lady. Breaking in to be among the animals in their cages. The gate swung open and Borodin trotted back to the motorcycle. Then they were inside, rolling down the inclined cement walk to the swan and duck pond, the gate gently swinging closed behind them.

Borodin negotiated the walkway and headed towards the cages that offered some privacy. He shut off the engine next to where the white Siberian tiger lived, an animal extinct everywhere but in zoos. The tiger did not appear in the enclosure, though there was a prodigious hunk of meat on its cement floor, the shoulder of some mammal, a horse, Sonya hoped. A piece of meat like that, boiled into broth, could have served the tenants of the fortress Borodin for a week.

Borodin dismounted and helped Sonya out of the sidecar. She leaned against its chrome strip, her ears ringing from the engine's uproar.

"I often come here at night to consider the possibilities," Borodin said, gazing at the empty tiger cage. "The site is unusual, I admit. These days, we are encouraged by the State to examine ourselves and identify our vices. Retreating to this place is one of mine. No doubt I have others, too, worse ones . . . But this is the only place I know where I won't be disturbed. I suppose I must find some comfort in the company of animals."

"Animals don't talk back," Sonya noted.

"But they do. As a matter of fact they make excellent debating partners. They take whatever side of the debate you need them to take. But first you must understand their words. They speak, yes, but in their language, and you must learn it."

"And when you understand it, what do they say?"

"About what?"

Borodin looked at her quizzically. He was not used to explaining himself. He was a communicator, but he had never had to communicate *himself*. Revolutionary charisma had always freed him from that dreary, individualistic task.

"About the possibilities," Sonya specified. "The ones you come here to consider."

"The possibilities?" he mused. "What possibilities can there be when there are winners and losers? You win, or you lose."

"And we are losing."

"At one point we believed in exporting the Revolution. We believed that there was something, something real, tangible, called the workers of the world. I travelled the globe for that belief. But the wind shifted, as it has tonight."

Borodin shrugged off the chill that had fallen on his shoulders despite his leather jacket.

"The Russian xenophobia from before the Revolution has returned, only this time it is wearing the cloak of the Revolution. Which makes it more dangerous. Mind you, with what is developing on our western frontier, there is reason to be vigilant."

"So there really might be spies the way Jack says? People like Pinsky?"

"Spies? There have always been spies. Or people lacking in zeal. As for your Pinsky . . . it's obvious that in another time no one would have bothered with him. Maybe he is, maybe he isn't . . . A spy for what? For whom? That is my first question. But that question doesn't necessarily interest everyone. In some quarters, a man can be a spy without being a spy for some particular nation or cause. This is a new and perverse kind of Platonism."

"And what goes for a man goes for a woman, too?"

"Yes, a woman, too. That is conceivable, though less likely. We are not completely egalitarian yet, not like in your country." Borodin laughed dryly. "Which is probably a good thing for women. As for Pinsky . . . think of him as a symptom."

Suddenly, Sonya reached up and clung to Borodin fiercely. Borodin and his coarse, oily leather jacket with the smell of Moscow on it, the closest solid thing in this desperate time. His tragedy dignified him. He was like a poised, careful, lucid acrobat about to tumble off a very high tightrope, who had known the outcome of the exercise ahead of time.

Sonya wrestled with the leather headgear that protected his eyes.

"Take those things off, silly! I don't want to kiss a man in a mask."

Ah, the not-so-discreet charm of Western women! They were unseducible, but they did make things easy for a man, once they decided on the object of their . . . Borodin hesitated to call it affection. He hung his headgear on the handlebars of the motorcycle. He caught a brief glimpse of himself in the little round sideview mirror. The man who peered back was decidedly perplexed, and had still not lost that grim twist to his mouth. Definitely not the face of a seducer.

A motorcycle parked in a zoo provides little comfort for lovers. Sonya Freedman provided the answer, unburdened as she was by the need to appear inexpert in these matters. She made a pillow with his blanket, then reached under her dress and freed herself from her underthings, but kept her shawl on against the raw air. Borodin loosened his rope belt and took down his trousers, then lowered himself into the deep sidecar. It was awkward, but possible. Then, like an angel from heaven, she descended upon him, wings spread.

"You have ingenuity," he complimented her.

"It is the only way to unite," she told him in sweet parody of his gallant, formal English.

When they were joined, the white Siberian tiger emerged from its hiding place in the pavilion into the cage behind them. Studiously, with mute animal comprehension, it watched through the heavy, reinforced bars of its cell as Sonya settled upon Borodin and rode him with surprising grace, considering their improvised bed. Borodin sat upright, a little awkwardly, his back straight, staring forward sightlessly, his hands under Sonya's dress, moving with her movement. It looked as though he were piloting his motorcycle from his seat in the sidecar. The white Siberian tiger observed the copulatory dance and ignored the hunk of meat, which was nothing more than the shoulder of an EOP that had turned a shimmering, rotten green. The animal itself was on its way to extinction as surely as the lovers it watched. It might have wanted to roar in affirmation of the human activity it was witnessing, but the procedure carried out on its vocal chords prevented it. No roaring was permitted within earshot of the Foreign Ministry.

Sonya and Mikhail Borodin had not come together for pleasure's sake. There are times when pleasure is not the point, and this was one of them. Their lovemaking was a political act, a sacrament by the losers, a way of admitting they'd lost. But with all that was strange and exotic and tragic—the winking, all-seeing lights of the Foreign Ministry, the tiger extinct everywhere but in this zoo, the impossible cocoon of the sidecar, the chill air on their faces and the heat between their legs—how could pleasure not flood through them? Sonya closed her eyes to shut out the tiger. Her pleasure was like tumbling down an elevator shaft where Borodin waited for her, a sword, a ghost, a black block of granite.

She would not let him go until false morning had begun to glow beyond the pointed pickets of the Zoopark's iron fence and he had delivered himself of all his seed. They heard the squawking disagreement of birds from the pond, as the nocturnals met the awakening day birds. Slowly, Sonya became aware of how uncomfortable it is to kneel on a half-naked man in a motorcycle sidecar.

She wrapped her shawl tighter against the pre-dawn air and slipped on her underthings in front of the tiger cage. The tiger appeared, attracted by the scent.

"Where to now?" she asked it.

"Pardon me?" said Borodin.

He was painfully extracting himself from the sidecar, obviously unaccustomed to such a position.

"I was speaking to an animal. I was asking about the possibilities."

"What did it say?"

"I don't know. I don't speak tiger."

Borodin came up behind her, kissed her hair, attempted to retie her chignon.

"That was beautiful," he told her.

"And necessary."

He held her breasts from behind as they stood before the cage.

"I wanted you from the first time I saw you," he told her.

"Back when you were the Messiah of Division Street?" she teased.

Borodin grimaced at the mention of the old days, and put on his headgear. Sonya sat back in what had been their lovers' couch.

The leather seat was slick with their juices. Borodin started up the engine and, as quietly as possible on a Soviet motorcycle with a misfiring engine and poorly refined gasoline, a battered muffler and a blown-out exhaust pipe, they eased out of the Zoopark and across the great cobbled square of the Foreign Ministry.

The ground rumbled beneath them, marking the subway's progress through the soft, treacherous, counterrevolutionary soil that underlay the city. They drove past the Barricades Station, grand and empty as it waited for the tunnels below to be completed, a monument in the neo-Greek style that Stalin preferred. A rotunda, columns, everything in perfect order.

Sonya and Borodin did not discuss. They kissed on the landing by the *Moscow Daily News* office, on the stairway, on the Street of the Heart. *Kiss*, Sonya recalled, was the first word of Russian Gesser had taught her on the *Île-de-France*. *Goodbye* was the second.

That morning the paper would be late, but who would notice?

11

THE GIN MILL CLOSES DOWN

Comrades continued to send their regards, but since their names were unfamiliar to Jack and Sonya, they had no more effect on them than did any of the other rumors of war and prison generated in the fortress Borodin. Lehto and Pinksy may well have never existed; Mafili's Law did. The two EOPs sent no word, no one inquired after them, and Borodin's attempts at locating them, or even discovering the nature of their crimes, were unsuccessful. There were so many such cases. And so many men named Pinsky, which did not help. At the Anglo-American Club, the rudderless choir sang on. Who could blame them? It was their nature to sing. And what they sang were the rollicking, undisciplined, nihilist tunes of their wilder days; they'd suddenly taken a liking to "Cakewalking Babies from Home."

During those Anglo-American Club soirées, Borodin looked on, dreamily watching Sonya's red chignon bobbing above a sea of faces he barely noticed, and wondering what a cakewalking baby was. He took comfort in his ignorance. If he didn't know what a cakewalking baby was, he, that noted Anglophile and specialist in all things American, there was little chance any political commissar would know, should the thing turn out to belong to the realm of Enemies of the People.

Poor Borodin, he was truly outside the current of the times. Too concerned with what words meant to realize that if there was one whose meaning was unknown, that in itself was criminal.

The three policemen arrived during a particularly raucous rendition of "Cakewalking Babies from Home." The long leather-belted jackets, the caps low on the forehead, the holsters making an ostentatious bulge under their clothes, looked distinctly out of place. It was funny: none of the members of the Anglo-American Club choir had actually seen a member of the secret police, yet they all knew to stop singing when the three men entered the room.

Their leader hopped onto the stage as the song tailed off.

"Excellent discipline," he said in the sudden silence. He surveyed the choir, the room and Borodin with predatory pleasure. "If only you had displayed such discipline earlier in your careers as builders of socialism. International builders of socialism, you call yourselves. As if such a thing could exist. You are adventurers, nothing more. Who leads this choir?"

There was no response.

"I asked you frightened little creatures who the leader of this choir is!"

Silence again. The policeman reached for his gun.

Gesser stepped forward. "I think they're trying to tell you that there is no leader."

The policeman's hand dropped. "Ah, there is one who talks Russian perfectly. Very good! It is unusual for a foreigner to speak our language. They say it is too difficult for them."

"I learned Russian the way you did—from my mother."

"Excellent! In that case, tell the choir they are leaving with me for a short investigation of their musical tastes."

Gesser did as he was told. He lent his tongue to the enemy. There's a danger in knowing too many languages. Sometimes you are forced to speak to people you would have preferred to ignore.

The choir shuffled timorously down the stairs, followed by the authoritative thud of the policemen's boots. They went unprepared, without their hankie packs, which most had ready under their beds. But their beds were upstairs, in the attic, in the fortress Borodin, and that might as well have been miles away. No one can be prepared all the time, especially when you don't know from which direction the attack will come, and when you have such meager experience in these matters.

On the first landing, in a mournful, minor key, in voices that would have made the black stones of the Kolyma weep, the choir began to sing:

> Say, don't you remember
> they called me "Al"
> It was Al all the time
> Say, don't you remember
> I'm your pal . . .

What would the pens of Tin Pan Alley have said had they known their inventions were being sung by a choir on its way to the Lubyanka? *Don't blame us,* most likely. *We got out, and we had the horse sense to stay out.*

Sonya turned to Borodin. "Can *all* of them be enemies of the people, all at once?"

But Borodin had slipped out the door.

That evening, in the chateau, in the upstairs fortress, Sonya Freedman reclined on the analysis couch and devised charges against the members of the Anglo-American Club choir. Seditious Negroid-Jewish music—no, wait, that would be a Nazi charge. Inability to speak Russian. Lack of discipline. Internationalism. Adventurism. Corruption, sabotage, counterrevolutionary activities disguised behind the off-key singing of "Cakewalking Babies from Home." She didn't know what a cakewalking baby was any more than Borodin did. See, right there, through that crack in the structure, that shadow of a doubt, that sliver of an entrance, that was where the enemy entered. *Cakewalk.* It could have been a code word for the fascist fifth column.

And why not?

She tried on the charges herself and found they fit quite comfortably. Part of Sonya wished she had been arrested with the choir. The wish was more than the guilt of the survivor, the one who'd been spared. She was exhausted from the suspense, from the effort of realizing that, yes, the impossible was possible, and not just for others, for her as well.

The attic was unnaturally quiet that night. Uncle Joe played dispiritedly by the cold kerosene stove, scratching at the floor for crumbs that might have escaped human attention. Jack was gone, too. After the choir was led away, he announced that this time someone had to go to the Lubyanka and ask after the comrades, and he was going to be the one. And down the stairs he went.

With so many tenants gone, Mafili was able to push her rag and stick into corners usually forbidden her. She finally made her way into the chateau, came to Sonya, stood above her, wanted to speak.

Instead, she placed her hand gently, maternally, on the back of Sonya's neck. There, she felt the extra bulk that was so sweet to the touch. Then she touched her stomach.

"You are pregnant, daughter," she told Sonya.

Sonya nodded.

"And the father?"

"He doesn't know."

Mafili nodded. That was the normal course of things.

"I always thought it was a shame to do without that pleasure, just because times are hard," Mafili said. "They are always hard, yet the world turns. God bless you."

Mafili bent and kissed her on the forehead, then the cheeks. Sonya reached up and embraced her, more fiercely than she had Borodin that night in the Zoopark, when she'd known she would get pregnant even before their bodies had separated. Sonya clung to Mafili, the only force that stood between her and oblivion. Mafili held her, then grew embarrassed and broke off the embrace, and picked up her rag and stick again. But before she continued her rounds, she told Sonya in primitive Russian that she would look after her, even if nobody else did, that she would raise the child, alone if that was necessary, and that she hoped it was a boy because, even in a society where men and women were supposed to be equal in their suffering, men, somehow, still controlled it.

In the middle of the night, Sonya was awakened by a tuneless rendition of "Cakewalking Babies from Home," a song that was developing nightmarish echoes.

The choir had returned triumphant, and they intended on everyone knowing it. Somehow, on the march back from the Lubyanka to Hertzina Street, they had bartered or bought a full liter of potato vodka.

"We went to the Lubyanka!" a voice shouted.

"And we even came back!"

"A first," the first voice jubilated. "A world premier!"

"Cause for celebration! So, we celebrate!"

"I'm celebrating by packing my bags," a dissident voice said glumly. "I didn't come here to get arrested for singing some silly *schwartze* song. Did you see the mugs on those bulls?"

"Yes, but aren't we back here, and free again?"

"Sure, for the time being. They don't want us here. Didn't they make it plain enough?"

"Now, boys, we're all on the same side here," came the voice of a peacemaker.

Sonya turned her head towards Jack's bed. Waves of nausea followed her movement. *Morning sickness*, she thought, *in the middle of the night*. Jack was gone. Still out on his fool's errand. In the state she was in, Sonya could spare only a passing thought for him.

Disturbed by the choir's celebrations, Uncle Joe skittered into the chateau, then stopped short to await Sonya's welcome. She patted the couch next to her and the monkey gratefully jumped up.

"Blessed be the Almighty, who hath created the fruit of the potato," the recent political prisoners blasphemed gaily from behind the sheets and partitions.

"How bad can it be? Here we are, after all."

"They let us go. It was a misunderstanding."

And so went the round of self-comforting justifications that followed the bottle, hand to hand, mouth to mouth. Whoever had dissented was silent, or too busy packing his bags to debate. When the choir burst into ragged song praising the virtues of the lowly potato, Sonya got to her feet, motioned Uncle Joe to stay, then smoothed the wrinkles from her dress. It's the middle of the night, I'm freezing and I'm sick, she thought. Do I have to be surrounded by madmen on top of it?

Sonya made it to the door unnoticed and stole down the stairway. On the landing, two floors below, no lights burned behind the door of the *Moscow Daily News*. Sonya stepped into the darkness. Habit guided her among the desks and long tables and Remingtons. At the rear of the office was a solid oak door with leather padding. Borodin's retreat. His waiting-place.

She pushed the door open and found Mikhail Borodin lying in lamplight, fully dressed, his eyes closed. His hands were crossed over his barrel chest. The scene was like a death watch. The corpse was present. Now, enter the mourner.

The bedside chair squeaked when Sonya sank into it. Borodin opened one eye.

"Sonya," he said dreamily. "How lucky I am that it is you."

"I woke you, I'm sorry."

"No, I never sleep. I was waiting. Waiting for you."

"The choir is back. They're drinking upstairs."

"They found something to drink? Let them drink, then. They are becoming good Russians."

"No. They talk too much to be Russians."

Borodin opened the other eye. "Well spoken." He smiled weakly. "I suppose I should speak more . . . personally with you. I promise I will. I will be less Russian. It won't be easy, not the way we have been made . . . Did everyone who went come back?"

"I didn't count them."

"It is no matter. The choir doesn't matter. The apparatus doesn't care about the cakewalking babies from home. What is a cakewalk, anyway?"

"I couldn't tell you."

"You must ask Comrade Gesser. He knows about such details of American life. My English is strictly classical. I am a classical man.

255

Your husband is a man of the people. By the way, where is he? Did he visit the Lubyanka?"

"No. He disappeared. They didn't arrest him. He disappeared on his own."

"A good decision, perhaps. But the night . . . It is cold out there. Cold, endless, endless night. Do you know how distant day can be?"

"I am learning, comrade."

A silence settled over the room. A silence of the night.

"If the apparatus doesn't care about the cakewalking babies from home," asked Sonya after a while, "what does it care about?"

Borodin gave a shallow laugh. "We have been working together too long. You are beginning to be like me, asking questions whose answers you already know. They are speaking to me, through the choir. The choir, Lehto, Pinsky, it is the same . . . ."

"Symptom."

"Yes."

"And what is the disease?"

"The disease? The disease?" Borodin's voice rose in a kind of outrage against Sonya's naivety. "The disease is death, woman!"

"And you are lying here, waiting for it."

Borodin sighed.

"The questions you Western women ask! Yes, I am here. You want me to go for a walk, like Comrade Gesser? You can call this waiting if you like. It *is* waiting. But what do you suggest I do? Escape? And where do you suggest I escape to? The United States of America, which I worked to unsettle? Fascist Germany? Scotland, where they broke my handsome nose in Barlini? Or how about self-imposed, internal exile: escape into my own country? Yes, the Soviet Union is a very big place. But I am a very big person. And here one doesn't just travel idly from place to place. This is not a country where hoboism is permitted."

Borodin sat up on his bed. He patted the pillow that cushioned his head from the wall.

"Soon, perhaps rocks will replace this soft pillow I have grown used to. So why don't I avoid this fate? Because it *is* my fate. This is my country, my place. I worked to build it. Its fate is my fate."

"I found it easier to leave my country. My countries."

Borodin reached for her and she came into his arms.

"Of course it was easier for you, that's normal. You were not a creator of that system, you did not build it and it did not build you."

He loosened her chignon. Her hair tumbled down, golden red in the lamplight, the softness that every prisoner misses most.

"Besides," he admitted, "part of me must actually like this."

"So it makes sense that if I'm not wedded to this country the way you are, I must still be able to escape it. If I wanted to."

"That is your decision to make. Surely you have had ample time to consider it. Of course, it is not your decision alone. It depends on your passport status, and the strength of your will, and the mysteries of the apparatus."

Borodin gathered in the harvest of her hair, curled and sculpted it and groomed her. He kissed and bit the nape of her neck.

"I love that chubby bit of flesh on a woman. At least you are getting enough to eat."

Sonya Freedman opened her mouth to tell him what she owed that extra flesh to, then changed her mind. They didn't have the leisure to speak of it. If there was need to, and opportunity, she would tell him later. He would be proud, no doubt. Jack she would tell, whenever he decided to return. He was different. He was a man of the people, he would know how to adapt.

Though perhaps Borodin did have some sense of Sonya's state, an instinct that was better than knowledge. He reached into the pile of books and papers by the bedside lamp and pushed them aside with sudden urgency.

"Here, a little token for you." He opened his hand. "If I am arrested, it will only be confiscated, and do no good for anyone, except for some policeman's whore. It is right for you to have it. I'm giving it back to its rightful owner. Like all of us, it has travelled a lot, and not always known where it was going, and what use it could have. And like you, it is beautiful and red and glowing."

It was as Sonya had imagined. Czar Nikolai's ruby. The Cape Haitian ruby.

"This stone has been following me around for practically the whole decade," she said.

"May it be useful to you. I suspect it will be more so for you than for me. Think of it as an insurance policy, like that passport of yours. It's the gift of escape, if you can ever use it that way."

That night she knew the luxury of a bed, a big bed with sheets and blankets and pillows and a backboard, and no bugs. As she drifted towards sleep with Borodin still resting on her, she thought briefly of Jack, and what would be if he came home in the night and found her couch empty. She did not stir. For once, let me have the grace of forgetting, she begged, and sleep granted her that wish.

When did Jack Gesser and Sonya Freedman truly know that things had gone terribly and definitively wrong in the workers' paradise? When Lehto, then Pinsky, then others sent their regards? No. It was when they themselves did. The horror that surrounds us is never truly real until it happens to us. Until then, we are the chosen ones. The spared. Others are cut down but we will live forever. Eternally spared until it is too late to see that such a fate cannot exist.

What was Jack Gesser's life like during his time of walking? Unspeakable, but free and full of lunatic hope. Unlike Borodin, he believed he could disappear into the country. Space would envelop him like a great cloak of anonymity. He had money in his pocket, he knew the language, no one knew him. In that splendid naivety, Gesser had never been more American.

The night the choir was arrested, he did do what he swore he would. He walked to the bottom of Hertzina Street, he crossed the top of Red Square, passed the Hotel Metropol and climbed the slope to the Lubyanka, whose pale pink facade dominated the boulevard. Gesser did all that, and when he came to the Lubyanka, he kept on walking. Wisely so. He decided he would walk forever. As long as he was on the move, out of the fortress Borodin, in the street, he was untouchable. He would stay there until the storm blew over. However long that took.

He walked with his head down. It was a kind of instinct, an ancestral memory, the way that survivors of dictatorships still talk with a hand over their mouths long after the hated tyrant is in the ground. As he walked, he looked exactly like an anti-hero from one of the books he'd read—and we know what becomes of anti-heroes in a country full of positive thinkers. At some point, he turned north, past the Zabatskaya residence for foreign idealists. It looked deserted—strange in this time when so many had to share the same room. He journeyed to the gates of the Loputchkha plant that had put so much metal into his lungs and bloodstream, then banned him as an undesirable. He stood before the factory and gazed enviously at the outlines of the glowing forges behind the dirty glass panels. But it was no place to linger; he moved on. Everywhere he went he marvelled at the absence of neighborhoods, of street life, of the places made for the random encounters that make up a city's fabric. The wind was cold, snow flurries fell in great squalls. That was just as well, for at the rate he was walking, he would have burned up like an asteroid had the weather been warmer.

He stopped to catch his breath in front of the Greek revival
gates of the Park of the People's Economic Realizations. He drew
his hand across his forehead; it came back smudged black. Last
summer's peat grime, still riding the wind. In front of the gates, a
bow-legged, potato-shaped matron was tending to the saddle
sores on the donkey that gave children rides among Stalin's neo-
classical temples. The woman's body proved it was possible to be
both fat and undernourished. It was the middle of the night, the
children were busy with their nightmares, the Park's temples
loomed dark and formless against the sky, but it did not matter: the
woman continued in the commission of her duties. Another ant on
the anthill, and a comfort to Gesser, for who would come to arrest
him, an innocent man, in front of witnesses? In the overgrown village there was always someone near. A vendor, waiting patiently,
unconcerned with sales. With a tree behind to lean against, or a
stool if he was particularly prosperous. Two patriarchs playing
chess with snow falling on their pieces. Sandhogs popping out of
the ground like primitive earth spirits. And the construction gang
endlessly tearing up the sidewalk in front of the Conservatory in
an act of State terrorism against music.

Gesser suffered most the pre-dawn hours. Once he raised his
tired eyes and saw a sign he first took for a mirage. There was a
rough drawing of a wine glass, and in Roman numerals the hours
of operation. A bar that did not open until well past midnight.
Amazing, thought Gesser blearily, that the State would permit
such a place designed for the inebriation of the sleepless. But when
he went inside, every pore of his skin buzzed with danger. Some
of the patrons were drinking; others were not. Strangely, the poorest seemed to be drinking the most, while the better dressed gentlemen sipped tea, or ordered nothing at all. As they abstained,
they waited for someone to utter something culpable.

Gesser moved on. Drink would have only diluted the madness of his exercise.

Unfortunately, it is impossible to live like this forever. If you are Jack Gesser, you must tell someone of your unspeakable new life. And then there is the problem of fatigue. Gesser was so nauseous with exhaustion that it finally overpowered his fear. Dangerously, he began to drift back towards the center of the city, crossing the Garden Ring, then the Boulevard Ring. He came upon the top of Hertzina Street and the *Pravda* mansion.

The next thing Jack Gesser knew, he was being shaken out of his scratchy straw bed by two secret policemen with corrosive onion breath.

"You can't be here," Gesser told them in Yiddish, the language of his dreams.

"Oh yes we can," one of them answered in the same tongue.

The shock woke Gesser up fully. He opened his eyes and looked into the pitted face of the Jewish policeman.

"Ein yiddish politzyhant?"

"We believe in the Revolution, too. Remember, it freed us."

The Jewish cop got Gesser onto his feet, perhaps a little more gently than his Gentile partner would have done. A small concession to his co-religionist. Sometimes, the polite torturer is crueler than his coarser brother.

Gesser took a step and stumbled. *The arrest pack*, he thought, and searched wildly for it. But it didn't exist, any more than this moment was supposed to. Sonya had a pack; he would take hers. But he couldn't remember where she kept it. Perhaps it was just as well she wasn't there to tell him. She was spared the spectacle of Gesser, naked and shivering, crawling around the dusty floor of the fortress Borodin in his desperate search for the little bundle. That is the problem with the hankie pack: rationally conceived, it cannot be found in irrational times.

Gesser cast around for his clothes, and though it was not yet winter, he knew enough to put on his longjohns and wool tunic and sweater and greatcoat, clothes for exile in the north, a place whose existence he had refused to admit until now.

"Who are his investigators?" Mafili asked Sonya.

"I don't know. I don't think he has any."

Mafili shook her head.

"That is a bad sign. He must have investigators. If he does not, he will be forgotten."

"If only Borodin were here!"

"Don't call upon the departed, daughter," Mafili advised her.

"Why didn't they arrest me?"

"You are only a whore of an Enemy of the People."

"Some whore I am! A pregnant whore!"

Sonya raised her arms to display her body. Nothing appeared any different. Only a practiced woman's eye such as Mafili's would have seen the signs.

"I still don't understand why they'd care about us."

"You have to truly be a nobody for them not to care about you. You have to be like me. It is a skill to be that low, and I have it. Otherwise, in our society, we care about everyone. Even the foreigner."

In the former fortress Borodin, there was not much left to do but speculate on these matters and play with Uncle Joe. After the choir's first trip to the Lubyanka, those who had decided to leave, and been permitted to, had done so. Those who hadn't now sent their regards. Or was it regrets? In the attic, only two women remained: Mother Russia and the pregnant Freedman. Two women and a monkey, the latter bewildered by the loss of so many of its playmates, and by the cold, slanting sleet that pelted the windows.

Mafili kept her promise. She looked after Sonya. Her first act was to accompany her to the Lubyanka. The two women were the first and only fortress Borodin residents to go to the prison of their own free will.

There, Sonya saw how delicate her position was. She had come to inquire after two prisoners. One was her husband, to whom she was not married: the EOP Gesser. The other was her lover, whose tiny seed she carried: the EOP Borodin. The State had some difficulty assimilating this information. Though its structures were labyrinthine, and ruled over by a Byzantine, it did not have classifications for the maze of the human heart and all its nonproductive labor.

At the Lubyanka, Sonya discovered how important her lover really was. At the wicket where the guards handled the prisoners' families, they refused to believe that she, a foreign woman, could be inquiring after Mikhail Borodin, *the* Borodin, or that such a man could have been held in their jail, where so many common criminals were locked up. One guard, who must have remembered the short decade of idealism after the Revolution when Borodin's star had burned most brightly, scoffed at the idea of his arrest. After that public ideological error, Sonya and Mafili never saw the man again.

At the prison wicket, Mafili flew into action.

"I swear on your mother's eyes that I'm going to gouge out that everything this woman says is true!"

The guards agreed to receive Sonya's inquiries.

"What is your relation to the EOP Gesser?"

"Wife."

"And to the EOP Borodin?"

"I am his whore."

"I have no such classification," the guard informed her. "I will put down 'sister.'"

"It's all the same to me," she assured them.

With their inquiry registered, the two women walked through the sleet back to Hertzina Street. Low winter clouds hovered over the city, leaden and ominous with snow. Under her shawl and shapeless broad coat and beaten boots, Sonya Freedman was beginning to resemble Mafili, at least from the back. As they trudged through the brown sea of mud and frozen slush, Mafili mumbled and complained about the state of everything: the sidewalks, the weather, the price of cabbage, the configuration of the universe. She was unhappy. Her code had been disturbed. From the safety of being a nobody, she had emerged to become a somebody: a person who goes inquiring after prisoners. If you look for trouble, you will find it. Now they knew her name. They knew she knew a foreigner.

But she'd had no choice. She had sworn to help a sister in need, even one lunatic enough to boast to the Lubyanka guards that she was an EOP's whore. That's how the contamination spreads— through human compassion. That's what the system counts on. Mafili found some bitter consolation in this thought. With things the way they were, lie as low as you like, sooner or later they'll spot you. In the early winter of 1938, trouble had a way of finding just those people who went out of their way not to look for it.

In front of the Conservatory, the street crew blasted on, digging the same pit it had filled the week before, shit-colored mud flying in great geysers out of the excavation and along the Street of the Heart. Mafili stopped and touched Sonya's stomach, as if it were wealth they both shared.

"You need a rest. Why don't you go listen to a concert? I'll go back and cook something."

There was nothing to cook, and no kerosene to cook it with, but why state the obvious? Mafili pressed a coin into Sonya's hand

and turned away, tramping up the street through the mud towards their lodgings.

The concert had already begun. The usheress gave Sonya the disapproving look she reserved for those philistines who arrived late. Sonya crept up to the highest rows of the balcony, where there were still a few free seats, the squishing of her boots and the creaking of the wooden steps sounding obscenely loud in this temple of quiet. She declined the offer of a program. It was of no consequence who was playing, and what the pieces were. All her concentration went to easing her wet boots off her feet without attracting the attention of her fellow music-lovers. The awkward bending process of the pregnant woman, the wrestling with the laces fused tight with frozen mud, the triumph and relief when the foot finally emerged from the boot.

To her terror, she saw that the pages of the *Moscow Daily News* she had used to line her boots were still clinging to the bottom of her foot-rags, in full sight of a row of concertgoers. The *Moscow Daily News*, a banned paper, its publisher an established Enemy of the People. She might as well have stood up in the middle of the pianist's recital and praised Hitler.

The strange and horrible logic of the State! Perfect, hermetic laws built on the absolute denial of chaos. The absence of accidents or chance occurrences. Total personal responsibility combined with the valuelessness of the individual. If a comrade had leaky boots and cold feet, and was using newspapers to alleviate the problem, as all comrades did, a page from a banned or disgraced publication in the boot could not be an accident. That page signified that the comrade was acquainted with the publication, had touched it, had *chosen* to put it in his boot. And, therefore, was guilty of everything the paper was guilty of. Because the truth will always come out, with the same dreadful stink of a cardboard sole and an unwashed foot-rag.

Sonya Freedman did her best to wiggle her foot back into her boot. Next time, use *Pravda*, she reminded herself. She glanced up and down the row. Had anyone seen her? Should she flee? Would she be followed and arrested?

The rest of the concert, with its brilliantly executed interpretations, offered scant solace.

Soviet logic was also at work in the tombs of the Lubyanka. Give us a man and we'll build you a case, the logic was called. A man's entire life is a document, and somewhere in that document is something culpable. You just have to know how to read it. Between the lines, if necessary. Jack Gesser, having been arrested, was guilty, but the State had nothing on him. Early on in his residence in the Lubyanka, his investigators came to request his help. As usual, there were two of them.

"If you have no trial, you will never be sentenced. Without a sentence, you will remain in this cell forever. If you do not have a sentence, you cannot serve it, you cannot finish it, you will be a prisoner in perpetuity."

The investigators' logic was unimpeachable. And it had powerful allies: the damp black cell, the salty food and lack of water, the sleep deprivation, the pants that, in the absence of a belt, kept slipping down to Gesser's knees.

"To have a trial, there must be charges. Even in your country it is like that."

"I'm a Soviet citizen," Gesser interrupted the investigator.

"Yes, of course. Otherwise you would probably not be here," the investigator smiled thinly. "You will devise these charges yourself, and we will investigate them and decide on the appropriate punishment."

Lazy dogs, Gesser concluded. Then the second investigator stated the ideological aim of the exercise.

"It is essential for you to display the correct self-critical attitude. We are not interested in results alone. We are interested in changing and improving the man. We are interested in the knowledge of the heart."

And with that, the two investigators swept out of Gesser's cell, into the light. Gesser noticed they had left pencil and paper behind. Not much of either, really. His self-criticism would have to be brief.

A less co-operative prisoner might have written *stick it up your ass* on the sheet provided. Not Gesser. He still had hope that his words could make a difference. And as one who hopes, he was ideal prey for his investigators. But don't blame him for that. In a windowless cell the size of an immigrant's trunk underneath the streets of Moscow, dying of thirst and fatigue, the first thing any of us would do is hope. Gesser picked up the sheet and pencil stub. He positioned himself under the crack in the stone wall through which a little light and air came in. In that grey rectangle in the larger black square of his cell, he sat and thought, *Whatever could I have done wrong?*

A less philosophical man would have asked himself, *What crimes will get me the fewest years?* Not Gesser. He reflected. For once, he had the leisure to think. Thinking was his freedom, his defense against insanity. His pride, too. He would leave something behind, the writings of an educated man who had been prevented from using his mind by the misfortunes of the century. He would give his investigators a dense page of confession and inquiry and let them puzzle it out. It would be his finest hour.

He took up the pencil stub. Too short, too dull to be used as an instrument of self-destruction, though had he devised some way of killing himself with it—swallowing it and choking to death, perhaps—the State would not have minded. Normally, it regarded suicide with the same disgust as did the Catholic Church. Unless, of course, it was politically motivated, in which case it was willing to assist.

Gesser touched the paper. Soft with humidity. The great negative heroes, from Dostoevsky down to Old Man Poklub, gathered silently at his side as he made his statement.

I returned to the Soviet Union to remake my past. It was a past of blood and burning, where a boy is made a man at a young age, by violence. The kind of past many of us had before the Revolution.

There, Jack thought, I have praised the regime. Perhaps they'll see the mistake they made in imprisoning me. But he had not confessed to any crimes yet. That was the purpose of confession, not just to praise the confessor.

Because I came for reasons that could be thought of as personal, you might find me guilty of idealism. But the Revolution is not an adventure for me. I have always supported the goals of the Revolution and sought in it the meaning otherwise absent from the life of a small man. Perhaps this is individualism.

Gesser reread. At least now he was confessing. That was a start. But something was lacking. Some detail that would set him apart from the great army of confession-writers. There was not much paper left, though.

Perhaps I would have been better off staying in the West, peddling watermelons off a cart. But watermelons are a waste of a man's life, especially an educated man. I considered going to California but I was sick at the very idea of watermelons. I came here instead, in good faith.

In good faith? The formulation was absurd; it was ahistorical. But he could not change it. The pencil had no eraser, and scratched-out words in a confession are not a good sign.

Somehow I ended up on the wrong side of the fence. How did that happen? Let me try to explore the question.

Gesser's confession ended there. Did the knobby point of his pencil give out, or did he run out of paper? Or did he realize suddenly, as he shivered in the damp cell at the sound of a fellow prisoner's screams, that this was no more than a cruel charade?

The answer to that riddle is in a file somewhere, still preserved today. The State, you must know, has a particular love for its own archives, even the most shameful sort.

12

ALMA-ATA

The blanket of snow on the Moscow streets deepened with each of the women's visits to the Lubyanka. The pilgrimage took on the quality of some quack therapy. You went to the prison, not for any reason that might influence reality, but for your own needs, to unburden yourself to someone who didn't care. For you, it was the only catharsis permitted. As winter wore on, Sonya realized she didn't give a damn about either man. She had been pushed past caring. She sleepwalked through a state of nonbeing, and she was happy for the Moscow winter that so expertly reproduced the season in her own heart.

Giving up hope is a necessary step. At a certain point, you must give in to despair and relinquish hope. Otherwise, you will find it impossible to live in times like these, moved by every random act of the State.

Sonya confided none of this to Mother Russia. Mafili believed in hope, or so she professed. Hope manufactured from crumbs, from dust, from dry skin-flecks. It is good, she told Sonya, that Gesser had at least been assigned investigators. The little man's case would be decided soon. Any decision is a blessing. A decision means a sentence, and every day that passes and the prisoner stays alive means that sentence is a day shorter.

The big man in the equation, the EOP Borodin, was a more delicate case. At times he seemed to have slipped entirely out of existence. Either he had never been arrested, or no reference to him could be found, or his case had already been disposed of, but was classified.

All of these were possible, even simultaneously.

"A bad sign," Mafili predicted.

Her words were a superstitious tag-line, a kind of verbal throwing of salt over the shoulder.

The troika of Mafili, Sonya and Uncle Joe clung to their attic real estate in the old fortress Borodin. As the year of grace 1939 began, the impossible seemed to have happened. They had been forgotten. How long can this go on? Sonya wanted to ask Mafili, but dared not. The question was the worst kind of blasphemy in the religion of survival—call it luck, if you will—that they were practicing. Below them, the offices of the *Moscow Daily News* remained locked, unoccupied, as if under quarantine due to ideological contagion. The city rattled on its way, the pipe-laying crews blasted away down the street in front of the Conservatory, but the attic was unnaturally quiet. Cold, Sonya discovered, has a silence to it unlike any other.

A monkey in winter, Uncle Joe had no appreciation of the kind of endurance the two women practiced.

"What's the matter with you? This can't be your first winter," Sonya said to him. Uncle Joe replied with a morose look. He was unhappy. He was growing thin; his coat, patchy. It wasn't the monkey's first Moscow winter, but it was his first in these circumstances. In better days, when he'd first come to the attic, there was always a cabbage leaf or a bit of tuber around the stock pot, and a jovial choir member to charm for the handout. Now, even the carrot and apple peel were forbidden him. They were dried in an enclosure especially designed to keep him out, and when they were ready, hot water was poured over them, and the resulting mixture drunk as tea. Once, Uncle Joe discovered a neglected section of spine from a smoked salt mackerel. The monkey sniffed at it, wrinkled up his nose from the greasy salt smell, then put it down. He was obviously not hungry enough.

In the false safety of their anonymity, they never had the chance to learn that Jack was going on trial. When he stepped into the Lubyanka theater that was the courtroom, blinking against even the yellow, low-wattage bulbs, he surveyed the room in despair. Sonya was not there; he deduced that she, too, had been arrested. The courtroom benches were filled with trial vultures. Those old crones, all female, or what passed for female, with nothing better to do than attend political trials. They were well served. They mocked his baggy trousers and the way he had to hold them up with one hand, they egged on the prosecutors, they demanded more outlandish accusations from them and more spectacular confessions from Gesser, and more outrageous punishment from the magistrate. In nearly every case, their wishes were granted.

One cold morning Gesser was standing in the Mayakovsky Yard with a group of Enemies of the People, awaiting transfer to the northern netherworld. The Mayakovsky Yard was not officially called that, and neither was it on any map or plan. The satirical minds of the EOPs had devised the name to honor the poet of the Revolution who had given himself the gift of death at the beginning of this terrible decade that had still not ended. With its typical taste for the symbolic, the Lubyanka had expanded to encircle his garret, and turned it into a museum.

Gesser and a few other prisoners, all ex-Americans who had returned to remake the Old Country, had gathered in the Yard to play a game. It was a kind of baseball, but without bases or a bat, and without umpires. The men divided into two teams, and a player on one side would throw a small frozen potato high against the wall of the poet's house. Normally, the potato would have been eaten, but among the men, it was agreed that they would spare it; never has one potato given so many men so much pleasure. When the potato came down, a player on the other side had to catch the ball. If he muffed it, it would fall for a single. Three singles and you scored a run. The players named themselves after the stars they had once seen play: Hack Wilson and his whisky jar in the ivy of Wrigley Field; Greenberg, the king of the Yid sluggers. To honor the late poet, the game was called Mayakovsky ball.

The opposing team had thrown its pitch and Gesser was waiting for the rebound off the treacherously pitted brick wall. Just then, from a top-floor window, a great shape hurtled down. It was a man, Gesser saw, no doubt an Enemy of the People like himself. A swan-diving man, a man who looked as though he were planning to gracefully enter a swimming pool at the end of his dive. He fell without wavering or any attempt to cushion the impact. That was how he hit the cobblestones of the Mayakovsky Yard at exactly the same moment as the frozen potato. Both shattered, though in different ways. The potato burst into countless frozen shards, like a ball of ice. The game was over. The man didn't break apart. His limbs splayed out in unnatural angles, and his head was completely turned around, as if he were looking behind to see whether he was being followed. He could not have wished for a more sympathetic reception party. Many of the Mayakovsky ball players had known him from the Anglo-American Club.

Gesser bent over the broken corpse. A thought occurred to him with the amazing clarity born of horror.

"My wife's lover," he said softly to himself, then turned away from the wreckage.

The ball players gazed upon him, the man who had exhorted so many of them to come here. They had no bitter thoughts or blame for the Messiah of Division Street. Together, they spoke this silent elegy, and that was all: *If I ever get out of here alive, I'll tell . . .*

The two women's wait came to an end that same week as a mean, frozen shower of white pellets whipped at them. Who is to say which is worse, the waiting or the verdict? Their turn came, they stepped up to the wicket, the guards paged through the big book of lost lives.

"Gesser, Jacob," a near-sighted guard read out, running his finger along the entry on the page. "Yes. Suspicion of adventurism. Plotting against the new reality. And profiteering in watermelons." The guard looked up. "Watermelons? Where did he find such things? Do you want to know the last time . . . ? Anyway, he's repressed for ten years, but you may send packages. That's a good sign for you. Next!"

Sonya could not speak.

"Borodin, Mikhail," Mafili said to the guard.

The guard returned to his registry.

"The Enemy of the People Borodin . . . Ah! Terminated."

"Terminated?"

"Yes, terminated. Deceased. Croaked. Kicked the bucket. Died of a heart attack while under interrogation. Next!"

The two women turned away to give the next in line her turn.

His heart gave out. His heart couldn't take it any more and it just gave out.
Sonya pictured his heart in his chest, his big chest that she'd clung
to in the Zoopark, where she'd laid her head and slept those last
nights in his room. The red vessels exploding and blowing everything inside him into the world outside, splattering the walls with
the soul and lost ideals of Mikhail Borodin. Mafili was nodding her
head and chewing her gums and leading Sonya away from the
wicket. They came to a halt outside, in the wide empty square in
front of the prison, as so many others before them had done. There,
the wind whipped feeling back into Sonya's cheeks. She, too, was
making some sort of sound with her mouth. It was vaguely musical,
a kind of empty, meaningless, repetitive, childish chant. It was "The
Bear Went over the Mountain"; it was getting to be a habit with her.

"We have to do something! We have to do something for Jack."

"Come, daughter. Think of yourself. Think of the child."

"That's what I'm doing. That's who I'm thinking of. The child
must have a father, even if he's only a ghost."

Mafili gave her a look, part pity, part contempt. This was no
time for the luxury of illogical thought or words with hidden
meanings, like poetry. Instead, say these words. Wall. Potato.
Kerosene. Boot. Rag. The secret police built their fortress and
swallowed up the house of the poet Mayakovsky. They display it
like a shrine to their crushed enemy. That's all good poetry does.
Keep busy surviving. Make that your poetry.

The bear went over the mountain . . .

Sonya and Mafili exercised their right to send packages to Jack.
The exercise of that right was designed to be as painful as possible.

First, there were the three trams. Each of them conspired to be
full, so that the hour-and-a-half ride was made standing up. Then
there was the post office of the Enemies of the People. Appropriately,

it stood in the center of a field of frozen mud in a distant suburb, so far from the city that a dense forest of birch shut off the horizon. The post office had to be distant so the contagion of the EOPs' families would not spread to everyone else. The field had to be muddy because of the tens of thousands of feet that scuffed and trampled the ground.

Then came the official boxes. They had to be obtained. And paid for. That was one line.

Then the official boxes, to be made even more official, had to be scored with the official State scratch. That was another line.

Then the contents of what was to be sent had to be inspected. That was another line, a particularly long one.

Then the contents had to be placed in the box.

Then the box had to be nailed shut.

Then the ends had to be sawed off.

Then the box had to be roped tight.

Then it had to be dispatched.

Every step required a line. To send a package took all day, sometimes two. That didn't matter, since they had no other productive tasks. One day, once a month, this was their day's work. Somehow, society needed them to occupy this position and play this particularly thankless role. Once a month, Sonya and Mafili stood side by side under the pale sun, in the snow, under low clouds, beneath a lightless sky. They did not speak. What was there to talk about? They could have spoken to others, but did not. The women they might have spoken to were all too weighted down by shame to lift their heads and meet each other's eyes. Those who needed to talk did so incessantly, and Sonya and Mafili believed such people to be dangerous, to themselves and others. Just hearing certain kinds of conversations, even by accident, could get you repressed.

But the letters and packages were important. Through them, Jack discovered to his amazement that Sonya hadn't been arrested after all.

After the first trip to the post office of the EOPs, Sonya's ankles swelled up as big as soccer balls. Insanely, she began to crave cottage cheese, which did not exist. She sat on the edge of the old analysis couch and cried.

"Next time, I'll go. By myself," Mafili told her. "It's no job for you."

Sonya shook her head. "I'll do it if I have to give birth in that field!"

"But the child . . ."

"I want the child to know!"

"The child will know, don't you worry. You don't have to tell children things, they know. Whether you like it or not. Even the unborn ones. Especially the unborn ones. Take my word for it, daughter. This child is for the future, not for you. Can you do one thing unselfishly?"

Sonya looked as though she'd been slapped.

With the right to send packages came the right to correspond. Once a month. But to pass the censor, the letters had to be in Russian, a language that Sonya could not write.

"I'll do it for you," Mafili volunteered.

"You couldn't," Sonya stammered.

"I couldn't? I suppose I don't know how to write?"

"No, no, it's not that."

Mafili glared at her, hands on hips.

"You couldn't write the things I want to say."

"I see," Mafili said. "Daughter, the things you want to say wouldn't pass the censor anyway. So don't get delicate. I'll help you. You just say it and I'll write it down. I'll put it in a way that will get through. Afterwards I'll show you how to make the letters. Then you can write yourself."

"It sounds like you've had experience at this."

Mafili's face closed up.

"No," she said. "It's just something we know instinctively."

The letters began as a kind of forced intimacy. A little like squeezing into somebody else's room. The way Sonya had to tell Mafili everything, then watch as she wrote it down. As she hesitated and wrestled with thoughts a Soviet woman would never have, and if she did, would never have spoken. As she wrote, Sonya followed her hand to learn to make the letters herself.

That correspondence was cement between them. Slowly, forced intimacy became real, as in an arranged marriage.

The art of living off nothing. The art of considering as food what you would have previously spat on. And the relationship, unexplored in history books, between the chaos and submission in Europe and the swelling of Sonya Freedman's belly.

One evening, with Uncle Joe looking on hopefully, Sonya and Mafili sat dining in the attic. The Mafili special was being served. A broth rich in nutrients, since many of the ingredients had come from the garbage cans of the Kremlin. How Mafili had penetrated the fortress, only the gods of starvation knew. Mafili could have slipped through a keyhole, she could have snatched a piece of stroganov off Stalin's fork before he could pop it into the opening beneath his crushed-caterpillar mustache, and have spirited it back to the attic soup-pot before the Great Leader had time to realize something was amiss. Food was food, and that creature whose foot was beginning to push against the wall of Sonya's stomach had to be nourished. The little being was as voracious as a tapeworm, and in the absence of doctors seemed to be in splendid health, judging from the commotion it made inside Sonya's body.

"Our little parasite," Mafili called it tenderly, as if she had participated in its conception.

From the way Mafili placed her hand knowingly, firmly, gently on Sonya's belly, it was clear she had had plenty of experience with maternity. What kind, when and how, and with what man, she never said. The particular man didn't seem to matter. Men come and go, swallowed up by the State, or drowned in a bottle. Perhaps she had had boys, perhaps they had been lost in one of the patriotic wars. She was the only one Sonya would let touch her in so intimate a way. Sonya had no patience with those hags who stopped her on the street, anonymous, toothless, sexless, embittered women, grasping at her stomach as if its contents already belonged to the collective. "Little Enemy of the People inside," Sonya hissed at them. "Mother the whore of two EOPs!" And the good Soviet women would retreat, hands over their own bellies, or ears, to ward off the contamination.

It came that evening. The knock on the door. They had been expecting it for so long that their vigilance had exhausted them, and they'd all but forgotten.

Sonya stood up and wrapped her dressing gown tightly around her throat.

"All the while we think we are making history," she spoke aloud, "and we don't notice the chains around our legs."

"Please be quiet, daughter," Mafili ordered.

She grabbed the most compromising object in the room: Uncle Joe the monkey. He was compromising because he was irrational; she stuffed him in a box and snapped the lock shut. Like a sleepwalker, she moved towards the door. There, she turned and considered the room. It was lousy with compromising objects, starting with the soup itself. Where had the ingredients come from? The salt? The pepper? The plates and bowls? The permission to exist?

The knock came again, louder this time.

"Why don't they just open the goddamned thing? It's not locked!" Sonya wailed.

She put her hand over her belly, as if to protect her little parasite from whatever kind of rape was to follow. She knew nothing of the protocol of victimization. How to be arrested, how to submit, how to have her dignity trampled, how to wear that smile of ironic submission when the ravens came to your door. It would have been good to have a man there—Gesser or another. Men knew instinctively about those things.

The policemen swept into the room, the last of the winter's snow riding on the shoulders of their leather coats. They examined the premises with disgust.

"As we near a state of war, there is no room in the capital for nonproductive individuals. You are to travel east, out of the way. There, you will be put to work in productive war industries."

"We have volunteered for Civil Defense work. That is productive," Mafili argued.

"There is no room in Civil Defense for the wives of Enemies of the People and their . . . keepers. How do you think we could trust such people, especially those who refuse to divorce their spying husbands?"

"I can't divorce anyone," Sonya told them. "I'm not married."

"Whatever moral outrages you are capable of do not interest us. Your documents are in preparation."

"Do you really think she can travel in this state? Aren't you policemen who are supposed to notice such subtleties? Don't you have any respect for the miracle of impending motherhood? Do we not call our country the Motherland?"

Mafili's speech caught the policemen short. They had, in fact, not noticed Sonya's state. It was not their habit actually to look at EOPs, their wives, their whores.

They consulted each other with a quick glance.

"Have your baby, then. On the day after its birth you'll go east.

And be quick about it, too. Otherwise we'll induce you. And if we don't, the German bombs will."

"We're not afraid of the fascist dogs," Sonya announced.

Just then, Uncle Joe chose to protest his captivity.

"What's that?" the policemen spoke in unison, drawing their guns.

"Rats," Mafili told them. "They're hungry, too."

The policemen decided not to investigate. Rats were not in their jurisdiction.

"I don't know why you're so eager to stay in this place," one of them said.

"The evil one knows is preferable to the evil one does not know," Sonya explained.

"Evil?" they echoed. "Now you are a priest as well as a whore?" They turned to go. "We will return to check on your progress. Think of us as your obstetricians." One of the policeman spat on Mafili's clean floor. "Just what the Motherland needs: the whelp of a Jewish-American whore and an Enemy of the People!"

As long as you're fighting them, you don't have to think. Your mind is occupied. But when they leave your flat and return you to what passes for peace, the real anguish begins. You wait for the warning signs. The footsteps on the quiet stairway, the suspiciously idling car in the street. Waiting is a full-time occupation. You take to your bed, and there you wait.

Amazingly, they didn't come back. Winter broke, timid spring arrived, summer began. Mafili stockpiled kerosene to heat water. She washed rags and tore them into strips. Perhaps if I never gave birth, perhaps if I held it inside, we'd never have to leave, Sonya speculated as she clumsily climbed the stairway to the roof. Uncle Joe tagged along, pulling on her skirt from time to time to remind her of his existence; he had become an insecure little primate since

Sonya's pregnancy. Several floors below, the offices of the paper were still padlocked, the ghost of Borodin trapped inside, like a soul within a putrifying corpse. Sonya stepped to the edge of the roof and leaned against the parapet. She looked west, past the curving ribbon of the metal-colored Moscow River. West, towards the war. A war, why not? Everything else has happened. Once, she and Jack used to enjoy debating the meaning of history, and how to get on its right side. But history is like a circle. You can't get on its right side because it has no sides. Then the circle opens up to reveal its true nature: it becomes a hole, and you fall through it.

She watched Uncle Joe skitter off across the roof, in search of something to climb on or hang from. On the roof of the next building was a giant pair of iron tongs, placed there by the Civil Defense volunteers. She crossed over for a closer look. She pictured the fire bomb launched by the Germans, how it would strike the roof and burn there, how she would grasp the device with the tongs before its evil fire could set Hertzina Street alight, then dump it over the side where it would fall to the pavement with a great explosion of phosphorence and chemical stink. The comrades below would cheer her, and she would be welcomed as a heroic defender of the city.

Fantasies of acceptance on the very eve of her exile! Poor, tireless human heart!

She strained to lift the tongs from the roof, but found they were much too heavy for someone in her condition. Something shifted inside her belly. She dropped the handle of the tool and hurried downstairs to have her baby.

When he came into this world on the analysis couch that had been covered with clean sheets, Sonya announced proudly, "I will call him Michael Mafili. After the father, and after you."

"You can't name a boy after an old woman."

"I can do whatever I want to. It's a mother's prerogative."

It was true. If you're in Sonya Freedman's position—whore to two Enemies of the People, a free woman who has fallen down a hole in history—you can name your child anything you want.

After little Michael Mafili was miraculously ushered into this world by Mafili's expert hands, as by a magic spell, the State apparatus forgot all about the inhabitants of the fortress Borodin. War broke out in Europe; given respite by the devil's bargain with Hitler, Russia prepared—or at least that was the logic of it. Protected by divine oversight, Michael Mafili grew. He crawled, then toddled through the fortress, accompanied by his shadow, Uncle Joe.

When the smell of war grew too strong in the west, Sonya carried out the last errand that would let her leave the city with a clear conscience. It had to do with Uncle Joe.

Sonya rummaged through the attic in search of a suitable container. She came upon the wooden box into which the monkey had been so unceremoniously stuffed the night of the policemen's visit. Uncle Joe had become spiteful and unmanageable since Michael Mafili's birth. The monkey was used to being the only plaything, mascot and court jester in the fortress Borodin. Now he had to share the spotlight with a being who, because he was human, was infinitely more charming.

Worse still, the little boy loved the monkey, and his love for the primate went unrequited. It was a bad lesson for a man to learn at so young an age. Besides, the monkey had become a sad sight. Once a clever, high-spirited plaything, he had become a starved, embarrassing appendage. All that having a monkey around showed was that the inhabitants of the attic were monkeys themselves. A monkey, as Jack had once pointed out, is no more than our reflection.

Sonya lured Uncle Joe with a promise of caresses, which had taken the place of food. The monkey came near and let her scratch the worn fur behind his ears as Michael Mafili watched, enchanted. When the monkey dropped his guard, Sonya whisked him into the box and slammed the lid shut.

Uncle Joe protested with frantic scratching and little yelps.

"Don't complain, things could be worse," Sonya told him through the closed lid. "We could have chloroformed you and turned you into a fur coat."

Out on the street, Sonya sang to Uncle Joe through the box in hopes of calming him. She sang softly, for foreign languages were proscribed on the streets of Moscow. Such languages could harbor secrets, as Sonya's did now.

"Poor little monkey," she sang to him, "poor little man. You've been cruelly repressed." She shook the box. "I could have boiled you into soup. Mmmm! Monkey broth! But don't worry, in my world we don't eat our pets. Not yet, anyway."

She crossed the Boulevard Ring and the Garden Ring, then began to sing:

> *The monkey went over the mountain*
> *To see what he could see, to see what he could see*
> *And all that he could see, and all that he could see*
> *Was the other side of the mountain, the other side of the mountain,*
> *The other side of the mountain, was all that he could see.*

Her little song kept the repressed primate reasonably quiet until she could reach the Zoopark.

The zoo was open, but empty. No one had a taste for staring at underfed animals in tiny wire cages. Besides, half the enclosures, the ones whose former occupants made acceptable soup meat, were empty. The poor zebras, boiled into broth. Perhaps, too upset to mate, the males and females had turned to devouring each other instead.

Sonya paused before the white Siberian tiger cage. It, too, was empty. Sent to Siberia, perhaps. I should have brought Michael Mafili here, she thought, and the sound of his name made her breasts leak with milk, setting back her attempts to wean him. I could have shown him the spot where he was conceived.

The door to the monkeyhouse was open and slamming in the wind. She entered. Half the simians began to holler and curse at her; the other half hid and cowered in their cages. It was not a happy place. She opened the lid of Uncle Joe's box with the tip of her boot. His head popped up, then he sprung out and perched on the edge of the open lid.

"There, now you're with your own kind," Sonya told the monkey. "Here's where we say goodbye. Don't blame me, you had a few good years."

Uncle Joe cocked his head at her words, then went to explore the monkeyhouse. He hunkered down and stared uncomprehendingly at the animals in their cages, as though they were a species lower than his own. At the door, Sonya gave him a last look. Uncle Joe was still contemplating the caged animals in a cloud of unknowing.

Uncle Joe had been Michael Mafili's favorite toy and only playmate. But when his mother returned without him, he made no protest. Already he was a good little Russian.

Sonya and Mafili's evacuation orders did not come until the last, most pressing moment. It was the time of the great flight, the evacuation, the debacle of autumn 1941, the last exile of nonproductives like Mafili and Sonya. They reported to Kurski Station, which resembled the dwelling-place of the demons of panic.

"We've been preparing for war for years. I can't understand why everything's so disorganized now."

Mafili shrugged. "Don't ask questions," she said.

Little Michael Mafili rode on Sonya's back to save him from being trampled by the crowd. No Muscovite wanted to leave the city. Leaving the capital on a train bound for the obscure edges of the empire was synonymous with repression—death, if you prefer. But the citizens obeyed their orders. They flocked to Kurski Station. And there they waited, as they had waited in their shared flats, for days, a week sometimes, for a train to be put together, an engine to be found, fuel to be located, a crew to be roused from drunken, exhausted sleep.

Sonya and Mafili were lucky. Their train had not been requisitioned. They pulled out of Kurski Station only a day late, but soon discovered that if it wasn't the train that had been requisitioned by the military, it was the track. A wet, wind-driven snow pelted the birches that had not even had time to change color before their leaves were ripped from their branches. They watched the storm from a siding. The day passed; they had made fifty kilometers at best. A troop train passed in the opposite direction, slow and deliberate. The faces of the soldiers were a frightening spectacle. Young beardless boys with blank eyes, squeezing cigarettes between their stubby fingers, the fear and imminence of death written on their childlike features.

The countryside fell silent. Sonya listened to the snow ticking against the window and the cooing of Michael Mafili in his sleep. Then their train maneuvered off the siding and headed southeast, towards Asia.

As long as the train moved, Michael Mafili was pacified. The blackout curtains on the windows helped him sleep. But the hours and days spent on the sidings were torture. His cries and complaints did nothing to ease the atmosphere of the overcrowded, blacked-out transport coach full of nonproductives heading into exile.

The coal stove that kept the samovar hot sent out noxious fumes that gathered and swirled about the ceiling of the unmoving train car. Michael Mafili was like a canary in a coal mine. As the oxygen level dropped dangerously low, he wailed desperately.

Once, when the boy was at his worst, a fellow passenger tilted in Sonya's direction.

"I have a remedy," he informed her.

He opened his rattly bag of provisions, which consisted of bottles of vodka corded as neatly as firewood.

"Potato," he said proudly.

Sonya took the chipped cup, and he filled it. She dipped her finger and rubbed the boy's gums with spirit. He tried to squirm free, but she held him fast. For good measure, to the man's approval, she drank off the rest of the cup.

She felt the passengers' censorious eyes in the darkness. To hell with all of you, Sonya thought defiantly. You're all nonproductives yourselves. If you weren't, you wouldn't be here.

Then, as coal smoke, boredom, the boy's crying and the sheer proximity of so many strangers combined to drive the whole coach crazy, the train resumed its journey into exile. Movement brought comfort to everyone.

They had no idea where they were going. Their official destination was *Transit*. Most shared a vague sense of guilt at having been expelled from the capital, even if it was to work in the relocated war industries. As the train rolled on, Sonya thought of Jack. Perhaps he had passed along this line, not in a blacked-out coach, but in one without windows at all, for he had become a nonperson, with the right neither to look out nor to be seen. Perhaps at one of these crossings he had tried to send word; perhaps he'd been able to scrawl a note on a scrap of paper and push it through a slot in the boxcar out into the light of the world. Perhaps someone had picked it up and mailed it.

She stopped herself. The process was vain, enervating and useless. An illustration of why one must relinquish hope. Little Michael Mafili stirred, bringing her warmth and comfort. She gazed upon him in the darkened car. He was the fruit of the mad logic of the time, but it never occurred to her to regret. In this world of dispossession, here was something that was hers.

They spent more time on sidings, waiting for troop trains heading west, than they did travelling. Sometimes they waited all day for the passage of a transport that turned out to be a rumor. One night, the man with the potato vodka discovered Sonya's thigh. "Pretty woman," he declared, and clamped his hand on her leg. He might as well have been patting a tractor tire. She looked through him and concentrated on the blackout curtain. An hour later, he realized his hand was missing. He went searching for it and found it on Sonya's leg. Surprised, somewhat offended, as if Sonya had put it there, he drew it away. He was the only one with such a generous stock of vodka, which he carefully rationed out to himself. The rest of the car lived on tea made of carrot peelings and apple skins. The sugar that made the concoction drinkable was gone. Sometimes, when the train idled on a siding, they were able to buy barley from the suspicious, grasping peasants and boil it into a grey, tasteless gruel.

One morning, Sonya raised the curtain and saw something she had not gazed upon since her childhood on the Hungarian plain. A horizon. For years the sky had been the place where rain and snow came from. Now it was a vast blue blanket that hung over the grasslands, an intense Mediterranean indigo Sonya had never seen before, a sky that was, for once, the ally of the earth. They had left Russia; this was another country. Tears sprung into Sonya's eyes.

Mafili nodded with satisfaction.

"Now we're getting to my part of the world," she said.

Later that day, the train halted beneath the shadow of a water tower. The brakes had barely had time to lock to the wheels before a market formed alongside their coach. Sonya watched in wonderment as vendors laid down their wares in the dust, men in sheepskin vests and baggy pants who walked bow-legged from days spent on horseback. The vendors swarmed around the train like Lilliputians around the prone body of a giant. Sonya slid open the window and spotted Mafili in the market chaos below, haggling with the shashlik sellers who had set up a grill in the shadow of the train. Mafili came back along the line of coaches, eyes squinting against the sunlight, searching for Sonya at their window.

Mafili handed up a stick of shashlik. She was smiling. For the first time she wore a look of pride.

"Food, at last," she said. "Real food."

Finally, Sonya understood why Mafili was willing to take on the dangerous job of befriending a foreigner. Mafili was a southerner. Azerbaijani, Uzbeck or Caucasian, she couldn't tell which. But she wasn't a Russian.

They came to their journey's end thirty days later, at dawn. When Sonya stepped onto the platform of the Alma-Ata station with shaky legs, trailing little Michael Mafili behind her, the first thing she saw was lemons. Five lemons in a white enamel bowl. Behind the bowl sat a cross-legged man with prayer beads and a skullcap. Sonya looked at the five lemons and decided she had arrived in paradise.

After a month in a train, travelling across the great grey impassive body of Russia, anything would look like paradise. This dusty trading post called Alma-Ata, where the Kazakh steppes met the mountains, owed its resemblance to paradise to the fact that it had been all but forgotten. Earthquakes, floods roaring out of the mountains, drought and wind had wiped its name from people's memory.

Then the new nations came. The town lived again.

The slave laborers, the deported peoples, the nations consigned to extinction, the product of the century's failed romance. All those who'd sent their regards. Who'd never expected or even wanted to live, and found themselves dumped at the edge of the Hungry Steppe. They discovered with amazement the beauty and generosity of the place, and the strangeness of the inhabitants. The tall, graceful, willowy women with swaying curtains of black hair, who expertly shot gobs of dusty spittle through their teeth as they strolled through the streets. Their men who ate mutton, dressed in sheepskins and played games with dice fashioned from sheep's thighbones. The wall of snowy mountains that sheltered them from the fanatics to the south, who murdered in the name of their prophet, and the Chinese wastelands to the east. The high, sweet, mild air. The apple orchards that climbed the slopes of the Tien Shan. The rows of poplars as alive and noisy as an aviary. The channels that ran through the town and carried the mountain runoff into the hundreds of garden plots, where lemon trees grew, and tomatoes and aubergines and courgettes, all fat and firm and sweet.

Alma-Ata. Never has a stranger place of exile been devised.

Of course, it wasn't exile. It was evacuation. Sometimes the distinctions become blurred.

Sonya and Mafili and Michael Mafili—for no one is too young to receive orders—received their residence assignment at the station. They set off in search of Kir Street. As they walked through the freshness of the early morning air, Michael Mafili stopped every few feet to gather the giant oak leaves that drifted gently down from the trees. The facade of the building that housed the city baths was more intricately ornamented and better cared for than the mosque, in itself a good sign. In the middle of the central park stood an odd wood building, a mixed temple to two jealous Gods, with Orthodox onion domes and Arabic arches, held together without a single nail. Under the gazebos around the church, swarthy men were already playing chess.

After journeying out of Russia, it is impossible to fully describe the sweetness of early autumn in Alma-Ata. Tears ran down Sonya's face as she walked. Tears for the gentleness of the air, for the graceful lines of the distant mountains, for the sheer remoteness of the place. *I am on the underside of the world*, she realized. *And no one knows I'm here.* She reached down for Michael Mafili's hand and squeezed it. The boy did not respond. He was busy admiring his oak-leaf collection. Why shouldn't he? Since losing Uncle Joe, he hadn't had a single plaything of his own.

A whitewasher swept past them, a man with almond eyes and a mustache of flowing black filaments. His hands and arms were stained blue with copper sulphate wash, and he was eating an apple that must have weighed a kilogram.

How could war ever come to this place? How could war invade this park where a man wrapped in sheepskins moved slowly under the willow boughs, sweeping the slender golden leaves out of the *arik*, the drainage channels, with a twig broom, then gathering them in a jute sack for mulch? Sonya listened in wonderment as the mosque sent out its mournful call to prayer, its strange and melancholy discords so much like the sacred music of her youth.

Suddenly she was possessed by the lunatic desire to be happy. It was the lemons' fault. To see lemons reminded her of the existence of happiness. To see the glowing mauve skin of the eggplant on a polished stone slab reminded her of happiness.

These are the counterrevolutionary movements of the heart. These are the aspirations that make you an enemy of the people.

Vigilance! Vigilance! the authorities had clamored in Moscow, vigilance against the enemies of the people, real and imagined. What the authorities really wanted was vigilance against the self. Not only must you throw a blanket over your head, or fall into induced sleep so your ears won't overhear some subversive conversation—you must also put your heart under surveillance of the strictest kind. Reduce your heart to a sliver, a bit of iron thrown off a lathe and stuck under the fingernail. Mafili said it best. You must be low, as low as a peat bog sunk into the earth.

I will not do it, Sonya swore. I am not a peat bog. I will not be a peat bog here in the land of the lemon and the aubergine.

A great and dangerous resolution for an exile to make.

The partition in the house on Kir Street was a well-worn sheet hanging from the center rafter, an enormous, rough-hewn oak beam. Michael Mafili discovered that by putting his eye against the sheet, he could see through the threadbare fabric to the other side, and the house's original occupant: a Kazakh woman who wore something that looked like a rug and whose name, incongruously enough, was Moonflower.

His game violated the protocol of forced sharing, and he was shooed outside. Outside into paradise, for the laneways of the town were perfect for the child explorer. Chickens pecked at his feet as he stole through the yards where mules were tied up, swishing their tails in the sunlight. Pump-handles creaked among the willows as he ducked low under drooping wires, for electricity had just come to the district, even if the water still flowed from outdoor pumps. The baked-mud houses were all wall and roof, with tiny windows tucked up under the eaves, which meant he could pass unseen from yard to yard. Their walls were washed lime green and iridescent blue. To the boy's eyes they were colored building blocks, with the most extravagant decorations, scrolls and curlicues on the awnings, gingerbread trim along the roofline, the timber-ends sculpted into points, all the shutters painted blue to keep the evil spirits at bay, for even far from the Lubyanka there was no shortage of such spirits. Michael Mafili lingered at the edge of a circle of chanting children. From their benches, prompted by their master's baton, they recited their lessons in flawless unison. He did not know the language, but he did know that languages you did not understand kept you on the outside, and that all around him lived such languages. Then and there, he chose English as his mother tongue and swore he would excel in it, for it was a language no one else could understand. It would be his revenge. His link with his mother.

They lived the life of the evacuee. Dangling, in suspension. The war was a rumor for them. It neared, it stalled, it retreated, depending on the day's gossip and the quality of radio reception. Others suffered more than they were; that was the extent of their concrete knowledge of the war. Mafili worked at a fertilizer plant that had been converted into an ammunition factory. Sonya looked after Michael Mafili. And since that was not work enough to earn her a ration card, she reverted to an earlier, less exalted trade: she took in washing. Her room was not the ideal place to wash clothes. It stank of rancid fried mutton fat and the dung fire used to cook it. Michael Mafili worked, too. He learned to stand in line with his card and receive his 400 grams of bread a day.

At night, when the boy was asleep, Sonya went in search of a place to think. The streets provided the only private place, now that late-arriving winter had finally swept them clean with cold. She walked through the town to the first slopes of the great Tien Shan range, where the orchards began. As she walked, she considered that line past which endurance ends. Not that things hadn't been worse or that she was particularly more despairing in the past;

she simply wondered if she had lasted long enough, and which of the many straws would prove to be the final one. For some, a child is a tether that holds us to the world. Sonya had come to consider Michael Mafili not as a child at all, but as a little man, a partner who happened to be smaller in stature. She treated him like an adult so he would become one faster, and free her to accept whatever fate was being prepared for her.

On the other side of the fence of iron pickets, in the darkness, stood the State orchard. In some trees the apples had been allowed to rot, and now they hung frozen to their branches, for most of the pickers had been shipped out suddenly to a destination more remote than Alma-Ata—the Kolyma, from which one does not return. Where there is a fence, Sonya knew, there is always a way under it. She found that place, a spot where rushing water had cut a gully under the pickets. She slid under the fence and went to one of the trees of frozen apples. They were as hard as snowballs and the noise they made as she snapped them off their branches as loud as a burglar alarm.

She slipped as many apples as she could into her pockets. Some went under her dress, between her breasts. She put one under her armpit to warm it faster, for she was hungry.

Thaw, you bastard, she told it.

The apple remained silent. It was exercising its right. It was brown and rotten and gave off the smell of shit as it thawed.

She ate it on the way back anyway, while it was still frozen, pretending it was ice cream.

The apple got its revenge. It gave her the trots. Only the peel was any good, and only for making tea.

First, the wooden sidewalks began to disappear. Then the fenceposts, followed by the crosspieces. Some of the apple trees in the courtyards were also converted into firewood in contravention of the law, for they were State trees. A burned tree will give no fruit, but no one expected to be around to see those trees blossom the following spring. Some of the smaller ones in the central park were sawed into logs during the night.

Michael Mafili joined the hunt for wood. He combed the yards and lanes around Kir Street, his sheepskin pants stiff with frozen piss, gathering twigs and branches and sticks neglected by the adult world. As he neared the house he'd shout, "Wood, wood!" in perfect imitation of the blunt, nasal Sangamon Street accent, the private language he shared with his mother, the language that kept everyone else out.

It was just as Mafili had said. You do not need to tell a child anything. Children automatically understand their situation and what is expected of them. Like collecting wood.

One night, when the smoke in the house became particularly noxious, Sonya stepped out onto the front step. Perhaps they were burning wood with paint or varnish on it. You couldn't always inspect every stick of fuel. Hardly anyone was on the streets of Alma-Ata after dark, which is why the man slipping among the houses along the lane caught Sonya's attention. He was carrying a sack over his shoulder. Sonya was willing to bet it held some kind of contraband, and whatever it was, she wanted a share of it. She threw on her sheepskin and fell in behind him.

The moon had risen over the Tien Shan to the east, a full silver moon, as cold as the mountains over which it hung. The man moved with his head down, his loping steps making her hurry. This comrade is in an irregular situation, Sonya thought. And so am I, following him.

They walked through the back lanes, avoiding the streets, until they came to a river whose water flowed under a thin dull sheet of ice. A footbridge spanned the river, and there the man put down his sack. He set to work on the bridge. He took out an iron bar and began prying the uprights from the transverse pieces, carefully so the nails wouldn't squeak in the clear, quiet night air. He drew a claw hammer from his belt and finished pulling out the nails with it, then dropped them into his pocket. With the nails out, the railing came apart easily, and he put the wood in his sack. Then he went to work on the other rail. The whole operation took only minutes. The man knew wood, what it would tolerate and what it would not, and how to keep it quiet.

When he finished the job and had his tools and wood stowed safely in his bag, Sonya stepped out from her hiding place. At the sound of her footsteps, he reached into his sack and drew out the crowbar and advanced on her, to kill or intimidate, she could not tell. Sweat was running from his cap band and his face glistened in the moonlight.

"Lehto the Finn!" she cried. "I thought you sent your regards."

He lowered the crowbar halfway.

"I remember you."

"Of course you do."

And Sonya began to sing, terribly off-key, "*Hey, don't you remember, I'm your pal.*"

"Jesus Christ! You, here!" He slid the crowbar back into his sack. "Yes, I sent my regards. I never thought I'd end up here. I figured they'd deport me, being a foreigner. But it doesn't look like too many of us are going home now."

Sonya nodded at the bridge. "That was quick work."

He considered his accomplishment.

"People can still use it. They just have to watch their step now."

Then he shouldered the bag and, together, they walked back towards Kir Street.

"What about your husband?"

"Gesser," she spoke his name. "He sent his regards, too. Like you did."

"Forever?"

"He got ten years."

"What for?"

"Plotting against the new reality."

Lehto did not even smile at the absurdity of the charge.

"You might not believe me, but ten years isn't too bad. He could always come back. With the war, everything is mixed up. Anything can happen."

"I don't care to think about it," Sonya told him.

He mumbled his apologies.

"It's not your fault." She touched him gently on the shoulder. "I'm just not used to talking about it. There's no sense in it. Nobody knows but Mafili. Who else should know? I never even said it out loud before. *He got ten years.* I didn't even know what it sounded like."

"Now you do."

"Yes. Now I know."

"What about Borodin? What did he get?"

"He got . . . He was lost."

"Forever?"

"He died of a heart attack while under interrogation."

Lehto snorted with laughter, the first loud noise he'd made.

"A heart attack? Under interrogation? Do you really believe that?"

"No," said Sonya flatly. "But that's what I say."

"All that proves is that he was important enough to murder, and not just to let waste away, like us."

They walked through the maze of laneways, back towards a destination neither was in a hurry to reach. She was comfortable by his side, though he was almost a stranger to her. In Moscow, she had scarcely known him. He was a voice in the choir, Pinksy's sidekick, who became a symbol as the first to have sent his regards. The one they had chosen to ignore, or explain away. Now, he had returned as her companion in exile, and that was a powerful, instant bond.

"When we win this war," she declared, "I'm getting out of this place."

Lehto smiled. "Of course. *When* we win it. Whoever *we* is. And assuming that *we* will let you go . . . I'm sorry, I'm offending you. But I'm in no hurry for the war to end. Sounds crazy, doesn't it? But they're so busy with their war they've forgotten all about me. When it ends, they'll return and swallow me up again. I'll be a prisoner. A real prisoner, not like I am now."

They came to her house behind Kir Street. Lehto bent over and opened his sack. He pulled out half the wood and handed it to her.

"There, it'll be a little warmer in your house tonight. It's clean wood, too. Now go put it in your stove."

As usual, Sonya Freedman did not do what she was told to. She didn't burn the wood. She hoarded it for that time when things would get worse. She didn't know when that would be, soon enough though, probably just after the last round of pain had subsided. And there was another advantage in hoarding. You didn't have to explain to anyone where the stuff came from, or share it.

Whenever he could, Lehto would stop by with an offering. Once there was wood; another time, apples. No use asking him where they came from. Michael Mafili's stomach did not ask when the unfrozen apples entered it, scarcely chewed at all. Sonya hid the firewood. Since everything inside the Kazakh's house was made of rough timber, it was easy to conceal Lehto's gifts. They went under the bed, under Michael Mafili's pallet, atop the rafters, wood masquerading as other wood.

Here was a new definition of privacy: a place to hide things. Your own thoughts, anything you do not want to share with others. Meanwhile, she burned dung instead of wood, as the needy of Alma-Ata did. It gave the apple-peel tea a particular tang she had come to appreciate.

Lehto appeared whenever he could. He would stand in front of her door at night until she noticed him, as she had the first night. She would take down her sheepskin and hurry outside, and they would walk as the trees tossed and cracked above.

During her weekly moment of solitude at the ornate Alma-Ata baths next to the mosque, Sonya realized how much she looked forward to those walks. To being alone and adrift under the enormous Asian sky with the stolid, reassuring presence of Lehto the woodcutter. At first, the two of them said little of importance. He described the primitive logging camp in the mountains above the town. She told him what little Michael Mafili had done that day. For a time, that was conversation enough. Then they began to talk about Moscow, and how they had come there. Tentatively, they moved to self-criticism. Not the State's stagey self-criticism that passed for truth and usually preceded annihilation, but a kind of understanding of their adventure, and the century's adventure, and the tiny part they had played in that romance.

Unclothed, Sonya Freedman was the wonder of the women at the Alataou Baths. With curiosity and admiration, the naked Kazakh women gazed at her breasts made more generous by childbirth, and her natural pelvic tilt. She returned their evaluating gaze, but did not feel the same way about them. The willowy Kazakhs, so tall and noble and graceful when they were wrapped in their colorful woollens and silk decorations, turned out to be long-haired boys when they took off their clothes. She considered their bodies, hairless but for a tongue of black fuzz at the parting of their greater lips. And their breasts—little buttons like the buds of young girls. Their beauty was in their carriage, their slender feet, the intricate arrangements of their wraps and their crow-black hair. From time to time, through the billowing steam of the baths, a Russian woman would appear among them, as out of place as a potato in a lemon grove.

Once, after Sonya had dropped her robe and prepared to immerse herself in the steaming pool, a woman approached her and spoke in Kazakh. Sonya understood not a word of it. She did what people usually do under the circumstances: she smiled non-committally and nodded. The woman reached out her hand and touched the scattering of freckles across her shoulders and the top of her breasts, as if to see what dye had been used to make them. Then she gathered a few strands of Sonya's red pubic bush. Sonya took a sharp breath of air. She felt flattered, she felt like a rare and precious object, but an object nevertheless; she did not know what she felt. The Kazakh twirled and rubbed the strands of her maidenhair between her fingers, as if testing the quality of some fine silk. I have heard of this taking place. Now she will make love to me, Sonya thought—but how? What must I do next? How must I submit? The Kazakh combed her exuberant red bush with her fingers, then gave her head a half-turn and shot a gob of saliva into a sweating silver spittoon nearby that was as big as a bedpan.

With her curiosity about Sonya's body sated, the woman retreated through the steam to her washing stall.

Later, Sonya sat rubbing her skin with pumice soap, feeling vaguely disappointed. Foolishly, she felt spurned. What is wrong with me? she thought plaintively, and gazed upon her body, the thing she had lost as a girl in Budapest, then rediscovered under Jack's possessive care, and was now losing again, out of neglect. She pictured her memorable transit through the Poklub flat with Spielerman's unspoken blessing, for he had feigned disinterest, then sleep, his mind on Miss Pearl or one of her sisters. That long hallway on Sangamon Street had led her to the baths of Alma-Ata. You never know where you'll end up when you agree to lie down in a new bed.

She rinsed herself with a bucket of lukewarm water, then inspected herself for bites. Thank God she had left most of the bugs back in Moscow! She'd been spared the worst. She knew of women who'd had to shave their heads, who looked like convicts, who looked like . . . like Jack Gesser probably looked.

Jack, whom, she was convinced, she would never see again. For how could anyone survive what he would be called upon to survive?

One night Lehto produced a treasure wrapped in brown paper. A piece of grilled mutton.

"I got it up in the hills."

Lehto tore the piece of meat in half, giving her the flesh and eating the fat.

"I have adopted the widow," he told her.

"I'm not a widow. I never—"

"Of course, of course, I forgot, you are beyond classification," he cut her off.

Since Mafili was working at the chemical plant that night, Lehto was invited in. Sex was something you had when you could. When there was room. When Mafili was at work. When Moonflower the Kazakh woman's snoring from the other side of the partition was deep and even. When the boy was at relative peace. Sonya, who still had a sense of occasion, lifted up her mattress, uncovered her cache and put some of Lehto's wood in the stove. He said nothing, but admired her foresight. She closed the stove door quietly to keep from waking Michael Mafili.

Lehto squeezed into her bed. They lay there for what seemed like hours, as if keeping watch over the night. He's a woodcutter, Sonya thought, though he acts more like the tree. She was close to sleep when he finally overcame his modesty. She helped him find his way, this big, uncertain bear of a man who had none of Gesser's superstitions or worshipful nature, and none of Borodin's tragedy. Lehto's love was clearly love made for exile.

Very early the next morning, Michael Mafili opened his eyes to see the Finn's big back as he headed out the door with an axe over his shoulder. He ran to his mother's bed, afraid she had been chopped to pieces by the woodsman, like in a fairy tale he had been told.

The boy noticed that the bed smelled different. He chose not to climb into it that morning.

"He's a friend of ours from Moscow, where we lived when you were very young," Sonya explained. "We're a little like family. He's helping us out this winter."

No one could have said how Michael Mafili felt, least of all the boy himself. But when he saw that his mother had not been chopped into pieces by the woodsman or eaten by wolves, he seemed reconciled to whatever life would deliver next. With that tacit blessing, Lehto began to visit as often as his job as State woodchopper would allow.

He and the boy sat in companionable silence as Sonya burned the rest of her hoarded wood. After all, winter was ending. The goal of life, Lehto believed, was to get on with people using the fewest number of words. Music was the cure for all things. Whenever Michael Mafili began to fidget, Lehto would open his mouth and sing, his big bass voice trembling with tales of birch forests and winter and wolves and falling through the ice.

One spring day he disappeared. He did not even have anyone to send regards for him.

"I know men," Mafili said in the gaping silence his voice had left. "Sooner or later they prefer the bottle. With us, they always wake up with themselves. They don't like that. They'd rather wake up with a headache."

"That's nonsense," Sonya countered. "He was deported and you know it."

"It doesn't matter. Deportations, executions, evacuations— they're all ways invented by men to run away from women."

And that was the closest Mafili ever came to talking about herself.

In the spring, all Alma-Ata travelled to the foot of the Medeo Road to admire the blossoming apple trees on the other side of the iron fence. Each tree was a heavy, snow-white carpet laden with sweet-smelling flowers. There was not a single person in the orchard.

The war remained something distant, drifting in from afar, like a bad smell on the breeze. Almost distant enough to be ignored, which is what Sonya did. But those schooled in the interpretation of signs, even without the help of a radio, could tell the tide had turned. It had to do with trains. The trains had come lumbering into Alma-Ata with equipment and technicians and scientists, entire factories, as the Germans threatened the oil fields of the Caucasus. Now those same trains moved back west with the same equipment and the same technicians and scientists, and laborers, too, as the Red Army began its push towards the Oder River.

Sonya Freedman didn't want to know about the war. When something changes, she reasoned, I will be informed. Probably by being placed on another train. She watched Michael Mafili dance along the iron fence, a flash of red and yellow and orange in the multicolored clothes she'd sewn him from job-ends she retrieved from the scrap outside a textile plant. The layers and colors made him look like a Kazakh. She watched this strange little secretive child she had borne and nurtured, and wondered how he could possibly live in a country like this. Then asked herself how he could live on Sangamon Street either, for that matter, under the pressures she had known there. At those times, weariness fell upon her, and she considered giving in to inertia and staying on here, and learning to live the way they do on the edge of the empire, in isolation and obscurity, taking the little pleasures of lemon flower and zucchini blossom when they came along. Above the Medeo Road magpies circled, calling raucously and mockingly as they flew above the iron fence that guarded the State orchard. In Alma-Ata even the magpie was a magical bird, with iridescent feathers making a blue flame at its tail. You'd have to be a bird, or a bureaucrat, to get into the State orchard and sample a State apple, unless it was rotten to the core and frozen solid.

Suddenly she saw Michael Mafili streaking through the orchard on the other side of the fence, in a running crouch, making for the nearest apple tree. Her heart froze as she saw a little group of Kazakh workers appear from under a tree. But they were passing a pipe from hand to hand, smoking hashish, and they didn't see the boy, or if they saw him, they refused to believe he was there.

Michael Mafili leaped, caught hold of a branch and twisted it off in a shower of white petals. Then sprinted through the orchard again to the fence and pushed his boneless eel body under an opening he had discovered. The next thing she knew he was skipping along the fence, displaying the blossom branch.

"They're going to turn into apples," he told Sonya with calm assurance.

The branch was young and green and supple. She wound it into a crown and placed it in her hair.

"I am the queen of apples," she told the boy. "The mother of apples."

"Luscious apples," he repeated. "Big, ripe, *luscious* apples."

They were walking back through the town towards Kir Street when a Russian woman stopped them. She had the chunky, sexless body and the closed face of a commissar. She pointed to the apple-bough crown.

"You are a saboteur of trees," she declared.

Sonya cocked her head, hesitated a second. She couldn't stop herself.

"You can smell my fanny crack," she said in English.

The woman took a half-step back, as if she'd smelled sulphur.

"A foreign saboteur of Soviet trees. I will report you."

"You can double-smell my fanny crack, too," Michael Mafili volunteered. *"Luscious!"*

He obviously liked the word. They lost the commissar in the central park by crouching under the low willows and darting out of sight. But the bloom was off the bough. The commissar really could report her. Someone like Sonya was findable. Everyone was findable. It happened that fast. You let yourself go, you made a joke, for some crazy reason you wanted to be happy. And you were caught.

A few days later, the ill-named Moonflower appeared from behind the partition with a box and proposed a bargain.

"I have this stuff," she said in her halting Russian, which was even worse than Sonya's. "I know it's food but I don't know what kind. They tell me it comes from America. But I don't know the directions. Tell me what it says and I'll give you some of it. Whatever it is."

Sonya smelled a trap. It was typical of the way they worked. "I don't know English. I'm Hungarian. Sorry."

Moonflower grumbled. She obviously didn't believe her, but had no choice. She picked up her box and shuffled off to her side of the partition.

"Egg Powder," the box had said. "Just add water. Product of the

United States of America." Word from home: powdered egg. What was the matter with American chickens? They gave egg powder, not real eggs? What good is an ally like that?

It was another sign to interpret. If a box of egg powder could make it to Alma-Ata, if the United States had nothing better to think about than sending powdered eggs to the Kazakhs, they must really be winning the war, and the Soviets, their faithful allies, must be winning it with them.

Alma-Ata was graced by a visit from some distinguished artists who had been travelling the evacuation circuit since the fall of 1941: the entire Bolshoi Ballet and its orchestra, right down to the stage sweepers and assistant apprentice seamstresses. By day, the legendarily beautiful prima ballerina Galina Ulanova would stroll through the central park, accepting the adoration and flowers of young exiles of all nations. Sonya still feared the nameless Russian commissar, so Michael Mafili was free to run alone through the park, trailing after Ulanova and her coterie. In the park once, he picked up a lump of coal that had tipped off a passing wagon. He looked at it, examined his fingers, noticed how it could write, then slipped it into his pocket. Something that extraordinary could always come in handy, for use or for barter.

By night, the Bolshoi would perform at the Kazakh People's Palace of Arts and Culture. Sonya never misssed a recital, especially since they were free. At the main door, the ushers looked disapprovingly at Michael Mafili.

"Don't worry, he'll be quiet, he loves the ballet. Ulanova knows him."

Then she rushed for a seat, secure in the darkness of the People's Palace. The offended commissar could be sitting a row away and not even spot her.

The music would begin, the corps de ballet would make its appearance, softening the terrain for the great Ulanova, and Michael Mafili would slip his hand into his tunic pocket. He would rummage among the folds of cloth of his torn pocket until he found it. His little lump of coal. He slipped it into his mouth to suck on. It kept down the hunger; that much he knew. What he didn't know, not consciously in any case, was that the rock was full of the vegetable extracts of its distant origins. Ancient vitamins and minerals that helped him survive, even grow.

As he watched and sucked, Ulanova took to the stage, putting her graceful body through that series of unnatural contortions and death-like flutterings known as classical ballet, going against every instinct the human body has about natural movement. The mastery of arti-fice was at the heart of her art; it was her life's pursuit. But in the dark-ened theater, safe from the commissars and the thousand other evil spirits, at least one person gave rein to his instincts. That person was Michael Mafili, sucking coal. Any number of mammals, not just the higher ones, will eat coal when pushed to it by starvation.

Sonya always chose an aisle seat to speed the transition to the lobby. Even before the curtain fell for intermission, she was on her feet with Michael Mafili ahead of her, pushing her way towards the light. Michael Mafili, of black mouth, returned his rock to his pocket before he came into the glare of the lobby lights. In the foyer, Sonya fell upon the buffet, stuffing squares of buttered bread and caviar into her and her son's mouth. When their mouths could hold no more, she made a stack of tiny sandwiches and retreated to the back wall. There, she slumped against the ersatz marble as applause thundered from inside the hall. It was every cultured com-rade's duty to applaud to the bitter end, to exhaustion, even at intermission, to show their appreciation of the State's gifts.

"I want more," Michael Mafili said, his mouth full.

The audience came streaming out of the hall, towards the buffet.

"Go get what you want. Hurry, now."

Michael Mafili charged into the crowd like a miniature locomotive, slipping between the legs of the cultured and the starving. Caviar was perfect cover for coal. Both were black. Both were nourishing. And in those days, coal was rarer than caviar, and worth much more.

Sonya turned her cheek to the wall. The cement disguised as marble cooled her fever. The foyer spun with the danger of detection and the smell of the commissar ladies, that distinctive reek of sweat and woodsmoke overlaid with cheap cologne that flaunted their privilege. She suddenly felt sick from having stuffed her chronically empty gut with rich food too quickly. Michael Mafili came skipping back, the light of recent combat at the buffet table in his eyes. He was holding sandwiches in both hands and somehow balancing a full glass of white wine.

"For grownups, that's what they said," he told his mother.

She saw with dismay the two textures of black in his mouth. There *was* a difference between caviar and coal. As always, first came the shame and pity at having to live that way, next the fear of being seen. She took the glass and drank it down. The wine was thick and warm and resinous.

A woman was hovering at her elbow. A Russian.

"Your son was very quiet in the theater."

Sonya supposed that was a compliment. "Yes. He is transfixed," she said.

"Ulanova is very beautiful, right?" the woman spoke to Michael Mafili.

The boy nodded and looked away.

"Someday," she predicted, "he will be an artist."

Like a dog sniffing for danger, Sonya took in the woman's scent. Menstrual napkins, no perfume. No danger. Not this time.

"Thank you," Sonya said dully. "But it would be better if he did something useful. A cobbler. A woodchopper. A tank-driver."

They did not stay for the second act. Her head spinning, Sonya hurried from the hall into the square outside, where the disappointed ones who could not get in loitered on the cobblestones, hoping for a glimpse of the glittering Ulanova and her dashing but cuckolded husband. No one paid any mind to Michael Mafili's black tongue. It was night.

But Sonya returned to the Palace of Culture. One time there were cucumbers in sour cream with dill. She almost fainted at the sight of the shimmering sour cream and the impossibly green herb. Another time there were smoked sprats. And aubergines and tomatoes beaten into a paste. The first act, the attack on the buffet, then flight into the warm, forgiving air. That was Sonya's appreciation of classical ballet.

Michael Mafili began wanting to stay for the second half. He had fallen in love with Ulanova. He wanted to be a ballet dancer. He wanted to be a swan.

At intermission, after her rush at the food table, Sonya retreated to the washroom to hide from the ubiquitous commissars. The woman who had complimented Michael Mafili on his silence approached him and his stack of sandwiches again.

"You've come back?"

The boy nodded.

"Ulanova is very beautiful, right?"

"I love her," he admitted.

The woman smiled. "That's very good. She is worthy of your love." And then: "Where's your mother?"

Michael Mafili shrugged. He'd long since learned not to answer a question like that.

"She isn't feeling well," he said, and turned away.

Safe in her stall, too scared even to piss, Sonya waited until the bell sounded and the crowd returned to the hall. She emerged to find the lobby empty but for her son.

"You didn't talk to anyone, did you?"

He shook his head. He'd learned to lie. They went into the theater. The second act had begun.

On the way home that evening, though he wasn't hungry, Michael Mafili took out his coal and popped it into his mouth. He truly was in love.

The inevitable happened. Michael Mafili was performing his Dying Swan on the beaten earth in front of his lime-green house with the blue shutters when something went terribly wrong. He lost his balance. His swan's wings touched the burning dung of the cooking fire where the samovar bubbled. He managed to rebound and roll away from the flames, but his foot hit the stand and knocked over the samovar. Its top flew open as it fell, disgorging boiling water everywhere, putting out the cooking fire and scalding Michael Mafili's cheek and neck and jaw.

Moonflower came storming out of the house.

"The fire! The fire!" she lamented.

She knelt over the shit-fire and tried to nurse the embers back to life. It was too late. They were drowned.

Next to her on the ground, Michael Mafili, young ballet dancer, lay screaming, the right side of his face a blistered red nightmare. His career as a dancer was ruined. He would never be a swan. Sonya and Mafili ran out of the house, Mafili carrying a slab of mutton fat she had been heating on the kerosene stove. Sonya swept him up in her arms as Mafili applied the fat to his scalded face. The boy screamed his pain and disbelief as the neighbors gathered around, nodding, as if they'd been expecting something like this all the while. They loved their children in Russia, but they expected them to take it like men.

Michael Mafili lay on his pallet that summer, a child in convalescence. His craggy skin opened and poured out pus, closed, then opened again. Sonya's center, her tether, her little man had been disfigured.

"I curse that witch and her samovar," Mafili said in low tones, but loud enough for Moonflower to hear through the tattered partition. "We should leave this place. Evil spirits are here."

Sonya nodded. She was too broken to say anything.

"Don't walk on that spot again," she advised her son the first time he ventured outside, his hand over the side of his face.

But there was not another half-room or even quarter-room free in the town. Little Michael Mafili, crippled dancer, had to learn to live with the bad spirits that had spoiled the ground before his door. In the park, Ulanova stopped favoring him with her sultry, theatrical glances.

An innocent young boy-dancer was scalded. His wound became infected. A lady commissar was spotted on the street. Was she the one who'd sworn to report her? A different one? It scarcely mattered. Sonya Freedman's resistance had been weakened, and all it took was one germ of madness to fell her. And those germs were all around.

She began waking up in a terrified, disassociated state. She would rise with a start, go to Michael Mafili's pallet and rouse him.

The boy would stretch with feline grace, then immediately put his hand to his jaw and touch his skin, just in case a miracle had occurred during the night.

No. Not this night. Then he would squint against the wavering glow of the kerosene lantern, and a second or two later he was awake and alert.

His mother spoke to him this way.

"When I am arrested, this is what you are to do. There is money sewn into my mattress—watch that the straw doesn't slice open your fingers. I have a few extra rubles, and a dollar or two. Who knows what a dollar can buy now? Who knows if people even know what a dollar is and where it comes from? My God, what a dollar used to mean to us . . . but still, it's important, a dollar is important because it shows you come from somewhere else, you know more than this, you *are* more than this, and that's important if you ever want to get out of here. Mafili will take care of you. She swore to me even before you were born. The best thing is to go up into the hills. Into the apples, but not too far up, it gets cold. I'm going to tell her all this, you can trust her, just don't show her the dollars. Maybe they're just souvenirs, like my passport, but you can never tell when a souvenir will come in handy. Don't worry. If I go, I'll be back. That's what they all say when they go off in the middle of the night. What else can they say? That's what your father said. Your putative father. But you'll see, I really will come back."

Sonya kept her promise. She did come back. Night after night after night. She'd awaken Michael Mafili, he would reach up and touch the crusty yellow and brown scab to make sure he was still himself, and satisfied that he was, he would settle in to listen to his mother.

"I've packed a little bag for you. It will be beside your bed. The usual things. We'll be prepared that way, you and I. But don't forget it. There's no sense being prepared ahead of time if you forget when the knock comes. Take your pack. Don't let them follow you. Go with Mafili into the hills. Take your sheepskin. You can trust Mafili. You'll see the Kazakhs in the hills but remember, they are good people. It's only when they have to squeeze in with us that they get the way they are. Even the nicest dog will turn cur if it has to share its house with a cat."

That was how Michael Mafili, surrounded by Russian and Kazakh, came to speak perfect English. Every night he feasted on his mother's words. He learned to love English because it woke him up in the middle of the night with secret, shared terror. During those nights, he had fabulous adventures in the Kazakh hills with Mafili, he saw the mythic snow leopard, he drank from the streams that flowed out of the Tien Shan, he caught their fish, he met the shepherds and ate their grilled, spicy meats, wrapped in sheepskin and the trust of old Mafili, until the day when his mother returned triumphant to claim him. He would be as good as the baby Moses in his raft of reeds!

The boy listened as intently as he could. His attention pleased his mother, and that was important for both of them. But sometimes her voice hypnotized him, her stories of preparedness and arrest and flight became like a lullaby, so predictable were they, so easy to anticipate, like a chorus in a song. As she talked on in her urgent voice, he would put his hand on his scar, his head would slump back on the pillow and he would fall asleep. As he slept, she would move on to other subjects. The matter of her life immediately before he'd come into it. It was better that he missed those monologues.

In the evening he went to bed willingly so as to be awakened again, and begin the story all over. Sonya never missed a night. She brought him ever better adventures and more daring plans— until the time Mafili caught her. For, as Sonya had said, Mafili really was someone to trust.

She loomed up by the bedside one night.

"Stop it, whatever you're saying! Stop it with those stories of yours! It's enough we live like this. You have no right to scare an innocent child out of his wits!"

Mafili was outraged. The boy was none too happy either. He wanted to know more about his brilliant future as a temporary orphan.

The next day, Mafili told Sonya, "I will not let you do that to the child."

"You don't even know what I'm saying. You don't even understand."

"I don't need to know the words to know what you're doing. This is no time for disorder. This is no time for self-indulgence."

A nocturnal struggle began between the two women. A battle of pedagogical method. Of two kinds of love. At night, when Sonya's dreams awoke her and she went to stand at the foot of her son's pallet, Mafili, too would stir on the rug she called a bed and emerge from her corner, silent and disapproving, her presence usually deterrent enough to stop Sonya's storytelling. So much attention for the heart and mind of one small boy in a nation of tens of millions of sufferers—no wonder Michael Mafili developed a vigorous sense of his own importance.

Considering how exhausted they were, the two women's vigilance was a miracle. Sonya fought off sleep, then rose and gave herself to those precious moments of delirium when her son belonged to her entirely, when her world became his, when the world she invented replaced the one outside the door. Soon, both women wore dark circles under their eyes. As the struggle went on, its nature changed. Mafili fought less for the boy's right to live without fear, and more for Sonya's soundness of mind. As she did, both women saw in their struggle an expression of love and comradeship.

Mafili's Law, Mafili herself came to see, had become invalid. Something better was replacing it.

She never was able to stop Sonya's nocturnal crusade entirely. When she worked on the night shift at the ammunition plant, or when her vigilance failed and she slep through, Sonya and the boy were free to feast on mad stories. In the end, a man appeared and accomplished what Mafili could not.

*　　　*　　　*

One morning in the heat of the summer, a man came and stood in front of the lime-green, baked-mud house behind Kir Street. He was wearing a curious dog-fur coat, puttees and surprisingly decent boots. The boots had been a going-away present for someone leaving the shadows, at least temporarily, to travel back into the light of the world.

Underneath the coat the man wore bindings of colored fabric, a mixture of wool and silk, as if he had despoiled some camel-driver of his finery in the Betpak-Dala desert on his way to Alma-Ata. The kind of cloth Sonya had used to piece together Michael Mafili's pants. A jute sack, which he wore as underwear, peeked out from his open collar, and a sheepskin hat was crammed onto his head, defying the heat.

The man was half northern woodsman, half Kazakh nomad. Which made sense, since those were the last two places in which he had sojourned.

He loosed the silk scarf he had wound over his nose and mouth on the transport across the desert steppe. His face was so pinched it looked as though it had been caught in a vise. The man was Jack Gesser, Enemy of the People. Clearly a man who had dared tangle with the century, and lost.

Sonya came out on the step, stopped and stared.

"You look like you've seen a ghost," Gesser told her.

"It's just that . . . well, they told me you got ten years. And for nothing!"

"No. Not for nothing. For nothing you get twenty. I got ten. Plotting against the new reality." He gestured around the yard recklessly. "This is it, the new reality." He squinted at Sonya, bringing her into focus. "You wouldn't be waiting for somebody else by any chance?"

"I'm not waiting for anybody," Sonya said flatly.

"Because nobody comes back."

"Yes," she said angrily, furious at him suddenly—for what, she didn't know, for surviving, perhaps. "Because nobody comes back."

He sat on a block of baked mud by the front door, a traveller without baggage.

"Nobody does come back, usually. But with these exceptional circumstances we're having, this war we're going to win, well, there are ways." And he began to recite, as if by rote. "First I was up north, cutting trees. Who knows where, some of the boys said in Karelia, but I have no idea where that is. Then it turned out Comrade Stalin needed help in his coal mines, what with the war. They used to drag the coal out of the mines on little cars pulled by horses, then by mules when the horses went, but they needed those animals at the front to fight the great patriotic war. So I got to do their job for them. Animals are valuable, unless you're the type that stands on two feet. That was Karaganda. Between white bears and camels, I'll take camels."

Sonya sat, listened, wondered. She had heard it said that when a man comes out of a camp alive, he comes out silent as a stone. The years are lost forever in his memory, cordoned off by the barbed wire of pain. This, so it seemed, was not the case with Jack, and it made her uneasy. The ex-prisoner's ashamed, shambling silence would have seemed more natural.

"How did I end up here?" he continued, answering a question no one had asked. "I fell through the cracks. Cracks I made myself," he added proudly. "There's always a way. First I was an ordinary EOP. When they sent me to Karaganda to be a mule, that meant I was on the labor front. When I was there, I heard about something called the education front. I figured that if an education front could exist, it must mean we were winning the war. I liked the way it sounded. *Education*. Clean, warm and dry. So I got my reclassification to the education front. When I heard that lots of nonproductives had been evacuated out of Moscow to Alma-Ata, I knew you were one of those, and so maybe you'd end up here."

There were more holes in his story than in the average pair of Soviet boots. But the sudden carefree shouts of children stopped her from asking any questions. Michael Mafili came tearing around the side of the house, chased by a Kazakh boy with a stick. Michael Mafili came to an abrupt halt. The other boy peeled off and watched from a safe distance. Michael Mafili looked at his mother, then at the man dressed as a nomad, then back to his mother again.

"This is your father," Sonya said to the boy.

Michael Mafili took out his rock and rubbed it. Then realized he was in the presence of a stranger, and pocketed it again.

"Okay," he agreed with his mother.

Then he dashed off after the Kazakh boy, who tossed him the stick and let himself be chased into a yard where a donkey brayed and stamped, wanting to join the fun.

Gesser's shoulders slumped.

"Well, congratulations are due." He stared at the beaten earth where the lithe little miracle had stood. "But I'm not the father."

Sonya shook her head.

"Then why did you say I was?"

"Because I'm his mother."

Mafili chose that moment to return from the plant. She took one look at the nomad and knew it was Gesser. She rushed to his side, knelt in the dirt by the cooking fire and kissed his hand. She raved on in her native tongue, pinching his flesh, calling on various orders of prophets and miracle-makers.

"Some people really know how to roll out the welcome mat," said Gesser.

*   *   *

It was Jack Gesser's turn to squeeze into the half-room in Moonflower's house. Michael Mafili lay on his pallet, pretending to sleep,
but all the while his jaws were busy working on his lump of coal.
Mafili tried to melt into the furniture. She was unsuccessful because
there wasn't any. On the other side of the partition Moonflower
muttered, complained, sniffled, hawked, made liberal use of her
spittoon. It seemed the further east you travelled, the more people
spat. In Alma-Ata, full equality between the sexes had at long last
been attained: the women spat as much, if not more, than the men.

Jack's arrival made Sonya part of some vague conspiracy, the
automatic result of two foreigners being in the same room at the
same time. She did not like it; it was an invitation for the lady
commissar to show up. As for Michael Mafili, he knew his midnight travels with his mother were over.

It was back to the fortress Borodin again. The blanket over the
head, the hushed voices, the itchy heat, the sour smell a frightened
body gives off. Speaking English wasn't protection enough. You
never knew. Neither of them had forgotten the little trick that had
been played on Koshgarian at the Leningrad customs house.

Jack wanted to hold Sonya. She let herself be held.

"I know it's not the same," he said.

"It's not."

"It'll never be the same."

"Of course not."

Sonya wasn't sure what she was agreeing with. But the statement was vague enough to be true, applicable to all things.

"Let me guess who the father is."

"One guess."

"Borodin."

"You win."

"What's the prize?"

"There isn't any."

"He's dead and I'm alive. I'm with you. That's a prize of a kind."

"Is it?" Sonya wondered.

Later she told him, "His heart gave out."

Jack said nothing. He pictured Borodin's final, graceful dive into death's arms. For a man who'd been pushed, as he always assumed he'd been, he'd fallen with great composure and self-control.

"Tell me how you slipped through the cracks," Sonya said. "Maybe I can do it, too."

"The system works perfectly only if you believe in it."

"If it was that easy, everyone would do it."

"Easy? Easy? I was unhappy being a mule in Karaganda. They strapped us to coal cars. We had to pull them out of the mine on rails. I tried the best I could. I wanted to be a good mule, God only knows, but I couldn't. The guards . . . urged me forward. When winter came I took off all my clothes and ran out of the barracks. I ate snow. Even that didn't work. I didn't even catch a cold.

"I had to think of something else, and I did. I told them I was a teacher. I knew that teachers had no business on the labor front now that the education front had been opened up."

"You had no papers," Sonya protested. "I suppose they believed you?"

"My papers were in Moscow. Nobody had any papers anyway. Considering the talent they had in those camps—violinists, chemists, poets—a teacher was the least I could have been. I spoke English to them, I gave them classes in it. So much English they got sick of it. I showed them my little hands and feet and my little bird-wrists and told them, See, aren't these teacher's hands?

"You are no good for a mule, they told me. Maybe you'll be worth something for a teacher. 'As a teacher,' I corrected them.

They hit me in the mouth and knocked out a tooth." Gesser opened his mouth and pulled back his gums, but the exhibit was lost in the darkness under the blanket. "I didn't care. They could have knocked out all my teeth. I got my transfer to the education front."

"What battles are you going to fight on this front?"

"Now that the capitalist dogs are our allies, we have to know their language. I'll teach English."

"Right! I can see it now, a whole school full of kids sounding like Sangamon Street."

Under the woollen blanket, Gesser struck a professorial pose. "I chalk up. I break first. I run the table. I do an eight-ball scratch."

"*Do* a scratch? That doesn't sound right to me."

"This is Soviet Union! One does not correct professor!"

Suddenly they were laughing. The protective blanket was all in disarray.

"Don't laugh," Jack said. "It'll give someone a trauma."

Sonya looked over to her son's pallet. Michael Mafili slept, rock under pillow. As for Mafili, she wasn't a child, she could separate herself from the trauma. Besides, she didn't envy lovers. Love just gets in the way of survival, that's what she said. Though she did make an exception for the love of a child.

She and Jack embraced. Silently. After a time he came inside her. Silently. They made love, if it could be called that. Barely moving. When it was over, and that happened quickly, she clapped him on the back in comradely fashion.

"Gesser the teacher. You're finally going to be able to use all that knowledge you've accumulated. That's why you came here, after all. You must be happy."

"Yes," he breathed into her neck, in an attempt at romance. "Right now I'm very happy."

"No, not *that* kind of happy. Really happy. Philosophically, historically happy."

"You're right. I tell myself I've been vindicated."

Vindication, they would discover, is a short-lived state. In the land of the New Man and the New Woman, you can never be vindicated for long. On the other hand, you can be rehabilitated. But that usually happens only after death.

In the morning, little Michael Mafili's teeth and lips were black with gnawed, nourishing coal. Papa was back.

As a confessed EOP, a convicted plotter against the new reality, Jack Gesser still belonged to the State, the way a requisitioned wheat field belongs to an army. Yet he had been recognized as a man of learning and paid to dispense his knowledge at a State institution. That was the paradox of the Alma-Ata chapter of his life. He responded to that paradox by becoming a believer in the Soviet system. How could he not be? As Sonya had said that first night, he'd always wanted to be a teacher, ever since that winter day he'd been chased out of the little theocracy of Soukenai.

The season that followed his return from the hell of the Karaganda coal mines was a time of reprieve. For Gesser, not for the Germans, who were trying to defend their capital with boys who hadn't shaved yet. Gesser went off to the Foreign Language Institute, returned with a pay packet for noble and ennobling work, steered his students through the lawless, shifting territory of the English language, took to teaching as a craft and mastered it.

"After the war, I'm going to start my own school," he told Sonya one optimistic evening.

"Good thing you're talking English! Do I need to remind you that the school belongs to the State, not the individual? You're displaying a capitalist mentality."

"You're right," he admitted, chastened. "In that case I'll work on improving the English section at the Institute. We'll be needing more teachers, more administrators. There will be room for you."

"I don't know about that," Sonya said evasively.

There were a few insignificant scrapes. Once, Moonflower, who had never forgiven Sonya for her son's dousing of the dung fire, complained to the district commissar that a foreign tongue was being spoken on the other side of her partition. Gesser was called in to explain himself. Confidently, he argued that as an English teacher, it was part of his job to use the language outside the strict hours of his employment. By doing so, he was displaying a zealous spirit towards the Motherland. Then he insinuated that he often heard Kazakh from the other side of the partition, and while English was the language of the Soviet allies, Kazakh was a vestigial Mongol dialect of a people who had shown their hostility to Moscow. The commissar dismissed the issue, telling both parties they had a duty to get along in wartime. No formal decision was made. When the war was over, and everything returned to normalcy, something could always be done.

That minor scrape did not keep Gesser from receiving his official designation as an English teacher. The prison camps were becoming a distant memory, a mistake, a misunderstanding that had cost him some time. He never spoke of the north or Karaganda except to describe how he'd slipped through the cracks, ones he'd made himself. He was beginning to tell the same story over and over again, like a veteran of some foreign campaign whose relevance has been lost.

Sonya had stopped listening.

Summer seemed to go on forever in Alma-Ata, the father of apples. With her son, Sonya liked to walk to the edge of the town and imagine where she was in the world. To the east was the Tien

Shan; to the south the Kirghiz mountains. The north, out of which Gesser had materialized, was a place she'd rather not think about.

Then there was the west. The west was the only way out. But it was still devoured by war, and there was nothing to do but wait for the Red Army and the Americans to finish the job.

The next move I make, she swore to herself and to Michael Mafili, I'm not going to end up in the wrong place at the wrong time.

BOOK IV

MOURNING THE G-MAN

13

TRANSIT

To each his moment of self-discovery, of finding out who he is and where he stands in the world. Michael Mafili had his on a train just outside Orenburg. A train running west, into the maelstrom.

He and Sonya Freedman had finished their journey across the great empty steppe. It seemed to Sonya that the war had brought no change to the landscape. This was the same desert she had endured, years before, in a dark coach, starving, with a desperate child. Except now, since Moscow had discovered how to make it bloom, some of the desert had been irrigated and made fertile. Grain grew where before only rocks had lain, strewn about as if thrown down by a vengeful heaven.

Russia propper began at Orenburg. The train halted there to take on supplies. The Russian passengers and crew were happy to have crossed the steppe; its hostile inhabitants had never converted to the religion of the Kremlin, thousands of kilometers away. As the train slowed, Sonya saw the market awaiting them alongside the track.

She pressed a few coins into Michael Mafili's palm.

"Go buy two sticks of shashlik. And tell the man you want meat, not fat."

The boy dashed off, dropped the coins, backtracked, picked them up, blew imaginary germs off them—"Germans," he and his mother called them—then dashed off again, happy with the responsibility. At times like this, when she had to confront the impassive, often accidental cruelty of the world, in something as insignificant as a vendor trying to pass off cubed fat as squares of meat because she was a defenseless woman, she was grateful for her son's precocious sense of responsibility. The boy's very existence was a kind of protection. Had he been female, it would not have been the same. A little girl doesn't have the same effect in Russia, and God knows, she felt in need of protection as she moved north and west into the old empire.

On this train, she had travelled with the reflections Lehto had shared with her during their strange, silent, comforting idyll. The war had made him free, he had said. During the war the State was occupied elsewhere, first in defense, then in revenge. Every case could not be looked into. People like her and Lehto and Jack were allowed moments of freedom that would otherwise have been denied them. Knowing the State, when it returned in full force it would no doubt blame them for taking advantage of its momentary lapses of vigilance.

Which is why Sonya left Alma-Ata, despite her love of the place. Which is why separation from Jack had been inevitable. Why stay in Alma-Ata and wait? Perhaps, given the distance, it will take them longer to get to you, but what does that change?

She hadn't asked Jack to take this journey with her. When she told him she was applying for transit back to the capital, he merely nodded. He was determined to be the new czar of English instruction in Alma-Ata, and was not about to surrender his hard-won position as a man of learning at the Foreign Language Institute for another round of sleeping on borrowed buggy mattresses in Moscow corridors. He was rising quickly in collective esteem at the Institute. His classes were the most popular, and it was agreed that he had an expertise that other instructors could only dream of.

The separation, Sonya discovered to her surprise, was painless. Years before, they had set out on this adventure for different reasons and now, finally, those reasons could express themselves. The break would be more painful for Michael Mafili, Sonya feared. But the boy made it easier on everyone. He must have decided that was his duty.

In the laneway behind Kir Street, by the pump, Sonya awkwardly and mendaciously began to explain to him why she and Jack had to part. The boy interrupted her.

"Mr. Gesser is not my real father," he told her.

It took a while before Sonya could answer.

"No," she said. "Your real father was lost in the war, right at the beginning. He never even got to meet you. Actually, it was before the war. He was killed by Russians, not Germans."

"How could that be if he was a Russian?"

"The Russians were busy fighting each other before the war came along. They only stopped when they had to fight the Germans. Now that they've beaten the Germans, they'll probably go back to fighting each other again. We don't want to be around when that happens."

The explanation was designed to get Michael Mafili on her side. She might as well not have taken the trouble. Like his mother, he was always ready to get on a train.

Leaving Mafili was more difficult. There was no conflict between them to make the parting easier.

Mafili offered to make the journey with her. Sonya refused.

"I can't take you away from here. This place is your country. Your real country. I'll always remember how happy you looked when we crossed into the south."

Mafili waved her off. "I like the train. You can relax on the train. It's not like you can relax in a powder factory that's always about to explode."

"I'll need you on this trip, too. But I'm not staying on in Moscow. I'm going to the West. If I can."

"Can you?"

"I did it once. I'll do it again."

The two women sat in silence at the table they'd set up in front of the lime-green house. Two cups of tea steamed before them. Real tea now, not from apple peels. The sounds of the laneway were timeless, almost enough to tempt Sonya to stay. Chickens clucked lazily, a donkey brayed, down the lane a man was praying noisily.

"What about Mr. Gesser?"

"I informed him."

Mafili affected a scandalized air for a moment, then laughed heartily.

"Now the women are leaving the men! The war really did change things."

Sonya joined Mafili in her laughter.

"What are you going to do?" she asked.

"Do? I'll stay here. I'll work at the plant. The war's over, they say, but they'll still be wanting plenty of bullets. They'll find somebody to use them on."

Together, the two women turned and considered the house that had sheltered them these years. The house? The half-room. The partition that swung with every breath of air that came through the open door. And, within the half-room, the screen with its Byzantine motifs and Kazakh scroll that served as a division between the matrimonial bed and the compartment into which Mafili and her little namesake were squeezed.

"I think it's better that a boy not grow into a man in this room," Sonya said.

"Not that a Moscow hallway is any improvement."

"No. But it's only one step along the way."

"I pray that it be so, daughter . . ." Mafili turned and discreetly spat on the packed earth. "You know, you have changed from the frivolous girl I first knew. I had never met anyone, still less a woman, who was so frivolous in such a precarious situation."

"But it paid off," Sonya pointed out.

"It did, I suppose, though I never would have thought so. You are very lucky. You have a child, you have enjoyed the love of men, you have been spared most suffering. Perhaps that is the Western way, to dance on the tightrope that one must walk. Had I known about that way, I might have tried it myself. Had I been capable."

"I'm sure you would have been."

"We'll never know." She rose and embraced Sonya across the rickety table. "Let those be our parting words."

Michael Mafili came running back through the corridor of the train, proudly brandishing the two sticks of meaty shashlik, grease running down his fingers and wrists. But there was a cloud of doubt in his eyes.

"Mother," he said gravely after they'd finished their meal and the train was rolling again. "Why did the shashlik man tell me that my God doesn't want me to eat this? Why did he call me 'Abie'? That's not my name. He doesn't know my name."

Sonya Freedman took a deep breath and cursed. *It never ends.* Her son's life was beginning in a world unimproved by time. The world that teaches us who we are by making us hate ourselves.

"God made a Covenant with the Jews, though no one really knows why," she began, a little shaky on her theology. "He chose the Jews to make this Covenant with, though they certainly didn't ask for the favor, they just happened to be there. They were always doubting. That's normal, who wants to bear such a burden? In the end, they had to believe, after God performed his miracles. So we are linked to God through the Covenant and the Commandments, which are holy, and through a lot of laws that don't always make much sense to us now, or that we couldn't obey even if we wanted to. Laws about the things we can and can't eat. We don't get anything special out of this Covenant, not in this world. On the contrary . . ."

Sonya paused. There must be a brighter side to this Covenant. No use sending Michael Mafili into life with a sense of doom. That would come to him soon enough, without her intercession.

"Your only job is to love God and be worthy of the Covenant," she told him. "If you do, that will be reward enough." Sonya thought a bit more; there must be something else she could say. "If you can love, that is the greatest reward. The way I love you."

The boy said nothing. His mother's emotion embarrassed him. He still didn't know what all this had to do with shashlik.

As they rode through the Ukraine, Sonya finally saw what the war had done. She understood why her request to return to the capital had been granted so quickly. *To return to productive life*, the wording ran. It was obvious that the capital, the entire country, desperately needed the productivity of people like her. First you need us, then you hate us, Sonya thought as she and Michael Mafili disembarked at the Kiev Station in the terminal shabbiness of postwar Moscow. Then after you hate us, you need us again, she silently addressed the press of grey faces under their cloth caps, their bodies wrapped in the grey shrouds of overcoats, the entire crowd a suffocating fog. What may I expect after this current round of need is over? Another slap across the face?

As they pushed their way out of the station, Sonya clearing a path for the boy, she was overcome by a new and violent sensation of hatred, the repudiation of all those years of trying to love these people and fit in with them. Hatred, she discovered there on the subway platform, was as liberating as intoxication. It *was* intoxication. She hated them, and now she could admit it. She hated the stink of rot and despair that emanated from their decaying teeth. She hated the way, when Michael Mafili was knocked to the ground, that no one slowed to help him back on his feet. She hated their fixed stares, eyes glazed, as if deep in thought, but they were only faking, and if they were thinking at all it was only whether to fart at the Kievskaya metro station or hold it till Park Kulturi. She hated the dull distrust that enveloped them all, for after years of being exhorted to vigilance, they were so exhausted they could muster only a vague xenophobia. She hated the women with heavy, bulky bodies—amazing when you considered how little there was to eat. She hated the men, weasel-faced and chinless, for whom maudlin sentiment induced by bathtub vodka replaced true feeling. She remembered when she had loved the Russian people, actually *loved* them, indiscriminately and promiscuously, on Kuznetsky Most in the winter of 1933, when a grizzled drunken soldier with a salt fish in his hand danced to the music of a wheezing street band. The only good thing she could find to say about them now was that little of this had been their fault.

No doubt these feelings were mutual.

Sonya and Michael Mafili passed the Conservatory. With grim pleasure, she noticed the sidewalk had still not been repaired.

How many years was it now? Then they were walking up Hertzina Street, the seat of the great romance. In front of the old fortress Borodin, she set down her bag on the pavement.

"This is where you were born. Your very first house."

The boy leaned down to rub his bruised knees. His colorful Kazakh pants were an embarrassment in this climate.

He looked up at the forbidding facade.

"Where do we sleep tonight?"

"Come on, follow me!"

Sonya grabbed her bag and his hand. Together, they stormed the *porte-cochère* and the double courtyard. She tried to make the climb up the wooden stairway to the *Moscow Daily News* into a game, but her febrile state frightened him. Children, she had forgotten, are natural conservatives. He watched disapprovingly as she went about forcing the door to her old place of work.

"There's no one living here now," she tried to reassure him. "We might as well use the space. Don't worry, I know my way around. Half the city is living this way."

The boy watched as his mother broke the pane of translucent glass and let herself in. They entered the antechamber where, several lives ago, she and Jack had stumbled in, two young lovers in search of a meaningful life. Sonya advanced. Michael Mafili waited by the door, ready to take flight. She moved past the Remingtons, their keys cloaked by a thick layer of dust. She touched them, then the layout tables, the desks and chairs. Michael Mafili trailed cautiously after her, through the two oak doors lined with leather, into his father's chamber.

He hung back at the entrance. Some unconscious interdiction weighed upon him. You do not go into a stranger's bedroom. You do not take the fabric of his sheets between your fingers, as Sonya was doing.

She turned and caught him studying her.

"You're right," she told Michael Mafili. "This is no time for a sentimental journey. We've got work to do."

Sonya Freedman had a little leather pouch she always carried. It hung between her breasts. She had taken it off three times since she'd been in the Soviet Union. For Gesser and Borodin, and to nurse Michael Mafili. The pouch contained the little red jewel Borodin had returned to her, and something more precious still: her American passport. Expired, true, but in her mind—and for the government of the United States of America, too, she hoped—forever valid.

On the strength of her expired document and the authenticity of her nasal Chicago twang, she marched through the gates of the American embassy. Michael Mafili marched with her, stateless, but with a father, she informed the vice-consul in charge of such matters, who had also been an American citizen, now unfortunately lost.

She sat in an office antechamber buzzing with listening devices.

"What makes you want to go back?" the vice-consul for immigration asked.

Sonya sat and stared at him. *Where do you live, on the moon, maybe?*

"I was travelling," she told him. "I got caught in the war."

"An odd place to go travelling, wouldn't you say?"

"That's what you'd say now. It didn't seem odd at the time. I wanted to see the world. I saw it, all right."

The vice-consul pointed crudely at Michael Mafili.

"What happened to the boy?"

"He got caught in the war, too."

Michael Mafili put his hand to his jaw. Whenever he forgot about the scar of pink skin the shape of Kazakhstan, someone always managed to remind him.

"Did you commit any expatriating acts?" the vice-consul asked.
"Pardon me?"
The official named them off. No, Sonya had not voted in another country's elections. There hadn't been any. Nor had she served in another country's military. She hadn't been allowed to. Had she taken on another country's nationality? No, unlike Jack Gesser. She worked her way through the list with a clean conscience.
"How can we get in touch with you?"
"You can't," Sonya said. "We'll stop by from time to time."

Sonya had decided that Jack Gesser would make a convenient father for Michael Mafili. It made a certain amount of sense as far as the rest of the world was concerned, and Jack was too far away to show up and dispute her claim. But when Sonya told the lie about him being lost, she did not know it would come true.

Or did she?

Once again, Jack Gesser's ideals and proud learning turned against him. Several years had passed since the end of the great patriotic war. The system had had time to recoup. One day, at the Foreign Language Institute in Alma-Ata, in the middle of a particularly illuminating explanation about the present perfect tense, he noticed a stranger at the back of the classroom. The present perfect is so important in English, he was expounding, because not only does it speak of an action that began in the past and continues unabated, it also describes an action that began and ended in the past, but whose effects are still felt. This is why we call it the tense of emotion. He trotted out his most successful example: *No one has ever loved me like you did.* Though you don't love me any more, he explained, and the action of loving is entirely in the past, the effect of not loving continues. Therefore, the present perfect is called for.

The stranger shifted his weight at the back of the classroom. An academic inspector, perhaps. Gesser felt a slight sick shiver run through him, for he had just committed a grievous grammar error. He had followed *like* with a verb; it should have been *as*. Bravely, he moved on through his explanation of the tense, noting how the present perfect demands a response or subsequent action of some kind. Notice the difference between *The prisoner escaped* and *The prisoner has escaped*, he begged his students. Whereas the first merely states a fact, the second implies the need for—

"It is no accident that you use prisoners in your example, comrade professor!"

The stranger strode down the center aisle towards Gesser, then leaped onto the platform where his desk stood. An odor of *rouliet* sausage emanated from him, that smug smell of someone who'd had meat for lunch. Too late, Gesser recognized him. The district commissar who had set aside the Kazakh woman's complaint about the speaking of English under her roof. Since that wartime interview, the commissar had forgotten nothing, and Gesser, everything.

"My dear comrades," the commissar addressed Gesser's students, who had witnessed and appreciated this kind of theater before. "The case of this so-called professor of yours was brought to my attention during the war by a patriotic woman of this city. Comrade Gesser was suspected of sheltering pernicious foreign influences."

"As a teacher of a foreign language," Gesser replied smoothly, "it is normal for me to be interested in things foreign. Otherwise, how could I do my job?"

A condemned man is not allowed to reason. The commissar ignored him.

"Comrade Gesser once boasted of being able to slip through the cracks of Soviet justice. You know what kind of animal slips through cracks. He did just that during the war, when the nation was busy repelling then punishing the fascist invaders. As the Motherland was occupied in patriotic war, Comrade Gesser was busy slipping through the cracks."

Gesser felt his bowels loosen. Instinctively, he crossed his thighs. He speculated futilely on who might have betrayed him, forgetting how often and to whom he'd told the story of his escape from Karaganda. Not Sonya, he hoped. There had to be some limits to betrayal. What about the Kazakh woman on the other side of the partition, one night in a fit of optimism, when the blanket slipped from their heads? That's all it takes. A man's whole life leads up to one indiscretion.

"Do you wonder how it is that a man simply shows up in a place," the commissar continued, "seemingly out of nowhere, far from his birthplace, without employment, and attaches himself to an institution like a leech, with nothing to offer but some easily transportable knowledge that can be packed in a suitcase and moved on, heedless of what is left behind? Yes, immediately you recognize the behavior of the cosmopolitan! Is Alma-Ata Comrade Gesser's natural place? Of course not! The cosmopolitan Gesser has taken advantage of the generosity of the Soviet State to come here and peddle his wares, this man of many passports. He is an intellectual adventurer. He has no love for our country. Ask him where he spent the war! The cosmopolitan and the Soviet man are incompatible. One is bound by love of the Motherland. The other is bound by nothing!"

"I got an A-5 in the study of Marxism and Leninism," Gesser offered in his defense.

"Of course you did. And a circus bear may be trained to recite a credo. We are interested in what is in your heart, Comrade Gesser."

It was then that he noticed the two members of the People's Militia at the back of the classroom, truncheons hanging loosely against their thighs, faces blank, waiting for the signal. *If I ran for it?* Gesser wondered even as the militiamen were moving towards him, one up each aisle in the theater of the temple of knowledge. The students looked on in total acceptance, waiting for a new teacher to appear who would certainly know less about the present perfect but whose ideological fitness was above reproach.

Jack Gesser was taken off to rejoin the shadows. The silent, shabby, shuffling army of ghosts.

In Moscow, thousands of kilometers from that Alma-Ata theater where a scene was played out that was being repeated all across the Motherland, the American embassy granted the request for transit to Sonya Freedman and Michael Mafili Freedman. Sonya and me. A little boy's passport was issued for me. I became an American, another in a series of miracles. No matter how many the State obliterates, there are always a few who make good their escape and return to tell the tale.

Jack Gesser was not one of them. The man who halfheartedly played the role of my father for a few of those Alma-Ata years, and whom I halfheartedly loved back. My putative father. *Requiem in pace*, proud, unbending butt of history's joke.

We continued forward, bending when necessary, my mother Sonya and I, westward through the disaster of Europe, towards something the vice-consul in charge of people like us called "repatriation." In Alma-Ata, surrounded by Kazakhs who were forced to make room for us, I suppose we must have yearned for Europe. Civilized Europe with her pianos and libraries and tearooms. Now, as we rode in a train past chimneys that had so recently smoked with the burning flesh of our people, I realized how lucky we had been. Praise be to Asia and Alma-Ata, father of apples, our protector!

Some of those who rode with us in that coach had been singed by the chimney-fires. Walking skeletons who'd left their hearts and most of their minds in this wreckage. As we travelled towards Vienna to be handed over to the Americans, then over the mountains into Italy, we would come upon a battle site, a town reduced to rubble where, it seemed to me, you could still smell the charred timbers and the stink of unburied corpses in the ruins. I would rush to the window of the coach. I was eager to see. Children are always attracted by disaster. Then I would notice I was the only one staring. Up and down the coach were rows of blank faces that had seen enough.

We idled in the harbor of a city the Americans called Leghorn, a name that still strikes me as unbearably funny. "The Americans," we called our saviors, forgetting that we, too, were Americans now, unlikely though that seemed. In Leghorn, I remember, my habit of stone-sucking suffered its first attack. I was playing along the waterfront, the site of our next point of transit, watching the fishermen bring in their catch. I especially liked the tender, many-fingered squid and cuttlefish whose bones could be made into toys, and whose flesh my God did not want me to eat. I did not listen to Him; I was too hungry. An Italian lady standing nearby inquired after me in a kindly voice, probably wondering why I wasn't in school like other children. Not only could I not understand her, I couldn't tell her so in any of the languages or shreds of languages I had at my disposal, for I had a stone in my mouth. Probably two, so they wouldn't get lonely. The good lady looked at my burned face and my Kazakh pants and must have decided I was some retarded urchin left to wander the streets untended. Perhaps, at that juncture, that was what I was. I was marched down to the Red Cross, examined and probed until the true pitiful nature of my case came to light—probably after they pulled down my pants. The Covenant will out!

Finally, my mother appeared to claim me. She was shown my stones. My beloved smooth sucking-stones in the scrubbed palm of the female health commissar. My mother shrugged, unimpressed. She must have known about my habit, and she did nothing to discourage it. No doubt she had a few habits of her own at the time.

The commissar was outraged by my mother's acceptance; she took matters into her own hands. She disappeared into a back room and returned with a jar of red powder, which she sprinkled liberally over my stones. I didn't know what to think. Perhaps the stuff was sugar. Sometimes people gave candy to poor lost children like myself. I popped the rocks into my mouth.

A second later my tongue caught fire. I spat the stones back into my hand and gazed at my former source of comfort that had so cruelly betrayed me. Meanwhile, the health czarina lectured my mother in Italian.

Back at the barracks where we were housed, my mother rinsed off my stones in a mixture of water and wine and returned them to me.

"Just make sure you don't swallow them," she chided me.

But before she placed the stones in my waiting palm, she added, "You're going to have to stop this, you know."

I nodded.

"You're an American now. They don't do this in America."

I promised I would stop, though I didn't see what all the fuss was about. After all, these weren't pieces of black, staining coal. I'd given that up. I'd made great progress, considering where I'd started from.

I told my mother all this. She smiled sadly, then promised I would make greater progress in the future, in the land of the living.

14

A JEWEL COMES HOME

The telephone rings in my flat in Montreal, Canada. A city made for the expatriate, the perplexed individual hanging between the Old World and the New. A city of minorities, where each one tries to out-minority the other in a comical ballet. Astonishingly, this is all done in an atmosphere of good humor.

It's been over forty years since my mother and I crossed the ocean together, back to Chicago. I, too, have changed countries in the meantime, though what I did was insignificant compared to my mother's journey. Chicago to Montreal is hardly an adventure, but I suppose I like peace and quiet too much to go wandering further. Can you blame me?

My mother is on the phone, summoning me to a funeral.

"Jacob Spolansky," was all she said.

She paused. In the silence her pause leaves, I am meant to use my memory. I obey, and, lo and behold, the barrel-chested Spolansky with his great crown of unruly white hair pops up. In my first memory, he has a posthole digger in his hands, and he is digging a hole in the sand to bury the garbage at our summer shack.

"The good G-man," I replied.

"A little respect towards the departed. You know, he saved our skins."

"I know. That's why I'm being invited to his funeral."

"You're so perspicacious. Actually, you're going because I don't want to go alone. So, you're coming?"

"Of course."

"There are airplanes," she suggested.

"I'll figure it out."

"Remember, this isn't a vacation, so maybe you can come alone. Unless, of course, your escort is somebody special. I wouldn't want to stand in the way of your happiness."

"She's always somebody special."

"Of course. Every woman is. With or without your participation. You know, I'll never understand how you get so many dates."

"It's the scar. You know women like a man with a scar."

"Stop it, would you? Nobody sees that scar but you!"

"Don't worry," I told her, "I'll come alone."

"Good. Because I'll need you. You know, Spolansky, he's the last one of the breed."

"There's always you, Mother."

"Shhh! Don't give Death any ideas!"

I set down the phone. *Jacob Spolansky*, I thought. I fingered my pale pink burn scar that, according to my mother, no one else but me can see—as if that mattered. Spolansky was the first one we went looking for when we arrived in Chicago, two DPs from the East, stumbling into the contentment of the American 1950s, into the unspeakable freedom and luxury that I still haven't gotten used to. My "dates," as my mother calls them—she enjoys exaggeration, and I won't take that or any pleasure away from her—no doubt have something to do with the shock of American abundance. My mother spent an unusual amount of energy looking for Jacob Spolansky. At first, I thought it was just to recreate the past, and feel closer to the old times. But my mother is too original for a motivation that simple. "He was one of the gang," she would tell me, "even though he never went as far as we did. He was too smart for that." And she would laugh. "I'll never forget the time he taught me how to play pool!"

Pool? I never saw my mother pick up a pool cue in her life. I figured there was something else, and that I was going to find out what it was. That's what funerals are for: to release the secrets. How many could be left after all this time? I wondered. I picked up the phone, still echoing with my mother's voice, and booked my flight for Miami.

It took my mother a while to find Jacob Spolansky in Chicago. When he finally did show up, knocking at the flimsy screen door of our vacation shack in the Indiana Dunes along the shores of Lake Michigan, it was already the first summer of my adolescence. It was also the first year of America's assault on the Reds within her borders, a charge led by Mr. McCarthy. Like him, I was vigilant, but for a different reason. My first year of adolescence was a period of watchful waiting, observing adult conduct, following the movement of women's bodies under their light summer clothes, hoping for a glimpse of them as they changed into their swimsuits behind half-closed doors. The doors were always only half closed in our cabin; we were a free-spirited bunch.

When the knock on the screen door came, I was the one to answer it. My mother never answered the door. The air was slow and hot, as it always is during the first summer of your adolescence. A man stood shirtless and in swimming trunks before me, as if he'd just stepped out of the lake. I had never seen him before. He, however, looked at me as if he knew me. As if he recognized me. Then he squeezed my bicep as if he were testing the material.

"Yes?"

"Is your mama in?"

He didn't wait for the answer. I let him walk by me into the house. The Indiana Dunes were full of eccentrics. Scientists who specialized in Rube Goldberg machines, socialists who painted watercolors of the Lake Michigan sunsets. With my own extraordinary status as the son of a lost father, I suppose I was a member of the club. My status earned me all kinds of special treatment. Especially solicitous, especially awkward, especially rough, depending on the guest.

And there were plenty of them that summer. It must have been particularly uncomfortable and hot that year in Chicago. There were continual meetings in our wood cabin. *McCarthy. HUAC. Silence. Squealer.* Those were the words being used. And this man was part of that crowd.

He came and stood before my mother in the front room. There was something urgent about his posture, almost threatening, but it was clear from their collusion that the threat came from elsewhere. With false poise, my mother took a sip of cold tea and set down her book on the Afghan that covered the arm of her wicker rocking chair.

"This gentleman's name is Jacob Spolansky," she said to me. "He's an old friend. No doubt he's here to help us."

I said nothing. I just naturally accepted that we might need help. And though I recognized that a boy might be better off outside in the fresh air at a time like this, I was allowed to stay. My

mother's favored pedagogical method was exposure. You permitted a child to hear and see everything, then let him figure it all out
later. It was a particularly radical method of education, though
now I suspect it had more to do with fatigue than choice.

"Please, sit down," she told the man.

He took a wicker chair that sagged under his weight.

"So, now, Jacob, what do they want with our pasts? Are they
going to throw us in jail?"

"I don't see how they can," Spolansky said carefully. "The
important thing is to be prepared."

"Prepared? Like with the arrest pack? The little hankie pack no
one can ever find when they need it?"

I didn't know what my mother meant. If Spolansky knew, he
wasn't letting on.

"They don't have anything to throw you in jail on. Your sins are
all in the past, if you don't mind me putting it that way. That's what
you should talk about. They'll want to see how much you'll tell
them. Talk as freely as you want about the past. About Berg's College, about Steinstein's—everything. They'll threaten to deport
you, of course, but I don't see how they can do that."

The world tilted, the floor fell away at the word *deport*. Our
shack separated itself from the solid, quiet contentment of a 1950s
American summer. I regretted not having a stone to suck on. A big,
nourishing black one.

My mother looked slowly towards the door, and the dazzling
surface of the lake beyond.

"So there really is nowhere to run to," she said softly.

Later that day, I stood at the top of the sand bluff overlooking our
shack, holding a strawberry ice-cream cone in my hand, waiting. I
had been shooed out of the house for their arrival. And they did
arrive. Two shit-brown, four-door Plymouths came up the sand track

and stopped before our cabin. Two FBI cars, just for us. We had to be something special. As I watched the G-men get out of their cars, tiny as ants, I worked over the ice cream. Strawberry from Johnson's Beach Hotel. The best ice-cream cones in the world.

Inside our cabin, my mother underwent the usual inquisition. Was she or had she ever been a member of the Party. And who else had been along for the ride. It never ends. If you've been on the wrong side once, you can never get all the way back. She appealed to reason. She'd been to Russia, she'd seen things the FBI men had only read about in books, she'd suffered, she'd deserted to come back here. Wasn't that proof enough? The two agents acted according to the script that Spolansky, ever the double agent, had prepared her for. They threatened her with stories of irregular and expired documents that could cause deportation proceedings, they took notes, unhappy with the outdated information she supplied them, then they went away. They must have decided that this eccentric, dishevelled woman living in a beachfront shack was not enemy enough.

The minute their cars disappeared past the hotel and back onto the paved road, Spolansky emerged from the cabin next door. *Debriefing*, they call it now. I saw him cross from one shack to the other, but I wasn't in any hurry. I hung around on the bluff and looked at the stupid lake. I went for a walk in the dunes and kicked sand at the poison ivy. My absence was my contribution to the family cause.

When I woke up the next morning, I could feel the cabin was empty. A house has a certain feeling when it's been empty all night. I had slept late, the room was full of hazy summer sunlight, and I heard the pop of a metal posthole digger hitting the sand. I went outside in the swim trunks I wore as pyjamas and saw Spolansky in the sandy no-man's-land out in front of the house. He was digging a hole for the garbage. A drawback to these inexpensive cabins: there was no garbage collection. Spolansky thrust the digger into the ground, worked the levers and dropped a neat cone of sand next to the hole. He was short but strong, his chest covered with matted hair and his back with bites and scratches. I wouldn't want to be one of the criminals he hunted down.

My mother stepped around the corner of the cabin where Spolansky had hidden during the FBI's visit. She was holding a paperbag full of garbage at some distance from her body so it wouldn't stain her dress. She saw me and stiffened with embarrassment. Then she must have changed her mind: a second later an expression of pride came over her face. At the time I was only a boy, but I knew what was going on without knowing. Since then, I've seen that expression on the faces of other women proud to have broken the rules. Everything in the world is in that look.

Jacob Spolansky, one in a series of fathers. I wouldn't have minded him, actually. Sometimes I get tired of the prestige of having a father who was lost to history. It's a lonely kind of prestige when it comes down to it.

That was a time of heroes and squealers. The 1950s. Now it's the 1990s. And I am going to Spolansky's funeral.

So secular have we become, thanks largely to the Revolution, that I was unprepared for the ceremony surrounding the mourning of Jacob Spolansky's death. People turn to religion in death, it seems; where I will turn when it's my time, I have no idea. It seemed to me that the only Jews left who knew how to act like Jews were in America. All the Jews in Russia knew about their Judaism was that they were persecuted for it, without obtaining any joy from the Covenant.

In a south Florida bungalow, the air conditioning mercifully turned off, the Spolansky family sat, barefoot in their dark suits, the lapels of their garments neatly rent by a straight razor. Their attitude of mourning was formal and dignified, and I felt the way I always do in the presence of those who know how to believe: ashamed, and morally inadequate.

An old woman sat on a straight-backed chair in the center of the row of mourners. I understood her to be Spolansky's widow. My mother took my hand, then began to move down the line. Her condolences were vague and distracted and a bit impersonal, as were mine. I didn't know these people.

All that changed when she came to the widow.

She bent over to kiss her cheek and express her sadness, but she still would not surrender my hand. The two wrinkled faces brushed together tenderly, and I distinctly heard the Spolansky woman speak.

"We shared Jacob. I know that," she said. "I could never bring myself to blame him, or you. It was his way of doing a job he never got used to, I suppose."

My mother clung briefly to the Spolansky woman. For an instant, they were the only two people in the world who mattered.

"Jacob did a lot of good in this life," my mother answered softly. "That's all that matters. And you helped him do that."

I saw the tendons stand out on her fleshless hands and the vein in her neck beat harder. Then my mother, Sonya Freedman, adventuress, conscience of the century, straightened her back and moved down the order of mourners.

Awash in tea and cakes and schnapps, we walked past my rented car and wandered aimlessly through this south Florida retirement farm. My mother considered the shut windows, the omnipresent rattle of air conditioners, the Oldsmobiles parked neatly in the driveways, the lawns kept manicured by Cuban help. I wondered how many Spolanskys lived behind these modest facades.

"So," she announced. "Now I am the last one."

There could be no contradicting her. There was only to listen. Everyone wants to be the last left standing; everyone wants to be the memory.

Then my mother drew breath and pronounced Jacob Spolansky's funeral oration.

"I was awfully fond of Spolansky. 'We have a lot in common, Jacob,' I would tell him. We were both people caught in the middle, choosing first one way, then the other. Though I was more impulsive than he was, I suppose. I acted, then tried to figure out what it meant afterwards. But we were both balancers. We used to talk it over out there in the beach cabin. Why we'd done what we did, what it possibly could have meant. We talked about it endlessly, the way some people talk about the weather. It was a kind of weather, I suppose . . . a giant storm. He and I weren't so attached to principles, the way some were."

She looked up at me expectantly. "Am I making sense?"

"To me you are."

"Some recommendation!"

I smiled, but she did not smile back. I knew she was thinking of those men of principle who were lost, Jack Gesser and Mikhail Borodin, with whom she had shared the years of tumult. And so the appeal of a Jacob Spolansky. A man who did what was necessary to get along, a kind of Spielerman minus the spats and clarinet and gross ambition, a man with a conscience who never sold anyone out to get to the top the way so many immigrants did, and who never complained about the difficulty of the path he'd chosen for himself. Not a bad-looking man either, which didn't hurt. That big, square body and great halo of curly white hair like the twirl on a soft ice-cream cone. And a healthy weakness for the flesh to go with it.

There. That's my eulogy for the man. May his name be remembered.

"Only poor Spolansky had a . . . position, and in America, that's important," my mother said. "A position," she added dreamily, "a position to maintain."

Then she stopped and gazed blankly at this unfamiliar neighborhood.

"Oh yes, there's one more thing," she said abruptly. "You know, when we came back to Chicago after the war, and you were such a confused little boy . . . I had one more problem to figure out. A dilemma. That's why I was so eager to find Jacob, I wanted to discuss it with him. You see, I happened to have a precious stone in my possession, a *very* precious stone. Actually, it came from the crown of the last Russian czar."

She stopped and waited for my reaction. I had none. I simply didn't believe her. A wispy old woman leaning against the fender of a rented car in Miami Beach telling you she had part of the Czar's crown jewels—it was not very credible.

"I really didn't know what to do with this thing. It was a keepsake of a kind. I found Jacob, I showed it to him, I asked him what to do. Now two of us had the same dilemma. Funny! A long, long time ago, he'd been after the very same jewels . . . and now they came and found him."

"What did he tell you to do?"

"He didn't *tell* me to do anything!" My mother looked offended. "We decided I should keep it. That poor stone! It kept going back and forth across the Atlantic, ending up in the damnedest places and circumstances. We figured it could use a rest."

"Like you, Mother."

She smiled radiantly and opened her hand.

"Here, take. Enjoy it, it's a present from your father. Before, you had coal. Now, you have a ruby. That's progress, I suppose."

I took the little red stone. It winked in the harsh sunlight. Winked ironically, I'd be tempted to say.

"I'll try not to swallow it," I told her.

"Go ahead, if you must. In any case, it's much too precious to do anything with."

And she laughed richly at her own joke.

"Well, it's time to get back to the business of living. And a busy bit of business that is." She looked down the street, in the direction of the Spolansky bungalow. "And I intend to live forever. Living's gotten to be a habit with me."

But Sonya Freedman, my mother, had one more surprise in store. As I held open the car door for her, she stopped in mid-movement.

"Are you unhappy?"

"Unhappy? About what?"

"Unhappy," she insisted. "Just unhappy. The thing does exist, don't try to deny it."

She sat down in the front seat, but left the door open.

"Remember how you used to chew rocks? Happy children don't do that."

"Really? I thought all children did." Then I opened my mouth and reached under my tongue. "Through a miracle of conservation, I managed to hold on to one," I told her. "It's right here, I put it away for safe-keeping under my tongue. You want to see it?"

My mother turned away in feigned disgust.

"Don't worry, I'll leave it where it is. If I take it out, I won't be able to talk. Now, you tell me to what I owe a discussion of my happiness."

"I was reading some psychological material lately, something in a magazine about emotions, or some such nonsense. You know, emotions, the latest product on the market . . . Anyway, there was an article about unhappy childhoods and how common they are, as common as colds, it seems, though when has a childhood ever been anything else? Anyway, the person was saying how they can spoil your adult life. I began to think about . . . the hard times we had when you were young, and then about all your different dates. All of a sudden, all by myself, I deduced that you might be unhappy."

She paused. I waited.

"So? Are you unhappy?" she demanded.

"I am the most fortunate man in the world," I told her.

And I believe it, even though she laughed at me. I bent to kiss her on the forehead. Her hair smelled light and dusty, like something from an old cedar chest. Her skin was like silky parchment on which the romance of the century has been written.

Like she says, Sonya Freedman will live forever. I will see to that.

ACKNOWLEDGMENTS

My appreciation to Fred Reed, who gave me the keys to the dilemma of history; and to Tatiana Pocherstnik, my guide to the overgrown village.

Thanks to the Canada Council and the Ministère de la culture du Québec for their generous support.

For permission to quote "Brother, Can You Spare a Dime?", lyrics by E.Y. Harburg, music by Jay Gorney, thanks to the Harburg Estate, and to Ernie Harburg of the Harburg Foundation for kindness beyond the call of duty.